THE EARTH DAWNING SERIES
BOOK ONE

MERCURY'S BANE

NICK WEBB

Summary: They're all gone. We remember them like yesterday: pieces of our stolen heritage. We remember a time when we were alone in the universe, safe and oblivious. But it's all gone now. We called them the Telestines, and in the face of their ruthless invasion we were powerless. By 2040, all the world's governments and militaries had fallen, and the remnants of humanity exiled to the solar system. We looked down on our blue planet, so close to our birthplace, so close to our home. But the miles may as well have been lightyears. Our anger smoldered in the darkness of space. On Mars. On Ganymede. In the dank crowded filth of the asteroids. We swore: we will take our planet back. And today, it begins. Our fleet is ready. Our soldiers determined. Earth will be ours again.

Text set in Garamond

Designed by Nick Webb

Cover art by Jeff Brown

www.jeffbrowngraphics.com

ISBN: 154401872X

ISBN-13: 978-1544018720

Printed in the United Sates of America

For J., L., and C.

Prologue

September 2nd, 2061
Near Denver, North American Continent
Old Boulder refugee camp

You could always tell a Jovian from a Martian, and a Martian from a Native—people who grew up outside the gravity well never seemed to be able to keep up. One's history with gravity was always the hardest thing to hide.

"Not much farther now." Thomas Pike hauled himself over a tumble of rock in the middle of the path and held out a hand to the soldier scrambling up behind him, huffing and wheezing.

To call this boy a soldier was a kindness. The kid couldn't be more than sixteen or seventeen, dressed in a shapeless shirt and pants, an insignia stamped hastily onto one sleeve. And he was far too thin under the raggedy uniform. The soldier panted. He'd been struggling within minutes as they climbed into the foothills. Only momentum kept him going now.

Momentum, and a dull, simmering anger that Thomas Pike understood all too well.

He'd never seen someone so weak. Did Earth have a lower oxygen pressure than the stations? Higher gravity? The kid didn't offer an explanation and Pike was afraid to ask. The thought of the habitats spinning endlessly through the solar system—through the darkness, in the darkness, breeding grounds for darkness—filled him with a fear so deep that he had no words for it. To live a whole life without wind or rain or sun....

Pike hurried to catch up. They had to keep moving; the kid had pressed on without him, despite his breathless pant. The path's loose rocks crunched reassuringly under Pike's feet. This was his planet. Humanity's home. He welcomed the rasp of the air in his lungs, scented with juniper, and the faint burn of the sun on the back of his neck. The storm in the mountains wouldn't reach them for a while yet.

They climbed in silence now for the sake of the young soldier, who could spare no energy to talk. Pike listened to the boy's ragged breath and counted the steps until they finally rounded the bend.

The kid gave a whistle. The Rockies rose to either side of them, peaks plunging into the churning clouds of the unseasonal storm. Below lay the camp: makeshift shacks and tents covered in camouflage. If someone looked very, very closely, they could see movement along the river, where Natives cultivated crops among the trees. Heh, *Natives*. That's what the Jovian soldier kid had called them. To him, Thomas Pike, this was home.

A light breeze, the first winds of the oncoming storm, rustled the trees, signaling to the workers tending the crops that it would soon be time to take shelter. Christina and Joanna were there now. Farming was a risky endeavor, but a necessary one. People gotta eat, aliens or no aliens.

But growing crops wasn't nearly as risky as what he and the soldier had just done. Pike had agonized over the transmissions to the Rebellion. If those transmissions were caught in one of the sweeps, the camp would be gone within minutes. But what was the alternative? Scrabble for a half-life, hidden in the shadows, afraid to show himself to the sky? Spend his days avoiding capture, all for living on his own planet?

The familiar rage kindled deep within his chest. This planet was his birthright, and he would see it returned to his children before he died. That was the promise he had made years ago, and Joanna, a hand on her round belly, had agreed. They named the child Christina, and she had Joanna's black hair and Thomas's golden-brown eyes. Then came William, and Joanna began to ask if they should take so many risks. Perhaps, she said, they should seek passage to Mars. Her sister was there, and said the sunsets were beautiful. Or the Snowball Moons of Jupiter. Or even Mercury—live with the Rollers. At least they had decent gravity, and mining was good, honest work. And there were rumors that the mines served the Rebellion, too. If they only—

In the end, he persuaded her to stay every time she asked. But she worried constantly. He hadn't told her about the message to the Rebellion. How could he? He pushed the guilt away and pointed into the distance.

"You can't see it today, but there's a base over there." He twisted to point toward a peak behind him. "Come down through the peak with the notch and it's due west."

The soldier nodded. He was scribbling notes on an ancient tablet computer he'd brought with him, and he took a picture of the peak for reference, for all the good it did. He looked back expectantly.

"If you follow along the mountains, you'll find more of their floating things. They're all up and down the range."

"We saw some coming in. They almost looked like the aid ships."

"Aid ships?"

The kid paused, clearly trying to figure out where to start. "Well ... they're not *supposed* to help us, right? We're supposed to be self-sufficient. But the stations really aren't self-sufficient at all, and some of the Telestines know that. There's one, his name's Tel'rabim, he sends aid all the time. He argues for us in their parliament, too, and—"

"I don't care."

The boy broke off, eyes wide.

"This alien, Tel'rabim, you say? He's not arguing for them to give Earth back, is he?"

Slowly, the boy shook his head.

"Then it doesn't matter what else he does. He can burn with the rest."

The boy nodded, looked back to his computer. "Right. Uh ... the big floating ships. Are they all labs?" The thin hand was poised over the keyboard and his eyes flicked up to meet his.

Pike only shrugged. He hadn't gotten close enough to tell. Half floating island, half airship, the estates were massive. Some were a swarm of activity, others simply floated up and down the mountain range, taking in the view. When one hovered above the camp, all activity ceased for those few days.

They froze—fearful mice hiding from the hawk in the sky.

But the Telestines would not always be the predators. That would change.

"What kind is that one?" The boy jerked his head.

"What? There isn't…." Pike looked, and did a double take. There, as the storm billowed over the peaks, he made it out at last: the heavy bow of an airship. His throat seemed to close. "We have to get back to the camp."

"What? Why?"

"That wasn't *there* this morning." Pike pushed his way back through the scrub brush, toward the path. His mind was racing with calculations. Would he be seen on the path? Speed and the chance of being caught, or a slow, careful descent and the chance of the airship seeing the crop workers instead? His breath was coming short with fear. "Where did it come from?"

"I told you, we saw it when we were coming in." The boy was running after him now. "Slow down, I can't keep up."

"No time—why didn't you *say* anything?"

"Your message said they were here often!" The boy was shaking his head.

"*On* the range, going up and down the *range*. Not here in the foothills!"

Christina was at the crop fields. Fourteen years old, in a growth spurt, and always hungry. She would be doing her lessons as she tended the crops. Joanna had been adamant that the children continue learning, even if they had to work to keep the camp running. But Christina was wild, and always had been: she would be taking any chance to slip out of the shelter of the trees and into the sunshine.

He'd chided her for that, but not enough. He understood

the yearning too well to yell at her when he should have. And now....

Pike's fists clenched. He tossed a glance over his shoulder and stumbled.

No. No, no.... The airship had come alive with activity. Fighter ships were emerging from its top decks, rounded and sleek. They swirled like a flock of starlings, and then—

"*No!*" He scrambled up, palms bleeding, and ran. The camp, the fields.

This couldn't be happening. They had never been seen before.

He had never sent a radio transmission before.

"Mr. Pike! Sir!" The kid, however frail, had youth on his side. He caught up, reached out to grab Pike's arm. "We can take some."

"What?"

"We can take some of the camp." The kid was pale, his blue eyes terrified. "Whoever's there, we get them onto the shuttle and we go."

"We have to get to the fields."

"There isn't *time*." The kid grabbed his arm and dragged him to a stop.

"Let go of me, or I swear to god I will kill you where you stand."

"There isn't *time*," the kid repeated. His grip was feverishly strong. "We have to get the people from the camp and get out."

"My wife is at the fields—my *daughter*."

"And your *son* is at the camp, right?" The kid met his eyes. "We can get them out. But not if we go for the fields."

William. William could get out, and then Pike would go to warn the others. There was enough time to slip into the woods and make for the field, and the other settlement beyond that. "Let's go."

They pounded down the hill in a rising wind. It might have been his imagination, but the bigger ships always seemed to bring storms with them.

Like the one over the mountains today. How had he not guessed what was coming? Pike swung around one of the trees, felt the skin come off his palm, and didn't care. William. He had to get to William.

A hollow boom echoed through him and he *felt* the fire tear through the trees miles away. The fact that he could feel the heat from that far away could only mean one thing.

His knees buckled with grief and the kid hauled him up. "Come on!"

"Fire." His voice wasn't his own any longer. "Fire." He couldn't find any other words.

"That's the fields, they haven't hit the camp yet. *Run!*"

Screams were beginning ahead of them. Pike ran, the impact jolting up through his legs. He couldn't feel his feet on the ground any longer. The screams were around him, piercing him, rising through the trees in a chorus.

They burst into the camp in a dead sprint, the kid waving his arms for the shuttle. It was hovering as the Rebellion soldiers shoved children into the hold desperately. One of them was trying to grab little William, hands up as the boy pointed a rifle directly at the soldier.

"You have to come with us." The soldier was pleading, her hands out to him. Her uniform showed bony wrists; her eyes kept going to the Telestine airship overhead, menacing and low.

"My sister is at the fields!" William, gangly, had every ounce of his mother's fierceness now. He backed away amidst the tents, eleven-year-old body shaking. "My mom is there. Don't try to stop me, I … I have to go to them. They need our help."

"William!" Thomas Pike's breath was coming in a gasp. He swayed as he made his way toward his son.

"Dad." William's face crumpled in relief. "They're saying we have to leave the others and—"

"Shhh. It's okay." Only it wasn't. Of course it wasn't.

He looked toward the fields, and smelled the smoke on the breeze, rancid with both scorched earth and flesh.

They were gone.

Pike swallowed, looked back to his son, and lied. He poured everything left into this one lie, eyes fixed on his son's. "There's another shuttle at the fields." He didn't look at the soldier, whose shock would give him away. He stared into his son's eyes and prayed to every god he knew to make the boy believe him. Another explosion rocked the ground and he held out his hand. "You have to come now, William. They already went. Your mother and Christina will meet us on the spaceship."

William wavered. He looked to the fields, and back to his father. "They're safe?"

"They're safe. *Please*, William. They'll want to make sure you got away too. Come on."

William's shoulders slumped, the rifle dropped, and Pike thought he would collapse from relief. His legs shook as the soldier grabbed him to propel him into the hold of the ship.

"No.... " His voice was weak. He couldn't live with what was coming. "I'll go—"

They didn't even listen. They shoved him toward the seat where William was strapping himself in and Pike knelt on the floor and buried his face in his hands.

The shuttle knocked everyone inside to the deck as it took off.

"Everyone hold on." The pilot's voice was desperate. "They're still focusing on the fields, we should be able to get out of here."

"What about the shuttle at the fields?" William twisted in his seat. His hands closed on his father's shoulders. "Dad—*Dad*—they said the Telestines are focusing on the fields, did the shuttle get away?"

He could hardly breathe for the ache in his throat. Pike picked his face up. "I'm sure they did."

But this time, the lie was not so successful. William's face went blank with betrayal, thin body rigid.

"You said there was a shuttle." His voice was rising. He tore at the straps holding him in place. "You said there was a shuttle!" He was on his father the next moment, bony fists flying. "You said there was a shuttle! You said! You *said*!"

Pain exploded across Pike's eye and he fought by instinct alone. The shuttle was swerving and the two of them rolled, William all bony elbows and pure fury, and Pike hit the floor. The pain burst through him as his hands moved to block William's strikes. But the pain wasn't from any blow. It was in his gut, in his heart. Every shriek from his son pierced his soul.

"You said!" William's voice was hysterical, his fists raining down on Pike's face. "You—"

A soldier wrapped his arms around William and pulled him off. The shuttle was shaking—a patch of turbulence launched everyone several feet into the air.

The side of William's head rammed straight into a corner of a storage bin above them. He fell to the floor, knocked out cold. One of the soldiers knelt next to him, scanning him with some sort of medical device. "He'll be fine. We'll have to watch for concussion...."

"Are you all right?" The woman's face was scared. Her hand clasped his. "Your eye is—"

Pike pushed her away and pulled himself up on the straps of the seat. He swayed as he made his way to the window. His fingers splayed there; the glass was cold on his forehead.

One could hardly see the camp any longer. It melted into the slopes of the foothills. Even the Telestines hadn't noticed it yet. You couldn't miss the fields, though, not as the fire consumed them. The trail of smoke was drifting in the wind, and beyond....

Pike felt his breath catch. The fighters seemed to be dive-bombing at the camp, plummeting down and pulling up only at the last minute. He strained to see what they were doing.

They were chasing people. His fingers clenched. The figures were tiny, and they were running desperately.

And the Telestines were taunting them. They zoomed low overhead as the humans fled. They were toying with their prey before they killed.

They were not just aliens. They were monsters.

His mouth gaped in a silent sob and he rolled his head to look away. Look away, so at least he wouldn't have to *see* the ruin of the camp. He could change nothing. He was powerless.

All of this was unfolding because he had thought, briefly, that maybe he wasn't powerless. That maybe his little camp could provide intelligence to the Rebellion, and maybe, just maybe, be the key to the victory of Earth's imminent war of liberation. The great war to come.

A temporary delusion.

Through the blur of tears, he could faintly see a massive ship hovering over Denver, shining and beautiful in the afternoon sunlight. He wondered if the Telestines there knew of the attack on the camp. He wondered if any of them had volunteered.

He looked back to his son's prone body on the floor of the shuttle. The boy's chest rose and fell, slowly. When he woke, Pike knew, he would be nursing a hatred that would take years to die—if it ever did. He was his father's son, after all.

One day, Pike promised him silently, *you'll understand.*

And I pray you can forgive me. Because I'll never forgive myself.

CHAPTER ONE

September 25th, 2082
Jupiter, Ganymede's L4 Lagrange point
Command Center, New Beginnings Station

"These numbers can't be correct." Laura Walker, admiral of the Exile Fleet, crossed her arms and frowned down at the printouts on the rickety table in front of her. A slight shudder shook the space station, which creaked and groaned in response.

"I double checked them myself." Commander Arianna King grimaced. "And this is a conservative estimate. If we expand it to those ships with minor problems—and those really should be checked over, too, ma'am—it comes to twenty-two."

"We'll stick with the biggest problems for now." Walker tried to keep her face impassive as she shuffled the papers, checking the ship names: *Jocasta, Valiant, Andromache, Intrepid,*

Pele.... Some of them were frigates, mostly expendable—insofar as anything in the fleet was expendable—but there were gunships and carriers on the list as well. The fleet was now precisely in the position she'd wished to avoid: forced to choose between defending the Rebellion bases at Jupiter, and defending the task force headed for Earth.

Fifteen ships out of commission. This was not a good day. If she had one wish—

She stopped that train of thought with a quick shake of her head. If she was going to wish for things, she wouldn't wish for a better fleet. She wouldn't wish for more reliable supply chains and shipyards and weaponry.

She'd wish for Earth back. She'd wish for the Telestines to have died when their sun exploded—or, at the very least, for them to have struck out in any direction but the one they chose.

The direction of Earth.

She couldn't have any of those things. What she *had* was a fleet in desperate need of repair, and a shipyard that was only just starting to get up to speed on metal-rich Mercury. It had taken five years to build the secret mines and shipyards kept hidden from the Telestines only by Mercury's intense glare of scattered sunlight—rumor had it that the Telestines knew about them anyway, and allowed their construction as a show of hubris.

Five years spent gathering up the last dregs of humanity who still remembered aircraft carriers and NASA space shuttles and engineering, finding the best new minds, and bringing them to build new ships, better than anything the Telestines would give them. If their luck held, those shipyards would give them a fleet that had a fighting chance against the Telestines. Unlike their current, rickety *Exile Fleet*.

"Admiral Walker?" said Commander Larsen from the sensor station across the command center. "I picked up that blip again. Just a momentary ping. But Jupiter's magnetic field is messing with the readings. Could be anything, still."

Could be anything.

"Don't let it out of your sight, Commander. And keep me apprised."

Could be anything, she repeated in her mind. Or it could be a Telestine fleet, come to end the Rebellion before it even got started. With any luck, it was just a cargo freighter, and Jupiter's insanely intense magnetic field was simply fooling their sensors, making it look like a massive Telestine fleet. With any luck….

On the other hand, the balance of their luck over the past sixty years had been terrible. The hand they'd been dealt had given them the invasion of Earth. She wasn't going to count on luck coming to their aid now. She sorted the papers quickly and tapped on one stack.

"These four, we'll handle here." She considered the rest, and tapped at each in turn. "These, send to Io Station. These, Soros Station at Ganymede. The last two ... we can't fix on any of our stations." She sighed, and tapped the map. The planets circled in a sped-up simulation, stationary and orbital defensive systems lit up in red. Her lips moved as she did a rough calculation in her head. "Wait a week and plot a course for Venus. That should put Earth's systems far enough out that it won't trigger anything. Our contact on Venus can get the ships up and running, or so he claims."

"Can we handle four ships here?" King frowned. She

pushed the thick braid of black hair back over her shoulder and thumbed through the papers.

Not really. "Yes," she murmured.

"And I thought Soros Station's engineering docks were out."

They were—several of the struts had broken, cutting the life support systems to the repair module. Whether it was space debris or sabotage remained to be seen, and Walker had sent one of her best representatives to make discreet enquiries. There were those—the current Secretary General of the United Nations being one—who believed humanity endangered itself with the Rebellion. They were so afraid of the Telestine weaponry that they would gladly submit to a slow death on the stations instead. Sabotage had taken down at least one Rebellion station, and it was the reason this one stayed hidden.

To humanity, New Beginnings Station was abandoned, a relic of the exodus. To the Telestines, who had named it— Walker still felt a surge of rage every time she had to speak the words—New Beginnings Station was just another human cage.

She had thought their operations on Soros Station were hidden, but she must have been wrong.

"Everything will be operational soon," was all she said.

"Soon enough?"

"Is there a better option?" Walker looked up, her face cold. She was losing her patience.

Commander King swallowed. "No, ma'am. Sorry, ma'am."

I don't want you to be sorry, I want you to focus on making this fleet operational. Walker turned her gaze back to the map. The mission needed to launch tomorrow, and she needed to make sure Rebellion assets weren't vulnerable after it left.

This mission was everything. Their best hope to get a leg up on the Telestines in the coming war.

If she *were* wishing for things, she'd wish for their contact on Venus, an individual whose name she could not discover despite her best efforts, to get a reliable tap into the Telestine communications systems. They'd been working on it for three years and hadn't managed it yet. When they did, the Rebellion might be able to learn just how much the Telestines knew of their activities. In dark moments, Walker feared that the Telestines knew everything, and that they tolerated the Rebellion because it was too weak for them to fear.

With any luck, though, what their contact had just found would be useful enough on its own: it was called the Dawning. It was supposedly the key to every Telestine weapons array in the solar system, the answer to all of their prayers since the loss of Earth. A stunning development, really. It changed everything.

They just had to get at it.

"What do you think it is?" Commander King had caught her staring at the intelligence briefing.

"Hmm? Oh." Walker frowned. That the Dawning existed seemed clear enough; their source on Venus was absolutely sure. What it *was*, exactly, was another matter. "I assumed it was a chip of some sort. Plug and play. Something their engineers use when they want to do maintenance or whatever."

"That makes sense." King lifted a shoulder. "I'd been wondering why anyone would make something like that. Seems like a risk."

"Every system has an access point." Walker smiled grimly.

The smile faded quickly, however. *Even ours.* In truth, their system had more than a few access points. The Exile Fleet had only a few rickety stations and a couple of scattered bases to work with. They couldn't let civilian habitats be a target, and that meant they got the most remote and inhospitable of stations. Like their fleet, the Rebellion's homes were much-repaired and chronically on the verge of breakdown.

When she looked up, it was clear Commander King's thoughts had followed a different path. The woman was smiling. When she saw Walker frowning at her, her smile grew.

"We're going to get Earth back. It's actually going to happen. I can't believe it. It's ... like a dream," King said. "I wish my parents could have lived to see this. They always hoped...." Her voice broke and she cleared her throat. "Sorry, ma'am."

Walker said nothing. Anything she said might raise false hopes. She clasped her hands behind her back as she looked over the resource lists one last time.

"All right. Before you send the *Jocasta* for repairs, offload the fighters, and transfer supplies to the station; half of them will stay here, flying patrol. We'll keep the *Ysabel* here, and the *Valiant* will take the rest of the *Jocasta's* fighters for the mission to Earth, and go on to Venus from there."

"You're sending a damaged ship on this mission?"

"We aren't going to get *him* down to the surface with gunships—we need fighters taking the hits. So it has to be a carrier, and the *Valiant* has the largest hold." She looked over at King. "And if we lose a carrier, I want it to be one that's already damaged."

King paled. Her throat bobbed as she swallowed

nervously.

Walker's mouth tightened. No one liked to talk about the possibility of losing ships, and that squeamishness did nothing for them. Lives were lost in battle. Ships were destroyed. Bargains were struck. How could her officers not face that simple fact? Humanity had lost its home in the initial attack sixty years ago. The first resistance movements had been cut down like grass—a metaphor she only vaguely understood— and now humanity tore itself to pieces in the tiny floating cages they called space stations. More were going to be lost before this was over.

Her people needed to prepare for that.

"It will be worth it," she reminded the commander, hating the necessity of the pep talk. It was difficult to inject any feeling into it anymore. "For a chance like this, any of us should be glad to lay down our lives."

King hesitated, but she knew better than to argue. She nodded wordlessly.

Walker would accept that. She handed the stacks of ship repair materials to the commander and gave a decisive nod. "Let's get this fleet fixed so we're ready to act as soon as we have the Dawning."

"Yes, ma'am." Kind snapped a salute.

Both women looked around as the station shuddered. The hull gave a screech of protest followed by the agonized squeal of the extending docking clamps. The phone on the table buzzed.

Walker picked up. "Yes?"

"Ma'am, Bill Pike is here, and the Secretary General is on the line for you."

Walker let out a breath she hadn't known she was holding. "Send Mr. Pike to the briefing room, and tell the Secretary General that I'll call him back. At *my* convenience."

Which would be never, if she had her way. She despised that man. He was spineless and craven; he had the ear of far too many wealthy citizens. There were even a few within the Rebellion who listened to his speeches on nonviolence and non-antagonism. With luck, however—there she went, hoping for that elusive good luck again—she wouldn't need him ever again. She might not have a strong fleet, but if they could just get their hands on the Dawning, they'd have a fighting chance —and if she got Bill Pike onto Earth, she knew he would not fail her.

Of everyone she might call upon, Pike knew best what happened when you lost to the Telestines.

Larsen glanced over again. "Ma'am, that ping just got a little bigger. It's not just a single ship. Most likely two or three."

A tingle went up her spine. They'd yet to have a major battle with the Telestines, face to face, fleet to fleet. She'd been biding her time. Waiting for the best moment. But it looked like her luck might be running out.

"All ships on orange alert." She held Commander Larsen in her steely gaze. "Watch it, Mr. Larsen, like a hawk."

CHAPTER TWO

Jupiter, Ganymede's L4 Lagrange point
Freighter Agamemnon, New Beginnings Station

"You're sure you want to do this?" Pyotr Rychenkov raised an eyebrow. Short but unusually muscular, blond, with the pale, striking eyes of his Russian ancestry, he was an imposing man when he wanted to be.

Right now, he looked skeptical instead.

"I'm sure." Bill Pike hoisted a bag over his shoulder, wincing slightly as the old scar on the side of his head and cheek ached. It always did when something changed. When he left behind people he cared about. "She wouldn't have called me here if it wasn't important."

Rychenkov snorted. "You're giving her far too much credit. Revolutionaries think everything's important." His accent made its first appearance, which always seemed to happen when Rychenkov got angry, and he gave a shrug. "Go, go. If you want, go. But come back alive, *da*? I don't have the time to train a new first mate."

Pike smiled and clasped his captain's hand. "Keep my berth open?"

"You think there are so many people who want to join the cargo guilds? Criminals, all of them." Rychenkov waved a hand. "Go. We'll be running the food shipment to Mercury like we planned."

The *Agamemnon*, or *Aggy*, as they affectionately called it, had been at a scheduled stop on Europa when Laura Walker contacted Pike. The ship's engineer, Howie Howe, was still back on Europa getting the ice shipment ready for loading into the *Aggy*'s cargo bay, while the captain had offered to bring Pike to the Rebellion's New Beginnings Station himself. Despite his contempt, Pike knew he was curious.

"I'm sure they'd let you look around if you wanted." A smile tugged at his lips.

"I don't want," Rychenkov said, prickly to the last. "Go. I'll see you soon."

Pike waved and ducked awkwardly out of the *Aggy*'s cockpit.

"Come back, *guapo*?"

He grinned, and turned to face the purple-haired woman working on the water recycler, sitting cross-legged on the floor.

"Calling me *guapo* with your husband in the same room?" *Guapo*. Handsome. Hot. Whatever—he still couldn't pick up half of the Spanish Gabi threw at him.

From the air duct above them came another voice. "*Guapo*? You should hear what she calls me. *Gordito*. Little fatty." James Carsen, Gabi's husband, popped his grimy head down through the open vent. It was literally the first time Pike had seen the other man without his cowboy hat on. "Just remember, she only insults the ones she likes. Right honey?"

"That's right, *feo*."

Pike grinned—he knew that one. Ugly.

"Hey, Pike," James's face turned serious, even though it was hanging upside down out of the vent. "Be careful. Don't let her ... you know. Just don't throw away your life like ... well. Just be careful. Got it, cowboy?"

"I know." Pike forced a smile. He didn't know. But Laura Walker had given him a chance at something he'd been longing for. A chance he simply could not turn down. "Bye. Say goodbye to Howie for me." And, turning back to Gabriela, "*Hasta luego*, baby."

She smirked. "It's *hasta la vista, baby*." But her smirk turned to a wistful smile. "Stay safe. See you soon."

Minutes later, he was escorted through the hallways of the station by two young Rebellion soldiers. Very, very young. Almost as young as that soldier twenty-four years ago that had been the harbinger of doom for his old settlement camp. And his family.

He pushed the uncomfortable thought aside and focused on the station. It was built in the old style: a raised lip at the bottom of each doorway, heavy doors resting against the walls and ready to create a makeshift airlock at any moment.

It had held some of the first shocked refugees from Earth. Thousands had been sent to the hastily-constructed, massive stations around Jupiter, Saturn, and Mars, as well as the first underground tunnels on Mars, Ganymede, and Callisto, and the dark holes burrowed into the concrete-hard ice of Europa, far away from Jupiter's intense radiation. Thousands more had died in the airless dark: life-support malfunctions, orbital decays, debris that tore away solar panels and shattered radiation shields. This particular station had survived, but the civilians had long-since fled.

He thought the station had been decommissioned. Doubtless the Telestines did as well. He wondered who had saved it for Walker to turn into the Rebellion's headquarters. He wondered what she thought of it. Did the rusted walls, the hurried, desperate construction, remind her of why they were here? Did she hope it would inspire the others?

Pike wasn't one to think that way, but Walker made him wonder things like that.

He followed the two young men through the boxy corridors and did his best to ignore the stares of the other soldiers passing by. Years on Earth, with fresh food and sunlight, had given him a broad-shouldered height rarely seen out in the stations. His patched-together clothing looked shabby next to their slate-grey uniforms.

The young men stopped suddenly at a nondescript door. One of them rapped on it sharply.

"Come." Walker's voice sounded clear and commanding.

They stepped aside and gestured: "Admiral Walker is inside, sir."

Admiral Walker.

"Thank you." He opened the door and entered.

Walker had been in muttered conversation with two other uniformed members of the fleet, but she looked up and smiled as he entered.

The smile transformed her. The years had not been easy on any of them; grey already streaked her dark hair, and there were lines around her eyes. Even the UV lamps they used to stay healthy couldn't keep the tinge of grey out of her brown skin. When she smiled, he saw exhaustion in her eyes—along with the fleeting glimpse of the child she'd once been on Ganymede Station. He could see her now, hanging upside down in the zero-g, telling stories of ship battles and victories only she could see. *Mind like a steel trap*, a few people had murmured. *An instinct for the fight. She might be the one to—*

Best not to say it. No one ever said it, not back then. When he and Walker were young, the Rebellion had been hopes and dreams, two ships and a handful of soldiers with bars sewn on their standard-issue clothes. But Walker and the Rebellion—or, in some circles, "those crazy bastards"—had built a fleet from wrecks and scrap metal, making full use of humanity's penchant for turning anything into a weapon, and Pike....

Pike still dreamed of Earth. He would have followed anyone who promised him skies and mountains again. In the meantime, he settled for life aboard a cargo hauler. It was cramped and the food wasn't great, but it was better than dying in the hopelessness and squalor of the outer stations, which was really all he could afford. Mars was out of the question. Venus, a pipe-dream.

Plus, people got all weird when they found out he was from Earth. That he was *a Native*. Rychenkov was the only man who'd ever shrugged his shoulders. As long as Pike didn't steal —or crash the ship—the captain didn't give a damn.

"Pike." Walker's voice called him back. Her voice ... and that smile.

"Walker." He couldn't keep from smiling back.

One of the soldiers looked sharply at him.

"Admiral Walker," he corrected himself.

"No need for protocol. You're not one of my soldiers." She ignored the others' looks and beckoned him to the table. "Come see."

A star chart moved slowly through the revolution of the planets before breaking off with a burst of static and returning to the start. Pike's eyes followed the progression of a single dot tracing its way out of Jupiter's orbit, swinging wide to gravity sling around Mars, and—he swallowed—stopping at Earth.

"There's a mission." Walker's voice seemed to come from very far away. "We need to retrieve something from Earth."

Earth. He didn't answer. He couldn't quite remember how to speak.

"Pike." She slid a printout across the desk. "This is what we're going for."

He didn't care, but he picked it up. His eyes tracked over the words three times until he could make sense of them. "Why is it called the 'Dawning?'"

"To be honest, we don't know." She folded her arms. "We just know the laboratory is somewhere near a mountain range. The ... Rockies?" One eyebrow rose at the name.

"Colorado," Pike murmured.

"You know where it is? You could find them?"

"I grew up there. And ... they're hard to miss."

Walker grinned at that, and one of the other commanders cleared his throat loudly.

"We need your ... firsthand knowledge ... to make this mission a success." There was the faint bitterness there that Pike had become familiar with over the years; those who had grown up in the stations never liked to talk about Earth, especially the ones who'd seen it. For some reason the people on Mars and Mercury and the Snowballs didn't have that problem. But station-folk? You never talk Earth with a station-dweller. The man's eyes swept over him coldly. "You will brief our mission specialist—"

"Pike will be the mission specialist." Walker interrupted her commander calmly. She smiled at him, and then at Pike.

"Ma'am, with all due respect, he is not a member of the fleet."

"I'm aware of that. However, he has firsthand knowledge of the terrain, he won't require any medical enhancements to compensate for the gravity, he has been fully vetted, and he has ... experience with weapons."

"He is not a member of the *fleet*." The commander leaned across the table, whispering as if the rest of the room would not be able to hear them.

"I'm aware of that," Walker repeated. There was an edge in her voice now. "Dismissed, Commander." Her eyes swept around the room. "All of you are dismissed."

They left, some more eagerly than others, and Pike studied the ceiling to avoid looking any of them in the eye. When they were gone, Walker sighed.

"Pike, you don't have to do this. You *can* be mission specialist if—"

"I'll do it."

"You're sure? If it's where you grew up, the Rebellion cell you'll be interacting with might be very close to where...." Her voice trailed off, and then strengthened. "To where your family died," she said simply.

He swallowed. He hadn't thought of that day in years, but he had thought of Earth. He had thought of the wind and the grass, the buzz of cicadas. He had thought of the breathless scramble up into the foothills on summer days.

"Technically my dad died on Johnson Station." He tried to grin. She wasn't buying it.

"Bill," she began.

"I'll do it," he said again. "When do we leave?"

"Two days. We're waiting for confirmation on the drop point. We'll need to escort you in and provide cover for the landing." She smiled wryly. "If only we already had the Dawning, right? We could make quick work of the whole alien Fugger fleet," she added, using the semi-vulgar nickname one used for the Telestines in the presence of children, which, in space on the over-crowded stations, were ever-present. And since they hadn't seen each other since they were children, it seemed appropriate.

"And the Telestines?" He raised his eyebrows. "What about their orbital defenses? This won't be a cakewalk. I've made cargo runs for the Fuggers before, and I've run stuff under their noses. Let's just say that they don't take kindly to human ships over Earth. They kinda have laws about it...."

"We're ready for them."

"You say you are. But are you prepared for the consequences?"

Her gaze was almost cold. "We will lose ships. And people. But this is our chance, Pike. Our chance to change ... well, everything."

His lips twitched, but his eyes were already fixed back on the mission map. He traced the ship's progress to Earth and hoped his death-grip on the table wasn't too obvious.

He was going home. After twenty-four years, he was finally going home.

CHAPTER THREE

Jupiter, Ganymede's L4 Lagrange point
Command Center, New Beginnings Station

"We need to draw the Telestines' attention to let our fleet get to Earth before they can mobilize a defense." Walker raised her hand to point at several glowing dots on the screens in the war room. One of the screens flickered madly, and she couldn't bring herself to feel anything beyond weary acceptance. Something was always breaking down here. The Rebellion needed mechanics—and plumbers, welders, and construction workers.

She reminded herself, again, not to wish for what she couldn't have.

If this plan worked, she would have more than she had ever dreamed.

"The scout ships are going ahead." She nodded at two blue dots entering the asteroid belt, then tapped several red dots. "These locations likely have sensor arrays. If we knock out *this* one, and create a diversion—more on that in a moment —we should be able to get the task-force through without being seen. Commander King, do you have a progress report?"

King winced and shook her head. "Nothing yet, but it'll take them a while to cross the asteroid belt. Everything we've mapped so far on this trip aligns with what we've heard from the transport ships, and we've been able to avoid a few sensor arrays we might not have spotted."

Walker nodded in satisfaction. Ten years back, the rest of the Rebellion leadership at Jupiter and Mars had told Walker not to bother seeking out agents within the other colonies. Those with enough fire to be loyal would always find their way to the cause, General Essa had said. No unnecessary risks were to be taken. The rest had agreed with him.

The rest, save those in this room today. Lieutenant Commander Scott Larsen had grown up with her on Johnson Station. Commander Delaney, already cast aside by General Essa as too old, had remembered the old militaries of Earth— and his dreams of the planet he had seen with his own eyes stoked Walker's resolve. Commander King, young and overlooked, had backed Walker time and again in increasingly bitter disputes.

There had been others, of course—men and women whose resolve could not hold, who were not willing to give everything to the Rebellion. Men and women who did not seem to care that humanity lay shattered and chained and starving, scattered throughout the solar system.

They were gone now.

She should be happy. The Rebellion was what *she* had

made it. Every success, however, had only been a thorn in her side. Guns, ships, uniforms, even *air* brought to them through a wildly inhospitable environment—none of these were victories she should have to win.

She closed her eyes and tried to drive all of that from her mind. They were close to their target now, but that was no excuse for nostalgia. She should focus on the mission.

"Admiral!" Commander Larsen's raised voice interrupted her brief reverie. "That blip from earlier? I've resolved it. It's Telestine, all right. A small task-force. Four ships."

Her spine stiffened again. "Course?"

He paused, working out the trajectories and numbers. "Not aiming *directly* at us," he looked up, with a note of fear in his eyes. "But ... close enough."

She sprang into action. "Red alert. Larsen, if they *were* to adjust course and come here, what's the ETA?"

"At their speed? Five minutes, tops."

Not enough time. Dammit.

She pressed the button on the command station that would link her into every Exile Fleet ship docked at New Beginnings. "All ships, depart immediately. Don't wait for your captains or crew members if they're on station. Leave now. Commander Larsen will feed you a course. Keep the station in between you and the incoming Telestine fleet at all times, and then swing around Jupiter. Aim for the north magnetic pole. That should shield you from their sensors. Go!"

She glanced around at the captains and leaders of her fleet assembled in the command center. There was no time for them to get to their ships. The crews were on their own. The Telestines had caught them with their pants down.

Never again, she resolved to herself.

Minutes later, Larsen confirmed. "Ships are away, Admiral."

"Our shuttles are humming and waiting for us, if we need to bug out," said King.

Walker nodded. Not yet—there was still the chance this Telestine task-force was just on a routine patrol, and not on a pre-emptive strike mission. "Hold here. For now. Larsen, track that task-force with every passive sensor we've got. No radar. We don't want to tip our hand and blow our cover. We're supposed to be an abandoned station, after all."

The minutes passed, and a deadly silence had descended over the command center. The assembled fleet officers, powerless to do anything other than wait, stood and watched Walker and her crew monitor the incoming threat.

"Any course change, Larsen?"

He shook his head. "Not yet, ma'am."

Another five minutes. The tension in the room was palpable. Walker felt she could cut it with a knife. But the stakes were high—as high as they'd ever been. They were on the cusp of launching the most important mission ever undertaken. If the Telestines wanted to cause the most damage, to nip the Rebellion in the bud, now was the time. If this was a pre-emptive strike, how the hell did they know?

Larsen looked up, the color beginning to drain from his face. "Ma'am? They've changed course."

CHAPTER FOUR

Jupiter, Ganymede's L4 Lagrange point
Command Center, New Beginnings Station

Walker sprang into action. "Everyone to the shuttles. Now."

The command center erupted in a flurry of motion. This was the moment they're drilled and trained for, but it wasn't going down as any had planned. They'd trained for battle, not immediate retreat. If this was an invasion, it meant they had a leak. A plant. Someone who'd betrayed them.

The command center was half empty when Larsen called out again. "Admiral! Their course change…." He stared at his console, poring over the numbers.

"Yes?" Her hand had been poised over the comm button, ready to send out a pre-recorded message to her contact on Venus. The one who'd given her the critical information about the Dawning. The one who'd helped her stand up and fund the new operations on Mercury. The pre-recorded message said simply, "*We've been discovered, and we're evacuating. Go to ground. Cease all comm traffic. We'll resurface and regroup where we discussed earlier.*"

"They changed course, but ... their new course is not toward us." He looked up, relieved. "Looks like they're aiming to pass by Io. With about a hundred thousand kilometers to spare."

She relaxed, though not completely. "Stand down alert. Cancel shuttle launches. Recall the fleet when the Telestine task-force has passed." She breathed deeply, not realizing how long she'd been holding her breath. "Looks like Pike gets his chance after all." She looked around at everyone composing themselves after the near-miss. "People, if this mission succeeds, if we obtain the Dawning, it's the beginning of the end for the Telestines. And the first step in our final victory."

"I still don't think *Mr. Pike* was the best choice for this." Commander Jack Delaney settled back in his chair and studied Walker, his old, wrinkled forehead growing deep furrows. He had been with her from the start, but lately, it seemed that nothing she planned was acceptable to him.

"Pike knows Earth," Walker said simply.

"So do I." The words came through gritted teeth. Delaney had been eight years old when the invasion came; he had survived the first exodus, and the filth and despair of the earliest settlements. No matter how he tried to mask it, Walker caught the bitterness in his tone when he asked why the younger generation fought for a planet they had never seen.

She never answered him when he asked. It would be too risky. For all his bluster, Delaney had a quick mind and a legendary skill for strategy. Anything Walker said might betray her. She could not risk him discovering her true intentions and motivations, which she would never admit to another living soul, until it was all over, humanity safe.

"Pike was born and raised in the Rockies," she said patiently now. "He knows where the Telestines have bases—"

"Where they had bases twenty years ago."

"—*and* he can survive without supplies," Walker continued. She did not bother to raise her voice. "He was trained to use guns since he could hold one. We just have to get him onto the surface."

She stared Delaney down until he swallowed and looked away. He could see the look in her eyes. He knew she wasn't going to entrust this mission to a man past seventy, his hair white.

A man who'd never held a gun until fifteen years ago.

For a moment, she felt a stab of pity. But not everyone was made to be a soldier. And dreaming of glory in battle was not worth more than victory.

"Any other questions?" Walker swept her eyes over the group.

There was a hasty murmur, some heads shaking, and for a moment—just one—she felt a wave of regret. She understood why so few questioned her, after all: her rise to power had been as careful as it was ruthless. She started with the cargo haulers, against General Essa's express wishes. Walker knew what too much knowledge could do to a person, and the transports that carried goods between the stations and the colonies had seen it all, from the palatial estates above Venus down to the worst of the stations surrounding Jupiter. They were the ones stopped for the petty indignities of ship inspections by both human and Telestine bureaucrats alike. They passed Earth time and again, a forbidden home, and they looked down at the blues and greens and knew it was forever lost to them.

It hadn't taken much for them to start turning over their data on the obstacles within the asteroid belt, or the patrol schedules of the Telestine ships around Earth, or the questions that betrayed just where the Telestines were watching for threats. When missions were suggested, it was Walker who knew which systems to avoid and which to target. It was Walker who could predict the defensive capabilities of the satellites in orbit around Earth. Her power within the Rebellion grew as she anticipated Essa's mistakes.

When Essa fell, at last, it was Walker who courted the youngest among the cargo fleet. Their parents, long since accustomed to passing the Rebellion intelligence, accepted the trade: send their children to the Rebellion and they received the promise of Earth in return. The new recruits brought with them contacts within the manufacturing sector—linked, however distantly, to the mines and shipyards on Mercury. When the Rebellion's ranks swelled and its fortunes rose, the officers knew who had brought them so far.

It was Walker who stepped into Essa's shoes, and Walker who now commanded the Exile Fleet. King and Delaney questioned her, but rarely—and the others never did.

"Good. King, keep us apprised of the scouting information. The rest of you ... it's time to make a ruckus. We want the Telestines distracted so they aren't watching our ships come in." She hit a button, and three separate systems came up. "The first diversion: we have maintenance problems on these stations necessitating food aid and some parts." She tapped at several dots, stations tentatively aligned with the Rebellion but without any Fleet resources aboard. "These issues fall within the parameters of the Technological Easement, and with any luck, Tel'rabim will handle the food side of things."

As much as she hated watching humanity bow and scrape for food aid, the fact was that they couldn't feed themselves. They needed the aid the Telestines gave them, and that was all on the discretion of what seemed to be the richest members of their society.

Yet another reason for this Rebellion: who could say when that charitable streak would end? Tel'rabim had been sending aid to humanity out of his own coffers for decades. Surely he —she was fairly sure it was a he—would tire of it someday.

"Communications about these issues should obscure any signals coming from our ships," Walker continued. "Please note that we are allowing these stations to handle all communications themselves, for the purposes of seeking UN aid to ensure Technological Easement." Her gaze swept around the table, meeting each pair of eyes. She did not have to remind them how important this was. If the UN found out about this mission, they were in for a world of trouble. The General Secretary would almost certainly do something, whether intentional or not, that would expose the scope of the operation.

"On that note, ma'am, we *have* arranged for Secretary Sokoloff to be occupied with a great number of requests from the outermost stations so that he doesn't get too suspicious about these." Larsen looked up to meet her eyes and nodded.

"Thank you. Meanwhile, a diversion ship will send a transport for the parts they're requesting, which will break down near—" she tapped the screen, "*this* sensor."

"That will mobilize their fleet into the asteroid belt, won't it?" Commander King frowned.

"They'll tell the Telestines they're doing the repairs themselves. The trick is, the sensor arrays become backup communications grids. If the ship signals for help, that hijacks the sensor's primary array. As long as our ship can keep it busy with transmissions about parts and repairs, we can get through the belt with minimal interference."

Or so their source on Venus said.

She *wished* she knew who that was. Whoever they were, they commanded a network larger than her own, and better connected—and if the cargo haulers knew who it was, they weren't saying.

Right about now, however, Walker was willing to take any ally she could get. She stared down at the maps and tried to keep her expression blank.

"Ma'am?" Commander King looked worried at her pause.

At her side, Commander Delaney watched Walker, his eyes narrowing.

"Right." Walker turned back to the screens with cold determination. "Now, the other diversions...."

I will free humanity from this hell if it is the last thing I do. Don't fail me, Pike.

CHAPTER FIVE

Venus, 49 kilometers above surface
Tang Estate, New Zurich

"Sir?"

"What is it?" Nhean Tang kept his gaze fixed on the blaze of sunlight outside his office windows. He had stationed his personal chambers at the top of the floating estate so that he would always be surrounded by a view of towering golden clouds. The estates on Venus were prized for precisely this view, and his was one of the finest. That he did not like the view was another matter entirely.

For him, it was a reminder.

He turned his head at last as the footsteps approached. "A detachment of the Exile Fleet has broken out of orbit around Jupiter." Parees, his aide, placed a document reader on the desk behind him.

"Yes, I know. The admiral informed me." Nhean sank his

chin onto one hand. His focus was split now, between the view before him—a lightning storm brewing in the clouds to the east—and the constant scroll of information on the screens to his left. Information was his lifeblood. It was the only thing that mattered. Bullets could be dodged. Money could be lost. Power could be bought. But information? Nothing mattered more. "Anything else of interest?"

"Some are concerned about her choice regarding a mission specialist." The aide considered. "And the *Valiant* is their escort ship. Internal reports suggest that it's damaged."

"Yes, she's asked us to see to its repairs, if it survives this mission." His voice was neutral. He was not pleased by the admiral's request, but he could hardly fault her for asking for his help—or for using a weakened ship for this mission. The odds that any of them would make it out of this gambit alive were slim.

Then again, he could have predicted her actions when he told the Rebellion about the Dawning. He had judged it worth the risk. He wondered if the rest of the fleet knew the dangers, and decided they likely did not. Laura Walker was not someone to risk a mission with too many facts, or too many people knowing said facts. He had never met the woman, of course, but it had not been too difficult to learn about her.

"Tell me about the mission specialist."

"William Pike," Parees said promptly. He clasped his hands behind his back, reciting information without looking directly at Nhean. "Approximately thirty-five years old, but his birthdate is unknown. Native of Earth."

Nhean's eyebrows went up. There were humans still living on Earth—a great many of them, in fact—but the bulk of them were in chain gangs, used for whatever purpose the Telestines deemed most expedient. Official human settlement was banned under the terms of the treaty that had been so carefully written and imposed upon the human race, a farcical invitation for the Telestines to settle Earth, acknowledging their technological superiority and thanking them for the great kindness of not wiping out the species. Some humans still remained, of course, in defiance of the treaty.

They were hunted like animals.

His eyes flickered. "Was there a recent escape I was not informed of?"

"He was given passage off earth twenty-four years ago. His family was feeding information to the Rebellion; they were found, and the colony was destroyed. Out of loyalty, the Rebellion saved as many from the camp as possible."

Nhean said nothing. His eyes were narrowed. This man, William Pike, knew Earth, then. No wonder the admiral had been so assured that she had a good mission specialist. And ... ah. Of course.

"He's not part of the Rebellion, himself, is he?"

"No." Parees hesitated. "He was a childhood friend of the admiral's, from Johnson Station at Ganymede. His current political views are unknown."

Had been unknown. Nhean smiled grimly. However careful he might have been in the past, William Pike was part of the Rebellion now. "Learn what you can about him. And find me a way to get in contact with him on the surface—*outside* the admiral's channels."

"Of course, sir." Parees did not protest; he never protested when Nhean gave him impossible orders. "Will there be anything else?"

"Tell me if any of the rest of the fleet starts moving. Otherwise, no. You may go."

"Sir." Parees bowed and withdrew, bare feet padding on the marble floors. If one looked only at him, in his sleeveless vest and loose pants, long black hair drawn back in an austere braid, one might think this a tableau from Earth itself, and not in a floating estate in the caustic atmosphere of another planet.

From the marble columns to the hanging plants, it was an image Nhean did his best to cultivate in every room but this one. The view here was too obvious for such a deception to be successful.

He swung his chair around and gave the screens his full attention. A few he moved to one side so that he could still catch a glimpse of the stock market feeds and the meager packets of information he was able to extract from the Telestine communication systems.

The remaining screens arranged themselves into a map. He could see the advance scouts of the Exile Fleet forging through the sensors placed within the asteroid belt. The Telestines, justifiably mistrustful of humanity in spite of its surrender, liked to keep tabs on the passage of ships toward Earth. Those sensors were the epitome of high-tech: small, easily overlooked, with self-destruct capabilities if anyone tried to take them apart. They were still, however, prone to debris collisions, and thus the catapult had made a surprising return to the human military arsenal.

The admiral's ships had been careful not to take out too many sensors in any one area. They charted a careful path indirectly through the asteroid belt. From the number of fighters accompanying the mission, it was almost certain that Admiral Walker knew some of the defenses that lay between her fleet and its home planet.

She did not know all of them, however, and it had not been in Nhean's interest to tell her. To do so would be to betray how much he knew, his capabilities ... and his limits. He had spent the past few years very carefully building a tiny arsenal of copycat satellites, working his way insidiously into the Telestine communication systems. He could quite easily access the peripheral systems, but it was Earth's defense he needed to crack.

For that, he needed the fleet. Nhean was not foolish enough to show his own hand just yet. Rebels with guns, making a terrible commotion on the surface of the planet and stealing all of the Telestines' attention, would make the perfect diversion.

And, if he played his cards right, he would have access to a man not as loyal to the Rebellion as to the *idea* of Earth. Someone like that could be the most useful tool of all.

Admiral Walker had no idea what she had just handed him.

CHAPTER SIX

Jupiter, Ganymede's L4 Lagrange point
Command Center, New Beginnings Station

Admiral Walker watched the view screen with bated breath.

It was finally time.

The entire command center fell quiet as they watched the ships come out of deceleration burn at precisely 0800 ship-time. The *Valiant* began its slow turn broad-side to the bright blue planet below. Walker had only been there once before, but like that time she now marveled at how the atmosphere seemed to glow like blue fire, compared to the sterile vacuums of the Snowball Moons of Jupiter.

At least, it felt like she was there. In reality, she was watching from the relative safety of New Beginnings Station at Jupiter. Thank god they'd stolen faster-than-light comm tech from the Telestines or this would never have been possible.

On the view screen it looked like the whole ship reverberated as the fighter bay doors slid open. She was, charitably speaking, an ugly ship, a refitted algae tanker that still smelled to high heaven in the fighter bays. She didn't need to be aerodynamic, and so she wasn't. Her hull was streaked and scratched, and her crew called her—however affectionately —"the Troll."

She had it where it counted, though. The old skim tubes for the algae harvest now provided the lateral thrust to spin the ship, and the seven tanks held forty-nine fighters, more than any other "carrier" the Exile Fleet commanded. Delaney sometimes spoke of old aircraft carriers on Earth the size of small space stations, and also of the starships humanity had one day hoped to send into space, floating cities with gardens and schools, made not just to support the basic rudiments of life but to allow humanity to flourish.

Walker paid more attention to those stories than she let on.

"Fighter bays reporting open." Lieutenant Commander Scott Larsen kept his eyes fixed on the text readout.

"Thank you." Walker rested her palms lightly on the desk.

"Fighters beginning launch," Larsen reported.

Walker kept her eyes fixed on the screen. The planet curved gracefully beneath the *Valiant*, deceptively peaceful. She gave a quick look, counting the soldiers watching here: King, Delany, and Larsen; Captains Noringe, Lee, and Kim; her navigator Ensign Harris—men and women from all walks. Larsen had been a friend of Walker's younger brother, one of the many children who played "Tag and Retake Earth" in the zero-g center of Johnson Station. Sara Harris had been raised in the relative luxury of the Mars settlement, and Ed Noringe, people whispered, was the heir to an estate on Venus. Walker believed it. He rarely spoke up, and when others mentioned the squalid conditions on the stations, he furrowed his brow and tighten his lips, as if he felt guilty.

On screen, the fighters began to emerge from the *Valiant*, taking up their formation in a three-dimensional wedge pointed at the planet's surface. Nestled among them was Pike's ship, a heavier fighter with a capsule strapped to the bottom.

Pike would have a rough, unguided landing, but they'd learned through trial and error that the Telestines didn't bother to shoot down objects in free fall. The Telestine sensors looked for the byproducts of propulsion, and accordingly, the Rebellion had designed its ships to tumble like asteroids, drift inert, and plummet into gravity wells.

The species they were up against had been in space since before the birth of Christ; humanity scavenged the scraps of their technology, some given, some stolen.

Every part of this plan had been tailored to fit their enemy's weaknesses. Like their ships, human technology was crude and limited, scarcely advanced beyond NASA's heyday in the last century. Hopefully it was good enough.

They'd soon find out.

"No engagement yet from defensive satellites. I suppose that's good, right?" Larsen's gaze went to the readout, as if checking whether this could possibly be correct.

Walker paused. No detection, no scrutiny at all? No Telestine engagement? She zoomed in on the wedge of the fighters and peered at a serial number.

"Fighter Eighteen. Give me its video feed."

"Yes, ma'am."

The officers all turned their heads to watch as one of the side screens came alive with the video feed. It was a grainy fisheye view. Earth appeared as a glowing arc at the bottom of the feed, and two other ships hovered just in sight out the windows. Walker's eyes picked out the somewhat larger shape of the ship carrying Pike's capsule. She folded her arms over her chest and tried not to tap her fingers.

A flare of activity on the screen drew everyone's attention.

"Defensive systems engaging." Larsen swallowed. He looked up at Walker, his gaze like steel.

She nodded. There was nothing to do now but begin. Retreat was not an option.

"Formation spreading." Larsen's voice almost trembled now. "Bunching toward the sites of engagement."

"They're doing well." Delaney said, gruffly, stroking the white stubble on his chin. He sounded impressed. His eyes met Walker's and he gave a nod. They had created this formation together and tested the fighter pilots on it. When she worried and wished they had the old military manuals from Earth, he reminded her that they would have been no use. Three dimensional warfare was new to humanity. Space is not the sea.

And, in any case, as always, there was no use in wishing for what they could not have. The Telestines had carefully destroyed the entire human military knowledge base, along with the militaries themselves. The records of bases and ships, all lost. Weapons, missiles, strategies, tactics, all gone. All they had left were traces of memory in those who had escaped the culling.

That, and instinct. And as a million years of survival had

proved, humans had excellent instincts.

"Dive."

She gave the order firmly, with confidence. Afterwards, her lips shaped silent words as she recited the Lord's Prayer. She kept her faith hidden, the cross below her uniform, the icons in the drawer of her locker, and she always prayed in silence. *God can hear you anywhere, Laura,* Grandmother's voice whispered.

Her fingers clenched against the desk.

A flicker caught her eyes.

"Air-to-air mass-drivers detected. One ship down."

The room went still. Walker swallowed, and then the video feed pitched sharply to the left. On the screen, the wedge lengthened and began to tip. The rearguard fanned out and arced away in their own wedge formations. Blips of light flared and disappeared.

"Second ship down. Two—no, three more." Larsen did not seem able to avoid giving an account, even though they could all see it. "Defensive systems engaging ahead of the scout group."

A flare of light showed in the video feed and the ship swerved sideways. At the edges of the feed, Walker could see the other ships bunch and exchange places.

Four minutes and nine seconds in. She tracked the progress of the lead group with her eyes. They were close to the stratosphere now. Close, very close. She looked between the feed and the screen. Dots were beginning to freeze in place as the ships that were supposed to monitor one another were blown out of the sky.

A massive flare of light to starboard, and the whole screen flickered.

"What the hell was that?" The words came out before she could stop them. She looked over at Larsen, who was staring, frozen, at the video screen. "Scott, what was that?"

"Two detachments down, ma'am."

She didn't understand him. "Two ships?"

"Fourteen ships."

"What? What hit them?" The satellites had defensive arrays, but nothing to take out fourteen ships in perfect unison.

"I ... don't know." Larsen's eyes moved to the screen. "They're ... forming up."

The wedge tightened and lengthened yet again. Walker zoomed in, fingers moving unconsciously. The fighters had formed a cone around the drop ship and they were putting on speed. They arrowed desperately down toward the surface in a swift glow of compressed orange atmosphere.

Two minutes and forty-eight seconds.

The ship at the fore burst apart in a cloud of debris and the formation spread to avoid the fallout before joining up again. The view of Pike's ship dropped away as their feed ship took the lead position.

Walker's hand was over her mouth. It was her own voice she heard in her head now, two weeks back, her own speech to the very pilots she was now watching die horrific deaths. *The Dawning gives us a fighting chance. If we want humanity to survive, the drop ship* must *get to the surface and steal that tech.*

They had believed her, those pilots. They had hurled themselves into the defensive arrays, they had watched their fellow pilots blown to pieces, and now they were fanning out around the drop ship for what cover they could find.

She had ordered missions before that claimed lives. Lone

scouts had died on the asteroids and moons that housed Telestine weaponry. Soldiers had gone and never returned. It was part of the cost. She had always known that.

It was a different thing to see it: to watch them stare death in the face and continue on, regardless. Her fingers were white where she clutched the desk. Two more red blips disappeared, and then three more.

Even Larsen wasn't counting any longer.

She could see Earth in the view screen. The Rocky Mountains rose like a spine from the flat plain as the ships hurtled down. The ground was rushing up—

"Drop ship...." He trailed off. "Hit. Drop ship has been hit."

Her body jerked reflexively at the sound of his words.

Larsen's shoulders slumped with relief. "Capsule intact. And falling in the planned trajectory."

She swallowed hard. The video screen wheeled as the remaining ships in the formation arced back up toward the distant bulk of the *Valiant*. A single dot showed the capsule falling, falling, and Walker had time to wonder what Pike must have thought as he watched the debris streak past him and the capsule jolt loose from the ship.

Did he know the drop ship had been destroyed?

The ships were accelerating as fast as their engines could go. She saw the *Valiant* began to move to intercept them.

"*Valiant*'s accelerating to match fighters' speed." Delaney murmured.

The carrier was growing closer in the view screen. All but one fighter bay was closed, a grim acknowledgement of the loss. The remaining ships were still putting on speed as they left Earth's gravity well behind them.

One more dot blinked out of existence, and the gaping maw of the fighter bay grew to enclose the whole of the screen. The video bounced as the ship hit the deck and slid, two more ships coming in behind, and the doors began to come down—

"Message from the captain of the *Valiant*, ma'am: *mission successful, capsule intact on impact.*"

Walker let out her breath slowly. "And the *Valiant*?"

"Heading for the nearest dark space in the Telestine sensor array before resetting their course for Venus."

"And confirmation from Pike?"

"Waiting on that, ma'am." Larsen's fingers were tapping at the feeds. It seemed like an eternity before he nodded. "Yes, ma'am. He's alive and on the surface."

"We did it." Delaney nodded at her.

Walker said nothing. Relief made her weak at the knees, and yet—

This was only the beginning, and if Pike failed, they did not have the resources to try such a thing again.

CHAPTER SEVEN

Earth
Mountains Near Denver, North American Continent

The capsule came loose from the drop ship with a terrifying sideways jolt and Pike felt the tiny sphere blow sideways into the sky. He was thrown against the web of restraints with bruising force.

He hated this. He hadn't thought about it much on the two-week journey aboard the *Valiant*, and then they'd brought him out to see the capsule and he'd had a moment of pure horror. It was tiny. It was unguided. And in the horror of the battle, watching the debris of the escort fighters streak past the tiny window as the drop ship wove through the air, he'd learned just how much he hated having no control at all over his fate.

He hated the thought of falling without guidance, trusting that the parachute and webbing would cushion him against impact and that the Telestines wouldn't bother to shoot him out of the sky. He hated watching the *Valiant* recede in his view screen.

And then he was cut loose with a jerk and something that felt very much like a blast. The capsule went into a tumble so quick that even the stabilizing gyroscopes on the webbing failed, turning him over and over in a slow arc. The window spun around him in a blur, first showing the spine of the leading edge of the Rockies rushing up far too quickly for comfort, then showing the receding chaos of the battle. The fighters were protecting his fall. He made out one quicksilver dart of a ship, and then the vision was gone and the next time his eyes tracked the sky, he could see nothing at all.

The viewport swung into view of the ground again, and he realized that he had never expected to fear this return. The briefings had all started with, *once you're on the surface....*

On the surface and not a bloody smear, presumably. If he lived through this, he promised himself desperately, he was going to be a changed man. He would—

Impact knocked the wind out of him before he could think of something to promise god. The webbing stretched down to allow him to slam against the floor of the capsule and started to fling him back up, and his body mercifully decided to lose consciousness before he could find out if he was going to hit the roof, too.

He came to still hooked in. Everything ached. There was the taste of blood in his mouth and a low droning in his ears. He clicked his teeth three times over the tiny pad at the back of his mouth to trigger the signal back to the *Valiant*. Was the ship still alive?

The droning was getting louder.

Droning.

Oh my god, the droning.

It had been twenty-four years, but there was no mistaking that sound.

Telestine engines.

He thrashed, looking around himself. He had to get out, but when he thought about releasing the webbing and painfully dropping onto the floor of the capsule, he flinched.

Ok, don't think about it. There was hardly time, in any case. He rocked himself forward in the webbing and stretched his feet to hit the bar at the back of the swing; they had wanted to give him something he couldn't press by accident on the way down, but he was fairly sure no one had thought about how painful swinging in the webbing would be after impact. It worked though: there was a mechanical hiss, and the webbing dropped him onto the ground.

Panic kept him moving as he peered out the least obstructed viewport of the three hatches. He cursed softly. If only he could see out, to know if they had a clear shot, see how close *they* were....

He *knew* they had the weaponry to vaporize the capsule where it sat, and that they very well might. Running was still his best bet. He punched the button for the hatch and hauled himself out.

The ships were behind him, still just specks in his view. There were two of them. Could they see him?

Just pick the best choice and run with it, Walker's voice in his head. *Just keep picking the best choice.*

That's all you can do: the best choice.

And in this case, the only thing that qualified his choice as *best* was that it was the least bad.

He took a breath of unfiltered air for the first time in two and a half decades, and then he took off. Pebbles slid under his boots, the wind added a strange sense of vertigo, and he forced himself not to look at the sky or the greenery as he ran, not to mark the shape of the peaks to his right.

There was no time for homecoming now. There was only the chase.

Did his sister Christina have time to run, all those years ago? Did she lie in the burning forest, still alive after the first bombs? Suffering, in dread fear? If only he'd just started running when he first saw the ship all those years ago, to warn her, to save her—

He'd long since buried those questions. He fixed his eyes on a shadow ahead, an outcropping of rock flanked by brambles, and prayed he could run faster, harder.

He dove and rolled. His body slammed against the back of the makeshift cave and pain burst across the bruises that were already there. A deafening droning sound was blotting out everything else now. Pike curled his head down and forced himself to stillness. If they weren't shooting yet....

The air was screaming, and he felt the hiss of gravel and dust across his skin. They were setting down nearby.

Moving as slowly as he could, Pike uncurled himself and peered out from under the rock. The ships hovered over the ground—the Telestine anti-grav tech was a closely-guarded secret. They were sleek silver wedges, metal layered to look almost like feathers.

Everything the Telestines did had that sort of beauty. And

there, getting out of the ships....

Pike's jaw clenched. He'd never seen a Telestine up close before, but the figures emerging from the ships were clearly not human. They were close though, and that was the most horrific thing. They walked with an eerily smooth gait. Their skin was so pale that it was a wonder they weren't burned in seconds by the strong morning sun. Slits lay along their necks that looked almost raw, and they had no noses to speak of. Where hair should be, the skin over their skull rippled. It was like a child's drawing, utterly grotesque, and yet, at the same time, vaguely graceful and beautiful.

And deadly. Utterly, chillingly, deadly.

What had he expected? They took Earth, didn't they? With hardly a fight. He should have expected them to look something like the animals here. Maybe under those suits, they had feathers like their ships.

The two of them fanned out. They couldn't seem to see his footprints, but they were swinging their heads, unmistakably intelligent. They had broken up the area around the ships into two halves and they were both circling. It wouldn't be too long before the nearest one reached the outcropping, and then....

Pike went still. From the way their heads bulged in the back, it seemed certain that their brains were in their heads. They might not be human, but severing the connection between brain and body seemed like a good bet for killing them. He'd have to move quickly, do his utmost to kill the one before the other heard. His fingers flexed, and then clenched into fists. Quiet, he had to be quiet. Who knew what they could hear?

And would he be able to overpower even one of them? By all accounts, they were at least twice as strong as the average human.

But he was more than twice as angry as the average human.

The roar of a gunshot startled him, but he didn't care who was shooting—he was just glad someone was. He saw the nearest Telestine jerk around, searching for the source of the sound. He didn't have to be Telestine to see the look of surprise—or shocked betrayal.

Rage filled him. How *dare* they look surprised? How dare this alien look around as if it hadn't been expecting someone to take a shot, when it wasn't even their planet to start with? How *dare* there be even the start of anger on the alien's face? They had killed, and killed, and killed, and they had the gall to look surprised that someone was taking revenge on them for all the killing.

He had to focus—he was never going to get a better shot than this. Pike launched himself through the brambles and into the alien's body with a primal yell. His fist shot out and connected, and there was the satisfying crunch of cartilage and bone under his knuckles. The Telestine went down and he was on top of it a second later, chest heaving as his fist slammed down over and over again. He didn't stop until the grotesque face stopped wincing—just a bloody pulp beneath him. He panted, and slowly stood up.

The body lay still.

CHAPTER EIGHT

Earth
Mountains Near Denver, North American Continent

"Hey." The voice was light, jolting Pike out of his reverie. He'd been looking down at his blood-covered hands. He didn't know what color he'd expected Telestine blood to be. Certainly not red. Red blood—that was a human color. It seemed profane that the alien bled the same as his mother and Christina.

He looked up. The man picking his way down out of the spires of rock nearby was probably only a little older than Pike himself. Brown hair with the first few streaks of grey fell long over the forehead, and the man's work-weathered fingers held the shotgun easily.

Confidently.

After the endemic ill health of the space stations, this man looked all at once weathered and hearty: skin with the pink no

Martian or even Venetian could match. Thin yet muscular, not like the billion or so Jovian humans clinging to life out on Jupiter's Snowballs, living on carefully formulated protein supplements and minuscule gravity. And yet he moved with an easy grace that only an Earther could truly have in a gravity well, and only Natives at that, not Drones—not the Telestines' slaves. He didn't seem at all winded despite the altitude. He stuck out one hand with a ready grin.

"Charlie Boyd. Are you Bill Pike?"

"I ... yes." Pike looked around himself at the bleeding Telestine bodies and the scrub brush bending delicately in the wind, and wiped his hand off before reaching out.

And then he saw the mountains, and the breath left him entirely.

There was no sight like this in the solar system, no hologram that made it real. Even Olympus Mons on Mars, though far taller, was a pale shadow to these. The peaks were impossibly sharp against the sky. He tried to orient himself, remember east and west. It was morning; the sun was still rising. A hawk soared high above as it hunted for breakfast, and the air....

The air was fresh. Alive. Pike felt something in him unknot. He wanted to cry.

He clenched his fingers and turned slowly. Plains, sky, mountains. There were animals moving below them, not stock animals, not animals in carefully constructed cages, going nowhere while their feet plodded on little treadmills. These animals just *were*. There was grass, a dozen kinds of grass, and different shades of rock, and even the browns and faded greens of the high desert seemed like an assault on the eyes after so many years on ships and stations breathing sterile recycled air.

"You were born here." Charlie came to stand beside him. He shrugged at Pike's questioning look. "The briefing said as much. When did you leave?"

"When I was eleven." That wouldn't mean much to him, but it didn't have to. "The Telestines found us. The Rebellion got us out, took us to Johnson Station. Ganymede," he clarified, when Charlie frowned. "It's a moon of Jupiter."

"Is that one out or in?" Charlie frowned.

Pike felt a stab of annoyance, quickly tamped down. "Out," he said curtly, assuming he meant outside the asteroid belt. It was his mother's annoyance—his mother, who had not wanted her children to grow up ignorant. Who said they had to know everything children were taught *Before*, so they could pick up where humanity had left off when the Telestines were gone.

His mother was dead, and those who hadn't cared as much as her were still here.

Whatever Charlie saw in his eyes, he didn't press the issue. "We should go. They'll be sending more ships soon."

"Should we ... destroy these?"

"No point. We used to try, but they have locators of some sort; the next ships always come right to where the last two were. We've got about half an hour, probably, to get back to camp."

Pike looked around himself. He couldn't see anything habitable nearby.

"It's there." Charlie looked satisfied. "But they can't see it, either."

That, at least, he could approve of. Pike smiled and let the man lead him down the slope.

"Do you go by William or Bill?" Charlie called over his shoulder.

"Pike, actually." His father had called him William, and his mother had called him Bill, and after the escape, he hadn't wanted to be either. While his father died a slow death from grief, alone in their apartments on Johnson Station, Pike had worked to forget everything about Earth, about Christina and his mother, about the Rebellion. He was Pike, he told his father, not William, and he let his lip curl in contempt when his father asked if he'd be joining the Rebellion. He didn't have to say anything to remind his father what the Rebellion had cost them. He hadn't been on Johnson Station when his father finally died, and he wondered sometimes if the man had thought of Christina and their mother at the end.

The guilt was familiar, but not so easy to dispel as usual. Maybe it was the mountains.

Maybe it was the shotgun in Charlie's hand.

Or maybe it was the thought Pike hadn't been able to banish in two weeks, wondering if his father would be proud to see him now.

He'd come here to see Earth again, he told himself. Not for the Rebellion. Maybe they'd save humanity, maybe not. He hadn't believed that was possible in years—too many people, too much despair, too many odds stacked against them.

He was just here to see home again. To see mountains. To breathe air. To feel sun. He wondered if Walker knew that, and felt a fresher guilt. Walker *believed*. He didn't want to hurt her, he told himself. He just had a clearer idea of the odds.

He realized Charlie had been speaking.

"Hmm?"

"I said, it'll take a few days to get to the lab." Charlie used the gun to point north along the range. "You can't see it from here, but last we knew it was moving away, up toward Laramie."

"One of *their* labs?" Pike raised his eyebrows.

"Well, sure." Charlie looked bemused. He gestured to the grimy clothes and the old-style shotgun. "Did you think *we* made the Dawning?"

"What *is* the Dawning?"

"No idea," the man said cheerfully. "That's your call to figure out, and frankly, none of my business." He sobered. "The rest of us, we're going for something else."

For the first time, Pike felt a flicker of unease. "What are you going for?"

"Rescue mission. We think there're people in the lab, too."

Pike stopped.

"We gotta keep moving." Charlie didn't turn to look.

"What do you mean, there are people up there?"

"I mean, there are people up there. In the labs."

"*Why?*"

The man tensed. "Nobody knows. But if you ask me? Experiments."

Did Walker know about that? If she did, she hadn't said so. He heard her voice as clearly as if she'd been next to him, almost amused: *What would it change, Pike?*

Maybe he didn't have a clearer idea of the odds, he thought. Maybe she just had hope. Maybe this was what his father had always called, inexplicably, a Hail Mary pass.

That was something to think over later. Pike looked to

where Charlie was picking his way down the mountain. The tension in his shoulders hadn't eased, and his face was tight with anger. When he caught Pike looking, the man's face twisted.

"Just ask. I know you want to."

He hadn't asked, because it didn't matter—and because he didn't want to know. Pike looked down at the ground passing under his feet. "Who? Who's up there that's yours?" he asked quietly.

"My wife. Our daughter." Charlie looked north, and his eyes were distant. "Three years ago."

Pike let his breath out slowly. He didn't want to offer false promises, but he knew that was what he was supposed to do. "We'll avenge them," he promised.

Charlie flinched. Then, defiantly: "I'm going to find them."

"You're—" Pike broke off. *They're dead*, he wanted to say. *Even if they weren't killed when they were taken, they're dead now. No one lasts three years in a Telestine lab.*

From the bitter smile on his lips, Charlie knew just what Pike was thinking. He didn't bother to argue. He just gave a shrug, artfully careless. *Who cares what you think?* his eyes asked.

They walked on in silence.

CHAPTER NINE

Earth
Mountains Near Denver, North American Continent

"Where are we going?"

"You'll want to see this." Eva, a blonde woman who looked altogether too small for the impressive array of weaponry she was carrying, led the way up the path as Pike struggled to keep up.

Behind him, the other leaders of the Rebellion cell talked amongst themselves in low voices. Their camp was only Rebellion members, no children. Some of the members appeared to be spouses, but there were few of those. At some point during the past twenty-four years, the Rebellion had learned the awful cost of its operations.

Pike tried not to feel bitter about that.

"Here we are." Eva held out a hand to pull him up onto an outcropping. "You're not afraid of heights, are you?"

"No." But the dizzying view was more seductive than he remembered. Sunlight dappled on the rough forest at the base of the foothill below, and he could just see himself spreading his arms and leaping....

He swallowed.

Eva wasn't paying attention, though. Her arms were crossed and she was staring out at the Telestine city, far in the distance, that hovered over Old Denver. Her blue eyes looked furious.

Pike remembered that look too well from his father. He had always dreaded coming up into the mountains due to the inevitable angry lectures about the Telestines taking the planet. Then, Pike hadn't cared much. The occupation was all he'd ever known, and as a child, it had been hard to mourn a city he'd never seen. He looked at their rough camp of forty and wondered how millions of people had ever lived all together, jumbled up in tall buildings.

Now Pike, a product of humanity's exodus despite his Native origins, forced himself to look at the ruins of the city and the Telestine station that hovered above it.

It was sleek with shining metal curved all along the bottom. Sunlight gleamed and the metal gracefully arced up into spikes. Along the top were their buildings. *Skyscrapers*, he recalled wryly. The Telestine buildings fit the description better than human buildings ever had.

"Look." Eva handed him a pair of binoculars. "Under the ... under their city."

He set the binoculars to his eyes and adjusted the view cautiously. It had been a long time since he'd been somewhere he could use binoculars—nothing on a ship was far away enough, and nothing in space was close enough.

For a while, he wasn't sure what he was looking for. He scanned past ruined structures, struts of metal and shattered glass that he could still only partially pick out. There was a tangle of green in the middle of the city, something that reminded him of the hydroponic air refreshers on the stations, but massive.

And then he saw it: movement. He squinted. It looked like one of the long repair bots, stretching up to the tops of one of the buildings.

"What is that?" He tried to dial in, but could not sharpen the view. He looked over at Eva. "Are they trying to repair the city?"

She laughed at that, actually laughed. The sound was harsh. "No. They're tearing it down."

"If we could just set that bot on their cities, we'd be good to go." He couldn't keep from smiling.

"It's not a bot." She didn't smile back. "It's a chain gang."

He frowned, shook his head. The term made no sense to him.

"Humans. Well, Drones. Chained together." She jerked her head at the city. "There are platforms all the way up that building, and every day, the humans walk up and demolish a little bit more of it."

Drones. Human, but not quite, it seemed. He'd only ever met one, and he was strangely passive. His personality a void. Rumor had it that the Telestines bred them. Docile, meek, unquestioning. Intelligent, but empty. The perfect slave.

Pike held the binoculars back up to his face. He scanned across the city. Now that he knew what he was looking for, he caught the flickers of movement on a few of the structures. There would be more of them than he could see.

"Why not just blow it up? They have nukes, don't they?" He knew that all too well.

"They're sensitive to radiation, too. Or so we think. Plus, they're taking the materials, melting them down. We think they're salvaging the city. Probably to build more of their own. Easier than mining and smelting the raw ore."

"That can't be worth it." They had the technology to extract minerals more efficiently than humans ever had, surely.

"Of course it can—when you don't have to care about the labor." Her eyes were fixed on the city, and though she could see nothing from this distance, he knew she was seeing the gangs in her mind's eye. "And they wouldn't want to ruin the view by tearing the ground open, now would they?"

He had no answer for that. There *was* no answer for that. Could a Telestine appreciate a view? For a free human, it was unknowable. "What are they building?"

"Their own city—we think." For the first time, she sounded doubtful. "To be honest ... we aren't sure. Sometimes it almost seems like we see military activity, but they don't have anyone to fight that we know of." She shrugged. "Serve them right if someone else came to take Earth from them, I guess, but then we'd be even worse off, wouldn't we? Better the enemy you know? I never know what to hope for." She cleared her throat. "Anyway, that's ... what's happening here. Just so you know."

"Where are they getting the people?"

She just shook her head.

"Seriously. Are they getting pulled off stations?"

She gave a bark of laughter. "No. Don't—just don't." She swallowed, and pointed north. "It's clear enough today, you might be able to see the lab."

He hesitated, but it was clear she wasn't going to explain any more. He raised the binoculars and adjusted them. The mountain peaks swung by in dizzying clarity, and then: the tiny shape of an airship.

They would be on foot going up into the mountains, he realized. They would watch the airship grow in their view until they were dwarfed beneath it. It would hang heavy over the mountains, the way the military ship had hung over the camp so long ago. He swallowed hard. "How are we getting in there? Are we going in some of their ships?"

"We can't work their ships." Her regret told him that they had tried it. "Best we can tell, they interface telepathically or something. Maybe it's a security system that only recognizes Telestine physiology. You get into the cockpit and it's all smooth. There's something that *looks* like a control panel, but nothing on it. And we've never seen them use one. We studied their bodies, but we can't tell much from that, either."

"So how're we getting up there?"

"We have some hovercraft. The Rebellion sent us two. Your drop ship was supposed to be a third, but after it got blown up…." She shrugged.

"What?"

"The ship carrying your capsule. They designed it for impact, it was going to free fall after you. But Charlie told us how it got blown up."

He remembered the jagged strut protruding from one of the sides of the capsule and felt a chill. He'd thought the holds just came off when the capsule released. Now the sideways jolt made more sense.

He couldn't think about it, or he'd be sick. "So what's the plan?"

"We stashed the ship north a ways. We'll go on foot, rendezvous there, and take the ships up. You look for the Dawning chip thingie and we'll run rescue missions back to the ground with one of the two ships—that way, you can still get off the lab as soon as you find the Dawning."

"You say chip ... you don't have *any* idea what I'm looking for, do you?"

She gave a helpless shrug. "I mean, I know it's a computer of some sort, but all of their computers we've seen are white cubes or smaller chips, and there's gotta be more than one in the lab, right? The information came from the Rebellion. We figured you'd know. We don't even know how you found out about it. The labs don't emit any signals that we can tell. Someone would have to be in their communications systems."

He sighed and rubbed at his eyes, handed the binoculars back to her. "Well, we'll have a couple of weeks to think about it." He gave one look back at the city, then turned and pushed his way past the other members to start back down the path.

A losing, suicidal plan. Why the hell had he agreed to come back?

That's right. Mountains. Air. Sun. Walker. Dawning.

It had sure as hell better be worth it.

CHAPTER TEN

Jupiter, Ganymede's L4 Lagrange point
Fighter crew locker room, EFS Intrepid

"A whole squadron." Dave Hernandez, or Fisheye to his fellow pilots, snapped his fingers and leaned forward to whisper meaningfully. "Just *gone*. Toast. *Jodido!*"

"Dammit, Fish." Theo McAllister gave the pilot an exasperated look, and could only guess the vulgar translation of that last Spanish word. He'd given up on trying to keep rumors about the last mission from spreading, but he was in no mood to let things get out of hand. His promotion to CAG was recent, but anyone and everyone knew the value of morale.

Morale Fisheye was currently destroying.

"They should know what we're up against, *che*," Fisheye protested. He saluted, though, and McAllister knew the pilot's protest wasn't sincere. He looked at the group, and then back to McAllister. "*Che, boludo,* Why weren't *we* in the first group?"

Che, boludo. McAllister had learned months ago that Fisheye calling him "swollen balls" was actually an endearment. "What, you wanted to be...." McAllister snapped his fingers, echoing Fisheye's earlier gesture. "*Jodido?* Screwed?" He gave a grin at the others when they laughed. "I'm sure the bastards would oblige." He headed for his locker at the edge of the room.

"Naw, we're just...." Fisheye clapped a couple of the other pilots on the shoulder and hurried after McAllister. He settled into a chair nearby. "We're on the flagship, you know? Should'a been us, *che.*"

"Like they were gonna send the flagship in for an early battle, guns blazing?" McAllister leaned in, keeping his voice low. "You know they aren't planning anything until Mercury is ready. They must have found something big. But you know we're gonna get our shot. It's not like the admiral's own ship is going to miss the show when we take Earth back, right?"

Fisheye snorted in agreement. Unbelievably skinny, with a shock of blond hair and the palest blue eyes McAllister had ever seen, the young man had found his way to the Rebellion from far-flung Pluto, and he'd never lost the look of some alien creature that had climbed out of the depths of the ocean, translucent and blinking. How he'd wound up looking like that, with a name like Hernandez and Argentine heritage to boot, McAllister had never figured out. Hell of a pilot, though, once you got used to having someone who looked like a ghost on your team.

"What's going on?" Tocks settled in behind them and leaned close. "Telling secrets about me?"

McAllister reached out to clasp her hand, then bump it in greeting, nodding as Princess, a rough-looking stubbled man, settled in beside her. The two were practically inseparable—they even looked like twins, even though they shared no family and had grown up on different stations: same thick brown hair, same black eyes, same olive skin. Originally, it had been Nick who had the nickname Tocks, always following the plan rigidly, pointing to his watch, and Rachel who was Princess—and then Fisheye had pointed out it would be funnier the other way around, and the names had stuck.

Nick had taken it well, after an initial bout of sullen mumbling and profanities.

"Just about your curious affinity for a dude that looks like your brother." McAllister leaned in toward her, eyebrows waggling slightly. "So? You into him? He into you? Come on, we need a distraction."

She smiled-lopsidedly, flipped him off, and said nothing.

"Right...." He grabbed another chair and sank into its sagging cushion. "Ok. Earth. How much do you know?" McAllister raised his eyebrows as he stared directly at the two newcomers.

"Nothing." Tocks gave a sweet smile. "No one on *your* crew would gossip, LT."

McAllister gave her a look. He'd been given strict instructions by the admiral not to let his crew spread rumors about what had happened on Earth, but both of them had known even then that it was impossible to keep that sort of news from spreading. For a fighter crew, gossip about other crew's mission was like candy. Or crack.

The door opened and Admiral Walker walked in. Everyone

went quiet and jumped up to their feet.

"Just ... do your best to look surprised." He threw the words back, pitched low, and snapped into a salute with the rest of them.

"At ease." The admiral laced her fingers behind her back, taking a moment to look them over. "By now, I'm guessing that all of you will know what occurred on Earth several hours ago."

There was a shame-faced mutter of agreement, and McAllister relaxed. The admiral wasn't mad. That was good—she might be five-foot-nothing if she stood up very, very straight, but she could be more imposing than anyone he knew.

She was an arresting figure, with eyes like fire and steel, even when calm, but now that he knew this wasn't going to be an angry meeting, McAllister couldn't keep his eyes on her any longer.

Not with Commander King standing at her side.

His eyes traced over King's small, straight nose, the heart-shaped face, black hair bound back in a braid and struggling to escape. She stared straight ahead, her at-attention pose perfect, but her cheeks took on a slight tinge of pink—she could feel him staring, clearly.

"—imperative that you follow the instructions of your CAG." The admiral's voice drew McAllister back to reality, and he looked over just in time to meet her gaze and nod seriously.

Fisheye elbowed him in the side, grinning—he'd caught McAllister staring. McAllister shook his head, glaring a reminder. Of the pilots in the room, McAllister was fairly sure that only Fisheye, Tocks, and Princess knew about him and Commander King, and he wanted to keep it that way. For one thing, the admiral wasn't one to tolerate this sort of thing. She'd have him shipped off to some other vessel in a second if she knew what was going on.

"Any words you'd like to say, Lieutenant?" The admiral was staring at him now, her face so bland that he wondered if she'd seen him staring, too.

"Yes. Thank you." He leaned forward so he could sweep his eyes around the room. He didn't dare look at King again. He knew his smile would give him away, if the discreet bulge in his pants hadn't already. Whatever he did, he absolutely could not, *must not*, think about how she felt this morning, stifling her laughter against his shoulder in the showers—

He cleared his throat.

"We've seen some of the tricks the bastards have up their sleeves now." He nodded at them and shot a glance at the admiral. "Sorry for my language, ma'am. Fuggers, not bastards."

She only nodded, holding back a smile. There was one thing you could always count on with the admiral: she hated the Telestines more than any of them. "Rat bastards will be fine, Lieutenant."

He grinned. "But this doesn't change anything," McAllister continued. He met the eyes of the others, holding each gaze until they nodded. Fisheye, Princess, Tocks. The handful of other pilots. "We didn't get into this because we thought we had better tech than them, right?"

There was a nervous laugh.

"We got into this because we know we're worth more than this. We know that if we train hard, if we go in there like I know we can, we're gonna blast 'em out of the sky and we're gonna take back Earth."

The cheer from his pilots made him grin.

"So we go back out today and we train." McAllister jabbed his finger at them. He scanned the back row for more nods. "We remember the ones who were lost. We honor their sacrifice. And we get ready for the Big One. You with me?"

The cheer came again, pilots stamping their feet, and McAllister nodded to the admiral. His smile faded slightly at the look on her face, but grew again as his gaze drifted past her to King. The woman was smiling, biting her lip as she clapped for his speech, and he knew she was thinking exactly what he was thinking. They'd talked about it in whispers, in her quarters: no more stolen moments, no more ships or stations, no more frickin' protein rations that tasted like fishy cardboard. Someday they'd built a real life together.

On Earth.

"Thank you." The admiral's voice cut over the cheering and she waited for it to die down. "As your CAG has told you, the next step, for now, is training. We're still reviewing the data from the last mission, and—" She broke off as an officer slipped into the room and came to whisper in her ear. "What?" Her voice was low, but McAllister caught the sudden anger there.

The officer looked as if he would rather be doing anything than delivering his message. He leaned even closer to speak the next few words.

"But that's—" The admiral bit off the words. She forced a smile for those assembled. "If you'll excuse me, something has come up. As soon as the review is complete, we will begin training on new maneuvers based on our analysis from the last mission. McAllister, you have the floor."

And she was gone, King at her heels, the door slamming behind them.

Something was up. Something big, to make her leave like that.

CHAPTER ELEVEN

Venus, 49 kilometers above surface
Tang Estate, New Zurich

"Just tell me what I'm looking for." The admiral's voice was halfway between ugly and desperate. "Oh, for the love of … look, we don't have the *time* to be checking every computer in the lab. The Telestines are going to mobilize as soon as the alarms trip. The team will be at the lab in three days, and they don't know what they're even looking for. I'm sitting on a message from the mission specialist right now, and they don't even have a guess."

There was a pause, and Nhean knew that she was staring at the message. He cast his eyes down at one of the screens. He knew the message she was looking at. He knew, in fact, every communication that had gone between the Rebellion outpost and the mission team.

None of us know what we're looking for, the message read. *Give me anything, any detail. The team is anxious, and half of them are planning to go off and look for kidnapped family members instead. I don't think I can stop them.*

His frustration was clear. Nhean felt some sympathy for that. But while there was only one mission for William Pike, there were many for humanity.

He wondered why they thought there were humans there at the research station—the target. He'd been toying with the idea of asking his Telestine contact if there truly was a human experimentation program. Tel'rabim was one of their greatest advocates within Telestine society—surely he'd throw him a bone, some snippet of information on the subject.

But if some of them had decided to use captive humans as lab rats, would they listen to a lone voice of dissent? Even one as powerful as Tel'rabim?

"Are you still there?" Admiral Walker's voice was curt. The FTL packet transmitter caused a slight waver in her voice where there was none; she'd hate that. Now that he'd given them the tech to speak with him—stolen off a Telestine satellite that had, as his father would have said, fallen off the back of a truck—she treated him as if he were one of her soldiers.

He did not bother to remind her that he was not. Their interests were aligned, but he was not a member of the Rebellion. He did not take commands from her. She could forget that at her peril.

"Yes." He kept his responses short. His voice should be distorted enough to be genderless, but the admiral was getting closer every day to learning his identity. The less audio he gave her to work with, the better. "I can only tell you what I know, and that is that the Dawning is movable. It has been moved between laboratories before."

"So it isn't the laboratory itself." There was relief in her voice.

"I did check that. To the best of my knowledge, no."

"But all we can do is *hope* that it's small enough to get onto a shuttle."

"Yes."

"And if it's not?"

Nhean settled back in his chair and fixed his eyes on the swirl of clouds outside the window. He waited until his anger dissipated before he spoke.

"If it is not, we will be in roughly the same situation as before."

"No, we will not." Her voice was flat. "We will have lost forty-six fighters. Almost five percent of my pilots. We will have tipped our hand regarding the fact that we *have* a fleet at all, and we will have a *smaller* fleet to use next time for an attack —an attack they will be better prepared to repel."

"Admiral, with all due respect, our fleet was so outmatched that no marginal change in their present defensive structure will make the slightest bit of difference. The fact that those fighters succeeded at all is a miracle."

A silent, simmering anger came down the line.

Nhean could work with silence. He pushed himself up to pace, hands clasped behind his back, eyes still fixed on the clouds. "Did you think the Telestines were unaware of our activities? Did you think they had not noticed our Rebellion?"

They was a silence. "Yes," the admiral admitted finally. "I did."

Nhean raised his eyebrows. At least it wasn't bluster. He had grown used to face-saving lies in the earliest permutations of the Rebellion, and it had been tiresome. General Essa had been the worst. At least Walker had a sense of pragmatism and dignity about her.

"They don't know where it is," Nhean said. "Or, at least, I am fairly certain that they don't. I am not certain they can reliably tell the difference between military base activity and standard station activity."

There was only silence.

"Admiral?"

"So you're telling me...." She took a deep breath. "That if they take revenge for our attack two weeks ago, it might be anywhere, and on anyone?"

He paused to stare at the communications unit on the desk, a half-smile on his lips. Their relationship was one of deception—a tenuous alliance at best. Every once in a while, however, the admiral surprised him. Now, panicked not that the Telestines might come for her, but that they might come for someone else, she surprised him a great deal.

He tried to reassure her. "For all we know, they may think that the attack two weeks ago was the entirety of our fleet. I think we can safely assume that if they truly believed any one of our settlements was a Rebellion base, the settlement would have been gone long ago."

"You're sure?"

"Insomuch as anyone can be sure of anything where the Telestines are concerned." He was giving away too much of his speech pattern. He paused to consider before he spoke again.

She interrupted his train of thought: "Our mission

specialist mentioned potential military activity on Earth. Could that be leading up to an attack?"

To tell her, or not? Nhean considered for a long moment. Yes.

"There may be a factional dispute going on within Telestine society."

"Really?" She sounded as if the thought had never occurred to her before.

"It's hardly out of the question." Simpler words. Simpler sentences. "Earth is not their home. I don't know if they all agreed that settling here was wise. I'm given to understand there's a cult of some sort—more than one perhaps, but it's difficult to know how similar they are in that respect. We see similar disputes among our people aboard the space stations and moons. Competing power structures. Groups with diametrically opposed interests. The Telestines could be the same. Which, if true, would be ... fortuitous. Competing interests can be exploited, after all."

"I hadn't thought of that." She paused, and he could see her staring into the middle distance. A still shot of her, a candid photo taken some eleven years back in the hallways of Ares Station at Mars, hovered on one of his own screens. He wondered what she looked like now. "How do you know about the faction dispute?"

He hesitated. The truth was that he didn't know, not for a fact. It was only a suspicion, a shadow in the data he saw. Instinct. And how could he tell if his human instincts could be trusted to shed any light on Telestine society?

"I cannot share that at this time."

"We are on the same side, are we not?" Her voice was

tight.

How little she knew. She, of all people, should have guessed.

"My sources remain my own, and the Rebellion, of all people, should understand the need for secrecy." He took a seat once more. "I am awaiting confirmation on several pieces of information."

"A factional war could be exploited." The words were a reminder and a test.

"Unlikely at the moment, if we can't figure out what the factions are or how to interact with them. May I remind you that we have yet to find a way to interface reliably with their computer systems, however reliably they can interface with ours?"

"What does that mean?" she said. The question was sharp.

"It means that the Telestines are eminently capable of interacting with us when they so choose, and they may, indeed, have been doing so for quite some time."

"We see their communications."

"I don't mean the broadcasts." Every year, or thereabouts, the Telestines liked to remind humanity of the treaty between them. There seemed to be increasing emphasis placed on the loyalty of the individual to the best interest of their species. That had been one of the first hints that all was not rosy in Telestine society, but that was not the matter at hand right now. Nhean looked at the communications unit as he spoke. "Haven't you wondered at some of the information coming from the Rebellion cells on Earth?"

There was a very long pause.

"How do you mean?"

He bit back an instinctive oath. She knew. He *knew* that she was well aware of what he meant. No one in their right mind, this high up in the Rebellion, would be unaware of the possibility he was implying. She just wanted him to say it outright. She wanted *him* to be the one suggesting it.

He hated soldiers.

If she wanted him to spell it out, she was going to have to work for it. "I *mean* that many of your cells still refuse to be identified. They're able to conceal their location. And their information is unusually complete."

"They could be reporting from within the labs. It's what I would do if I were in their position."

Was it? He wondered. "If they're in the labs, they're working only with Telestine equipment." He was losing patience with this game. "And that's impossible, as we well know. I think you understand the point I am making, Admiral."

She ignored that. "If they're surrounded by Telestine technology, they might well have figured out how to use it," she retorted at once.

That was an intriguing thought. In the meantime, he was not going to continue to let her dance around the issue. "Do you not think it possible, Admiral Walker, that some of your sources are Telestine?"

"No," she said flatly. "Why? Are some of yours?" Accusation was heavy in her voice. *Traitor.*

He did not particularly care. A great many people might call him that before this was done. In the meantime, he would not let her take some imagined high road. "Telestine sources could be useful. You were the one who suggested exploiting the brewing factional conflict."

"Not by working *with* any of them."

"Any benefit to them in the short run would surely be outweighed in the long run."

"Even so." Her voice brooked no argument. "None of them can be trusted. To them, we are insects. Do you truly believe any of them would help us?"

"Some of them do. There have always been factions of humans who advocated for other species—why not Telestines advocating for us? Tel'rabim—"

"No." A flat denial.

He took a deep breath. "Admiral, are you quite sure that your principles aren't harming the Rebellion?"

She cut the call at that, and Nhean's eyebrows rose. Interesting. Very interesting.

He strolled to the window again to look out at the billowing orange Venetian clouds, and asked himself the question he asked every time he spoke with her—the question the rest of the Rebellion seemed not to think to ask: what was Admiral Laura Walker's endgame?

It bothered him that in five years, he still had not come up with an answer.

"Sir?" Parees had appeared silently, as he always did.

"Yes?" Nhean did not look over.

"We're detecting Telestine fleet activity near Jupiter."

Nhean froze. "Jupiter? How did they get there without us knowing?"

But it would have been easy—far too easy. Who knew the limits of Telestine technology? They had given humanity the dregs, and what they kept for themselves....

Now, he shook his head. "Warn them. Warn Walker. And

get me whatever feed you can on the Telestine communications. We'll help the Rebellion however we're able to."

Laura Walker's end game was no longer important. He might not trust her with a fleet—but humanity could not afford for it to be destroyed.

CHAPTER TWELVE

Jupiter, Ganymede's L4 Lagrange point
Command Center, New Beginnings Station

The room was silent. Everyone looked studiously away from Walker as she rested her fists on the desk. Her chest was heaving. Telestine sources? Did their source on Venus not understand what the Telestines had done to humanity? Did this person honestly believe that she would trust a Telestine with anything?

"Ma'am." It was Commander King. "Even if the Telestines are behind some of our intelligence, even if they're just trying to get us to take out their enemies in other factions, we'll take them down."

"You think it's good that we would fight for them in their faction wars?" Her head swung, and she was pleased to see King flinch at the look on her face. "Spend our own blood to buy them victory?" She could barely get the words out. "Show them *our* ships?"

"Any ship we take down now is one less to take down in the final fight," Delaney offered.

"The final *fight* is supposed to happen with their defensive grid down, they aren't supposed to have fighters in the air at all!"

The room fell silent.

"Our sources are not Telestine." Walker cradled her elbows in her hands as she forced the words out. "I refuse to believe that. We would know." She swept her eyes over the room and the others nodded quickly. They knew better than to disagree right now. Every one of them met her eyes and she knew from the tightening of their lips that even if they did not believe her, they would not speak of the suggestion again. She could live with that. Her eyes fixed on Larsen, whose gaze was firmly fixed on his screens. "Larsen."

He looked up and seemed to see the tension in the room for the first time. He looked around himself and cleared his throat awkwardly.

"Uh, it's just—I am getting the weirdest feedback coming in on our systems. It's like the outpost on Adrastea ... disappeared? Not quite disappeared. It's like trying to look at something through steam, you know? Lots of static."

"Solar flare?" offered Captain Noringe.

Larsen shook his head. "Adrastea is the second closest moon to Jupiter, so it's tidally locked and the sun is completely blocked out for the next hour. It couldn't be a flare...."

The rest of the officers looked at one another. When the line on the desk rang, everyone jumped.

Walker reached out to open the call. "Admiral Walker."

"The Telestine fleet has found you." The distorted voice was back, calm. "They seem to have appeared near Adrastea and are sweeping the system. I don't know if they know where the fleet is, but they'll find you soon."

"Clear the station." Walker heard her own voice speaking. "Delaney, King, with me to the *Intrepid*. You too, Larsen and Harris. Noringe, Lee, and Kim, to your ships. Everyone take your direct reports. Larsen, sound the evacuation order. Everyone *move*."

"What do we do when we're there?" Ensign Harris had stood up, but she was frozen there.

"Evacuation first." Walker's voice was sharp. "Get the station between us and the Telestines, dump all the thrust you can to get around the side of the planet, and then cut your engines." If they were drifting, giving off no signals, there was a chance the Telestines wouldn't see them. "Let's not be sitting ducks."

"Yes, ma'am." Larsen punched a code into the computer and the klaxons wailed to life. "People should be leaving the shuttle bays any moment now. It's a red alert, no one should be stopping for anything."

"Add a timer. We can't afford to wait."

"Yes, ma'am." No one moved.

"*Now!*" She jerked her head at Delaney and King to follow her; Harris was already moving.

New Beginnings Station was far from full; thankfully, King had suggested long ago that they should keep as many people on the ships as possible, even while docked at the station, and have the shuttles on constant alert and ready for the rest of them, in order to be able to leave at a moment's notice. *Maybe the only ones who will die today will be the officers*, she thought with black humor. Walker took the corridors toward the heart of the ship and the ladders that would lead them to the shuttle bay.

The countdown was flashing there on the walls—5:35, 5:34, 5:33—and Walker nodded in satisfaction to see the groups emerging at a jog from hallways nearby. No one was carrying anything, and no one was panicking. They drilled new Rebellion soldiers obsessively on the layout of their ships, and the soldiers now made their way to their assigned shuttles without shoving or jostling, though a few called goodbyes to one another.

"What's going on?" A new soldier paused in the doorway of Walker's shuttle.

Walker pushed him inside without answering and pointed to one of the seats. She strapped herself in and watched as the other officers did the same. She caught Harris's eye as the door of the woman's shuttle closed, and they both gave nods.

In a way, they had been waiting for this since day one. It was almost a relief that the Telestine attack had finally come.

Or, it would be if they didn't all die in the next few minutes.

"Ma'am." Delaney settled next to her. He pitched his voice low. "Do you have a plan once we get to the ships?"

"Yes." And no one was going to like it. She shook her head at him. "No details yet. Still working on the specifics." She didn't need him arguing with her while she thought.

"*All shuttles loaded.*" Larsen's voice sounded, incongruously, from the pilot's chair and over the linked intercoms. "*Depressurizing shuttle bay.*"

She heard the shuttle bay doors begin to open and the shuttle rocked on its mooring as the air blasted out into space around them. Larsen was taking this as quickly as he dared.

"*Godspeed and good luck.*" Larsen's voice was quieter now. "*Hope to see you all soon.*"

The answers came back quietly; the pilots were very aware that they might be emerging from the station into a war zone. Given what they knew of Telestine weaponry, the station was no safer—but the illusion was there. Space never felt quite as big as when you were in a shuttle.

"*No activity showing in the immediate area.*" Larsen's voice was a bit too relieved for Walker's comfort. She didn't want him spooking the rest. "*Engines are spun up, maneuvers will begin as soon as shuttles are aboard.*"

Thank god they had drilled for this. Walker clutched her fingers around the harness and stared straight ahead as the shuttles split off for the ships. The *Intrepid* loomed through the windshield of the shuttle. Her eyes traced over the lettering as she gave a silent prayer. Did the Telestines understand the way humans named ships? Did they realize that this was an expression of hope? Of defiance?

It seemed like an eternity before the shuttle thudded down in the bay, and Walker's eyes snapped open; she must have closed them to keep her face calm.

"Everyone stay put. Delaney and King, with me to the bridge. Larsen, come with us as soon as you can." She punched the button to open the shuttle as soon as the light flashed green, and made her way across the bay at a dead sprint.

By the time they emerged onto the bridge, all of them were panting. Walker saluted at the duty officer and took her place at the control table as he melted away. She nodded to the pilot.

"Make for Earth."

The woman pivoted in her chair. "*Ma'am?*"

King's jaw had dropped open.

"Admiral—" Delaney began. His voice was tight.

"What other option do we have?" Walker looked over at him. "They know about us now. They came to fight us. We don't have the fuel to run anywhere else, and we don't even know if we could outrun them." She made a calculation in her head. It was time for specifics now. "Tell the *Washington* and the *Pele* to hold them off, and get the rest of the fleet to Earth." She said a silent goodbye to Brown and Kim, and straightened her shoulders. There was only ever the best choice. "We have to be there when the defense grid goes down."

Now it was all up to Pike to find—and figure out how to use—the Dawning.

CHAPTER THIRTEEN

Jupiter, Ganymede's L4 Lagrange point
Fighter Bay, New Beginnings Station

Mechanics were yelling, pilots were sprinting between the ships, and the deck chief slammed Eric Barker's windshield closed so hard it bounced up again.

"*Hey.*" Barker grabbed it and hauled it down. "Don't get me killed."

The chief didn't seem to hear him. The man barely stayed to make sure the shield was in place before he was off the ladder and hauling it to the next fighter.

The robotic tug dragged Barker's ship into the airlock chamber and he looked around to see who was assembled. They would be the second group out. Two wings were already flying, and Barker's crew had just been coming off duty when the klaxons sounded.

"What's the word, Woof?" Whiskey, one of the older

members of the team, leaned to catch his eye as she slid into her cockpit. The ships' engines were beginning to flicker to life as the tugs zoomed away and the back of the bay—a heavy door burned black with the fire of a thousand launches—came down.

"Bastards found us, that's all I know." Barker ran through the ready checks, his fingers shaking. He'd flown hundreds of patrols, had even seen Telestine carriers and fighters drifting nearby, but he'd never engaged. *No one* had ever engaged before, unless you believed that ridiculous story about the *Valiant* launching an attack on Earth.

He didn't.

"And we're supposed to ... take them down?" Whiskey's wingmate seemed as uncertain as Barker was himself.

"That's what we make the big money, boys." The red lights began to flash, signaling decompression. "All right, team, get your ships ready to fly and listen up."

A chorus of *ayes* came back down the line.

"The fuggers found us. I don't know how, but you know how important it is that the fleet gets out of here. We don't, there's no Rebellion anymore, *capisce*?" He waited for the agreement. "Our goal is to take out any of the fighters heading for the capital ships. They're pushing off now and they'll go to drift around the edge of the planet and get out of sight of the Telestines. We'll keep the bastards occupied here and meet up with them at the rendezvous point."

"That better be one close rendezvous point." That was Whiskey. He could see her raising her eyebrows skeptically.

He didn't respond as the door opened and the fighters sped out into the black, falling into a wedge behind him. Truth be told, he wondered the same thing himself. If their ships left them, they had no cover from the cannons, and they didn't have the inertial dampeners to match the acceleration the capital ships could pull—or the fuel to get out into any of the three "dark spots" humanity had found: dead zones in the Telestine surveillance.

He hoped there were more than three.

"Right now, we focus on the mission." His voice was curt. "Bank starboard and go down; we'll come up from under the *Pele*."

They obeyed without a word, and he felt their fear thrumming in the air.

"Don't know about you, but I'm glad to be taking a shot after all this." He tried to keep his voice light.

Whiskey, thankfully, picked up the lead. "How many times we seen them go by? Man, I was tempted. *Bang bang*, fuggers. Now we get to shoot back, eh?"

The chatter began, nervous jokes between the pilots.

And then they came up from under the ship and the chatter stopped.

He'd seen Telestine carriers. Of course he had. If you lived on a station and you looked out, you were bound to see one eventually. They wanted humans to see them, after all. The things were made to look imposing, a regular reminder of just how outmatched humanity was. *To remind us of our place.*

And he'd only ever seen them from a distance, silhouetted against the red-orange bulk of Jupiter—or drifting out in space. Up close—

They took your breath away.

Three carriers loomed over them, impossibly large. Next

to them, New Beginnings Station looked like a shoddy, battered little toy. The *Pele* was even smaller than that, for all that it dwarfed the fighters, and the *Washington,* beside them, was one of the smallest capital ships they had. The rest of the fleet....

Was gone.

That was when he understood, and from the silence on the line, he realized that the others knew too.

He and his pilots were the sacrificial lambs. The ones who stayed behind while Walker drove the getaway car.

Damn her.

And god bless her.

"Fugger formation to port." Was that his voice? It didn't sound like it. He wasn't even aware that he'd been tracking the progress of the Telestine ships, but it seemed that his body was continuing on as if there was any point at all.

There *was* a point. Purpose came back in a rush, and he turned his head to look at the distant specks of silver against the heavy curve of the planet. The fighters cut between them, roaring overhead, and Barker forced himself to replace the hollow punch of betrayal with something more, something different. What had he said, the day he told his parents he was leaving Johnson Station for the Rebellion? *Getting Earth back is worth more than any single one of us.* They'd been listening to the Secretary General's speech, he remembered. It was that speech, reminding them to follow the laws of the treaty—to not *rock the boat*—that had caused something to snap inside him. *If we stay like this, out in the black, we'll all die.*

He'd already been as good as dead the moment he was born on one of those stations. Like hell he was going to let death scare him now. And that boat? He wasn't going to rock it. He was going to crash it. The secretary general could go to hell.

"You all see the *Intrepid* over there?" He knew his voice was shaking. He was doing the best he could. He could feel his hands moving like he was in a dream, righting the ship and taking preliminary aim at the Telestine formation in their sights.

Whiskey picked up the lead again. "Yeah, chief. We see it."

"That ship has the admiral on it." He banked hard to port and slammed into high acceleration, sucked back in his chair as their formation shot toward the Telestine ships. "She's going for Earth. Maybe not today, but someday. You heard about that mission they launched a few days back? Well, that was just the first piece. Admiral Walker's going to take back Earth someday —and we're going to make sure she survives long enough to do that."

There was a long pause, and he blinked rapidly. His vision was blurring.

"Aye, chief," Whiskey said softly. "Let's teach these bastards a lesson."

The *ayes* trickled in, some voices shaking, others numb.

The shooting started, tiny bursts of warm fire in the darkness and cold, and the formation swerved loosely to get out of the way. But defense wasn't enough, and those *ayes* weren't good enough, either. "So what're we gonna do?"

Nothing. They were avoiding fire, but there was no life in them.

Shit. They were going to die and there wasn't going to be any point to it.

The alien formation was coming up and Barker let loose a stream of bullets. He held his breath as they were lost in the black, and then the Telestine fighter at the front of the wedge burst into a hundred shards of silver.

"I said, *what are we gonna do?*"

"Fuck 'em up!" The shout came back, hoarse, from Fighter 8.

"What're we gonna do?" He pounded on his windshield for emphasis.

"*Fuck 'em up!*" The whole wing yelled the response back at him.

"Hell yeah we are! All fighters engage, let's make 'em sorry they found us!"

The roar of their approval was deafening. The formation split into four pieces, and Barker yanked on the yoke to take his group straight up. A formation of Telestines coming in hard to pick off the human fighters from above scattered in confusion and Barker heard his wild laugh echoing over the comm lines. "You like that?"

Almost beside him, one of the Telestine ships shattered and spun. He had time to see the fracture, a white cockpit, and his ship was already past the lost fighter as Whiskey gave a yell of satisfaction. They came up and around in a tight arc to dive down on the Telestines.

"They're coming around!" said fighter five.

"Not fast enough—get 'em before they can get us in their sights." His fingers closed around the trigger. He hissed in disappointment when one of the Telestines swerved out of the way of his bullets.

"Chief." It was Whiskey, uncharacteristically quiet as they

wove through the chaos outside.

"Sec. Come here, you fugger." Another burst of rounds, and the Telestine swerved again. "Come on, almost got you—*yes!*" He pumped his fist in the air. He was still grinning as he flipped the switch for a private channel to Whiskey, Fighter 2. "What is it?"

"The *Washington*." Her voice was soft, aching. Whiskey was fiery, grey streaking her brown hair, but she could drink any one of them under the table, and she told the dirtiest jokes he'd ever heard. Ace pilot, he'd said it a hundred times; she'd turned down the role of CAG at least twice. Now all that was left of the Whiskey he knew was the aim with which she took down one Telestine, and another, and another. She looked over at him, a tiny figure in her fighter, and then looked beyond.

He knew what he would see, but he followed her gaze anyway, and the sight was like a blow. He swayed sideways as the ships banked into another formation and the *Washington* came directly into view.

It hung at an angle, slowly spinning, struggling to compensate for the engines that had been shot to hell on its starboard side. Cannons still fired, but the decks surrounding the gunnery showed gaping holes. Fire flickered in its windows, and its hull was streaked with black. Telestine fighters plunged toward the carrier and sped away as their bombs pierced her hull. It was a terrible thing to see, a beautiful ship—beautiful to him, in any case, her rough jumble of parts the effort of blind hope and hundreds of mechanics—mobbed by fighters, dying by slow inches. Captain Kim didn't have a chance. The *Washington* was dying.

He didn't give an order. He didn't have to. There was no

going home to their ship anymore, and if there was one thing he was sure of, it was the raging fury of the rest of his wing. They accelerated so hard he heard a few heads other than his own slam back against the headrests. The rest of the groups swam back into formation in a three-dimensional arrow.

The thing he wanted more than anything was to climb out of the cockpit and lash out with his hands. He wanted to drive a blade into one of these bastards and see them bleed. He wanted the impact of his fists and a blade, and blood, and their screams in his ears, and if all he had was this trigger and the missiles under the wings, it was a poor consolation—but their deaths would do.

If he was dying here, he was going to make it hurt for them first.

He'd make them bleed.

He fired a missile and saw the rest of his team do the same. The missiles were for capital ships, and the Telestine fighters didn't stand a chance. They did not so much explode as vanish, dust rather than shards in the black.

Too quick, too easy a death. He looked up, teeth bared in an animal grin. "Come on, team. We're taking the carrier."

No one even questioned. They arced right and shot up at the belly of the ship. Missiles blazed as the wing shot and banked again; a gaping maw exploded where the missiles connected with the Telestine ship and it rocked in place, escaping air pushing it into a spin before the engines compensated. He could feel it watching him like a malevolent beast.

"Anyone know where the CICs are on these things? I think it's time to do a *guided* missile run."

From the dead silence, he knew no one had mistaken his meaning. They didn't have guided missiles.

"Up top, chief—I think, anyway. That's the Telestine way —always on top." Whiskey's voice was professional. "I'll come with you—I've got half my missiles."

"I've got some missiles still, too," someone chimed in.

The rest of the group fell away from the three of them as they streaked toward the top of the ship. Barker looked back once to see them each in their own path. They'd picked targets, they were ready to give everything they had. Lights flickered up on his screens as his team armed their missiles one by one. He flicked the cover on his up and hesitated a moment. His finger trembled when it came down on the button; a moment later, the warning beep showed him that Whiskey and the other pilot had done the same.

"Hit at three points, or join up?" Her voice was deferential.

The fore of the ship grew in their view as he considered his answer.

"Together." It wasn't going to make much of a difference.

Debris shot past them. He turned on his wide-channel comm to listen. He could hear Captain Brown of the *Pele* yelling orders, another wing of fighters calling to one another.

Collision course, his screen flashed. He canceled the alert. His hands were shaking; he took them from the yoke.

"Barker?"

He looked over. "Yeah?"

"Good speech."

He managed a smile. "Thanks. Honor to fly with you, Whiskey."

"Same, chief."

He did not watch his death coming. He turned his head to look at New Beginnings Station, a shattered husk of what it had been, solar panels floating in shards nearby, tumbling to catch the light of the planet. Other Telestine carriers surrounded it, unleashing hell. *Hellfire and brimstone*, he thought suddenly, the phrase from his youth surfacing unexpectedly. He looked at the place he'd called home, the creaking hunk of metal that had been just enough to keep them alive, and just enough to kill them.

And then the Telestine carrier blotted everything else out, and he leaned back in his seat as his fighter slammed into the CIC, two kilotons of explosive energy ripping through the hull.

CHAPTER FOURTEEN

Earth
Mountains Near Denver, North American Continent

By the third day, they could reliably see the laboratory without binoculars. By the sixth day, it was possible to pick out its shape: almost round at the base, with elegant structures stacked atop the high-tech-approaching-wizardry flotation devices.

Pike, who had once seen the estates on Venus, described them to the soldiers with him as they walked.

He tried to explain, but there were few words to describe the way it felt to descend into that hellish atmosphere, all boiling clouds and jets of superheated air—at least at the lower altitudes. And one time he'd accidentally strayed too low, trying to avoid official detection on a smuggling run. The *Aggy* withstood the pressure—and, thank god, most of the heat— but there was no way to miss what was happening outside in the boiling Venetian maelstrom. It took no special knowledge to look at that place and know that it was wildly hostile to life, though the denizens of the luxury estates assured Pike that the view was an acquired taste, and highly prized.

The soldiers seemed to find his descriptions of the Venetian atmosphere more interesting than the estates. Pike supposed he understood that. He'd had a sense of almost visceral revulsion the first time he stepped foot on the polished floors of one of the opulent floating mansions. Everything clean, gleaming.

And the rest of humanity practically imprisoned.

"Telestine pets, those Venetians," one of the soldiers muttered. "If they'd helped us, maybe we could take down these ships rather than trying to get up to them."

It was hard to argue with that. The tech for those estates was Telestine through and through, and only the richest of humanity had been able to settle on Venus. The tycoons, the upper echelons of the UN—hell, even the pope. Supplied by the cargo guild and waited on by servants, the rich on Venus seemed a universe away from the rest of humanity. Walker had mentioned that some of them served in the Rebellion, but Pike wondered if that was only wishful thinking.

This whole mission was wishful thinking. Pike edged his way along a narrow ledge toward the resting spot their guides had chosen. His breath was coming short. Between acclimation and growing exhaustion, it was difficult to tell if his situation was getting better or worse. Even the fact that he was keeping up seemed like a mixed blessing. He didn't understand why he was here, lugging a rocket-propelled grenade launcher on his back. He'd been working his way to a good life of honest commerce and mostly-honest smuggling on the Aggy with his fellow crew mates, and he'd thrown it all away for this?

Mountains and trees. Remember Pike, mountains and trees.

"Rest up." Eva handed him a mostly empty water skin. When he looked at her with a wordless question, she jerked her head toward the laboratory. "We're almost to the shuttles."

It would be awhile longer until they actually entered its shadow, but the floating lab already seemed to draw all of the light to it. It sat heavy in the air above the next peak. Then Eva's eyes fixed on something out on the plains and he turned to look.

Holsteins. When the Telestines first arrived and the human solar diaspora started, Pike's father said, they set all of the food animals loose. They wanted herds out roaming the land, like nature intended, only they hadn't quite realized that the animals they found in the warehouses weren't the same as the animals that had freely roamed—so for a few years, all they got to watch were majestic herds of chickens wander back and forth. Whenever he told those stories, Pike's father had laughed until he cried, gesturing with his elbows and neck in a wild imitation of a chicken strut.

The chickens had mostly died off over time, but some of the cows and pigs survived. Many of those were surreptitiously tended to by humans now.

Eva's voice called him back to the present.

"We're close enough now that we're probably going to trigger their defensive systems soon." She grimaced. "We made better time than I expected. I thought we'd be able to get the fighters and get up there from outside its defensive range."

Pike only nodded. He went to return the water skin to her,

but drew his hand back as he caught sight of Charlie standing alone at the edge of the camp. The man had been silent on the climb, and Pike had rarely seen him either sleep or eat. He carried the water skin over now and held it out.

Charlie hesitated before accepting. He had spoken little to Pike since their first meeting near the camp, when Pike had guessed at the other man's true motivations for participating in the raid. But in the end, he couldn't blame the man. Family first. Blood first.

"Thanks." He drained the last of the water and held the empty skin back out. "There's a creek ahead, we'll be able to refill there."

Pike nodded. His eyes followed Charlie's to the laboratory. He had not wanted to ask, but he supposed he should know what he was in for before they got to the ship. "You think they're up there?"

Charlie looked at him wordlessly.

"Your family," Pike clarified.

"I know what you meant." Charlie's gaze clicked over Pike's face, calculating. "Why?"

"You never told me about them."

"Wasn't much point, was there? You think they're dead." The man's mouth twisted. "You're not going to get me to give up on them, though."

"I know." Pike set the RPG launcher down at last. "So? You think they're there?"

"To be honest ... I don't know what I think." Charlie's voice held an ache. "I don't know where they were taken. I don't even know who took them. We were hunting one day and when we came back, they were all gone."

"We?"

Charlie looked back at the group of soldiers and pointed to his chest, then to two others. "Me. Hank. Eva. We all joined up after that. We'd said we wouldn't bring any harm to our families by taking risks, but once we didn't have our families anymore—" He caught sight of the look on Pike's face. "What?"

"Nothing." Pike crossed his arms. He felt the other man's gaze linger on his face. "My father didn't take your precautions. Brought the Telestines down on us."

Charlie was silent for a moment. "I didn't take risks," he said finally. "Didn't bring the Telestines down on us. But it didn't matter in the end. Sometimes fate frowns equally on the wise and the stupid."

Pike turned back to the camp. He refused to listen to this again—it might as well be his father standing there, reminding him that humanity was dying. Pike hadn't listened to the man's entreaties then, and he wouldn't listen now.

Charlie's voice stopped him in his tracks, though.

"Diana was three days old when they got taken."

Pike looked over his shoulder. Charlie was staring at him.

"Three days. And Tara couldn't even walk yet. It was a hard delivery, but we thought they were going to pull through. I left her at the camp with Samantha, Hank's wife. Hank was a doctor, a real one. We thought they were safe. We were too far away when we saw the ships leaving. We thought they'd just been shot, and in the end we went back to bury them— wondered what we had to lose now that they were dead. And their bodies weren't even there. They'd just been taken. When I joined the Rebellion, that's when I found out about the labs."

"They might have been taken for the disassembly."

"Who takes a baby for that? And Hank's wife was pregnant, too."

Pike rubbed at his head. "I'm sorry. But—"

"Do you have a kid?" Charlie challenged him. "D'you have a wife waiting for you in the Rebellion?"

"No." There was only one woman he'd ever thought he might be able to love, and her only love was the Rebellion. It was just as well, really.

"I'm doing right by my family," Charlie said fiercely. "That's all. That's all this is. Look down on it if you want, but I'm trying to get them free. If you can't understand someone doing that, why are you here?"

I wanted to come home. Mountains and trees. But that was an insult to the rest of them here. He couldn't say it. Pike met Charlie Boyd's eyes, and for the first time since he left Earth, he began to wonder if something had been missing from his life all these years. He wondered, finally, what would have happened if the Telestines had never come for them all those years ago. Would he have ended up joining the Rebellion? Would he be fighting for a daughter and a wife taken to the labs?

He didn't have time to wonder for long. The ground next to him exploded, and the *hiss-crack* of Telestine guns reached them a second and a half later. Blown sideways and nearly off his feet, the side of his face blistering, Pike grabbed the RPG launcher and ran for the outcropping of rock nearby. The Rebellion soldiers were yelling to one another, but he didn't hear screams.

Hopefully that meant no one was injured, not that people

were dead.

A hand reached out and grabbed at his through the flying dust and rock, and Charlie hauled him to safety. He was bleeding, but there was an incongruous grin on the man's dirty face.

"It's finally starting." He hauled the launcher out of Pike's hands and began loading it. "Thank god. I hate the waiting."

For the first time since he'd been back, Pike laughed. He actually laughed. His hands fumbled with the launcher.

"Me, too. Let's get up there and finish it."

CHAPTER FIFTEEN

Earth
Mountains Near Denver, North American Continent

The bullets were coming fast enough now that the echoing reports overlapped. The sound was deafening. The ground nearby tossed up burning chips of rock, and he couldn't even spare the time to hope he'd still have hair on his arms by the end of this.

"It's loaded!" Charlie yelled, over the noise. "Brace me!" He took aim, Pike's hands on his shoulders, and the RPG hurtled away with a jolt that sent them both stumbling backward.

Another hollow *boom* sounded behind them and Pike ducked instinctively as a grenade shot overhead. His head whipped around to follow it, and his mouth dropped open as it spun toward a Telestine fighter. Closer, closer, and the ship swerved at the last second.

It didn't swerve quite enough. The grenade caught it on one wing and sent it spinning down into the foothills, black smoke trailing behind it. There was a ragged cheer behind him, but a distracted one; the soldiers were already loading the grenade launcher again.

They fired, and fired, over and over, until Pike was fairly certain he was never going to be able to hear anything ever again, and he was keeping himself going almost entirely with the thought that every grenade he shot at the Telestines was a grenade he didn't have to carry for another day's worth of hiking.

"Keep going!" he heard dimly. "They're launching more feathers! Our ships won't be here for a few minutes, keep going!"

"Did she say *feathers*?" Pike yelled.

Charlie shot again before answering, and grimaced. The launcher was ensuring he would have bruises tomorrow. He turned his head back to nod as they loaded the launcher again. "Yeah, like the ones that shot you down. Feathers, because of the pattern on the outside. The other ones—the black ones—don't look like that."

"Other ones?"

"Yeah, they have different kinds. Maybe they do different things, I don't know." He shot again, and took the last grenade from Pike. "All right, brace and—"

One of the fighters buzzed low over them, out of nowhere, and Charlie's shot went wild. He tumbled, taking Pike down with him, and both of them looked up to watch the grenade streak away into the sky. A fighter—feather, Pike reminded himself—had just dropped from the belly of the floating lab and was still apparently finding its bearings. It swerved desperately to get away from the grenade.

It swerved *up*, and every one of the humans on the ground winced as the feather sliced directly into the hull of the lab. A few moments later, the sound of tearing metal reached their ears.

"Holy *shit*," Charlie muttered. "I wonder if it—"

He didn't get any farther than that. With an agonized groan, the airship tilted. It hung askew, and the sounds of desperate clanking carried on the wind.

The bullets ceased.

Silence. Pike looked around himself, certain for a moment that he had finally gone deaf, but there were no explosions—nothing remained but the now-silent airship and the smoke beginning to trail from the open gash in the underside of the hull.

"Run." Eva was behind him, her hand on his arm. "*Run.*"

"What?"

"Leave the launcher! Run!" She took off down the hill. "The shuttles! Go!"

It took a moment for him to make out a path, and he still wasn't entirely sure he wanted to follow her. "Why are we still going up there?"

"Because it's going to crash." She tossed a look over her shoulder.

"I know, that's why I'm asking!"

"The Dawning is still *on* there. And … just come *on*!" She hurdled a bush and stumbled a bit on the landing before hauling herself up with a wince. "Now!"

"Right." And the humans, of course, the ones being

experimented on. Wanting to leave was a cowardly impulse at best, but he couldn't shake the thought that none of them wanted to see what was up there. None of them were going to be able to forget it.

"Wait." Eva skidded to a halt. The others streamed past them and she turned to watch them, distracted. Her hand was on his arm, her eyes distant. "What if...."

"What?" He saw the others hauling tarps off two small shuttles. "What is it?"

"The Dawning. If it's a key to all of the defense network, what if that means it keeps the network up?" Her face twisted. "What if we *let* that thing crash?"

He looked up at it. Was it dropping in altitude?

It was.

"We can't take that chance," he said finally. "We have to go. If it can take down the networks, we can't take the chance that destroying it will do that."

Her hands clenched.

"*What?*" he pressed her.

"I don't want to lose my team for a mission we can't complete. We're not dying for nothing."

She was picking a *hell* of a time to bring that up. He shook his head. "No time for that. We have to move. Come on." He saw her waver, and lifted his shoulders. "At least three of your team think their family might be up there. There's no way you're not losing at least them, and a shuttle."

"Dammit." She blew out her breath. "You're right. Come on. Just between us, though?" She gave him a sideways look as she jogged down the hill. "I kinda thought you'd take any opportunity to be out of here. To go make your cabin in the mountains and have your life on Earth like you always wanted."

"Yeah. So did I." He'd never been good at lying, even when he really should.

"Why didn't you just head out then?"

He thought about it, silent as they tried to move as quickly as possible without slipping on the shale, but he didn't have an answer. He shook his head. "I ... don't know."

"You'd better figure it out," she advised him.

"Why do you care?"

"I care," she said grimly, "because a lot of people join up, and then there are bullets coming at them and they don't think it's a good bet anymore, and they leave other people in the lurch. Maybe it's the first battle, maybe it's the fourth, but they go, and we're always the ones who die for it. And you may be the one the almighty *Rebellion* sent to help us out, but I'm not risking my team for you, and I'm not risking my home for you. We're the ones who have to live with the consequences. You got that?"

"Yeah." He was oddly comforted. "And ... thanks for not making it about honor and duty, huh?"

"Not exactly a different speech, but sure." Her shoulders shrugged and she held out a hand to haul him into one of the shuttles, hidden by brush under an outcropping of rock. "There, that's your seat, strap yourself in and put in your earpiece. We'll need a way to communicate while we're up there."

"Right." He settled into the seat with a jerk as the shuttle took off and plugged the earpiece in. He turned it on with a button press, and a moment later, a man's voice crackled in his ear.

"*Hello Mr. Pike.*"

"Hello? Who's this?" He assumed it was one of the other fighters in another shuttle, about to give him instructions.

But the buzz—the background noise of the transmission was ... off.

"*That's not important right now. You're the only one that can hear me, so listen carefully.*" The voice paused, as if waiting for him to speak. "*Mr. Pike, I'm going to help you find the Dawning—without my help you surely will not find it. And in return ... I hope you will consider bringing it directly to me once you have it.*"

CHAPTER SIXTEEN

Earth
Mountains Near Denver, North American Continent

"Who are you?" Pike repeated. His voice was trembling with anger.

"Pike?" Eva frowned over at him. "Are you getting interference?"

"Mr. Pike, I have my reasons when I suggest that you don't tell her what you're hearing."

Pike hesitated. He didn't have to do what the voice said, he reminded himself. It was human, it knew about the Dawning, and it was offering to help. He'd cut off the call when he had what he needed—until then, he'd work at finding out just why this person wanted him to betray Walker. He nodded at Eva. "Some interference, but it's fine."

The voice paused. He could almost imagine its owner smiling. Could he sense what Pike was thinking? *"Thank you.*

Judging by what I know of you, you're going to want answers as to why I'm doing this, and why I'm requesting what I am. Unfortunately, I can't give them to you just yet."

Judging by what the voice knew of him? That meant he had to be somewhere in the Rebellion, didn't it? Only Rychenkov and the Rebellion knew he was here, and Rychenkov would never tell. He might disapprove of Pike's current activities, but the man was as loyal as they came.

"Mr. Pike?"

"That sounds like your problem," Pike said simply. He pitched his voice low. "Last I checked, you were the one who needed me."

"And we're operating over a line that could be tapped at any time." The voice seemed neither surprised nor perturbed by Pike's sentiments. *"I can offer you two assurances: first, that you will come to no harm if you bring the Dawning to me; and second, that I have humanity's best interests at heart."*

Pike considered this, and the shuttle gave an unpleasant sideways lurch.

"I can't get the doors open!" The pilot twisted to look at Eva. "They're not responding to the codes."

"Tell him to try reversing the code and re-entering it."

Pike closed his eyes for a moment. He had the feeling that this was only going to lead further down the rabbit hole. "Try reversing the code," he called up the front.

"Uh ... sure. One second." The pilot punched in the numbers, and a screech of metal rewarded them. "That worked. How'd you know to do that?"

"Recent Rebellion intelligence."

He hated this. "Recent Rebellion intelligence." The words

were grudging, and he dropped his voice again; it didn't take much not to be heard, what with the shuttle bay doors opening so loudly nearby. "It's not really Rebellion intelligence, is it?"

"*I think you know the answer to that. Now, Mr. Pike, do we have a deal?*"

"Maybe."

"*I see. But, may I ask ... why, exactly are you here?*"

Pike fell silent. His spine had stiffened.

"*You aren't a member of the Rebellion,*" the voice told him. "*You have no known political sympathies beyond an old friendship with the admiral—and with the state of humanity at present, I'm sure we all have an old friendship with a revolutionary. So why are you here, on one of the most dangerous missions the Rebellion has ever launched?*"

"I didn't say no quick enough and fell bass-ackwards into it." He *really* wasn't good at lying.

There was a sharp, brief laugh on the other end of the line. "*An acceptable answer, Mr. Pike.*"

"If we're going to keep doing this, could you call me Pike?"

"*Very well.*" The man sounded amused.

"*By the way, you'll want to turn right out of the landing bay, not left, and then up the first two flights of stairs you find. It may be on that level. If not, I have some further guesses. I'll be in touch.*" The line switched off.

Pike weighed his options. Somehow, the play-by-play offered by the voice was oddly reassuring. When diving into a pit of certain death, it seemed like a good idea to have someone who appeared to know what was going on. Even complete strangers.

"Are you talking to someone?" Eva leaned forward to call

the words across the shuttle, and even then, he had to strain to hear her over the screech of the doors.

He decided not to answer. "Where are we going when we get out of the shuttle?" he called back.

"The Rebellion map shows labs to the left. I thought we'd start there."

"What's to the right?"

"We don't know, we only got a partial map."

"Maybe we should start there." On the other hand, maybe he should have a good follow up before he started talking. "If they don't have maps there, its probably the important stuff."

To his relief, she bought his ad-libbed reasoning. "Sounds good."

He had a bad feeling about this. For one thing, he was pretty sure he could hear the faint sound of someone chuckling in the earpiece.

The shuttle landed with a thump and they piled out into a landing bay that tilted farther than Pike was comfortable with.

Shit.

"Come on, let's move!"

He had no idea when he'd become a mission leader, but people seemed to fall in behind him without complaint. They followed him into the corridor outside the shuttle bay, and he didn't even pause when he saw Charlie split off to the left with Hank and a few of the others.

Eva watched them go, but she nodded when she saw the look on Pike's face. *There's no saving them,* her eyes said. "Right. Let's go."

They steadied themselves on the wall and took the stairs at a gingerly pace; it was harder than it looked to climb a slanted staircase. Pike kept his rifle up as he climbed, ready for Telestines to appear in his sights, but there were no running footsteps ahead, no alarms, nothing to indicate that the Telestines on the ship either knew about the intruders, or sensed anything amiss.

"I don't like this," Eva murmured, and he couldn't help but agree.

He stopped dead when he emerged from the stairwell. Eva ran into the back of him and pushed her way past, only to stop with a muttered oath.

It was an eerily empty room, wide open, with only a featureless white cube in the center of it. The ceilings stretched high above, and the skewed angle of the floor only made the whole thing look stranger. The walls and floor were the same gunmetal grey, and a flight of stairs led up to the floor above.

"Is that it?" Eva edged toward it. The cube was easily four feet to a side. "How are we going to carry it? How do we *use* it?"

"I ... don't know."

"That's not it. That's a communications array. Keep going. Up the stairs."

Pike only narrowly kept himself from asking how, exactly, the voice knew the difference. He was saved from offering that knowledge himself, however, by one of the other soldiers.

"That's just a comm box."

"He was in one of the labs at one point," Eva murmured in an undertone. She looked over at the soldier. "Is it going to hurt us?"

"Nah. But you can sometimes get 'em to do stuff. Like this. Watch." He picked his way across the floor and slammed the butt of his gun into the cube.

With a hiss, eight doors opened around the walls of the room.

Pike jumped and swore, and Eva looked around as the floor tilted another few degrees.

"All right, split up. Everyone remember your path back, and give a call if you find anything."

"I'll go up the stairs." Pike didn't wait for an answer, but just took off at a run.

He slowed as negotiated the difficult incline on the stairs. There were still no Telestines, and that was beginning to bother him. When he reached the top of the staircase, the hallway split in three directions.

"All right, what now?"

There was a pause. *"Go straight. End of the hall, break the door down. And ... it's worth saying that I'm not one hundred percent sure what's in there."*

"That's ... not reassuring." Pike crept down the hallway with his borrowed rifle up. He hadn't been able to practice on it much, and he was beginning to wish he'd brought his own gun. He was going to kill Rychenkov if the man had touched his baby.

If he got back.

He reached the door. Pike took a deep breath, steeled himself, and punched his foot into it with a roar.

He saw a single chair by a large window. A lone figure looked around at the sound.

The figure was not a Telestine.

She was young—at a guess, somewhere between sixteen and twenty—with pale brown hair and lips as bleached as her skin. From the beige clothing she wore to the pale sweep of her eyelashes, nothing about her seemed to have any color at all.

Except the eyes. The eyes were jet black, and older than death.

Pike stopped. "There's a girl."

"*And?*"

"And that's it."

"*It can't be.*" The voice sounded genuinely bewildered. "*I can't be reading this wrong. It's supposed to be in there.*"

"Shit." Pike looked around himself. The room was manifestly empty, and the girl was still staring at him with those eyes. Outside, human fighters shot past the window, some pursuing silvery feathers, others pursued by them. Flaming debris hit the window and he jumped.

The girl didn't.

Then the station shrieked and tipped, and Pike made what he swore later seemed like a good decision at the time. The station was crashing, and the Dawning was nowhere to be seen. He could go down with the labs, or he could get out and make a plan B. *Just make the best decision,* Walker's voice said.

"Out of time." His voice was curt as he pressed on the earpiece. "All teams evacuate, do you read? All teams get out, the lab is *going down.*" He held his hand out to the girl. "We have to go. The ship is crashing. Come with me."

CHAPTER SEVENTEEN

Earth
Mountains Near Denver, North American Continent

"We have to go." Pike spread his fingers. "You're going to die if you stay here." They had room for more in the shuttles; Charlie had made sure of that.

Whoever she was—an experiment, a captive, a stolen child?—she remained where she was. Those black eyes watched him and she did not so much as flinch when the ship shuddered again. She didn't trust him, Pike realized, and why would she? If she was here, the Rebellion had already failed her.

When had he started thinking like that?

He lowered the gun and braced himself against the door. His mind protested in panic that he didn't have time for this. Their pilots were dying out there, and if the teams were evacuating, who knew if they'd wait for him? He should go, and she could follow. If she had any sense. But he didn't want to leave her here alone—what if she'd been with the Telestines her whole life? What if she still expected them to help her?

"I'm Bill Pike," he said, gesturing to himself. A thought occurred to him. "I'm here to look for the Dawning."

She cocked her head and her eyes sharpened.

"I'm human," Pike said earnestly. In a less lethal situation he might have pounded his chest and said, *Me Tarzan, you Jane.* He continued, "and so are you."

The smile was sudden, and almost impish. Her lips curved and he flushed in embarrassment. So she did know she was human, and she apparently knew English.

He shrugged. "Just checking."

She said nothing, but the smile stayed.

"Do you know where the Dawning is?" Pike asked her. They didn't have much time.

"*Pike. Pike!*" The voice was sudden and sharp. Static was claiming it now, and Pike yanked his hand away from the doorframe with a hiss as he heard the crackling of electricity coming from some unknown source. "*Pike—*" Static claimed the man's voice. "*—her and get—*"

"Are you there?" He turned, pressing his fingers into the earpiece. The hallway behind him was still empty, and despite the chaos outside, nothing stirred behind him in the station; he could not even hear the voices of the others. "I can't hear you."

Static was his only answer, static and distorted syllables: "*—out of there!*"

Well, that fit with his plan.

"No more time." Pike beckoned her. "Are there people in

these other rooms?"

She shook her head.

"Come on, then. Stay behind me."

He went down the hallway as quickly as he could, rifle up. He checked twice and found her close behind him. She didn't seem particularly worried; when a ceiling panel cracked and dropped, she batted it away from herself without even looking. He stopped when he saw that, and she watched him silently. Eventually she raised her eyebrows, as if to note that he was the one saying they should go.

That was a fair observation, he supposed. He crept down the stairs with his weapon up, and looked around at the room. For a moment, nothing seemed wrong, until—

The doors had closed.

"*Shit.*" He ran for the cube and slammed his rifle into it. He was looking around desperately. The doors weren't opening. He slammed the rifle down again, again. Which side had the other soldier used?

Fingers closed around his sides and firmly ushered him out of the way. The girl crouched down and stared at the featureless white cube. She craned her head to look at each part of it in front of her, searching for something. Her hands came up, palms flat on the white material.

Pike swallowed hard. He hadn't noticed in the cage room where she'd been kept, but a thin web of ugly scars traced over the backs of her hands and disappeared up into the sleeves of her beige shirt.

Static burst into his earpiece again, but this time, he could not make out a single word. He winced as the voice repeated whatever it had been saying, and gave an anguished look at the featureless walls around them. The doors had disappeared entirely. He fumbled at the earpiece to find a volume dial, but it was smooth.

Had this been the Telestine plan? Lure attackers in and trap them in the building? He strained for the sound of screams or a cry for help, and heard nothing at all. Had there been traps waiting over the doors, or—worse? Did the rest of the soldiers not realize yet that they were trapped? Would they only realize when they tried to return to the shuttles?

A hand wrapped around his and tugged. The girl was apparently done looking at the cube.

"My friends are in there," Pike said, pointing at the walls. She shook her head.

"Are they dead?"

She hesitated, then she tugged on his hand again and looked toward the shuttle bay.

"We should go?"

She gave him a look, jerked her head at the tilted floor.

"Right. Come on." He paused. "You wouldn't know where the Telestines are, would you?"

The hollow *boom* of an explosion sounded outside and she gestured toward it.

"They're all out there? Their scientists fly fighter jets? Really?"

She shrugged.

Static roared in his earpiece again, making him wince. This time it didn't stop. Useless. He ripped it out and took off for the shuttle bay; quick steps behind told him that the girl was following.

He swallowed hard when he saw the bay. Smoke was

beginning to drift across the floor, and flames were licking at one wall. Both shuttles were still there.

"I should get the rest of my team," he told her. It was a useless sentiment; he had no idea where they'd gone, and he'd barely seen the tiniest piece of two floors. The station must have ten at least.

Her eyes met his, and there was no judgment there. She looked sad.

"They got me here," Pike told her. "They...." He swore silently and stared down at the floor, indulging in a quick moment of regret. Eva had been right.

The Rebellion had sent him, and he had failed—and her crew was going to die for it.

A hiss of machinery caught his ears, and he picked his face up in time to see the girl climbing into the shuttle. As if to validate her decision, the whole station dropped several feet, taking his stomach with it.

Instinct got him into the shuttle and he found her at the copilot's chair, hands pressed on the control panel, brow furrowed. She looked up at him in mute appeal.

"Don't worry, I got this." Rychenkov was going to make himself sick laughing when Pike told him that he'd flown a shuttle.

Pike could hear him now: *You? How are you still alive?*

Well, he supposed he might still kill them. He took one last look out the windshield of the shuttle and brought up the screens. The code was still there and he entered it again. Behind them, the doors slid open. He waited, foolishly, hands on the controls, and the girl watched his hands.

At last, seeing his hesitation, she reached out and placed

her hand over his, dragging back firmly. The shuttle skidded awkwardly across the floor toward the empty sky, and Pike nodded.

Time to go. He looked down at the controls and backed them away, out into the battle. Better to take his chances there than be on the lowest floor of a crashing ship.

He was about to get his apprenticeship in flying.

CHAPTER EIGHTEEN

Venus, 49 kilometers above surface
Tang Estate, New Zurich

"Pike—*Pike*!" Nhean tore out the earpiece and threw it. "Dammit."

"What's going on?" The admiral's voice crackled over another line. "I can't get the feeds from any of them. Do you know what's happening down there?"

Her voice was breaking, and he closed his eyes.

"There's a shuttle leaving. Protect it at all costs." He opened his eyes and tracked her position. Good—nearly to Earth after a week of burning halfway across the solar system from Jupiter. But after the disaster at New Beginnings Station he wondered where she'd set up headquarters next. It was clear the Rebellion was going to be needing more help in the very near future. Help only he could provide.

"The team got out?" Relief was obvious in her voice.

He hesitated. "Just—your mission specialist."

There was a long pause, and he could see her looking at the names and pictures of the soldiers who had gone on the mission. The ones who wouldn't come back. Quietly, she asked the only thing that mattered: "Did he find it?"

He stared out the window at the billowing golden clouds, not wanting to say anything at all.

"No, but he found us someone who might be able to find it. Or possibly recreate it. Protect the shuttle." Nhean swallowed. "If we let them shoot it out of the sky, we are all lost. We need to get to them as soon as possible."

A pause. "Acknowledged. Given the Telestine response during Pike's insertion, this is going to be one hell of a fight. A fight I was hoping to have with the Telestine defense grid *down* because of the Dawning, not still fully functioning."

A good point. It was decided then. He'd have to reveal part of his hand to Walker, and the Telestines. "I'll take care of it. I can temporarily disable one of their satellites. The one in geosynchronous orbit roughly over Denver. You'll have a few minutes to get your fighters down there to protect Pike's ascent, but only a few minutes."

Another pause. "But won't that tip your hand to the Telestines? Clue them in to how much you've infiltrated their systems?"

She was good. Perceptive. He supposed it was why she was the leader of the Rebellion, and no longer sharing the position with that buffoon, General Essa. "It will. But for the Dawning, it's a risk we'll have to take."

He had to find a way to get in touch with Pike. The man had no idea what he'd found.

Nhean's hands were white knuckled on the arms of his chair. Now that he knew there had been a human in the same room as the Dawning, he could track her through the data. And no matter how many times he looked, those data kept saying the same thing; this girl always came with the Dawning when it moved. She was its caretaker, bound to it in some way.

And if she was loyal to the Telestines, there was no telling what she might do next.

CHAPTER NINETEEN

Earth, Low Orbit
Bridge, EFS Intrepid

"Protect the shuttle—all fighters, protect the shuttle."
Walker kept her voice steady through sheer force of will. Her
eyes were fixed on the array that hovered over the desk, the
bulk of the Telestine station tilting crazily and the fighters
buzzing between it and the sharp spine of the mountains.

And hurry it up, we only have a few minutes before we have to get
out of here.

She already knew they weren't going to make it. The
window was closing on the dead space in the Telestine array—
courtesy of Nhean—and there was no way the fighters could
make it out of the gravity well in time to get back to the
Intrepid. They would have to go to ground with the Rebellion
cells and wait until the ship came around again.

If the entire Telestine fleet mobilized, this party was going to be over in a hurry. And the horrific loss of New Beginnings Station, the *Washington*, the *Pele* … Captain Brown and Captain Kim….

The cost they'd already paid was too high for them to fail now.

She signaled for the pilot to begin spinning up the engines.

"*We're on it, ma'am.*" McAllister's voice was steady through the commlink. "*We're signaling the shuttle, but he's not reading us.*"

"I know." She cast a look at the earpiece and her eyes closed in pain for a moment. *Pike, I am coming for you. Hold on.* "Just do what you can to keep them off him."

"All right *che*, I'm drawing them off." Fighter seven peeled off from the group and shot through an approaching formation of feathers. They swerved away from him and regrouped, and he guided his ship up in an arc to shoot directly at the station. "Let's see how you like this, fuggers." His voice was a low mutter. "Everyone else, get them while they're distracted."

"Fisheye!" The call came from the CAG. "Back in formation!"

"With all due respect, *che*, it's gotta be one of us."

There was a pause.

"Then it'll be me," the CAG said simply. "Break off, Fisheye."

"Oh, no," King whispered. Her face had gone grey and her hand covered her mouth. "No, no."

Walker shot her a look and shook her head. There could be no weakness from them now. The pilots could not hear any doubt, nor they could hear grief.

Nothing was important right now beyond the shuttle.

Pike had found ... well, something. She had spent her life trying not to be blinded by hope, but right now, Walker could not keep it from welling up in her chest. She bit her lip, felt the skin break, and bit down harder until she was sure she could speak steadily.

"Give us the view from fighter seven."

The video feed was sudden and disorienting. The pilot—Dave "Fisheye" Hernandez, the screen read—had gone into a spin as he arrowed up toward the formation of Telestines. He was refusing to break off the attack, Walker saw now.

"Fisheye!"

"Gonna get my shot in, LT. And you have a life to build after this—I'm free as a bird, *che*. After this it would be back to Pluto, and that ain't no life, *boludo*."

Across the table, King's eyes were bright with tears. Her eyes were fixed on the holograph of the other fighters, not the video feed from Fisheye.

There was no time to wonder about that now. Walker turned her gaze to the video. Bullets streaked away from Fisheye and one Telestine was blown sideways into another.

"*Yes.*" Delaney's voice was soft. His fist pounded against the desk.

"Come on," King whispered. Her lips pressed together, holding back a softer entreaty. Her head was half-turned; she wanted to look away from this. "Come *on*."

The video feed jerked sideways and righted itself, but the ground was curving up slowly into the view.

"Shit!" Fisheye's voice was frantic—and then furious. "Like hell I'm not taking a few more of you with me." The video swerved to point straight down at the ground, and the ship gathered speed before the pilot must have yanked the yoke up, relying on aerodynamics and lift to right the fighter. With newfound speed, the ship arced up into the sky and the single working engine spun the ship to point up at the formation streaking by above. The dying fighter let loose a stream of bullets and a missile, and then it was falling away, falling, falling.

"Cut the—" But Walker's command was too late. The feed burst into static and the whole bridge crew flinched. She had to distract them. She cast about for something. "Give me numbers. How many of ours left, and how many of theirs?"

"Five of ours left, ma'am, plus the shuttle." Larsen met her eyes. "McAllister, Tocks, Princess, Morrison, Vu. And eight of theirs."

His face was white with shock. Two weeks ago, they had never lost a fighter in open combat. Now they had lost … too many. And the officers had seen them die.

It would be worth it, Walker told herself. She seemed to be reminding herself of that a lot these days.

"The CAG is moving to the fore," Larsen reported. "He has three on him."

"The other five?"

"Random, they don't seem to know who to shoot at."

"Tell our fighters to keep one guarding Pike, and the rest should get those three, before—" She broke off. *Before our distraction gets shot down.*

King's hands were white-knuckled around the edge of the table.

"Yes, ma'am." Larsen was murmuring into the earpiece. "They're on it."

The specks of green, all but one, swung around to face the

formation of three red dots. They couldn't see bullets on the hologram, but it was clear a few moments later that all of them were shooting. The Telestine formation spread, and one blipped out of existence a moment later.

The CAG jerked his ship hard to port, in an arc that must have had his muscles screaming. A nod from Walker put his feed up on the screens. They could hear him swearing under his breath as he climbed toward the structure.

"Two more down—"

Larsen's words died. On the hologram, the Telestine ship tilted further to the side, flickered, and plummeted straight for the mountains below.

"Holy shit," Delaney murmured. His eyes were wide. "It's going to—"

It disappeared in a mad flicker against the mountain range, and Larsen's fingers stabbed at his screen to bring up a video feed from one of the pilots. The CAG's ship shot over the wreck that smoked against the mountainside. It was collapsing in on itself as they watched; flames shot out of the tangled wreckage of the sides.

"We should call the fighters back." King's voice was expressionless now. "Did the rest of the team get out of the lab?"

"Not that I know of." Walker met her eyes. "It's possible, though. Pike's communications were knocked out. Maybe theirs were, too. If—"

A light flared on the screen and the bottom dropped out of her stomach.

No.

"The shuttle's been hit, ma'am." Larsen looked up at her.

She could only shake her head desperately. This couldn't be happening—to have the Dawning, and then to lose it.

And Pike with it.

A voice crackled to life: the CAG. "The shuttle is falling, but not destroyed. Fighters to me, get those feathers out of the sky. Just like in training, boys."

Walker's fingers were splayed over her stomach. Horror was making it difficult for her to breathe. *Pike.* The future of the Rebellion was plummeting toward the ground below and all she could think of was Pike.

Pike, who would never be down there if it weren't for her.

Delaney's eyes held a warning for her, reminding her to show no weakness in front of the crew, and she drew herself up slowly. Her fingers found the desk and she forced herself to stand straight. No weakness.

"McAllister, get out of there."

King took a sharp breath.

"Ma'am?"

"He's falling. The best we can do is leave it alone—otherwise they know we're still invested. Get out of there, the window's closing." *And we can't afford to lose any more of you.*

"Yes, ma'am."

Three feathers swam into view. Shots streaked away, and one exploded in a cloud of silvery debris.

"All fighters, pull up." McAllister's voice was steady. "We're going back to the nest."

A light blinked out. *Sarah Morrison,* the holograph read. *Age 22, Johnson Station.*

Walker swallowed.

"Everyone keep going!" The CAG's voice was desperate.

"I'm dropping back, I'll cover you."

Walker watched as the other ships overtook him, and the whole formation put on speed. He'd turned his guns; two Telestine fighters blinked out behind him.

One left, and the CAG's view screen turned as he guided his ship in another whip-fast turn; they heard the dull thud of his head hitting the side of the windshield.

"No," King whispered. She looked at Walker. "Tell him not to do this." Her voice was pleading. "He has to go with the rest."

Walker said nothing. Her eyes fixed on the Telestine ship and she steeled herself for an impact she would never feel. Its guns were swiveling as it swerved, suddenly facing its opponent. It had seen McAllister's ship, and she could only hope it had realized what was happening too late. Missiles burst across the screen, lighting it to a brilliant white, and the feather tumbled out of the sky, smoke trailing from its wings.

There was a cheer from the bridge crew.

"Ma'am." The CAG was breathing hard. "It's done."

"Come on home, McAllister."

"We don't have the time," Delaney hissed. "There's Telestine cruisers on the way."

"I'm not leaving him down there."

"Coming as fast as I can, ma'am." The voice fuzzed out and returned. "Just so you know, I got a look. The shuttle crash-landed. It was still maneuvering. It looks like the hull is still intact. There's a chance—"

The voice cut out.

Everyone on the bridge turned to look at Walker, and she, in turn, looked to the holograph.

"He's still climbing."

"We have to *go*," Delaney said again.

"He's still climbing." She bit the words off.

"Approaching atmo break." Larsen's voice was quiet; he didn't want to intervene in this fight.

"Vent bay four and open it. Close bay two as soon as the other fighters are in."

Delaney's hands were clenched.

Closer McAllister climbed, and closer.

"Ma'am, there's a satellite coming into range. Probably has some offensive capabilities."

Delaney shot her a look and Walker ignored him. *Come on.* She bit her lips to keep them from moving. *Come on, McAllister.*

The light disappeared on the screen and King's shoulder's hunched.

"He's aboard, ma'am."

"Get us out of here." Her voice was crisp. "Now."

CHAPTER TWENTY

Earth
Mountains Near Denver, North American Continent

Later, he would remember nothing from that day. The crash took the memory of the Telestine ship, of Charlie disappearing into the labs. It took even the choice that had led him to take the shuttle and go with his one fugitive.

But that day, he remembered all of it, and it played in a sickening loop in his unconscious brain: abandoning the ship, the girl dragging his hand on the controls to launch the shuttle, and the chaos of the battle. He remembered the first strike and the shuttle tumbling before the guidance systems righted it, and his desperate attempts to guide it down to the ground as the battle raged overhead. Debris fell nearby every few seconds as ships blew apart. He tried not to look—at one point he's seen the charred body of a pilot.

It had all gone wrong, the Dawning was lost to them, and

then the ground was rushing up quicker and quicker and he only had time to look over at the girl sitting next to him and say, "I'm sorry."

Then there was a burst of pain, a terrible brightness, and then the world went black and the whole sequence started again as his brain tried to find some way out of what he'd done. Stay on the Telestine ship? No, it had crashed as well, the team was dead.

Don't go to the ship. He should never have gone to the Telestine ship.

He should have never responded to Walker's desperate request.

The first thing that let him know he was awake was the frantic beating in his ears and feeling the pressure of his body slumped forward against the restraints. The acrid smell of smoke filled the cabin and he heard a crackle that sounded very much like fire.

He could taste blood.

He tried to remember how to pick his head up and settled for rolling it sideways instead. Wrong way, that was the wall. He rolled his head the other way, trying to ignore the way his stomach rebelled.

She was sitting calmly. Her eyes were open, and her hands were wrapped around the restraints at her shoulders. She was so still that for a moment he thought she was dead, and he gave a croak, a desperate attempt to say he was sorry, he'd thought she would be better off in the shuttle.

He jumped when she looked over at him. Her head had slammed against the wall at some point during the landing; her forehead and cheek were beginning to bruise a deep red with mottled purple. There didn't seem to be much of anything in her eyes as she unhooked herself and came to check him. Her fingers poked at his ribs, tipped his chin up. His head slumped once and she drew her hand back as if she'd been burned.

She thought his neck was broken, he realized. He picked his head up and shook his head. He had the sense of forgetting something.

"Amright," he slurred. *I'm all right.* Nothing was coming out the right way. "I'm ...." Better. What couldn't he think of?

She shook her head and fumbled at the clasps.

He realized that he was listening for something. Other fighters. "More of 'em? Fighters. Telestine." His voice was still slurred.

She shook her head and caught him as he slumped forward. There was a wiry strength in her as she leveraged him out of the chair and half carried, half dragged him into the main cabin. Her arms gave out when she tried to lay him on the ground. He could feel the effort it took for her to lift him, but she didn't make a sound. Not even a grunt.

She might not have flown a shuttle before, but she had watched when he came into the shuttle, and now she jabbed at the buttons to open the door. When they didn't open, she thumped the control panel, her brow furrowed in frustration, and Pike felt his lips crack as he smiled—it was nice to see she *felt* something, at least.

Hitting the control panel, however, seemed to work. The doors creaked, hissed, and sprang open. Pike froze, but there was still no drone in the air, and the view outside was only rocks and scrub brush—no Telestines pointing guns at them.

That was good. Pike wasn't sure he could stand up. He

watched the girl peek out of the shuttle and look around, and then she came back and stared at him in evident consternation.

What she lacked in strength, she made up for in determination. She pulled on his wrists to haul him upright and braced him on her knees while she eased around the back of him, then heaved him over to the doorway with her hands under his armpits.

This wasn't, Pike reflected, extraordinarily good for his pride. Rychenkov would laugh at him. Also, Rychenkov would laugh at him for crashing the shuttle, which was allowed to be funny now that they weren't dead.

Having deposited him mostly upright, the girl crouched in the doorway and contemplated the sky. It was getting dark, he realized.

"Night soon," he managed. "Cold." He summoned every ounce of determination, and banished the last of the fuzziness from his brain. "We should stay here until morning."

She looked over at him. He could see her considering, and then she nodded. The suggestion seemed to meet with her approval.

"I'm sorry I crashed the shuttle."

She shrugged. It was almost like she was saying, "it happens, you know?"

"I'll get you someplace safe," Pike managed. "The Rebellion has a camp north of here ... I think." Lord knew, the camp to the south of them was gone. Every member of that one had been on the airship when it crashed. He looked down at his hands, bruised from the impact. "Do you think any of them survived on the ship?"

She looked away at that.

His lips tightened. "Right. I'll get you ... to the other camp. Soon. We'll make it, I promise."

She looked back. Her black eyes were clear, assessing. She was waiting for him to remember something. He tried to think back to what he'd said to her. There wasn't much of it.

"The Dawning?"

She nodded.

"It was on the ship." He didn't want to think about it, but he had to face facts. "It's gone."

She shook her head, frowning.

"There's another one?"

Her frown deepened at that.

"You know where it is?"

She sat back on her heels, eyeing him.

So she didn't want to tell him. That was all right. He'd just have to hope she'd tell someone else. "Okay. We'll get you to the base, all right? They'll be able to get in contact with the admiral." For the first time, he felt a stab of something like hope. Maybe they could still find it.

Maybe they could all still make it out of this alive.

Don't give up, Walker.

CHAPTER TWENTY-ONE

Earth
Mountains Near Denver, North American Continent

The night passed slowly. Search lights swept across the
mountainside, looking for survivors. Pike slept fitfully. Every
once in a while, the light passed directly over the shuttle and lit
the windshield a brilliant white, light that spilled into the
interior. He would wake and find his mind a bit clearer. The
girl was always awake, sitting against the closed shuttle doors,
her gaze fixed on the back wall.

"What's your name?" he asked her once.

She didn't answer.

On another waking, soaked in sweat from a nightmare he
couldn't remember: "How did you end up in the labs?"

She didn't answer that either.

Each time he woke, his mind was clearer. Sometime before
dawn, he pushed himself up and leaned his head back against

the wall of the shuttle. The imagined voices of the trapped Rebellion soldiers were ringing in his head, a relentless reminder of the lives he'd left behind. What few words they'd spoken to him during the two weeks of their acquaintance were stamped in his memory now. He could hear Eva's warnings and Charlie's defiant assertions. They'd resented him and everything he stood for: a Rebellion that wasn't even based on Earth, run by spacers, with terms dispatched like edicts to those on the ground.

Their fears about him had been well founded. He had to acknowledge that.

He looked over and saw the girl watching him. Her eyes were sad.

"I left them to die," he told her.

She didn't look away. Her head tipped up in a wordless question.

"The rest of my team. On the Telestine ship. There were ten of us. You heard me call for them, but they didn't answer. I left them there to die," he repeated, almost defiantly.

He expected an automatic protest, the words etiquette demanded. She would tell him that they had already been dead. Or she would tell him that he would only have gotten himself killed too if he'd gone after them. Those were familiar words by now; his fingers clenched.

She didn't say anything.

"I don't even know why I'm here," Pike told her. "I wanted to see home, but that seems stupid now. I lived without it all these years. Space wasn't as bad as my father said it would be."

While his father sickened and died on Johnson Station,

Pike had joined the half-feral gangs of children who played "Hide and Retake Earth" in the labyrinthine corridors, holding mock airship battles in the low gravity rooms and debating the futures they could have: trader, cargo pilot, vacuum welder, exterior mechanic. Everyone wanted to be an exterior mechanic, clambering around on the outside of the station to fix solar panels and hull dents.

His planned future: farmer.

The other kids laughed cruelly.

She still hadn't said anything, and he felt obliged to fill the silence. It felt strange. He was normally the one who didn't talk.

"I was born on Earth," he explained. "Not far from here. Maybe a few miles north. We're close. I don't think the camp exists anymore—it got hit by the Telestines." He saw a question in her eyes. "My father was working with the Rebellion. The day they came to get information from us, the Telestines came too. The Rebellion soldiers took as many of us as they could on the shuttle. My mother and sister ... they didn't make it."

She curled her knees up and wrapped her arms around them. Her black eyes were steady.

"I didn't want to be part of the Rebellion after that," Pike admitted. It felt good to say it. In the past few weeks, it had been manifestly clear how unwelcome that admission would be to his compatriots. It was a lie of omission, but still a lie, and it ate at him.

The girl didn't recoil. She gave a minute nod instead, one that said she had heard him and she was considering things.

It was enough. "I still don't want to be, actually. Or ... I didn't." After today, things seemed more jumbled than before. "It seemed like too big a risk. We have a life out there, and we don't really have enough ships for a rebellion. When Walker told me about the plan, I didn't even listen. I just wanted to come back and see the planet, to see mountains and trees again, and I felt like ... I'm human, right? When the head of the Rebellion says they need you and you could save everyone's life, you can't say no, can you? I just didn't know that what we were trying to do was even possible, that's all." His lips curled with irony. "And it wasn't. We couldn't even get one piece of tech out of a lab." He glanced sideways to look at her. "If it weren't for you, we wouldn't even know we could still get at it. Do you know what it looks like? The Dawning? Were they developing it there?"

A pause, and she nodded.

"What is it?"

She shook her head. Finally, she shrugged.

"I'm hardly going to tell anyone," he pointed out. "And it's not like I shouldn't know, in any case. I did come here for it."

She gave the ghost of a smile at that, but another Telestine plane shot overhead with a flash of light in the cockpit and they both instinctively stilled.

It was reassuring when she did things like that, Pike decided. It reminded him that she was human, which seemed an odd thing for him to keep forgetting.

He tried to be fair about her reticence. She didn't know him from Adam, and he had shown up with the group of people who crashed the ship she was on and delivered her to a very dubious safety.

He let his eyes drift closed; he was getting tired again.

"I've missed Earth," he told her. It seemed like the most honest thing he'd said in years. "I liked running cargo ships. I liked seeing Jupiter. Didn't like Mars. Venus was weird. Never been to Saturn or Neptune. But Jupiter...."

The sight of Jupiter, blocking out half of the black, always sucked the air right out of his lungs. "I liked seeing Jupiter every time. It's basically humanity's home now. The stations and the Snowballs—Callisto, Europa, Ganymede. Cargo was a good trade. Smuggling even more. Everyone needs things. We brought water from Europa sometimes—they hauled it up to the ship and crated it there, these huge blocks of ice on a chain."

She was watching him, swaying slightly side to side. He could see her trying to picture it. She seemed like she might smile at any moment.

"Maybe I'm supposed to feel like we're going to die if we don't get Earth back," Pike admitted. "I'm not sure I do. I've never just believed that. My dad used to talk about NASA and America and McDonalds and aircraft carriers and ... those were just words to me. I don't like them being here, though. I don't like them having our planet and just running us off. And...."

The truth seemed too deep to admit, but she was waiting for it silently, black eyes expectant.

"I don't think I can leave again," Pike admitted, "and know I can never come back. This was supposed to be my home. I was going to get Walker the Dawning, she'd do her Fleet thing, and then after all the Telestines were dead, I'd come back. And then I'd farm. I'd farm."

He didn't understand until that moment. All these years,

he'd known the Rebellion as rage: his father's twisted grief, a shell of the strident anger he'd carried with him on Earth; Walker's cold, calculating fury; the traitorous whispers he heard on every long pass between Jupiter and Mars—the aeons of black there seemed to drag confessions out of anyone.

His Rebellion wasn't about anger. All those years he'd spent shoving the Rebellion away, too weary to let that ceaseless rage eat him up with the rest of them, he'd forgotten the only thing that mattered: Earth. He wanted Earth back so badly he ached with it.

"The Dawning...." His voice trailed off in a croak. "The Dawning was supposed to help us get Earth back. A stupid computer chip." He eyed her carefully. "It's not ... *inside* you, is it?"

She shook her head violently. *Ok then*, he thought, standing up and offering her a hand.

"Come on. We've sat long enough. If we don't move, they'll find us."

CHAPTER TWENTY-TWO

1 million kilometers sunward of L1 Lagrange point, Earth
Deck 5 hallway, EFS Intrepid

Commander King was waiting for him in the shadows of
the hallway outside the landing bay. She waited, composed, as
the medics came and examined his head and made him count
backward and say how many fingers they were holding up.
They asked him what he remembered, and he said nothing,
because he knew the truth would frighten her: the *Intrepid*,
impossibly small against a darkening sky, too far away to reach
as the satellites came online nearby and he thought he might as
well have gone out in a blaze of glory with Fisheye, or stuck
around to help the pilot of the shuttle. How he'd gotten back
to the ship he didn't know, and he didn't care much, either. All
he remembered was the hollow feeling of following the
command to return, wondering why it even mattered when a
life could get snuffed out that easily.

Then the medics were gone and it was just him on the floor, still in his flight suit, and her waiting silently.

She knelt at his side after a moment.

"She held the ship for you," she said finally. "The admiral."

He opened his mouth to ask her why she was telling him that, and realized that she didn't know what to say right now, either. He looked up at her familiar face with its faint dusting of freckles over the bridge of the nose and reached out to pull her close. His arms were too tight around her, he knew, but she was squeezing him back just as hard. After a moment, her torso shook and he felt tears on his neck.

"I made it back," he said irrelevantly.

Irrelevant, because they both knew, now, that he was never going to make it. How could he possibly survive, when the Telestines could take out fighters so readily? If he didn't die in the next mission, he'd die in the one after that.

She pulled away and ducked her head as she wiped her cheeks. When she looked up, her face was absolutely composed. She took a moment before she spoke. "I'll follow you."

He didn't understand for a moment, and then it hit him in the gut. If he died, in whatever battle, she intended to go, too.

"No." His head was moving of its own accord. "Baby, no."

"Did you just call me *baby*?" She gave something that might have been a laugh.

He laughed, too. Sort of. "It felt like that kind of moment."

She reached out to press her fingers over his. "I'm not afraid."

"You're not a fighter pilot, either." He met her eyes.

"You'll be in command of a battleship."

"You think all of our ships are going to make it?" She gave a rueful smile. "There are going to be some who shield the flagship in the final battle. Some who shield the Dawni—" She broke off. "I'm not afraid," she said again.

"I am." He shook his head. "I am. Ari—sweetie—don't do this. When I go—" He broke off when she put her hand over her mouth. "It's going to be okay," he tried to tell her in spite of the hand. He hadn't realized before today how sure it was that he'd die here, like this, but with that knowledge had come some measure of acceptance. "You're going to be okay, Ari. You're going to find some nice guy and—"

"Don't." She shook her head fiercely. "If...." Her voice trailed off and she looked over her shoulder. A single set of footsteps was approaching.

They both knew who that was. The quick, measured footsteps were like a unique fingerprint. He squeezed her fingers. "Go. I'll catch up with you later." His voice was low, and he watched as she hurried out of sight around a corner.

When he looked back, the admiral was there. Her hands were clasped behind her back, the way she always stood. He wondered if she ever relaxed, and decided she probably didn't. Her eyes were cool on his.

"Is that going to be a problem?"

He went cold. How she'd guessed, how she'd known about him and King, he didn't know, but it didn't matter. "No, ma'am."

"Good." She seemed to take the words at face value, and she came to help him up from the floor. "The medics tell me you have a minor concussion. You'll need to rest for about forty-eight hours, but after that you'll be good to go."

"Do we have forty-eight hours?" He reached up to scratch at his head and winced when his fingers touched the bruise.

She considered, and then lifted her shoulders. "No way to know."

"Any word on the pilot of the shuttle?"

Her face went still, and he knew he'd made a mistake of some sort.

"No," she said simply.

"Ma'am, are we allowed to know what we were doing there?"

It was way out of line, but she nodded. "You've more than earned that, I think. You have a right to know what you put your life on the line for. On that shuttle...." She considered. "No, in the lab—we'll start there—was something called the Dawning."

The word King had almost uttered. He waited for more.

"It may be the key to undermining the entire Telestine defense grid. We have reason to believe that it—or a crucial component of it—made it onto that shuttle."

His jaw had dropped open. He had not doubted that there was a reason for him to be out there, but he would never have guessed that it would be something like this. "That would put us close to—"

"Yes." She cut him off with a nod. "If we can retrieve it."

"Get me back out there."

"You're injured, McAllister. Rest."

"I...." He didn't want to rest. He didn't want to think. If he stayed in a hospital bed, he was going to be thinking of Fisheye.

Fisheye, who had died without ever knowing any of this. He'd sacrificed blindly.

She saw his face. "That wasn't why I came. I came to say—I'm sorry about Hernandez. I know the two of you were close."

There was a lump in his throat. He nodded jerkily. "Thank you, ma'am."

"I want you to remember why he died." She spoke quietly.

"To save me." And he was never, ever going to be able to make up for that.

"No." Her eyes were like chips of stone. "He died because the Telestines have enslaved us. He died for humanity."

He could not look at her. He drew himself up, trying to use etiquette to keep from breaking down.

"We have no time for guilt, McAllister." Her voice seemed to come from far away.

He nodded silently.

"Avenge him."

"I will." He swallowed. "Ma'am. I'll get Earth back for him."

She hesitated, but only for a moment. "When every fighter of theirs is out of the sky, and every carrier is downed, he will be avenged. Remember that they did this to him."

CHAPTER TWENTY-THREE

Earth
Mountains Near Denver, North American Continent

It took Pike most of the next morning to realize they were going in the wrong direction.

Everything had started out well enough. At some point in the night, the patrols seemed to have ceased and it was safe to be outside again. They watched the smoking wreck of the airship on the mountain below while they ate an uncooked food cube from the shuttle's emergency bag. The girl gave him a look that said she was trusting him that this was safe to eat, and he'd better not be messing with her. She appeared manifestly unimpressed when he pointed out that with the airship so close, everything was going to taste like smoke, anyway.

The Telestines hadn't, apparently, stopped to take care of anyone in the airship, or even bother putting out the fire. Why would they? The thought was bitter. It wasn't their planet after all. What did they care? They only would have bothered if it marred the perfect view from Occupied Denver.

He was limping, and she strapped the emergency pack to herself before they set off, holding out a hand to help him over a rock and onto a makeshift path. That, he realized later, was where he went wrong. She chose the path, and he followed.

It wasn't like he didn't have clues, of course. He knew the demolished laboratory was to the south of them, and it took them a good hour to get past it. He didn't put the pieces together, however, until about an hour after they'd stopped to take shelter from the sun. Without a chance to fill up the water skins, they couldn't risk direct midday exposure—something the girl already seemed to know. She led them down the slope to a promising-looking partial cave surrounded by withered trees and a dry creek bed.

They didn't talk. She, apparently, *couldn't* talk—or so he was coming to believe—and he was too tired to do anything but watch the thin, scraggly shadows make their way across the ground. At one point, he craned his neck to see the distant bulk of the ship. He supposed he should tell the nearby Rebellion cell about the thing, on the off-chance that they could salvage some of the tech. He'd heard about the interface problems, but surely they'd figure it out sometime soon. He tried to mark where it was in his head. Fifteen kilometers north? Eighteen, perhaps? They'd be able to see it, anyway. It wasn't exactly small or hidden, and the smoke was kind of a dead giveaway.

The girl had shoved herself up and wandered up the hill somewhat. He didn't look, trying to give her privacy, and was surprised when she came back with berries. She held them out with a smile.

"You can't eat those." He shook his head. "They're poison."

She looked at the berries, then back at him, surprised. She disappeared again in a little puff of dust, and was back a few minutes later, with what looked like a collection of every plant she could find. She spread them out and pointed to them one by one as he searched his memory.

"That's edible. So's that, but there's nothing to it but to fill up your stomach, and only if you boil it. Not that one." He saw her mark the shape of the leaves carefully, and approved of that. She could learn. "That one makes a tea you can use when your stomach is upset. That one's poison. That one's not poison, but you don't want to use it too much. And dogs can't eat it."

She frowned at the mention of dogs.

"Four legs, furry." He shook his head at her wide-eyed expression. "Not bears. Dogs aren't big. Maybe half your size." Few places had them anymore, though. No good way to breed hunting dogs in space, his father had said, and if a dog didn't hunt, it was just another mouth to feed. Probably had them on Venus, though. They have everything on Venus.

Pike watched as she leaned forward to study the plants again. He wondered if she'd been marking the shape of the mountains as they came south. Probably.

South. His head whipped around to look at the smoldering airship wreck, and he swore with all the inventiveness of a lifelong cargo hauler. When he looked back, the girl was watching him warily.

"We've been going south?"

She nodded.

He felt his anger start to rise. She must have been waiting all morning for him to figure it out. "You *knew*? You knew I wanted to go north."

She nodded again. Her fingers played nervously with the leaves.

"You took me south on purpose, knowing I wanted to go north."

A nod. She didn't seem particularly sorry, which only made him angrier.

"Without discussing it at all."

Yet another nod.

"I suppose you had your reasons."

His tone was like acid, but she smiled when she nodded this time. She settled back against the rocks, seeming pleased that he'd figured it out. The smile, he thought, was entirely too smug.

"I hope they're good ones." He settled back in the shadows, cursing himself. "Is there a closer Rebellion base this way or something?"

She hesitated, and he wondered, suddenly, if she was taking him to the Rebellion at all.

"During the ... break-in—" he wasn't quite sure what to call it "—there was a man guiding me through the labs. I don't suppose you'd know who that was...."

She frowned at him in a way that suggested he might be going crazy, and he had a memory of breaking down the door.

He'd been alone then—of course she would think he was crazy.

"Not ... *with* me." He gestured to his head. "In my earpiece." He began to regret not taking more care of it after ripping it out of his ear. Rash to lose tech just because it was malfunctioning. He knew better.

She gave an eloquent shrug, as if to say that he should probably know his own coworkers.

"He wasn't part of the Rebellion. He said he was only talking to me, and he knew a lot about me. He knew more about the layout of the labs than the rest of them there, and he asked me to bring the Dawning to him instead of Lau—instead of the admiral."

This, at last, seemed to interest her. She sat up, eyes narrowed speculatively.

"Any ideas who that might have been?"

She pressed her lips together, deep in thought, and seemed to consider this. One hand motioned for him to keep talking.

"I really don't know any more. He promised me he had humanity's best interests at heart, and that I wouldn't be harmed if I came to him."

She tapped her own chest questioningly.

"I don't think he knows I took you. He was guiding me to the Dawning, and when I got into the room and you were the only thing there, he was confused. I lost contact with him."

She considered this.

"Can you tell me anything about what we're looking for? You don't think it's gone. Was it a program?"

She bit her lip, shook her head—but in a way that suggested he was close.

"So it wasn't one of those cube things."

Another shake.

"Just tell me something, anything. You know about it, right?"

She hesitated. Again, she shook her head. *Almost*, the gesture seemed to say. But "no" still seemed to be more accurate than "yes."

"And you don't know who the man is, either." More a statement than a question, and he wasn't surprised when she shook her head. "I guess I'd figured ...." Pike shook his head. "I have no idea how you would know who he was. I just thought maybe you might, since you didn't seem to think much of the Rebellion."

Silence. She didn't look at him.

"Although I suppose we share that."

She looked over at him, expression unreadable under a sunburnt nose.

"As much as I hate to admit it, though, if you know where the Dawning is, maybe it's best we *do* take you—"

Pike froze.

The girl looked over at him questioningly.

"There's someone nearby."

She shook her head and moved her hand to indicate either a mouse, or a monstrously large spider. Pike shoved that unpleasant image out of his mind.

"No, it's ... stay here." Very carefully, he eased himself against the edge of the rock and peered out.

Directly down the barrel of a shotgun.

CHAPTER TWENTY-FOUR

Earth
Mountains Near Denver, North American Continent

"Up. On your feet."

There were five of them, all men wearing faded plaid shirts and patched jeans with leather boots, and they all had shotguns. Their faces were weathered, the sort of weathering you couldn't avoid in the mountains, and their fingers were rough from work. None of them looked the least bit friendly.

They did, however, look unsettled by the girl. It was probably her eyes. She didn't seem worried in the slightest, staring at each of them in turn as if she were taking a tally of qualities, and moving on to the next with a faint nod.

"So who the hell are you?" The one who'd hauled Pike up held his gun easily, ready to point.

"We're with the Rebellion." He judged that to be safe enough. These men didn't look like Drones who'd lived in captivity, and they didn't seem the sort to stare at the sky and dream of escaping off-planet, either. He figured they'd be sympathetic to the Rebellion.

He was wrong.

"So, *you're* the reason there's a crashed ship and fuggers swarming all over our ass." The man looked deeply unimpressed with this state of affairs.

The girl nodded. Pike gave her a look that said she wasn't helping, and she shrugged. *It's true*, her eyes said.

The man was looking between them, eyes flicking back and forth.

"Blake'll want to talk to you, then."

"Who's Blake?"

"None of your damned business." The man jerked his gun south along the range. "Get walking."

"All right." Pike limped his way around the outcropping. "But I'd like to point out that we didn't know anyone was here."

"Yeah, well, that's how you don't get your camp blown up by the Telestines, isn't it?"

It was hard to argue with that. Pike set off and the girl followed, slipping the straps of the emergency pack over her shoulders again. Now that she'd taken the time to assess each member of the group, she didn't seem particularly interested in any of them.

"So how'd you crash the ship?" one of them finally asked, about half an hour later. Pike was glad for the distraction. They'd been walking in silence, with the occasional stumble and oath. The men had stopped pointing their guns at the captives, but they weren't tolerating a slow pace, and his leg was killing him.

The girl looked over in interest, as if she'd been wondering the same thing.

"Not on purpose," Pike admitted grudgingly. "We were shooting at the feathers and one of them crashed into it."

"Feathers?"

"Their planes. The ones with the metal that looks like—"

"Ah, yeah, those ones." The man nodded. "Better than the black ones."

"What *are* the different kinds?" It was not inspiring that this man seemed to know more than the Rebellion.

"There's the ones you call feathers. Not nice. They shoot things, but they generally don't care 'less you get real obvious-like. They spend a lot of time shooting rocks and trees and shit." The man shrugged, as if to suggest that no one could understand the Telestines and no one should try. "They go with that type of ship, the pretty one, and you know you're having a quiet day. Th'other type of ship, now, with the bays and the fighters and all—those ones are dead black, and they fly silent."

"I don't remember those."

The man frowned at him, but didn't ask any of the questions he clearly had. "They're new. Stop here."

"What? Why?" Pike looked around himself at the barren slope. "Your camp is here? You can't possibly be that good at camouflage."

"It's not *here*." The man jerked his head as the youngest member of the group—or least weathered, at any rate—set off into the trees at the base of the hill. "We're not gonna show you where it is, we're not stupid."

"What d'you think I'm going to do, call the Telestines on you?"

"Given that that's the only thing we've ever seen you do, yeah." The man sat on a nearby rock. "It'll be a while, you might as well sit."

Pike was only too happy to take that suggestion. "Don't suppose you have any water."

The man hesitated, but pulled out a water skin and handed it over. "Make sure she gets some, too." He waited until Pike had leaned over to hand the skin to the girl, then beckoned him close. "What's her deal? She don't talk?"

"Maybe she doesn't have anything to say to you," Pike suggested. He handed the water skin back and smiled sunnily. He was under no particular obligation to be polite, he figured.

It was, indeed, a while until the runner came back. The man with him—Blake, they had said—was weathered, clean-shaven, with eyes as piercing a black as the girl's. His hair had gone entirely white, and the sun had weathered his skin to a deep brown. He stopped a few paces away and studied them.

"So who the blazes are you?" he said finally.

It was odd, but Pike had relaxed for the first time in years. People on the stations didn't talk like this. Blunt speech seemed to be a thing for cargo haulers and Earthers, and even cargo haulers were circumspect about any number of things. Maybe the sun brought it out in people, he thought.

"We're the only survivors of that thing." He jerked his head at the distant wreck and warned himself not to get too comfortable. These people would just have killed them if they were seriously worried, but there was only so much he could say.

"They had you in the labs?" Blake's bright eyes sharpened. "You got tracking chips or something?"

Pike's head whipped around to stare at the girl, horrified. She shook her head, and he raised an eyebrow. She shook her head again, more emphatically this time.

"Apparently not."

"She's from the labs, then. What about you?"

"I'm with the Rebellion." Out of the corner of his eye, he caught the girl watching him. Her face was still and her eyes were disappointed.

He knew what she wanted him to say.

"All right, I'm not actually with the Rebellion."

The mean's fingers tightened around their guns.

"I'm here because I knew someone there and they thought I'd be a good fit for this. But I know the mountains. I was born north of here, but the camp was destroyed about twenty years ago now. Swore I wouldn't get involved in the Rebellion, but...." He rubbed at the back of his neck. "Here I am."

"Why?" This man wasn't impressed by maybes.

Pike looked up and met the girl's eyes again. *Tell the truth.* He could almost hear the words.

"I don't know. I came back because I wanted to see Earth. Told myself I understood how things were, the Rebellion wasn't strong enough to beat the Telestines. Told myself there was no point in trying to change it yet. Came here because they could get me home. See the mountains again. Trees. You know ... air."

The men nodded at that.

"But...." Pike swallowed. "We're looking for a weapon." He knew his voice had changed, and he could see their wariness. "It exists, I swear it does. It's called the Dawning, and it can bring down their entire defense grid. I didn't think we could do it. It was supposed to be on that ship and she and I got out while it crashed, but she knows where it is and ... well."

"Well, what?" The man was still staring at him.

Everyone was staring at him, and it occurred to him now that perhaps one of the reasons he liked cargo hauling was that there generally wasn't anyone looking at him. No one to harangue him. He hunched his shoulders.

"Look. I don't know if this is going to work. Odds? It won't. What we've got, it's nothing compared to their tech, I know that. But she says she knows where this thing is, and if it works, we actually have a shot at taking Earth back." He tried to keep the words back, his father's words, but they pushed their way out anyway: "We're all gonna die one way or another, right? They're gonna kill us. Some people die on the stations, some on the Snowballs when vacuum seals break, and some people die here when they hit the camps. Maybe I'll take a few out on the way—and maybe I'll take 'em all. Probably not, but ... now that I'm back, I think I'd rather try than live out my days wondering."

There was a long silence.

"Well, you didn't bullshit me." Blake was staring up at the sky. He looked back to Pike. "So thanks for that, boy."

"Boy? Really?"

The man closed his eyes and sighed. "You were born on Earth and you don't know to shut up when your elders are talking?"

Pike shut up.

"That's better." The man looked around himself again. "Here's the deal. I don't like the Rebellion. They start a lot of shit they can't finish, if you want my opinion." He gave a laugh. "Hell, you're getting my opinion whether you want it or not. But. I like you." His eyes narrowed. "Maybe not. I like her, though. She doesn't lie."

"She doesn't talk," Pike pointed out.

"You do, and she got you to tell the truth, didn't she?" Blake didn't wait for an answer. "Any case, you didn't lie. Probably won't work, you'll probably die. But you're willing to put your life on the line, and the truth is, I'd like my grandkids to grow up without these fuggers around. So I'm going to help you out."

Pike felt his eyebrows shoot up.

"Don't make a big deal out of it—it won't be much," the man advised him. "Food. Shelter. Oh, and I may, just *may*, have a stolen Telestine shuttle laying around. Fancy Telestine tech and everything. We can't use it—never figured out how. So we stowed it for a rainy day. I figure your girl there might be able to … do something to it? Consider it yours."

"A shuttle?" Pike couldn't keep the amazement out of his voice.

Blake had the stoic look of a father on christmas morning. "Come on. Let's get you some food before you head out."

CHAPTER TWENTY-FIVE

1 million kilometers sunward of L1 Lagrange point, Earth
Outside the EFS Intrepid

"Accelerate! Go, go—don't ease off, *push* it!" Tocks's voice echoed down the comm lines. "Come on, newbie, you fly like my grannie!"

"He's doing pretty well. Maybe someone should get your grandma a fighter of her own." Princess sounded like he was grinning as he guided his craft in a smooth arc next to the newbie's shaky efforts. He and Tocks were flanking, giving the newbie the experience of flying point in a formation.

McAllister hung below, watching through the windshield as the makeshift formation came through. Tocks and Princess deposited the newbie in a loose group of fighters and waved the next in.

There was no substitute for experience. They had training programs, of course, a VR headset and a mockup of the cockpits that got new recruits ready for the multitude of switches and thrusters and roll maneuvers. You couldn't get the g-forces in a simulation, though, and you couldn't recreate the feel of being very, very small in an enormous universe.

They weren't going to get experience with atmosphere this way, of course, but it was the best McAllister could do for them right now. The more familiar they were compensating for the g's and learning which button was where without looking, the better they'd be in the pulling roil of Earth's atmosphere.

"McAllister!"

He looked up and swore. The next newbie in line had been doing fine until he tried to pull up—and went down instead. Now he was hurtling toward McAllister's fighter, wobbling as he tried to adjust.

"Hold course, newbie." He gunned his engines, pulling to starboard to avoid.

"I've got it," the newbie called back. He tried to adjust and swerved right toward McAllister's escape vector.

"I said *hold course*!" The yell came from deep in his chest. He yanked the controls up and shot out of the way by scant meters. He pulled the fighter around, cold with fury now. "I want you dead in the water, newbie. What the *hell* did you think you were doing?"

"Theo." Princess's voice was quiet.

"No. He's good enough to be in a plane, he can explain himself. So? Huh, newbie?"

The newbie held his fighter stable. His voice was barely audible. "I was going to pull up, but the controls aren't quite like the simulation."

"You ran a training maneuver out here earlier, right?"

"Right. I just … I didn't think. I'm sorry, sir."

"Sorry," McAllister said, his heartbeat pounding in his ears, "is not *good* enough. *Sorry* is going to get your ass killed. You *and* your wing mates, you hear me, pilot?"

"I just panicked when I brought the plane the wrong way, and—"

"You can't panic! You don't *get* to panic. Panic is a luxury we don't have out here. You want to panic, you stay on the colonies with the rest of the civilians, because we don't need you here. You hear me? You panic, and you're out. Done."

There was a long silence.

"Get back to the ship." McAllister's voice was hoarse. "Everyone. We're done for the day."

No one protested that they hadn't all gotten to go yet; after McAllister's outburst, he knew no one particularly wanted to go anymore. The team launched into motion silently and he watched them go. Tocks began to talk them into the approach, voice even. If she disapproved of what he'd done, he knew she'd never say it on an open channel.

Princess, though, hung back. He watched with McAllister as the newbie slid into place at the back of the group. The wings were still wobbling a bit.

"How you doing?" Of course. Princess on a private channel.

"Don't."

"He's not Fisheye, dude. He was never gonna be Fisheye."

McAllister could feel himself shaking. "I said, don't—"

Princess interrupted. "You remember that bar out at Neptune? Horvath Station?"

McAllister looked over at that. The further out you got in

the system, the worse the drinks got—and the more people drank. When the sun had dwindled to a vague spot of light in the black and all you could see out a single window was unending darkness, the stations turned into an enclave for the half-alive. The people worked because there was nothing else to do. They hauled themselves through zero-g with grey, papery skin. They ate protein rations that had expired a long time ago.

But *man*, could they drink—a fact the team had discovered on one of their longest-ranging patrols aboard the *Pele*, back when she was still disguised as a cargo hauler.

"What about it?" McAllister asked now.

"You remember that chick Fisheye was with? I *think* it was before you took your flight suit off." His voice took on a stoic edge. "Also before you kissed me."

"I *said* I was sorry about that."

"Yeah, well. Dude's gotta do what a dude's gotta do."

McAllister tried to remember back through the blur of that night. "The girl Fish was all over? Brown hair? I thought it was Tocks for a bit."

"So did I. I was pissed. Anyway, I haul him off her and go to punch him in the face, and the girl said to me, she says—"

McAllister started to laugh. He could remember it now: the smoke, the laughing, Princess going to beat the shit out of Fisheye and Tocks trying to hit Princess over the back of the head with a chair to slow him down. Turned out that maneuver doesn't work so well in zero-g with two pilots drunk off their asses. "She says, oh *hell* no, that's my sugar!" Princess descended into laughter after mimicking the woman's heavily accented voice.

McAllister leaned back in his chair and laughed. He dimly heard Princess's voice continue.

"And then the next morning, we tried to fly a patrol and you landed your damn fighter on an *asteroid* and broke the wing off, crashing it, trying to get it up again."

There was a silence. McAllister's laughter faded and he looked over. "What's your point?"

"I'm saying if it was Fisheye sittin' where you sittin', and *you'd* scratched that maneuver back there, you know what he would've said."

Because he *had* said it, two years ago: *Che, boludo, McAllister. Let's hope the Telestines fly like you do. Come on, I'll buy you a coffee.*

McAllister rubbed at his forehead. "Right."

"The kid's nervous," Princess said quietly. He started his acceleration toward the ship and McAllister followed along. "Just give him some time to get up to speed."

"Princess."

"Yeah?"

"He doesn't have *time* to get up to speed." McAllister tightened his hands around the controls. "He pulls that shit when we're in a battle, his wing-mates are going to die."

"Yeah, well." Princess watched with a critical eye. "Stuck his landing here, didn't he? Anyway, how long were you really planning on living?"

He had a point.

CHAPTER TWENTY-SIX

Earth
Mountains Near Denver, North American Continent

"You done yet?" Pike pitched his voice to carry up the hill, between the thin trunks of the aspen, to where the shuttle sat. They'd removed the tarps and dead branches covering it, hiding it from casual view and from searching Telestine eyes overhead. The girl had disappeared inside more than an hour ago, fiddling with the computers as he made one last repair to one of the thrusters, and they were nearing the launch window now.

Every day, he hoped to hear her call back to him, but every day, he expected that a little bit less. He smiled when she stuck her head out of the shuttle and gave him a thumbs up—a gesture she'd learned from the inhabitants of the camp, along with an impish appreciation for foul language.

She looked so pleased with herself that Pike stepped up

into the shuttle to see her handiwork. He remembered her helpless confusion in the Rebellion shuttle, but it was clear that she learned quickly.

He couldn't for the life of him tell what she'd done, however. He gave an automatic smile and a silent prayer that whatever she'd done wasn't going to drop them out of the sky as he ran through a few of the pre-flight checks quickly.

Everything *seemed* to be normal....

"Sit tight. I'll be right back." He jumped down and waved to Blake. The man was hauling supply packs through the woods toward them, and Pike hurried to help. "You didn't have to do this on your own."

"Young man, will you kindly stop insinuating that I have one foot in the grave?" Blake, Pike was beginning to suspect, was prickly out of habit, but the man had a tart humor that Pike hadn't found anywhere since he left Earth.

He was going to miss this place.

"Don't look like that, son." Blake gave him a look. "You'll be back."

"I will?" Pike grinned as they reached the shuttle.

"We're not exactly on all your fancy networks, now are we?" Blake began unloading the packs, handing provisions up to the girl. "So someone's going to have to tell us when the Telestines are gone."

"And here I thought you'd notice when they stopped wandering up and down the mountains."

"Don't be a smart-aleck."

"Sorry, sir." Pike gave a conspiratorial grin up at the girl, and was pleased to see her looking fondly at Blake.

She, like Pike, seemed at ease here. Whatever she'd hoped

to find when she came south, she'd been pleased enough to wind up here, and she'd approved of their plan to take the shuttle up to the Rebellion fleet.

If it was still there. The odds were quite low, actually—Pike looked up at the twilight sky and felt uneasy, not for the first time today.

Blake saw the look.

"Don't think about it," he advised. "You're a country boy at heart. You know there's no point in worrying about things you can't change, eh?"

"Then why am I worrying about it?"

"Because you've been up *there* so long that you don't pay attention to what you learned down here anymore. You got all caught up in their plans. They're not your kind of people."

You can't argue with that, Pike considered as he loaded the last of the rations. Plain potatoes and dried strips of meat weren't much in the way of variety, and he was certain they didn't have the perfect balance of chemicals Pike was used to in his food—but he was looking forward to them all the same. He missed having food that could be different day to day. Since he'd been back, he'd had fiddleheads and snake meat, beef, eggs—it seemed some chickens had been saved after all—and apples from a tiny orchard at the base of the camp. They even had cider that slid across the tongue with a fizz; the girl had looked *very* surprised at that.

He told himself that he was fixating on the food because he didn't want to go, and knew it was true. He couldn't shake the feeling that as soon as he saw Earth dwindle away in the shuttle's windows, he would never see it again.

"All loaded up." Blake nodded at him. "Best go now, boy.

There's not much of a window. The next Telestine satellite array flies by in another thirty minutes."

The inhabitants of the camp, careful as any human settlement, had mapped the comings and goings of the different patrols. Every once in a while there was a dark space, and they'd found one now. As far up as the eye could see, there shouldn't be anything in the sky for a few minutes. Once they got past that ... well, Pike would just have to trust the old claim that the Telestine defensive systems only shot things coming in, not things going out.

He'd also have to trust that the Exile Fleet was still there. That Laura hadn't abandoned him.

One thing at a time. He took his helmet from the girl and strapped it onto the makeshift suit. Like the shuttle, the suits were old, but while metal could be fixed, there was no technology here to make the suits airtight again. He was only putting on the helmet to make Blake feel better.

"Thank you for everything." He clasped Blake's hand.

"Don't get sentimental on me, now, boy." Blake bobbed his head and stepped back. "But thank you for giving an old man hope." He looked back to the camp, where his grandchildren were playing, oblivious to the grown-up drama playing out here. "Give those fuggers hell, eh?"

"I'll do my best, sir." Pike ducked into the shuttle and stood aside for the girl to wave as the shuttle door closed. He sighed when he flopped into the seat. "Well, let's get this show on the road. The sooner we get going...."

The sooner we can die when this piece of shit blows up.

She laughed silently, shook her head at him. He knew she could hear the words he hadn't said.

"Well, I'm glad you have a good feeling about this."

She settled back in her seat, cross-legged, the very picture of contentment. She reached out for the dashboard, which lit up at her touch, and she pressed a few buttons only she could see. The lights flickered, she scowled, then thumped the console firmly with her fist. The lights steadied. She turned and grinned broadly at him.

"We're … not going to die, are we?"

She shook her head cheerfully. Another touch, and a control stick extended out of the console in front of Pike. He shrugged, and after she ignited the engines, he grabbed a hold of the controls.

As he guided the shuttle up out of the trees and out of the sight lines, she took her helmet off. The sunburn on her nose was peeling, but she didn't look troubled, even when she craned to look up at the sky.

Pike guided them as close to straight up as he dared. The air buffeted around the shuttle as currents pooled and shifted, but soon the shudders became smaller. The air was growing thinner, and soon it began to darken around them. His ears popped, one of the jarringly human aspects of leaving atmo and the shuttle's life support not compensating quickly enough for the inevitable micro leaks in the hull seams.

They were close to the border of the atmosphere when the alarm systems blazed to life, beeping frantically. His head whipped around, searching for the source of the sound. No. They were in a dark spot.

But he could hear the drone starting—and here, he couldn't exactly get out of the shuttle and beat the Telestines to death with his bare hands.

No.

The girl reached out to lay her hand over his. She gave a little half-smile.

"It's *not* going to be okay," Pike retorted. He reached for the controls—

Her grip was always stronger than he remembered. She dragged his hands away with a look and jabbed her finger at his chair.

"If they see us—" he began.

The finger jabbed again.

The Telestine ships shot overhead with an imagined burst of sound, black shapes that blotted out the stars they could see flickering above them. Their wings curved wickedly; the beauty of the ships seemed like an insult right now. The wedge passed narrowly overhead, three ships, five, eight.

They didn't change course, didn't even swerve. Their pace stayed constant as they shot away cross-ways, disappearing into the last wavers of the atmosphere, and Pike tried to remember how to move. He couldn't breathe. He was still picturing their ship shot out of the air and tumbling, with the wedge accelerating behind to blow them to pieces.

In fact ... was this a dream? Was he dying right now, and his mind was just making up the idea that he was still alive and ascending?

How would he know?

He looked over to see the girl peering after the Telestines.

"Was that something you did?"

She nodded.

"You worked that into the computers?"

Another nod, this time with a shrug. *Close enough,* her

expression said.

"Can you teach the fleet to do that?"

This time she shook her head emphatically. *No.*

He had the sense that Walker was not going to take that for an answer, but they'd deal with that problem when they got to it. He reached up to begin the scan, and paused.

"Think it's safe to look for the fleet?"

She nodded.

"All right, then." He sent out the first ping and settled back in his chair.

The time limit came, and he sent the second ping. They were still ascending, and he peered around as best he could. He couldn't see any satellites. Then again, the thing about being on a planet was that you forgot just how big planets were, and how much larger a reach technology had. The satellites might be so far away that he couldn't see them—but that didn't mean they couldn't see him.

He pressed his lips together as he sent the third ping. They wouldn't have left entirely, would they? Abandoned the mission, gone back to Jupiter? But the thin hope that had held him together was fraying. How *could* the fleet stay here? Where would they hide? And why would they, if they'd thought the mission had been a failure?

His eyes drifted closed. What in the seven hells were they going to do now?

The shuttle, apparently, had thoughts on the matter. It shuddered, banked, and a course popped up on the screen. Pike stabbed at the course correction before shooting the girl a look.

"Want to tell me where we're going?"

She shook her head, eyes worried. It hadn't been her. She didn't know where they were going.

That wasn't reassuring.

And then the radios came on.

"*Hello, Mr. Pike.*" The voice was amused. "*I'm glad to see you alive and well.*"

"Who is this?"

"*Did I not make an impression the last time we spoke?*" The voice was a bored drawl, with all the elegant tones of the rich.

Pike froze. It couldn't be. And yet, he remembered it very well now: that affected voice, guiding him through the labs. "You hijacked my shuttle?"

"*Not at all, you still have complete control. However, I've taken the liberty of inputting the directions to a rendezvous point.*"

"The Exile Fleet is there?"

"*I....*" There was regret there. "*I don't know what to tell you, Mr. Pike. I'm afraid some of the Exile Fleet may have been lost in an attack on Jupiter. The rest seem to have fled. I'm still trying to determine where the survivors may be. We can ensure that you will be safe, however. I will see you soon.*"

CHAPTER TWENTY-SEVEN

1 million kilometers sunward of L1 Lagrange point, Earth Bridge, EFS Intrepid

"We're going to have to be careful with this." Delaney was chewing his lip as he stared down at the plans. "I don't think it's wise."

"'Wise,'" Walker pointed out, "would have been not joining the Rebellion."

"Wise" would also cover *not* dropping Pike on Earth, *not* attacking the laboratory for the Dawning, and *not* preparing to go back in any capacity until their fleet at Mercury was done. Walker knew what she was supposed to be doing: abandoning the plan that had so clearly failed, and going back to the plan she'd spent years crafting. They'd have a fleet with a fighting chance soon. They should use that and go back to Earth with guns blazing.

Instead, they found themselves hovering in the nearest dark zone, hoping that no passing Telestine patrol would see them, and hoping against hope that some signal would come from Pike.

And they were making a new plan: take out the hubs of Telestine activity, hit them in their very centralized city centers. Telestines didn't seem to have the urge to roam, to live alone. It was convenient—if the rest of the Rebellion was willing to sacrifice Earth's cities, that was, and they were being far too stubborn about it.

"There's a middle ground," Delaney began.

"This is what we're doing." Walker did not look up. She had no time to indulge her officers' worries these days. If they didn't like the way things were headed, they could leave.

There was a long pause.

"I'd like to speak to the admiral alone," Delaney said finally.

The rest of the officers filed out of the room. Delaney didn't outrank all of them, but as one of Walker's first recruits, and as the oldest by far, he had de facto seniority. When they were gone, he strode to the door and locked it for good measure before turning to stare at her.

She still did not look up. This had been coming for days, and she had waited with weary acceptance. There was no adrenaline in her, no fire. Her fingers found the chain under her uniform and pulled it out. Holding the cross in her hand offered her no comfort, and yet she could not seem to stop doing it.

Pike. Her heart squeezed and she looked up at last to meet

Delaney's eyes.

"What the hell is going on with you?" he asked her bluntly.

At least she didn't have to sit through a pep talk. That was a relief.

"What do you think?" Once, she would have spat the words at him.

Once, she would have cared.

"I think we launched our first mission, without much chance of success, it failed, and it knocked everything out of you." The words were brutal. He stalked back to the table. "Now you're planning something that, frankly, should get you hauled up for mass-murder. I told you I thought it was unwise so the others wouldn't think I was challenging you—that was more than you deserved. I'm not going to stand by and watch while you nuke our cities, and frankly, I think if one failure is all it's going to take for you to get *here*, you can get out of the way and let someone else lead this thing."

That got her back up at last. "The Rebellion is mine."

"Then lead it! Because you're not, and god knows humanity deserves better. You remember everything you threw in Essa's face when you took the Rebellion from him? People dying in the halls of the stations? Remember that now. So a team died. Ships were lost. We knew that was coming. Not a person came here who didn't see their death on the way. Did you think *we* are going to make it through the final battle?"

"Of course not." Though she was fairly certain she was envisioning a different final battle than he was.

"So what is it?" He braced himself against the desk, arms crossed. "Because from where I'm standing, we never had a good shot at this. From the beginning."

"And you didn't think to say something?"

"As I recall, you *knew*. You knew when you got into this that it was a long shot we'd ever take Earth back. Frankly? We got further than I expected. I thought we'd be dust by now. I thought we'd be dead in orbit around Jupiter. When that attack came at New Beginnings…." He looked away.

"What? We don't have all day." She looked down at the map of the Telestine cities. *We've got cities to nuke. I need to show humanity that Earth—*

His voice dragged her back to reality. "That was the first time I thought we had a goddamned chance."

That stopped her. "What?"

"Landing the drop ship, it took something out of you. You hadn't watched your teams die before. I wondered if you had it in you to lead. And then when the attack on New Beginnings came, you turned around and you made the best choice you had. You sent your friends to die because you needed to— because the Rebellion needed to survive. And that's when I realized we still had a shot at winning against those bastards— when I realized we had an honest-to-god leader on our hands."

Walker looked down at the desk. They'd had a funeral ceremony for the crews of the *Washington* and the *Pele*. She'd spoken over the radio while the rest of the fleet hung in shocked silence. The stakes hadn't been real before. They wondered which of them might get sacrificed next, and she got the sense everyone had been a bit relieved when she'd led the *Intrepid* into Earth's orbit. King hadn't said a word about it, and neither had Delaney.

It had never occurred to her that he was proud of what she'd done.

"Was the Dawning the only thing keeping you going then?" Delaney couldn't hide his contempt now. "Five weeks ago, we didn't know it existed. We were outmatched then, too —but you weren't making plans like *this*." He stabbed a finger at the desk.

You have no idea. "What do you want me to say?" Walker shook her head at him.

"I want you to explain why you're taking the chance of nuking the cities we're supposed to live in when we go back to Earth!"

"I'm going to kill the Telestines." That was all she was prepared to say. "Do you have a better plan to do that?"

"Biological weapons," he said promptly. "EMP. Something to take down their computer systems."

"We don't *have* biological weapons, nor the capabilities to research and develop them. Lucky for us, Little-Boy-style uranium nukes are a cinch—we can hit them with a small EMP, at least. But we just don't have the time to be sitting around researching biological and wasting precious—"

He waved his arms wide. "Then we wait until we do have them! So a few million more die while we wait. Millions have already died. They've already lost their shot at Earth. We aren't trying to help anyone who's alive right now—we're playing the long game for all of humanity. Do you even understand that?"

Better than you.

She met his eyes and knew her gaze was cold. "Believe me, I do."

"Then why the hell are you risking an attack now? You think you'll get them to pick up and leave?"

"No." She dropped her head into her hands. "I want to kill

enough of them that we *can* take their defenses out."

"Misjudge that and you put them right in humanity's position," he warned her. "You don't want them to have nothing to lose. That's where we are, and it's what makes us dangerous. It's supposed to be *our* edge. Leaving enough of us alive to fight, and to hold grudges—that was *their* mistake. Let's not make it ours too."

Her fingers clenched the desk. For so many years, they had accepted her reasoning. They had gone along with her plans— as they needed to. She saw the patterns no one else did. She saw the picture no one else was willing to see.

And now, at the very end, they were fighting her on it.

She had to be calm. She had to convince them.

"Every generation we wait, we get farther from our memory of what we need to know," she said quietly. "You still remember aircraft carriers. You remember NASA and … and … frozen yogurt and chewing gum. How many do? How many remember what we had the promise to be before this? We're living on scraps. If we wait now, we will be crushed. The Rebellion will be gone, and how long will it be until someone revives it? A hundred years? A thousand? We'll be lucky if we survive another two generations out there on the stations and the Snowballs."

"We will always fight," he assured her. His face had softened, though. "Walker, I promise you. That is what humanity is."

"Humanity is *dying*," she told him simply. "There may not be enough of us. Deep down, you know what this is. This was them killing us without killing us. This was them stripping everything away so that, as we died, we couldn't mount a defense. We need to move *now.*" *While humanity still remembers enough of what it was to grasp at the future that will save us.*

He wavered, and before he had a chance to formulate a retort, there was a pounding on the door.

They exchanged a heavy glance, and Walker went to open it. "Yes?"

"There's a—there's a—" The communications officer had clearly run all the way from the bridge. "There's a shuttle leaving Earth," he managed at last. "Just got a tight beam message from one of our cells in the Rockies. They report that Pike left a day ago."

A day ago. Relief almost made Walker's knees buckle. *Pike.* For five days, she had told herself he was dead. Now she had proof he was a alive. Or rather, *was* alive a day ago.

She hadn't planned on it. She had convinced herself he was dead. It was the only way she could go on, and not knowing made a pit open beneath her feet. He was dead, she told herself with one part of her brain, while with the other she told herself that she'd given him the best chance there was to survive. If he was dead, he wasn't alone on the surface. If he was dead, he wasn't in danger.

They'd seen the coming and going of a dozen Telestine patrol groups from their vantage point of their hiding place a million kilometers sunward of Earth, washed out by the glare of the sun, and every day the last rays of hope had faded from her mind.

But now....

Now, he was alive. Alive, and with something their source swore could lead them to the Dawning. How it had been saved, she did not know. She did not even know what it was.

It was a chance. She had, on the desk before her, a bloody plan to put her final endgame in motion.

The endgame she'd confided to no one.

But with the Dawning, she had a chance to do the same—and spare the bulk of her forces in the process. Dammit. There was only ever the best choice.

"Deploy the fighters, and tell all ships to spin up. We'll be making a hard burn for Earth. Exactly how long ago did the shuttle leave?"

"Twenty three hours." The communications officer was getting his breath back. He slumped against the wall. "It's out of range of our sensors now, but it was just a shuttle. It didn't have the range to get *anywhere*."

"Any shuttle should have at least that much air. He'll have taken cover somewhere, behind an asteroid or next to a satellite or something. He'll know staying there's the best way for us to find him. Let's go."

"Is this safe?" Delaney's voice was quiet.

"You have two options." She straightened her top. For the first time in days, she felt like herself. "That shuttle may have the Dawning on it. It's either this, or the nukes and total war, which, at this point in the construction of the Mercury shipyards, I'm not confident we will win. But as long as the Dawning could be ours, I'm putting my bets on that."

He met her eyes for one moment before his jaw clenched tight. He nodded once.

"Good." Her voice was crisp. She held out a hand to haul the communications officer upright. "Come along. We have a weapon to find."

CHAPTER TWENTY-EIGHT

Near Venus
Shuttle

From the rendezvous point, it took two days to get where they were going, wherever that was. With each hour that passed, Pike revised his estimate on the location of their destination. First it was more likely an asteroid, then Venus, then Mercury—or Earth again, for all he knew.

He would have had a better idea if the rendezvous itself hadn't been so strange. The ship that met them was not only unnamed, flying without transponders, it didn't appear on their scanners at all until they were almost on top of it. It was a ghost, and Pike, who thought he had seen every invention humanity could dream up, had the horrified thought that this was a Telestine ship.

It didn't seem to be when they got inside. The furniture was scaled for humans, not Telestines, and every inch of it was gorgeous. Light came from glowing glass orbs. The floors were polished, and there were carpets. Carpets on a spaceship—he'd never seen anything so ridiculous. There were full-sized beds in each of the rooms, made up with silk sheets, and a full spread of food had been set out.

Hell, the artificial gravity felt like a full g. Not like the tenth g most pieced-together human ships had. Telestine artificial gravity tech was a wonder, but terribly energy-intensive. He wondered if there was bacon too, as long as they were dealing with luxuries here.

The luxuries didn't quite make up for the fact that they were clearly trapped, however. Pike spent the better part of two days pacing around the ship, looking for a way onto the bridge—there was none that he could find, and no one else seemed to be there, but the voice on the comm assured them that all was well, and that in fact he might have found details about the location of the Exile Fleet. In the meantime, they should enjoy the journey. There were books, movies, music.

It made him nervous as hell, though the girl didn't seem to mind. As Pike made his rounds through the common room, she sat with an ever-growing pile of books. Sometimes she seemed to be looking for something specific, and he would find her poring over books on medicine, history, weaponry. Other times, she'd be curled up with a novel, looking up occasionally to watch him.

Meanwhile, the more Pike thought, the more he was sure he'd made a terrible mistake trusting this person. When at last the ship docked, his whole stomach turned over, and he tried to decide whether or not to hold his gun as the doors of the shuttle bay opened up. In the end, he settled for resting his hand on the grip. They knew he was a Rebellion soldier, after all.

"It'll be okay," he said to the girl in an undertone.

From the look she gave him, she didn't believe him at all. Well, neither did he.

And then the doors opened, and his grip on the gun tightened by reflex.

A lone figure stood waiting for them. The man's long black hair held a faint curl, and was drawn back in a low ponytail down his back. His vest was white, as were his loose pants. He was very clearly unarmed, though Pike knew that being unarmed didn't necessarily mean the man wasn't dangerous. Indeed, this place probably had enough automated security to vaporize them on the spot.

He glanced past the man, to the windows beyond. They were on one of the floating estates of Venus.

The figure bowed low. "Mr. Pike, welcome. I am Parees. If you would accompany me?" He came up with a faint smile, one arm gesturing to the end of the docking bay.

"Come on." Pike jerked his head.

The girl gave him a look.

"I don't like it, either." He gave a shrug. "But they've definitely got the upper hand."

"Mr. Pike." The servant's voice was calm. "This way, please. All will be explained."

It took effort not to roll his eyes at the inlaid floors as he followed the servant out of the docking bay. Venus was meant to be the height of luxury, but surely no one needed marble on the lower decks.

Doors slid open for them automatically as they walked. The docking bay gave way to a hallway of deep blue, video screens giving the illusion they traveled through the poly-glass tubes in the oceans of Europa. None of the denizens of Venus would actually go to such a dangerous place, of course —but the view was extraordinary.

They must be in one of the cities, not a lone estate. He could hear the crush of humanity vibrating through the metal. Stations were never quiet, even on Venus. It was part of why he'd become a cargo hauler, desperate to escape the pressure and the smell of so many bodies in such a small space. They'd never known anything else.

He'd known Earth, though. Mountains, trees—he immediately banished the painful nostalgia. He'd abandoned his home, again, and thinking about it made it worse.

An elevator decorated with a truly obscene amount of gold filigree awaited them at the end of the hallway.

"It will be only a short journey," Parees assured them. He swiped his hand over the terminal and stood back as the doors closed.

Pike waited, gritting his teeth at the music. It didn't matter whether one was in the mines or the most luxurious place in the solar system, apparently—elevator music was just universally terrible.

The doors opened onto a flood of intense golden light. The girl winced.

"Mr. Pike," the familiar voice greeted them warmly.

Pike squinted into the light, trying to make out anything beyond the blaze.

The figure resolved as they were ushered out of the elevator: a man with short black hair and the light suit favored by the inhabitants of the Venusian estates. Atmosphere could be corrected, but it was always warm here. Sweat was already sliding down Pike's back.

"It is good to meet you at last." The man smiled. "I am Nhean."

Pike said nothing. He could think of nothing to say. The man was greeting him with the warmth of a host, but they had never met—and Pike didn't have the thing this man so desperately wanted.

Why were they here?

"You will have questions, I think." Nhean stepped back and gestured to a table laden with food. "Please, eat. Ask. I will answer what I can." He cocked his head to one side. "And who is this?"

The girl gave him a wordless look before going to the table, almost ostentatiously turning her back. If she had been a soldier, Pike would have known what to make of the gesture: utter contempt for her opponent's abilities. As it was, he was left to wonder.

Nhean had only smiled at her silence. He looked back to Pike.

"You will surely want for some food as well, yes?" He strolled toward the table at Pike's side. "Tell me, what questions do you have?"

What the hell is your game? "You said you might have picked up the trail of the fleet. Does the Rebellion know I'm alive?"

"No." The answer was quick. Nhean's face carried a trace of regret. "Soon, I promise. You see ... I have some questions to ask of you too, Mr. Pike."

Nhean paused, and picked up a strawberry from the table. Good god, a *strawberry*. He popped into his mouth, and smiled.

"Questions, and a favor."

CHAPTER TWENTY-NINE

Venus, 49 kilometers above surface
Tang Estate, New Zurich

"A favor?" Pike stared at the man, incredulous.

"Yes." Nhean met his eyes.

"You're joking," Pike said flatly. "You brought me here on a ship worth more than some stations to ask for a *favor*?"

"Yes."

"I'm listening." Pike heard the bitterness grow in his voice. "And please, don't call it a *favor*."

Nhean considered this with a small frown. He seemed surprised by Pike's frustration, but then, rich people always were. Rich people thought money fixed everything. "What would you call it?"

"You brought us here without any real recourse. You might be pretending we're friends, but we don't know each other, and she and I have nowhere else to go. It's not a favor, it's an order."

Nhean looked surprised at that, and Pike wasn't sure if he wanted to laugh or cry. Rich people were crazy. Or woefully naïve.

His host considered for a long moment before raising his voice to call the servant back from the door.

"I'd like to speak to Mr. Pike alone, please. If you'd escort our other guest to her rooms?"

"No," Pike said flatly.

"Mr. Pike, she will not be harmed. Miss, you are quite safe, I assure you. I must speak to Mr. Pike alone, but I will see you later at dinner."

"You don't have to go," Pike told her.

She considered this, examining Nhean with sharp eyes, and Pike was pleased to see that the man looked uncomfortable under her assessment. Whatever she saw, it was enough. She shrugged and turned on her heel to leave with the servant.

As the door closed, Nhean let out his breath slowly. "That's the girl you found in the lab? She doesn't look lab-grown."

"She isn't."

"Mr. Pike—"

"Just Pike."

"Ah, yes." Nhean paused, and when he spoke again, his voice was flat. He sounded uncertain, and a bit frustrated. "Here is the whole of it: I've been tracking the Dawning since before I knew what, exactly, it did. All I knew at first was that it was important. Very important. There isn't any foolproof way to intercept Telestine communications, however, and the ones pertaining to the labs operate on an entirely different system than the standard military communications. To be frank with you, it's not even clear if the two systems are ... allied with one another."

"How can research and development not be on good terms with the military?"

"What we don't know about Telestine society is, quite frankly, almost everything." Nhean met his eyes. "At this juncture, it makes sense to question every assumption we have about them. I don't know, in fact, if the Dawning was developed by the military, or if it was developed as a check on the military."

Pike considered this. "Why is it called 'the Dawning'?"

"Because that's what I named it."

Pike did a double take.

"You didn't think the Telestines would give it a human name, did you?" Nhean's eye twinkled for fraction of a second. "Its real name is a Telestine word, of course. Dawning is ... well, it's the closest translation I can make."

Pike shrugged, and repeated, "So why is it called the Dawning?"

A pause.

"I don't know, and that worries me."

Pike considered this as he went to the table. There was some kind of bird there, roasted—a ridiculous extravagance when most meat could be lab-grown. He tried to figure out how to eat it and wondered why he would want to if it was filled with bones. He vaguely remembered a few roasted birds on Earth, long ago, but even then it was a scarce luxury. For Christmas. Once every three years.

"The reason I asked to speak with you alone is the same

reason I scanned your shuttle on the ship—and the reason I overrode your guidance systems." Nhean glanced at the far door and looked back to meet Pike's eyes. "The girl you have with you has, to the best of my knowledge, been in those labs for many years—and she has always moved with the Dawning."

Pike considered this. "So?"

"So she has something to do with an experimental Telestine system, and I don't even know who built it. Why she's involved is a complete mystery to me. She may be its operator, which begs the question of *why*. What capabilities do humans have that Telestines don't? If Telestines are capable of working it, then why aren't they doing so? Most importantly of all— what does she *think* about it?"

"If she knows what it is, she might well be working for the Rebellion," Pike said at once. "She could have earned their trust and—"

"Mr.—" Nhean broke off, and breathed. "That is a pleasant dream, but let us look at the facts, please. The Rebellion is small. How many have found their way into its ranks—a few thousand? Ten thousand at most? And that's people raised by humans, told by human parents and human friends that humanity is enslaved. People who see that every day."

"What's your point?" Pike's voice was harsh.

"My point is that as far as I can tell, she may have been raised by the Telestines. Do you really want to place the hopes and dreams of humanity on her allegiance?"

Pike went hot, and then cold. "She's had plenty of chances to turn me in. She could have hurt me, she could have taken out a whole camp—the ones who got us that shuttle."

There was pity in the other man's face. "With all respect ... you're not the biggest prize she could take down. The Rebellion itself would make a better target, don't you think?"

Pike swallowed.

"It's one of the reasons I had you brought here rather than letting you go to them. This isn't even my estate, and it's still a risk." Nhean's eyes caught the flash in Pike's face. "What is it?"

"We passed Telestine fighters on the way out of atmo and they didn't stop us." The words were bitter. "They didn't *stop* us. I should have known. I thought she cloaked us somehow, but...." He turned away.

"What type of fighters? Out of curiosity."

"The black ones with the curved wings."

"Interesting." Nhean looked down at the floor. "I think you understand my caution now, why I wanted to speak to you alone. I wanted to know what, if anything, she'd done to the shuttle."

"So she's a Telestine spy."

"She might be. For all we know, there is some loyalty in her. For all we know, she's lived a life of pain and she hates the Telestines as much as we do. The question is how much loyalty she has, and how far it will hold."

Pike looked out at the clouds. "So now what?"

"We question her."

"She doesn't talk."

"She doesn't *want* to talk. But ... she can be persuaded." The words were said delicately, but the implication was clear. Nhean was not yet willing to trust a woman found in Telestine labs.

"No." Pike felt horror seize him. "If you ever want her to be loyal—"

"We don't have much *time*," Nhean said quietly. "The fleet was there to help you at Earth because their location near Jupiter was compromised. They've already lost two carriers and many of their fighters, and they are on the run. If we don't get the defensive grid down soon, we won't have a fleet to capitalize on that. Give me a better option and I will use it." His eyes seemed sad, but his jaw was set.

Pike searched for an answer, but came up blank. And his last sentence reminded him of Laura. "There is only ever the best choice."

Nhean nodded as if in agreement. "But we may not have a better option. The Exile Fleet is already coming up on Earth."

"Walker's going back to Earth?" Pike's spine stiffened. "Why?"

"Either to pick you up—they probably detected your shuttle leave—or...." A shadow passed over his face.

"Or?"

"Or she's beginning her assault on Earth. Prematurely."

Pike shook his head. "No. She wouldn't do that."

A raised eyebrow. "Wouldn't she? You know her best, after all."

He forced his back to relax, but couldn't dispel the ache in his stomach. "How long do you think they can hold out?"

CHAPTER THIRTY

Earth, Low Orbit
Bridge, EFS Intrepid

The fleet decelerated hard, right to the edge Earth's exosphere. Only the *Oksana* held back, her fighters out, bays open on the off chance that Pike's shuttle was just hiding behind an orbiting asteroid or defunct human satellite, as the rest of the fleet made a diversion in the fore. Walker marked the progress of the fleet against that lone, tiny dot.

Come on, Pike. The *Intrepid* lurched as the engines roared to life and Walker gripped the desk as the room rocked. The ship dropped altitude and she let out a sigh of relief when they came to a relative stop a moment later as the engines pushed them into orbit at the upper reaches of the atmosphere.

On the other side of the desk, Delaney looked like he might be sick. Telestine-made inertial dampeners helped with acceleration—or they tried to—but for some reason the stolen

Telestine tech struggled to make deceleration comfortable. It felt like none of them had been able to take a full breath since Walker gave the order.

And she couldn't let them stop to enjoy the moment, either.

"Larsen, give me news."

"Right." Larsen's fingers danced over the screens and his lips twitched. "Looks like we managed to get under the radar *and*—are you ready for some good news?—I think we took out a Telestine satellite on the way in. *Without* puncturing the hull," he added.

"I was going to say...." Walker allowed herself a small smile. She kind of wished she'd saved this maneuver for the final battle against the Telestines, but it was impossible to deny how satisfying it was to screech into the atmosphere of her home planet at full burn, and take out a few Telestines on the way. "Are they regrouping?"

"Their units are all full of chatter, that's for sure. Broadening the sensor sweep." Larsen waited, jiggling his foot with impatience. Around the bridge, the rest of the crew was also adjusting to the lack of extra g's, with excess energy made manifest in pen tapping, nervous smiles, and a great many people stretching hugely.

All of the nervous activity stopped when the klaxons came on.

"We're detecting five fighter detachments, ma'am." Larsen met her eyes. "And it looks like we might have a carrier coming as well."

"All right." Walker laced her fingers behind her back and gave a silent prayer. "Let's take out those detachments before the carrier arrives, and make a lot of fuss while the *Oksana* finds our payload. Fighters out, and dive." It was time to see if McAllister had gotten his new trainees up to speed; she could only hope that he had.

"Yes, ma'am. All fighters launch. Say again, all fighters launch." Larsen held up one finger toward the *Intrepid*'s helmsman. His lips moved as he counted the fighters now streaming out into the holographic view. "Bays one through nine empty. Bay ten. Bay eleven. *Valiant* reporting all launched. *Brama* reporting all launched." He looked up to meet the helmsman's eyes. "Dive."

The *Intrepid* gave a groan ... and dropped.

Delaney clutched the desk with both hands and started into a whispered Lord's prayer, Larsen turned vaguely green, and King stared straight ahead as if she would only keep it together if she pretended all of this was normal.

"Altitude three hundred kilometers and dropping," Larsen reported a bit faintly. "Partial burn beginning...." His face split into a smile. "All Telestine formations scattering."

Walker fixed her eyes on the hologram and watched as the Telestines shot out of the way of the falling carriers.

"They're regrouping behind us."

"Hard burn!" she called back. "*Now*!"

"Yes, ma'am." Ensign Harris, their helmsman, slammed her hand down on the controls with evident pleasure. Landing, she had told Walker, was perfectly fine. Flying was perfectly fine. Dropping the carrier out of the sky and cranking the engines on the way down, however, was not her idea of a good time.

"They're coming for us," Larsen called. On the screen, the

Telestine fighter groups had reformed and they were making a slow arc to come down toward the carriers.

"Well, let's say hello." Walker gave a small smile. "Start with the cannons."

"Cannons primed and ... firing." Larsen tapped his screen, and lines appeared on the hologram, streaking away from the *Intrepid* and the *Brama*, too fast to track with unaided eyes.

"All units repeat. Fighters stay out of the way. Pick 'em off as they come out." Walker watched the Telestine fighters scattering desperately as the cannon fire began. "You don't like that, you bastards? Then get the hell off our damn planet."

Delaney grinned.

"Seventeen enemy fighters down," Larsen called. "Twenty-two. Twenty-nine. Thirty—ah, hell. The carrier's here, and it is *not* happy to see us!"

"Duly noted—Harris, take us *up*. Yes, right into the rest of the fighters, if you have to." Hopefully they weren't going fast enough for a hull puncture. Hopefully. "All fighters climb, you aren't going to do anything against that thing."

Now they came to it. Delaney met her eyes across the desk and nodded.

Walker swallowed. "*Brama,* do you read?"

"We read, admiral," said Captain Noringe.

"Is the nuke primed?"

She'd heard the stories of the terrifyingly powerful hydrogen-based thermonuclear weapons humanity had built before the Telestines had arrived. Tens of megatons each. But she didn't have the luxury of fusion bombs, or plutonium, for that matter. Just simple gun-style uranium weapons at a few hundred kilotons each. Quick and dirty. Hopefully enough to both take out a Telestine cruiser, and, at this altitude, effect a halfway decent electromagnetic pulse to knock out electrical systems on the ground below.

"Yes, ma'am. Ready for launch; we're just out of range."

"Hang back. We'll cover you. Shoot as soon as we swing wide. *Jocasta, Andromache,* hope you're ready."

"We're ready, admiral." The voices were tight with anticipation.

Walker watched the formation close around them on the screen. The *Jocasta* came to rest a scant distance above the *Intrepid,* with the *Andromache* below.

"Broadside," Walker called. The ships began to turn as they banked toward the carrier, all guns firing. The first round of Telestine missiles slammed into the ship and through the rumble she heard klaxons echoing on the *Jocasta*'s comm line. "We're closing, keep firing, keep firing, keep—all right, move!"

The ships pulled apart. The *Jocasta* was limping, but the captain had the ship at full burn. No one wanted to be around for what was coming.

"The *Brama* reports the nuke has launched, ma'am." Larsen's voice was quiet.

Whether the Telestines guessed what they were facing, Walker didn't know. The ship began to slow, however, and turn.

It wasn't quick enough. With a boom they heard through the hull of the *Intrepid,* the carrier flashed out of being on the hologram. The computers flickered, the rudimentary EMP shield they'd devised taking the brunt, and Harris was already turning them to streak out of atmo.

"Any more contacts?"

"None yet."

"And the EMP?" It was the whole reason for that ill-advised maneuver in the first place, dropping down precipitously into the atmosphere to add more EM fuel to the nuclear fire, and possibly take out Telestine electrical systems on the surface.

Larsen was shaking his head. "No effect that I can see, ma'am."

Damn. So there went one potential tactic. The Telestine EMP shielding tech was as good as their own, apparently. But she wasn't surprised.

Larsen looked pained. "News from the *Oksana*."

"Yes?"

"They aren't seeing that shuttlecraft anywhere. Either it's hiding from *us*, it already left, or...."

"Yes?"

"Or it's already been taken down."

Walker looked back at the screen. No one had turned the hologram off, and Earth was receding behind them. She narrowed her eyes and considered. Her lips moved in a silent litany: *no despair, no hope*. When the answer finally came to her, she almost did not believe it. Hope could kill a person, she'd always known that.

But it made sense, it checked out.

"I don't think so," she said aloud.

"What?"

"I don't think the Telestines got to it. They didn't have much notice that we were in the vicinity—how'd they get a carrier in position that quickly? No, I think they know someone was flying around here, maybe drifting with their engines quiet. I think the Telestines were waiting for them to

run out of air and come down. The question is ... who was it?"
She looked up to meet Larsen's eyes. "And where in hell did
they go?"

"I don't know, ma'am."

"Well, we're going to find out somehow. Pike is alive. The
Dawning isn't lost to us yet."

CHAPTER THIRTY-ONE

Venus, 49 kilometers above surface
Tang Estate, New Zurich

"So." Nhean sat behind his desk and inclined his head. "Let us speak about what you know of the Dawning."

The girl stared back at him warily, then looked toward the door.

"Mr. Pike is not here." Nor was the man aware of what was happening at present. Nhean had judged that to be the best option. The man was likely to be squeamish if this progressed beyond simple questions.

Nhean, however, had long since accepted that possibility.

"Tell me about the Dawning. We have reason to believe it wasn't destroyed the way we thought it was. You always moved with it. Where did it go this time? Why were you there, where it should have been?"

She crossed her arms and stared at him, and his irritation

grew.

"Do you understand why you are here?"

Nothing.

"You are *here* because you have a key to something that could save humanity. Do you understand? We have been given the keys to spread ourselves across the universe, and yet we are watched, we are limited, we are *caged.*"

Still nothing.

"Did you know that humanity has often had labs like the one you grew up in?"

Her eyes grew wary.

"We didn't do the things like what were done to you." He paused, his desire for accuracy at war with his best interests. "Usually," he conceded. "We studied things like propulsion, agriculture, military development—anything and everything. Do you know what we study now?" He waited until she shook her head. "Nothing," he told her flatly. "We study nothing. The Telestines believe that any innovation will lead us to war against them. It's impossible to stop all of it, of course— there's always a mechanic somewhere that can make a spaceship run better. And designing new rudimentary nuclear missiles has been a priority for Walker. But it's better for them to feed us these things, to squash the universities and laboratories we build, than it is for them to deal with a populace that can think and invent for itself. Meanwhile, they keep inventing. Do you know all of the experiments they performed on humans in that lab, or just the ones they did on you?"

She sat rigid. He knew he was giving her more information than Walker would have been comfortable with. But before information, came trust. And barring trust … enhanced questioning.

"It occurs to me to wonder: do you know how they make human slaves? The ones some of us call *Drones*?"

The wariness grew.

"I don't think you do. You're clearly not one of those. So, let me tell you. They're bred in tanks. There's nothing wrong with that, of course—just an old-fashioned revulsion. Humans can be quite primitive in some ways, wouldn't you say?"

She said nothing to that, and it occurred to him to wonder if tank breeding seemed normal to her. What would a person raised in that environment think of normal birth? The thought was intriguing.

Not important.

"But the humans made in those labs don't come out like other humans. It's hard to know what it is—genetic engineering, gene selection, drugs. It's one of the things we could study if we had the facilities for it, but to be honest with you, I'm not sure I'd want us knowing. The *how* of it isn't important, though. They're … docile. Very docile. Drugged after birth, at least, if not before. Even when they aren't, they don't do much of anything unless they're told. They can't fend for themselves—their will to survive, the same will that makes it possible for us to live on orbital stations and hostile planets, is practically non-existent. The first ones we rescued off of Earth were a tremendous failure. After the second group, we knew it hadn't been a fluke. They're all like that."

She looked away. Her lips were pressed together. He was getting under her skin at last.

"You aren't like that," Nhean said.

Her head jerked up.

"Were you grown in their labs, or were you taken from human parents?"

Nothing. She looked down at her hands.

"You've been trained to use their technology, haven't you?"

Her head shook, but there was no truth there.

"Why, exactly, don't you trust me?"

She only met his eyes briefly before looking away, but her gaze was defiant now.

"You know what they did to you, don't you? Even if you were asleep, the scars should tell you. You're full of machinery."

She sat back, arms crossed.

So she did know.

"Although it appears to be inert," Nhean observed. He tried to keep the irritation from his voice now. He had scanned her surreptitiously, pored over the data as many times as he could, and he still could not figure out what the Telestines had put in her. For all he could tell, it was simply an enhanced skeleton.

Except he knew it was more. What *was* it? Short of taking her apart, there was no way to tell.

She shrugged.

"My dear, what do you think is going to happen here? Do you think I am a Telestine agent, sent to test your loyalty—or worse, kill your species? Do you believe I am planning to wipe out humanity? Believe me, that is not my plan. I want the Telestines gone, and humanity in control of Earth again."

He watched her for a moment, and pushed himself up to

pace around the room. "I spoke of science and technology. I did not tell you how deeply it offends me that we cannot pursue that. It is what we *are*. The way we have survived for so long is through innovation. We learn, we adapt. To cut us off from that and from our planet in one stroke is to deny us a part of ourselves. Surely you, held in that lab, watching the experiments with a human's mind but kept from your family ... surely you understand that."

She bit her lip.

"There is a Telestine military base on the moon," Nhean told her. "It contains access points that can tell us more about the Telestine defense grid. If you don't think you can get us to the Dawning...."

She only looked at him.

"...then perhaps you can help us infiltrate the lunar base," he finished.

Nothing. Of course. He was beginning to tire of this, but it was imperative that she not know that. Not yet.

"Mr. Pike tells me you were almost intercepted by Telestine fighters on your way off Earth."

She looked at him sharply. There was betrayal there.

"They didn't see you. Why?" He made sure his voice was sharp.

She folded her arms.

"Did they not see you, or did they let you go?"

She wouldn't even look at him now.

"I will not tolerate traitors," he told her softly. "The slaves, I pity. They had no choice. They aren't even entirely human. You, however—*you* have been given every opportunity to help your own kind, and you will not do it."

Her head shook—just once, an abortive gesture.

"No, that's not true? Or no, you won't help us? Which is it? The first or the second?"

She said nothing, and he crouched down next to her chair.

"We don't have the technology the Telestines have," he told her simply. "We don't have the technology to take our planet back without great uncertainty and great bloodshed. All we have is you." He stood and smiled. "I trust you will help us as much as you can. In the meantime, dinner is ready. I will join you presently."

She nodded, warily. Her face was a puzzle as she left the room.

Parees lingered in the doorway after she had gone. His eyes met Nhean's, and the men both nodded before the aide closed the door quietly and left.

I trust you will help us as much as you can. Nhean looked out at the view of the towering dark yellow clouds, and then to the spires of the main city. Even from here, two panes of thick glass and hundreds of yards away, he could see the seething motion of the city's populace. It never stopped. He often wondered how streets had looked on Earth—if they were ever empty, if there was space that was not crowded with a mass of humanity. Here, there was no natural process to ensure that the scrubbers kept cleaning the air or the cooling and heating systems did their work. There were always people awake, and so all of the aspects of life continued on as well: the cafes, the transit cars. On the other stations, crowded almost to the point of system failure, the hallways were always congested and filthy and loud. And on Venus, those not rich enough for their own floating estates ran stock exchanges that never closed, manned the hospitals, played endless rounds of poker in the casinos....

He would not be sad to see the last of this place. Nhean rubbed at his face. He had to focus.

The girl. How much *could* she help? He had planted the seed in her mind, but he might not have time for her to decide to help on her own.

He didn't need her cooperation, he reminded himself. He had *her*. He had the machinery inside her. His fingers clenched. If necessary, he could deconstruct her piece by piece. It wasn't something he looked forward to—Nhean was not a man who enjoyed pain, in himself or others—but it was something he would do without hesitation.

For Earth. For humanity.

But not yet. He nodded decisively and made for the dinner hall. To do so would be to make an enemy of William Pike, and that was an enemy he could not afford at the moment. If anyone could discover the truth behind the admiral's motives, if anyone could guess what her end game might be, it would be the man who—if the information Parees had found was accurate—still loved her.

It was a fine line to walk, but Nhean was used to that. He was accustomed to charming secrets from the tongues of his enemies, and William Pike did not even think of him as an enemy yet. A thought occurred to him, and he paused outside the dinner hall to motion to Parees.

"Has there been word from Tel'rabim?"

"None yet, sir. The lines are completely closed."

"I don't like this," Nhean murmured. "He's never closed our backchannel before."

Parees only bowed his head. He did not promise to bring

Nhean information immediately; they both knew he would do so. He did not promise Nhean that all would be well; they both knew there was no guarantee of that. Over the years, Parees had come to anticipate his employer's needs exactly. He bowed and withdrew, and Nhean strode into the dinner hall to greet his guests.

Twelve hours, he decided. The girl had twelve hours to offer information of her own accord.

Then he would take it from her.

CHAPTER THIRTY-TWO

Venus, 49 kilometers above surface
Tang Estate, New Zurich

He didn't like any of this. Pike paced around the set of rooms he'd been given and tried to shake his unease. He's seen the girl at dinner, perfectly healthy. They'd had a leisurely meal and had been given separate rooms—which made sense, of course. Nhean had taken him aside to tell him that they needed a plan by morning.

But the more he thought, pacing up and down on the exquisite floors, the more it seemed to him that something was wrong. This *wasn't* his world and these weren't his kind of people. Blake had been entirely correct about that. He didn't understand the way they worked. He couldn't get a straight answer out of Nhean about ... anything.

But he could fix that problem. The door to his room wasn't locked, and Pike grabbed his rifle before slipping out into the darkened hallways. He half-expected to see someone waiting outside his rooms, but Nhean was apparently not worried about Pike leaving. Where would he go? Jump out into the golden clouds?

Nhean knew Pike had nowhere to go—and that made Pike furious. Pike looked around and set off in the opposite direction from the main rooms.

He wasn't entirely sure what he was hoping to find. A journal, with all of Nhean's secrets laid out neatly in one place? He grinned. That wouldn't be half bad.

The floor sloped down gently as he walked. The estates on Venus, especially in the cities, used many levels rather than large ones—although even Pike's rooms were larger than some of the ships he'd served on in the cargo guild. He was, by his estimation, four levels down when he heard the clank.

He'd heard that noise before, though he couldn't remember where. There were two parts to it, three if you listened carefully. It came again and he frowned. There was one door for this level, only a few feet away. He put his hand on the knob and pulled.

If this were Nhean's own estate, Pike had no doubt that he would have been locked securely in his rooms. The private estates had their own security systems, their own house-loyal guards. If Nhean had taken the risk of bringing them to his estate....

The door came open with a jerk and Pike stopped dead on the threshold.

The room was in chaos. The girl had clearly been trying to escape. The bed was on its side, pieces of it ripped off—she had been trying to find something to wedge into the door, he guessed. Her room had nothing that might be easily used that way.

By design, he was sure.

"Are you hurt?"

She shook her head.

"I think we should go."

And? her eyes asked him.

"I don't know. We just have to get out of here." The more he thought, the clearer it seemed. Everything was off about this, just subtly, just enough to worry him. Pike grabbed her hand and hauled her up. He searched around on the floor for a weapon of some type and handed her the dull knife from the bowl of fruit nearby. "It's not much, but it's something. Come on."

He took them down the ramp rather than up, on the hope that it led down to the docking bay. It did, though the door there wouldn't budge. She pushed him out of the way and felt over it with gentle fingertips, and whatever she touched, the door slid silently open for her. She pulled him down the hallway, breaking into a run.

The ship was still there, silent and empty. Pike hadn't appreciated how big it was when they arrived, but it went up at least four stories, and extended back until it disappeared in darkness.

Thankfully, the crew was absent and the cockpit was empty. Pike punched at the controls at random until something turned on, and gave a silent sigh of thanks when the ship's protocols opened the docking bay doors as well.

Taking a deep breath, he engaged what he thought were the maneuvering thrusters, and with a jolt the ship lurched off the deck, nearly crashing into the ceiling before he arrested the ascent. He tried hard not to clench the controls, but he noticed his knuckles were white. He guided the ship back slowly out the bay door as the girl peered at the computer, lips pursed. Every once in a while she would tap something. She was searching, but for what, he didn't know.

Pike checked the fuel gauge as they zoomed away from the city, and finally remembered to breath. Good. There was enough to get them to fuel stations where he was known.

That was a risk, however. He sat back in his seat, and was surprised to see the girl lean forward to punch coordinates into the guidance systems. He studied them for a moment.

"Earth?"

She shook her head.

"The moon?"

She nodded.

"Is that where Nhean wanted to go?"

Another nod.

Only then did it come crashing down on him what he'd done, and he put his face in his hands.

These aren't your kind of people. What had he gotten caught up in? He'd been raised in a place where mistakes meant death, where people talked straight with one another because there was no reason to do otherwise. He didn't understand a world where Nhean claimed to be doing the same work as the Rebellion but wouldn't trust them, where Walker had shadows behind her eyes.

He didn't want to know if the girl who had saved his life was a Telestine agent.

He had to. He picked up his head and wiped the

coordinates out of the computer with a few stabs of his fingers.

"Are you trying to help us get Earth back?" he asked her. "Or are you one of theirs?"

Her face went white. She stared at him like he'd slapped her.

"Look, I don't know what the hell is going on here." His voice was rising. "I don't know who you are. All I wanted to do was get back home, and then when I found you, I thought maybe we had a shot. I just don't trust that guy." The words sounded idiotic. He forced himself to look at her. "So when you say you want to go to the moon base—is it to destroy it? Or to get the information we need to get these fuggers off our planet and take it back?"

She nodded.

"You think he's telling the truth about that?"

She sat back in her chair. Her nod this time was quieter. As if she was working something out.

"Why?"

She didn't have an answer for that, of course.

"All right." Pike clenched his hands and tried to think.

"I have to make a call. Let's hope he was lying about the fleet being missing, because we really need some backup."

CHAPTER THIRTY-THREE

1 million kilometers sunward of L1 Lagrange point, Earth Bridge, EFS Intrepid

"Pike?"

"Oh Laura, thank god." Pike's voice was scratchy. She heard him let out his breath in a whoosh. "Please tell me the fleet is okay."

Walker sank back in her chair. She was alone in her quarters. No one could see her break down. She pressed the heels of her palms into her eyes and took a moment to steady herself.

"The fleet is ... holding." He didn't need to hear the worst of it, but she couldn't bring herself to lie outright to him. "After we couldn't find you we fled back to our favorite hiding place in the glare of the sun. What happened to you?"

"Have you ever heard of a man named Nhean Tang?"

"No, but give me a moment." Walker pulled up one of the

databases and began a search. "Anything more you know about him? I have a few records, one on Ares station, one on the cargo freighters, and—" Her breath caught. *Venus*. Technical analyst and head of a small company called Data Enterprises. "Oh, my god. He's our contact on Venus."

"Let me guess." Pike sounded so bitter that she swallowed hard. "He's the one who told you about the Dawning."

"Yes." Walker had the sense of an immense pattern swinging into place. She could still only grasp the merest part of it, and yet what she could see made her start to question everything. Data Enterprises—she'd never heard of it until now, but from the data file, it looked to have its fingers in a lot of pots. Connections to several large banks. Cargo freighter construction companies. The Venetian branches of the Catholic and Mormon churches. The Dalai Lama. The cargo guild. The UN. Shit. She did not like this in the least. But Laura Walker had never been one to run from facts, though. "Tell me everything."

"He contacted me during the raid on the laboratory," Pike told her bluntly. "He wanted me to bring the Dawning to him, not to you."

And Pike's shuttle was coming at them *from* Venus. Her heart contracted.

"Did you?"

"No! No. Well...." He sighed again. "Not exactly. We didn't find it."

"At least he was honest about one thing, then." She could hear Pike's same bitterness echoed in her own voice. "Start at the beginning: what *happened* at the lab?"

"We damaged the lab in the first attack—your fighters

must have seen it crashing—so we split up to try to find the Dawning. Nhean somehow hacked into my earpiece—from Venus—and guided me to where his intelligence said it was. I got to the room and the only thing there was a girl."

"A *girl*?" Walker tapped at her earpiece. "Did you say a girl? Like, a kid?"

"Yes, a girl. Not a kid—older. Maybe nineteen or twenty. I couldn't just leave her, so I brought her with me. Our ship crashed—you know that—and we had to get off-planet. By the time we got a shuttle up though, he'd decided she had something to do with the Dawning. He told me Jupiter had been attacked and the fleet was on the run, and to come to Venus." There was a pause, and she could just see him rubbing his forehead the way he did when he felt out of his depth.

She almost smiled. She had missed him.

"I suppose that was all lies," he said quietly. "Dammit. Walker, I'm not cut out for this—"

"Not all of it was lies." Walker considered. "After we got your capsule down, they traced the fleet to New Beginnings. We lost—well, it's not important. But we lost too much, and we've been on the run, that much is true. He just didn't tell you that we were nearby. We didn't abandon you there, Pike. We were waiting for you." *And planning to make the Telestines pay.* He didn't need to know that, though.

"I should have waited." Pike's voice had the same flat tone he always used when he was angry with himself.

"You didn't know." She knew from experience that she'd never convince him, not where his own failings were concerned, but she could at least try. "You did the best you could, under the circumstances. In any case, there was a fight on when we arrived, so maybe it's best you weren't there." She sighed. "You're coming back, though? You'll meet up with us?" She wanted to see with her own eyes that he was alive.

"Not just yet. Remember that girl I mentioned?"

"Yes." A stab of—what was this, jealousy? Walker gave a fierce shake of her head at her own foolishness.

"I think he was right about her," Pike said. "I think—I think she actually can do things with their technology. At one point, a whole squadron passed right by us because of something she did. I don't know what, but ... look, he mentioned a lunar base, one of *theirs*. If we can get onto there, there's a chance she can get us the same information we'd have had with the Dawning."

Walker froze. Reason returned slowly with each breath, in the mantra she had repeated for years: *Think logically, don't be seduced by hope or fear, pick the best choice, keep moving.* "She thinks she can do that?"

"I ... think so?"

"Well—can she or can't she?" She frowned at the comm unit. "She's with you now? Put her on."

"I can't really do that. I'll explain later—"

"Why not?"

He hesitated. "She, uh, doesn't talk."

"Doesn't? Won't? Or can't?"

"I don't know. Can't, I think. Listen, Laura, I think we've got a shot. I really do. If the fleet can cover us...."

There was a pause. When his voice came again, it was muffled, as if he'd put the comm unit down. "We can't possibly get in there on our own," she heard. "We don't have guns on this ship, we *need* the fleet." A long pause. "You honestly think we can get in there alone? And that's a better option than going in with their cover?" he said, obviously talking to someone else. She heard him sigh.

Walker looked heavenwards and prayed for patience.

"Pike."

"One second."

"No. Not 'one second.' This is a military operation. The Telestines are watching *very* carefully. The operations that got you on-planet, helped you at the lab, and tried to retrieve your shuttle later? They've put the Telestine fleet on alert."

When he spoke, his voice was a jumble of emotion. "It'll be okay. We can get in there alone."

"I can't allow you to try that." She spoke sharply. "Good god, Pike, *think* for a second. If the shit hits the fan, you're on a ship with no guns, and there isn't a way in hell I'll be able to get in there to help you in time."

A long pause. He must have covered the comm unit this time, because she could hear only the faintest sound as he tried to persuade his companion of something.

"Pike. *Pike.*"

He wasn't listening anymore. With an oath, Walker grabbed the comm unit and made for the door. They hadn't gone far, and she was going to meet him at Earth, no matter what he said.

"All right." His voice came back in her ear. "Look, what if you come in from one of the dark zones and get into the shadow of the moon? Stay on the far side, set down in Mendeleev Crater. Their satellites won't be able to catch sight of you there. Maybe."

"They might see us on the approach." But it was a

murmur, not a denial—and they didn't have the resources for a full-scale battle again, unless they threw everything they had out there. "Can you give us any shielding on the approach?"

"Let me check." It seemed as though his voice turned away from his comm. "Can you get the satellites not to see the fleet coming in, even if you're not at the control panels yet?" A long pause. His voice returned, louder now. "Yes. That way you'll be close enough to help, but not in their line of sight."

"And you aren't going to let me talk to her?" Walker rounded a corner and returned a salute distractedly as several junior officers fell out of her way.

"It's not—you'll understand when you meet her." There was a pause. "Walker—I know this is a military operation, but you've already lost ships. You lost some getting me on the ground, too, didn't you?"

"That's not important." She could hear the guilt in his voice.

"I'm just saying, if we can do this without risking the fleet, isn't that worth a shot?"

"Pike...." The doors to the bridge slid open and she crossed into the room, uncomfortably aware that all of her crew had turned to look at her. "What is a fleet for?"

"But if you—"

"It's time, Pike." She heard the tremble in her voice and took her place at the desk. "If she's what you think, the fleet needs to be at Earth to capitalize on that intel. Because once she does her thing, we might not get another shot."

Silence.

"Right," he said finally. "Promise you won't get yourself killed, okay?"

"I promise." The lie came easily.

"Right," he said again. "See you on the other side. "

The call cut, and Walker looked up at her crew.

"Pike has made it off Earth." She paused as a ragged cheer went up. "Better still, he believes he may have found something very close to the Dawning. He will be landing at the Telestine's lunar military base to attempt to deploy it, and we will be on hand to get him out if it does not work—and capitalize on it if it does."

"What did he find?" Delaney, ever practical, narrowed his eyes suspiciously.

"A girl, raised in the Telestine labs. We believe she may have the capacity to interface with their technology."

Delaney's eyebrows shot up.

"Set a course for Earth. Maximum thrust." She glanced at her command console, mentally doing the math for the million-kilometer trek from their hiding place in the glare of the sun past the L1 Lagrange point. Five g's, nearly three hours.

"Ma'am." Larsen swiveled around in his chair at the comm station. "Our contact on Venus is on the main line."

Walker paused to consider this. She didn't know his endgame. Or even his motivations. And she was tired of depending on someone else.

"Tell *Mr. Tang*," she said finally, "that we do not require his assistance for now."

CHAPTER THIRTY-FOUR

Venus, 49 kilometers above surface
Tang Estate, New Zurich

"Dammit." Nhean slammed his hand down on the desk as the line went dead. His pulse was pounding. *Dammit, dammit, dammit.*

They'd told her.

This was a risk he'd taken, he reminded himself. Childhood friendships were strong, unpredictable, and Pike was more protective of the silent girl than Nhean had anticipated. If Nhean had just played a stronger hand, taken the precautions to hold them....

But Pike was Earthborn. A Native. And a cargo runner. If anything would have made him a certain enemy, it would have been a cage of any sort. Locks on the doors, overriding the shuttle's guidance systems—none of that would have done anything but earn the man's enmity.

Nhean allowed himself a wry smile. He had been pleased when Walker put such a chaotic piece in play, and now it turned out she had gambled better than he thought. He shoved the thought away. He would not wallow. He had played this wrong, and all that was left was to regroup. He needed to count his assets and start again.

The shuttle tipped as Parees guided it through the storms near Nhean's private estate, and Nhean glanced out the window at the airship, only partially visible amongst the clouds. He reached out to open a line on the comm unit.

"Parees, take me to the shipyard."

"Yes, sir." Parees changed the shuttle's course without question.

Nhean looked back at the information on the desk in front of him. It still didn't make any sense: he was seeing a sudden flurry of questions over the Telestine network, but no answers. Tel'rabim had disappeared from contact at the worst of times, although it was difficult to imagine that he would willingly give up information of this importance even if Nhean could contact him. It was one thing to sympathize with another species, and entirely different to admit to a military failure.

But this was maddening. No matter how many times Nhean went over what he was seeing, the same pattern always emerged: they were combing the area near the Rocky Mountains with increasing desperation, looking for....

The Dawning.

That they were searching for it too was clear—but why, Nhean could not imagine. If it had been moved before the lab crashed, they should know where it was. If it had crashed on the lab, they should know where it was. More to the point, they didn't seem to want anyone to *know* they were looking for it. The communications were heavily encrypted, and he caught references to stealth systems on the Telestine ships flying patrol. He'd looked at *that* part quite a few times, wondering if it was a mistranslation—perhaps they were searching for stealthed human ships.

They weren't.

It all made sense, it all *had* a reason, it had to—but what? He forced himself to sit back in his chair as he considered.

Why did Telestine ships try to keep themselves invisible to their own kind? A power struggle within the Telestine military? Possible. A classified project? Also possible. The faction dispute—

"Sir, we're approaching the shipyard." Parees's voice was entirely neutral. "Do you want to dock?"

"No. Hold us here." Nhean strolled to the window. His shuttle was built in the same style as his estate: sweeping lines and floor-to-ceiling windows that were utterly impervious to the atmosphere, a feat of engineering humans had been trying to achieve for years. He waited for the clouds to shift, and his breath caught.

Before him lay one of the few sights that still moved him to awe.

The fleet hung mostly hidden in the atmosphere, appearing and disappearing in the swirl of the wispy upper clouds of the storms. They were nearing dusk, but work was still going—he could catch the faint spark and glint of welding. The ships were sleek and fast, the sort one might mistake for Telestine transports, but they weren't Telestine.

They were *his*—he had spent over half his fortune on

them and called in most of the favors the elite owed him—and they were as close to perfect as he could make them. Their guidance systems were built to detect Telestine scans and adjust course accordingly. Their propulsion was finer tuned even than the Telestine wrecks he had recovered, and their life support systems were the most efficient ever seen. They could be remotely guided—a perfect weapon—designed to do the most damage to the opponent and the least to humanity.

And each of them carried the Seed—or would, as soon as he could be sure that it would work. The Dawning was his key, and the Seed ... the Seed was his revenge. Tel'rabim might speak of prosperity and equality, he might make entreaties for medicine to be delivered to the outer stations, but it was not enough. Humanity should not have to scramble for scraps, and when Nhean took down their computer systems one by one and dismantled their cities and loaded *them* onto ships, they would learn what they should have known from the start: as long as humanity existed, they would be planning to take Earth back.

His hands clenched and he let himself smile. The fleet was almost whole. He might have lost the girl, but there had been plans before her, and he could still use those.

Not to mention, the Dawning might still be up for grabs.

He frowned, and then his head turned sharply back to the desk. A thought was dawning.

"No," he murmured to himself. No, it didn't make any sense that the Telestine military had lost an integral piece of their technology. That was too ... easy. It didn't fit. It didn't make sense at all.

Unless ... the factional conflict. What if it wasn't just a

conflict, but a brewing war?

The whole of it hit him in an instant, and he didn't even feel himself cross the room. It took him two tries to press the button.

"Get me back to the estate, and the get the admiral on the line." His voice was shaking.

"Sir, the line isn't receiving communications."

"Then *hack* it if you have to." Panic shortened his breath. "Hack it, do anything you have to, get us in contact with them and tell them they *cannot* take the lunar base. They must abort, and abort *now*."

CHAPTER THIRTY-FIVE

Near Earth's Moon
Tang Shuttle

"This was a bad idea." Pike's voice was barely a whisper.

The girl shook her head without looking over. She had not looked at him in nearly an hour. Her fingers were busy at the ship's controls, sometimes moving dials for no reason he could understand and sometimes simply laying her palms flat on the screens.

Whatever she was doing, it was working, but unfortunately, "working" meant that their ship was now passing through one of the most intense concentrations of the Telestine fleet Pike had ever seen. Aboard the *Aggy*, they had been ordered away from Telestine military exercises in space—humans were not permitted to watch those—and he had seen, once or twice, the carriers that patrolled the solar system looking for violations of the treaty. Neither of those experiences were anything like this.

The shuttle's camera telescope zoomed in on Earth—it seemed as if the entire Telestine fleet was hanging outside Earth's atmosphere. Carriers. Dozens of them. Set like black dots against the swirl of clouds and oceans below—a hurricane was forming over the Atlantic—and the smaller ships swarmed around them like bees to a hive. Shuttles were carrying soldiers between the gunships and the carriers, fighters were flying patrol, and some of the smaller ships seemed to be practicing maneuvers in the empty space above the fleet.

Not a single one of them seemed to notice the human ship passing far too close to Earth. Good thing the shuttle was tiny, and black.

"This was a bad, bad idea," Pike repeated.

The girl gave him a look.

Hours passed, and the blue globe shrunk as the gray moon loomed large in the front viewport. They swung around the edge and watched as the Earth dropped below the horizon, and before he knew it, they were almost there. He fiddled with the controls and managed to initiate the deceleration burn.

She sat up in her seat to watch as the lunar base approached and pointed to its three main docking bays. On three splayed fingers, she indicated the middle bay and gestured for Pike to take the controls.

"We're landing *at* the base?"

She stared at him wordlessly.

Pike blinked at her. She blinked back.

"A bad, bad, *bad* idea," Pike muttered to himself. There was a Telestine patrol crossing beneath them, black shapes silhouetted against the dark lunar surface, and he held his breath until they were out of sight.

He also held his breath for most of the docking process. The docking clamps came out gently to grab the ship and pull it in, and the ship thudded into place a moment later. A green light blinked at him to let him know a docking seal had engaged. Her eyes were closed, as if in deep concentration—had she done that?

It was this easy? It was actually *this* easy? He craned to peer at the computer systems and could not tell for the life of him what she'd done.

He glanced at her. "You want a weapon?"

She opened her eyes and pointed to his knife, her hand out, palm up.

"I suppose that's fair if I get the gun." He handed it over. "Do we go left or right when we get out?"

She shrugged.

"So you're just going to wander until you find things?"

The look she gave him said this was mostly correct, and he sighed.

"All right. You haven't been trained in combat, have you?"

A blank stare. He wasn't sure if that meant yes, or no. Better err on the side of safety.

"So I need to go first."

She blinked. She had apparently not considered this.

"Unless you're actually invisible to Telestine eyes as well as their ships."

She shook her head sadly.

"All right." He held up two fingers and twitched them forward toward himself. "This means to go from wherever you are, to me. Until you see that gesture, you stay put. I'll move ahead, and when it's safe, I'll make that gesture. When you get to me, you tell me where to go next, okay?"

She nodded.

"And for the record? I don't like this."

She spread her hands with a shrug. What other options did they have?

It was a good point. Pike motioned for her to stay where she was, and opened the docking bay doors below. They waited, breathing as silently as possible, at the edge of the hatch, listening for any change in the bay outside.

The footsteps into the bay were immediate; someone had been waiting for them. Pike caught the girl's eyes and held a finger to his lips for silence.

Her grin was just as impish as it had been all those days ago, and a moment later, he realized the foolishness. He stifled a laugh and held up a hand for her to stay.

There was only one set of footsteps, slowly circling the ship. Pike retrieved his knife from the girl's hands and crouched down as carefully as he could. He must not make a single sound. The Telestine knew something was wrong. He had to die instantly, before he could call for help. Though the fact there was only one might mean they were short-staffed.

The alien came around the bend near the stairs and the knife left Pike's hand the same instant. It caught the Telestine in the throat and he went over backward, clutching at it, eyes wide with shock. He was dead before he hit the floor and Pike threw out an arm to keep the girl in place. If anyone else had heard....

Seconds passed. Ten, then twenty. Pike counted slowly against the racing of his heart.

No one else seemed to have been there to hear the thud,

but Pike still took the stairs carefully, wincing at every clang. He searched the body carefully, took what looked like an ID card and the Telestine's rifle, and gestured to the girl to follow him.

This is too easy, the voice at the back of his mind whispered.

In the hallway outside the docking bays, she paused to consider, and went to examine a computer terminal on the far wall. She stared at it for a very long time before nodding decisively and jerking her head left. Her gestures showed him a path: the second right, and straight on from there.

Pike looked around himself before answering. "How far?"

She held up her thumb and forefinger a scant distance apart.

"Well, that's a relief."

"*Pike.*" Walker's voice was soft in his earpiece. "*Are you there?*"

"Yes. She thinks the access point to the defense grid is close."

There was a pause, and he could see Walker biting her lip in his mind. She got protective at times like these. When she said, "*Good luck,*" he could hear every entreaty she wanted to say, but was holding herself back from. There was a pause. "*We're nearly to Earth—nearly done with our decel burn—and we're keeping an eye on their fleet. I'll tell you if it looks like anything's happened.*"

"Right."

They could hear the distant sound of activity above them, but this floor seemed to be empty. The girl guided him quickly down empty hallways and past cross corridors while Pike looked up frequently and prayed for the Telestines to decide that the docking bays didn't need patrols.

The dead end was sudden. A white wall dropped down in front of them with a hiss, opaque and shining slightly in the light. There wasn't so much as a millimeter for him to wedge his fingers into. It was—what *was* it? An airlock door?

Pike swore with all the inventiveness of a cargo hauler. When the girl nudged him out of the way, he was still swearing. He had not come this far to stop here.

And then she laid her hands flat on the wall and it lit up like Christmas.

Pike stepped back with an oath. Her head was bowed, her eyes closed, but her fingers were moving. A green line followed her right index finger, and tiny blue lines trailed from the fingers on her left hand. They moved like an orchestra conductor's, drawing patterns he could not see the whole of, and the computer panel flashed and glowed in response.

"*Pike.*" Walker's voice was urgent.

"Uh-huh?" He couldn't look away from the sight in front of him.

"*The fleet over Earth is ... dead.*"

That got his attention. "Wait, *what?*"

"*They're just ... everything stopped.*" Her voice was incredulous. "*I don't know how to describe it. It's like ... it's like....*"

The bottom dropped out of Pike's stomach. He looked over at the girl, still summoning information out of the Telestine computer grid.

Jesus, Mary, and Joseph, it had been in front of them the whole time.

"Oh my god. It's the Dawning," he said quietly. "The girl. *She's* the Dawning."

CHAPTER THIRTY-SIX

Earth's Moon
Telestine Military Outpost

"*You're kidding me.*" But from the hollow awe in Walker's voice, Pike knew that she didn't doubt it.

"We have to get her out of here." Pike reached out to haul her away from the computer grid and froze. He didn't want to interrupt what she was doing. If the fleet came back to life, they were beyond screwed. "I am getting her out as soon as I can. Can we hitch a ride in any of the carriers? The shuttle should fit—"

"*Check your ship for coordinates for a rendezvous. We'll meet you there.*" Walker sounded eminently satisfied. "*Right now? We have a fleet to take out. They're sitting ducks. We can't pass this up.*"

"Walker—"

"*We don't have time for this.*" She cut him off brutally. There was a noise, and he heard her voice, distracted, as she snapped at someone else. *"I don't care if he says the sun's exploding, I don't trust him. Pike?"*

"Yeah? Is Nhean trying to contact you?"

"Not important. He says we shouldn't be doing this."

"Why?"

"I have no idea. Look, there's another fleet inbound behind this one, coming from the other side of Earth's orbital space—the new fleet seems unaffected by whatever your girl did. We need to take these ships out before the other ones get here. It's a shame she didn't take them down, too, but maybe when they get in range...."

Something niggled at the corner of Pike's mind, but he could make neither head nor tail of it. Something wrong, something that didn't quite add up....

"I'm getting her out of here." He knew better than to try to talk Walker out of something when she was determined. The woman was as stubborn as an ass. "I'll meet you at the rendezvous point."

The line went dead without a response and Pike reached out hesitantly to tap the girl on the shoulder.

"Hello?"

She shook her head.

"Look, I'm sorry I didn't realize what you were. We have to get you out of here, though. Walker's fleet is going to destroy the Telestine ships."

She looked around at that, smiling. Evidently, this had been what she was trying to do on her own. She took her hands off the computer grid.

"We have to leave now," Pike explained. "Did you hear the conversation? No? There's another fleet inbound, and it's not disabled."

He looked around them, down the hallway, waiting for Telestine soldiers to show up at any moment.

Except they didn't. *What the hell was going on?* This was too easy.

The look she gave him was affronted. She turned back to the computer panel, searching the surface intently. She shook her head. Her lips were moving. Calculating? Praying? They were moving too fast for him to be sure.

Whatever she was looking for, she found it. Her fingers moved in a blur, and she looked over at Pike with a question.

"Walker. Any change on that second fleet?"

"*What?*" There was a pause. "*No, nothing.*"

"Right." Pike shook his head at the girl.

She slammed her fist against the computer, clenched her hands in the hair at her temples. She paced, considering, trying to make sense of it all, and Pike's own sense of wrongness grew.

And then, suddenly, she had the answer. He saw it hit her —her face changed from confusion to….

Horror?

She grabbed his hand and took off down the hallway with surprising speed, nearly hitting the wall of the cross corridor at the turn. They pounded toward the ship, Pike's breath coming harsh.

Still, no one stopped them. The base seemed to be empty. They turned again, panting, out of breath, before finally bursting back out into the landing bay.

"You know," he managed, "this would be a real good time for you to start talking!"

The look she gave him was anguished, and he wished he hadn't said anything. She hauled him into the ship and punched her hand down on the seal. *Up, up, up*—her hands waved him up the stairs, toward the cockpit.

Whatever the girl had realized, it was bad, he knew. He had to warn Laura. "Walker." He was holding the earpiece to his head as tightly as he could. "Walker, you have to get out of here."

The girl nodded at him.

"*We're finally taking these bastards down. It's like target practice out here.*" Her voice was fierce. "*Whatever this is, it can wait.*"

"It can't, get out of there!" He skidded into the cockpit to take a seat and did a double take as he stared over at the girl.

She was curled into the copilot's seat, staring up in horror. Her hands were balled into fists, and there were tears in her eyes. Overhead, formations of black Telestine ships—not feathers, but the other kind—were streaking past on their way back to Earth, toward Walker's fleet supposedly beating the shit out of the dormant Telestine military.

And he *knew*.

"Oh, my god. Walker, *Walker*, listen to me. It's a trap."

"*What's a—how do you know?*"

"It's a hunting trick." He looked at the fleet in horror as he pounded the button for a dock release. "You put out a lure—a chunk of meat, a worm on a hook. And then when your target is distracted...." He looked up. "That's when you shoot. They planned this. This was how they were going to get us."

The girl was nodding her head furiously. There were tears running down her cheeks and her eyes closed.

"Hey." Pike reached out to shake her. "There's a reason

you can't do anything with these other Telestine ships, right? The dark ones?"

She nodded.

"But we have to get away from them."

From the look she gave him, they weren't going to make it.

"Stay with me." Pike's fingers tightened on her shoulder. "I am not dying here like an animal in a trap. We are getting out of here, you hear me? Give me anything. Where do I go when we undock?" If he *could* undock. The ship wasn't releasing. He gunned the engines and yanked, and the ship came free of the docking port with a mighty screech—he hoped he hadn't ripped a hole in the hull. Soon, they were pulling free of the Moon's weak gravity and swinging back around the horizon. Earth rose slowly above it.

The rendezvous point was halfway in between. He gunned the engines up to the limit of the inertial dampeners, watching as the velocimeter rushed up to dizzying speeds.

She pulled herself together, looked around. Earth was above ahead of them, slightly to the left. If he peered closely enough, he thought he could just barely make out the fireworks of Walker having a field day with the dormant Telestine fleet.

"*Pike!*" Walker's voice.

"What?"

"Do you know a man named Charlie Boyd?"

Charlie? How in the hell.... "He was with me on the mission. He died in the labs."

Walker blew her breath out in a sigh. "*So he's legit. Turns out he didn't die—and there's a freighter coming out of orbit, Rebellion piloted. If you can make it to their cargo hold, they can get you out of here. Apparently they can burn to ten g's for some reason—they must have stolen Telestine inertial dampeners. They'll get you to Mercury.*" Her words were suspicious.

"Mercury?" Of all the godforsaken planets in all the systems in all the universe....

"*I'll explain later. Just get yourselves the hell out of there. And Pike?*"

"Yeah?"

"*You protect that girl at all costs. She's the best weapon we've got right now. We've already destroyed nearly half their fleet because of her, and ... I want to destroy the rest. Keep ... her ... alive.*"

His throat closed. On the sensor display he watched the non-dormant Telestine ships—the black ones—advance on Walker's fleet. "Will do. Good hunting."

CHAPTER THIRTY-SEVEN

Earth, Upper Atmosphere
EFS Intrepid

The silver Telestine carriers tumbled gently below. After the first shots tore through the fleet with silent explosions of debris on the video feeds, it felt almost cruel to keep shooting. The ships were defenseless. There were sentient lives aboard.

She had kept shooting.

The first volley was for her sister, dying of an infection in the darkened hospital wards of Johnson Station.

The second was for Pike's sister—a little girl who'd been hunted down and killed, not because she interfered with anything the Telestines did, but simply because she'd been born and dared to live free.

The third volley was for Delaney's twin, a boy lost in the initial bombardment sixty years ago.

She recited the names every night, knowing how many she was missing. She listened to the soldiers when they spoke. Every indignity, every slow death, every shadowed gaze. She remembered it all.

And yet, if Pike was right, even this tiny victory had been a lie, a trap.

If she got out of this alive, there were going to be no nukes. Nukes were too quick, even their tiny uranium-gun-style warheads. Nukes were a mercy.

She was going to make it hurt when she took Earth from the Telestines.

There would be blood.

"I want a full carrier frontal spread formation. Maximum offensive area. Take out as many sitting ducks as we can." She kept her voice crisp. "And all ships, acknowledge: the Dawning is on that shuttle coming in from the moon. There is nothing more important than getting it safely to Mercury." Flawed or not, working or not, that girl was the best chance they had of getting into the Telestine weapons systems again. And maybe all their other systems. As soon as they plugged her into the new Telestine black fleet, they'd have a fighting chance of taking down the rest of the Telestine grid and wiping the aliens off the map.

"Yes, ma'am," said several officers at once.

The black ships streaking toward them were entirely different than the dormant carriers. There was no mistaking the sleek look of everything Telestines made, but where the powerless carriers and their fighters were a breathtaking gleaming silver, the ships presently breaking out of the atmosphere as well as rushing toward them from the moon were a heavy, light-grabbing obsidian black.

"Those incoming carriers look deadly, but if they're anything like these silver feathers, we can take them." Delaney murmured. "But who has two kinds of carriers?"

Walker didn't bother answering him. "All batteries fire when ready, alternate ammunition against the sitting ducks and torpedo countermeasures against the incoming hostiles. Fighters stay out of the firing lines, but focus on the smaller gunships."

She watched on the screen as the fighters swung wide. Larsen had coded anything not moving as a target; the first fleet was green and unmoving; the second, red, and steadily moving to intercept.

"I'll bet you there was never even anyone on those ships," Walker murmured.

"These aren't salvaged carriers." Delaney was shaking his head.

"So?"

The conversation was forgotten—everyone flinched as an enemy warhead hit one of the countermeasures.

"That ... was nuclear." King looked up in mute appeal, face turning an ashen white. When the screens flickered with the EMP, her fingers clenched into fists.

"Their missiles are guided, ma'am." Larsen was pale. "We have to get out of here."

"We can't," Walker said simply. "Launch more countermeasures if you have to, increase the ratio two to one. Train some mass-driver ammo at any warheads that make it past the countermeasures."

The ship was shuddering as isolated rounds streaked

through the cover of their fire and the countermeasures, but the hull was holding for now.

"Remember what we are." Walker raised her voice. She looked around the room. "We are a shield. We knew when this began that we might have to give our lives for this effort. Today, we shield the Dawning—a woman who might be able to work with our new fleet at Mercury to end the Telestine occupation. It is our duty to stand between her and the fleet pursuing her."

There was a murmur of assent from within the bridge.

"As soon as we have confirmation that the ship is away, we will get out of here," Walker promised them.

The murmur of assent was a little more emphatic this time.

"Good." She nodded. "Delaney. What were you saying about the fleet?"

"Ah…." Delaney's eyes were locked on the booms and flashes on the hologram. He tore them away with an effort. "Right. Building a fleet this large is not a small matter. Assume no lives were lost. Well enough. But this is a big sacrifice for them. You don't just throw away capital ships like this. Something … deeper is going on here."

Now Walker understood what he had been trying to say, and her frown deepened. The yelling—communications officers shouting headings to gunnery sergeants, engineers calling desperate commands up to the bridge—faded as she concentrated.

Delaney was right. The Telestines always came for treaty violations at once, with no trial and no waiting. They'd come for the Exile Fleet at New Beginnings as soon as Pike was on the surface. There was no way they could have built this sacrificial fleet—the bait—between now and then, and why would they throw it up into the atmosphere as a con and then bring in a whole new fleet to attack the Rebellion, when they could have simply fired on the Exile Fleet as soon as it arrived? They were missing something.

"There's always the possibility that they thought we were better armed than we are." Walker's mouth twisted in a bitter smile. "They didn't think our whole fleet would be just this." There was a certain delicious irony to that.

"I don't like it," was all Delaney said.

"Neither do I, but it's what we have to work with." Her eyes caught a flicker of movement on the screen: one of the Telestine carriers changing course. "Larsen, they're trying to get around us. Set us on a collision course."

Ensign Harris did a double take. "A collision course, ma'am?"

"Chicken. See if we can get them to blink. To pull off first. And tell gunnery to keep launching countermeasures ahead of us. We don't want to get out of our own shield."

Harris knew better than to object. "Yes, ma'am."

"The human freighter coming off Earth reports that they're closing on the shuttle," said Larsen.

"Keep me updated."

On the hologram display, the *Intrepid* tilted and began to climb out of the gravity well. They were putting on speed even as the Telestine carrier did. It was banking higher and higher, trying to get around them.

"Stay in their face," Walker called to Ensign Harris at helm.

"Yes, ma'am." Harris's tone was glum. The *Intrepid* had been her ship since she first joined the Rebellion.

Walker looked away from the woman's pained face. Too many years as a shadow military, never engaging with the enemy—that was why they had this reluctance.

With luck, she wouldn't have to fight it much longer.

"Ma'am, shuttle has docked in the freighter, and they're making for the L1 Lagrange hiding place."

"Good. Larsen, wait for them to hit six g's and then get us out of here. Everyone disengage—disengage!"

"Ma'am ... *they're* disengaging." Larsen was punching buttons. He looked over at the hologram.

Everyone looked.

"Well ... that's ... eerie," Delaney murmured.

New red dots appeared on the hologram map.

"They've launched satellites!" Larsen's call was sudden, sharp. "Hard to tell, but ... it looks like a new defensive array is coming online, countdown timer indicates...."

"Get out of here. All ships, hard turn and accelerate. Tell the fighters to go, we'll pick them up when we can. Go! Everybody *move*!"

Inertia mashed them sideways and down as Harris obliged, pushing the *Intrepid* to the edge of her inertial dampeners. Walker hung on grimly, and tried piecing the puzzle together. A dead fleet as bait, another fleet engaging and disengaging, launching new satellites, a weaponized human girl that didn't entirely work....

Not one single piece of this made any sense.

"Ma'am." Larsen had struggled his way to her side. "Call for you. I think you'll want to take this."

With deep misgiving, Walker picked up the earpiece. "Yes?"

"*You've touched off a civil war.*" The voice was male. Light, but grim and emphatic.

"Who is this?"

"*Your contact. Surely you didn't think I'd keep using a voice scrambler now that you knew who I was.*" There was annoyance there. "*If you had listened to me, I could have kept you from doing this.*"

"Doing what?"

"*Come to Venus; I'll explain there. I'm sending coordinates.*"

The line went dead.

You've touched off a civil war. The words repeated over and over in her mind.

That wasn't a bait fleet. That girl with Pike was … not the Dawning.

And whatever factional divisions existed among the Telestines, Walker had just chosen a side. And done its dirty work.

"Oh my god," Walker whispered.

CHAPTER THIRTY-EIGHT

Halfway between Earth and Venus
EFS Intrepid

Barely two minutes after Pike had joyfully shook Charlie's hand and they'd begun their hard burn for Mercury, Walker had called them back and insisted that they dock instead at the Intrepid, which was itself making hard burn for Venus. She wouldn't say why. But the cold steel in her voice made him realize it wasn't a request.

Not that she was his superior officer or anything. Still, when she got like that, he knew it was best to play along. *We need to finally meet this Nhean*, she'd said, and left it at that during their brief conversation.

Now, hours later, they were docked with the Exile Fleet's flagship halfway to Venus, and finally getting settled in after their orientation briefing from the deck officer.

"Here's my turn." Pike jerked his head at the corridor that

led to the admiral's quarters. "I'll catch up with you soon."

"Saw a game room with a card table." Charlie Boyd gave a rakish grin. "Play you later?"

Pike said drily, "I don't risk my luck against guys who've survived what you just walked through without a scratch." But he gave a mock salute, and clasped the other man's hand. "I'm glad you made it."

"As am I." Charlie tipped an imaginary hat and strode away, whistling.

Pike, staring after him, felt a deep twist of sympathy. There was nothing to be said at times like these. Charlie's eyes were shadowed, a look Pike knew all too well. The bright smiles, the bravado, the offers of card games and shitty alcohol —he'd seen all of it as a cargo hauler. There was always some new recruit running away from a past life.

Charlie wouldn't have come off planet unless he believed, at long last, that his wife and daughter were lost to him. He'd survived the crash of the labs, but the rest of the team had been lost—and the rumors of human slaves held on the station seemed to have been just that, rumors. His survival was as miraculous as it was cruel, and Pike knew the haunted look of a man with lives on his conscience, and nothing left to live for.

Pike's face was almost as grave as he pushed open the door of the admiral's quarters.

She looked up at him dully.

"Laura?"

The sound of her name seemed to shake her awake. "What's happened?" Behind her desk, Walker stood. "Is it the girl?"

"No." He looked away, irritation at her single-mindedness warring with the urge to cross the room and wrap her in his arms. He held himself still through force of will. "The man who piloted that ship—Charlie Boyd? He lost his wife and daughter. He's not doing too well. As you'd guess, I'd expect."

Walker looked away with a sad smile, and Pike followed her gaze to the neat shelves and open closet with its spare uniforms. The *Intrepid* was a refitted cargo hauler, and she didn't have enough possessions to fill the quarters of a hauler's captain. There were no pictures on the wall of children or grandchildren. There were no scattered drawings or the knick knacks most humans kept. She lived a spartan life, like she would only reward herself with any possessions once she could store them in the only place that really mattered: a home on their own world.

"There'll be time to help him, after the war, I suppose," Pike said awkwardly.

"Sit." She gestured wearily. She seemed to be trying to pull herself together. "You want some whiskey?"

"Real whiskey?"

"What's real whiskey anymore?" She raised an eyebrow. "It gets you drunk. Take it or leave it."

Drunk? Laura Walker had once been a woman who didn't get drunk. He looked closer and saw the desperation in her movements. What had *happened* after the battle? He thought it had been a success.

He wouldn't ask directly; she would come to it in time.

"I'll take some." He settled into the one spare seat and took the tiny glass from her. She made sure their fingers didn't touch. "So."

"So." She settled in; it took visible effort for her not to let go. "Nhean thinks the Dawning is the girl. But I'm not so sure." Her face was expressionless.

"Oh?" He'd left her in the cargo hold, unpacking the Rebellion ship.

"Why a human girl?" She was walking him through something, he could tell.

But he'd been thinking about the same thing, in any case. "Why any of this?" he countered.

Her look said she had her suspicions, but she wasn't ready to share them yet. "You think she can learn to take down the real ships?"

"The ships she took down *were* real ships," Pike insisted. "Ask Charlie if you want—the silvery feathered ones, they said those were worse than the black ones."

She had nothing to say to that. She took a sip of her whiskey and leaned back in her chair, eyes distant.

"I don't like it," she said finally. Her gaze met his, and he saw the depth of her worry there. "I'll be honest with you. I *don't* like that she took you to the lunar base and she took down half the fleet. I don't like it at all."

"If you had seen her, you wouldn't doubt her." Pike heard his voice rise and forced himself to sit back in his chair. "When the ships went down, she was *glad*. But she looked furious when she saw those other black ships."

"Looked?"

"She doesn't talk."

"And why is that?"

"How should I know?"

"Think simpler. Think about what she is: a precious

resource we spent lives to acquire and protect, again and again. A tool ... a woman who was supposed to be able to disable all the Telestine forces, but who ... didn't."

He knew where this was going. "She isn't working for *them*."

"Say you're right. Say you know beyond any shadow of a doubt that she wants to destroy the Telestines." She held up a hand. "At this point, I'm even willing to believe it. But you say she was horrified that she couldn't take down the rest of the ships. What does that mean? Does it mean she thought she could? Does it mean she tried to do so and something— something programmed, something she can't control—kept her from doing so? Why did she fail? We don't know. What we *know* is that she was raised in a Telestine laboratory and she was not the resource we thought she was." She paused, adding, "in either form or function."

"You knew that when you protected the shuttle." Pike's face was white.

"Because she is still, in whatever way, a good chance. If nothing else, the ways they modified her to interface with Telestine technology can be studied."

His blood ran cold. "Studied?"

"What do you want me to say, Bill? What would make it sound *kinder* to you?" She put the glass down at last and leaned across the desk to stare at him. "You've traveled with her. You've become fond of her. But this isn't ... a normal ... girl," she said, emphasizing the words.

He had the vivid memory of the girl thumping at the control panel. He could see that sudden, amused smile in her eyes. She was *human*, he wanted to insist. She was human in ways even a Telestine lab couldn't touch. She would never betray them. But he caught himself: betrayal was a hallmark of humanity, of course.

"You've been speaking to Nhean," he accused her.

"Yes. He advised me not to allow her on the bridge, that was all. He says he will explain more when we see him. But, Pike, *think*. There's more to this."

"Tell me."

"I'm afraid...." She looked away. "I'm afraid I'm jumping at shadows."

"Tell me," he repeated.

She drained the glass and grimaced. "Nhean claims there's a civil war beginning between the Telestine factions—and that *we* kicked it off. I fear that we accidentally chose a side—or were manipulated into choosing a side—and did someone else's dirty work."

The realization was as swift as it was devastating. Two fleets, only one of which had been destroyed.

"She was made to destabilize one of the factions."

She waved her hand a few times, motioning his reasoning forward.

"And ... and *we* were the tool her makers used to ... unleash her. She was the bullet, we were the gun. Her makers look innocent, and ... heroic, for fighting us off."

"Yes." Walker gave a despairing laugh. "Yes. We just ... we just helped someone annihilate the main Telestine fleet. I blew it to hell. I mean, don't get me wrong—it felt amazing. But...."

"Fewer Telestines to fight in the end," Pike offered. It was the only thing he could think of.

"You think so?" She raised her eyes to his, and there was a

yawning abyss there. "The Telestine fleet came for our labs and it came for our military ships, but it never came for humanity. They always focused on military targets and ignored civilians. Do you think you can say the same for whoever we just put in power?"

CHAPTER THIRTY-NINE

Venus, 49 kilometers above surface
Tang Estate, New Zurich

"*Earlier today, the humans, in a gross and egregious violation of their treaty with us, launched a premeditated attack that crippled our defensive fleet. Their technology has advanced past the fair limits stipulated by our treaty. The humans, not content with the resources and aid we have given them, have decided to act with aggression. They have chosen war. Even now, their fleet is massing for another attack. Lend me your support, and I promise to end this aggression by whatever means necessary.*"

The words, read aloud in a too-smooth computerized voice, echoed off the marble walls of the study. Walker listened with her head bowed. Three of her officers stood with her, the gunmetal grey of their uniforms lit gold in the piercing light from the windows.

Pike stood alone.

"His name," Nhean said quietly, "is Tel'rabim."

Walker started at the sound of the name. "No."

"Yes."

"Who's that?" Pike was beginning to feel irritated by all of this. He didn't know the first thing about politics, much less alien politics. Why was he here?

"Tel'rabim has long been one of the most generous advocates for humanity." Nhean settled into his chair. "I communicated with him regularly on any number of issues: medicine for outer colonies, enhanced Gileadi Gravitation field-forming technology. He advocated for us within the Telestine government—or so I was led to believe."

"He was your source, wasn't he?" Walker almost spat the words. "You told us of factions. You told us that it might be worth it to take their help. And you've been communicating with a man who wanted to kill all of us."

"Communicating, and using his communications to begin reverse-engineering the Telestine computer systems." Nhean looked at her without remorse. "Every communication I could convince him to make directly to me gave me more of an insight into their encryption, their FTL radio technology. It was through that process that I found my window into their defense network—or what I thought was their defense network."

"Speak plainly." Walker had gone to the window. Now she tossed one blazing glance over her shoulder.

Pike couldn't help but agree with her sentiment.

"It turns out that he was quite the scientist. I'm beginning to think he may have been the one behind the modification of the human slaves. As should also be clear by now...." Nhean looked around the room wryly. "The Dawning was his invention."

"She's not an invention, she's a human." Pike knew his voice was too loud, all wrong. He looked down when the others turned to stare at him.

"She was once. She may not be anymore."

"She's *human*." The words came out through gritted teeth.

"Mr. Pike, there is more than your personal sentiment at stake." Nhean's voice was uncompromising. "She is a weapon. Presumably, if she had not fallen into our hands, he would have used her against the Telestine military himself. It would have been a bloodbath. I would not expect to be able to wield such a weapon without collateral damage."

Pike opened his mouth to argue, and Walker cut him off with a swipe of her hand.

"Why would he use a human?" She sounded genuinely curious.

"I wondered the same. He may have been supplying technology to the Telestine military; he had called a meeting with some of their top brass to discuss a new weapon he was developing. It's possible he could have deployed her while he was there, and used his control of the defense grid to force them to hand over the ships. My guess—and this is only a guess—is that humans have some innate quality that Telestines do not, that enables them to control a greater flow of information if they're somehow "modified" to be able to interface with the systems."

"My question is whether her inability to take down his ships is programming," Walker murmured, "or hardware."

"Precisely." Nhean nodded. His gaze went to the door as

his aide slipped into the room.

All heads swiveled, but Parees only gave a single nod to Nhean.

Pike felt a flicker of surprise when the man's shoulders slumped. Nhean's eyes closed.

"Forgive me for not opening with this." He spoke quietly, and as he moved to his desk, he was walking like an old man. He sat heavily. "After the … incident, I wanted to be sure that my information was accurate."

"Tell us." Walker laced her hands behind her back.

"Another communication went out to the Telestine government, sent after the one you heard. I had it translated, then checked and retranslated…." For the first time since Pike had seen him, Nhean did not look composed. He looked lost.

"Not saying it won't make it not exist," Pike suggested. It was his father's advice, and it surprised him to hear the words coming out of his own mouth.

Nhean gave a tired smile. "You are correct, Mr. Pike, of course. Very well." He took a deep breath. "Tel'rabim has suggested to the Telestine government that humanity, in its current form, is nothing more than a drain on their society. Any human who lives long enough wonders why we were left alive at all, in this crippled state. During the initial invasion, a large contingent of Telestine society spoke out against genocide. They believed it was too strong, too barbaric an action to take." His face twisted. "They were content to kill us more slowly, of course." He looked away, and took a moment to compose himself. "But it is impossible to deny that humanity has been costly to them. We provide very little to them beyond the slave labor it takes to disassemble our own cities for them. Tel'rabim has told them that extermination is the only answer. Quite accurately, he believes that we will never stop trying to take Earth back. He needs little help making a compelling case that we are too much trouble—especially in light of the last battle."

Walker looked down at the floor. Pike saw her face twist.

Nhean's voice was surprisingly gentle. "I believe he would have come to this point in any case. Once he controlled their fleet, no one would truly have been able to oppose him."

"He aided humanity." One of Walker's officers, Delaney, shook his head. "Why change his mind now?"

"Change his mind?" Nhean laughed. The sound was not pleasant. "What did he get from our leaders? An exact idea of the things that hurt us. A thorough accounting of how many citizens were where. He's been merciful for so many years— when *he* speaks against us, many will follow. Only Nixon could go to China, and all that. And they will know exactly where to go to carry out his plans. Plans I now believe he has held from the beginning. Plans to exterminate humanity."

"Where will he begin?" Pike tried to steady himself. None of this could be real.

"I don't know." Nhean met his eyes. "He's very ... methodical. But I don't know." He brought up a map of the solar system on a wall screen with a flick of his fingers. Human settlements glowed blue, primarily on Mars, the moons of Jupiter and Saturn, a dozen or so larger asteroids, with smaller smudges marking the estates on Venus, the newer settlements at Neptune and Mercury, and even the far-flung outposts at Pluto and the other tiny Kuiper colonies. "I don't know his plan—but by the time he's done, the only humans left will be the slaves he keeps—and I rather think they'll outlive their usefulness as soon as our cities are gone, don't you?"

CHAPTER FORTY

Venus, 49 kilometers above surface
Tang Estate, New Zurich

Pike was most of the way to roaring drunk by the time Walker arrived at his quarters. From his place, slid down in one of the armchairs, he waved a crystal decanter at her with careless grace.

She stopped just over the threshold with a smile, and the door slid closed behind her with a little *snik*.

"H'lo." His voice was slurred. He managed to extricate himself from the chair—a complicated feat, by the looks of it —and tried to retrieve a glass for her from the table. When the glass tumbled to the Persian carpets, he stared at it with the grave acceptance of the inebriated. "Real whiskey," he explained as she came closer.

"I'd expect no less from our host." Walker dropped into the opposite chair and tried to hide her grin.

"Gimme some of that." She took a different glass off the tray—a metal tray not so different from what one would find in any house in the slums of Ares Station, truth be told—and held it out.

He poured very carefully, with a frown of concentration.

"Wait. Don't move." Walker drained the glass and held it back out. "I have to catch up."

He gave her a smile at that, innocently pleased. He poured again and sat back with a *thwump* against the cushions.

"W'happened after I left?"

"When *did* you leave?" Walker frowned. "We looked up and you were gone."

"Didn't know anything." Pike gestured with his own glass and then stared sadly at the rug, where some of his whiskey had escaped to seep into the carpets. "Oh...."

"If you're worried, I'm sure Nhean can send you the cleaning bill." Walker pushed herself up and pried his fingers off the neck of the decanter. "Give it."

He stared after it sadly.

"Not a lot happened," Walker said with a shrug as she poured herself another drink. She promised herself that she was going to savor this one. She put her boots up on the carved table—jade? It looked like jade—and tipped her head back on the chair. Even the ceiling was exquisite, printed with an arabesque pattern that was oddly soothing.

Soothing, yet still obscene. Ninety nine percent of humanity suffered in the low-gravity slums of the solar system, and Nhean had jade tables and real whiskey.

"We all gonna die?" he asked. But his tone suggested it wasn't a question.

NICK WEBB

She picked her head up to stare at him. He looked morose at last, and he shrugged at her look.

"'S a good question," he insisted.

"Well, we're not planning on it." She was nettled, but the feeling was distant. "It's really no more likely than it was a few weeks ago, anyway. Nhean thinks we have a bit of time while this Tel'rabim makes sure he has Earth locked down. If he sends his whole fleet after us before making sure the military is completely under his control, could be a ... what do you call a coup of a coup?"

"Return to normal," Pike said promptly.

"Right. That. So we're trying to slow that down. Nhean is releasing communications this man had with him, anything to make him look bad—and putting a message in a whole bunch of their networks that the weapon that took down their fleet was his."

"They ... won't believe that," he said. The looming specter of death seemed to have sobered him up somewhat. He raised an eyebrow and twitched his fingers at the decanter.

"I'm still catching up," Walker said, with great dignity.

"Fine. I'll get the vodka."

"Since when do you drink vodka?" She craned her head to follow him as he went to the sideboard.

"Since flying with Rychenkov." He managed to retrieve another decanter and a few more glasses, and made a mostly-straight path back to his chair. He poured and held up one of the glasses. When she took it, he clinked his. "*Tvajo zdarovye.*"

"I'm not even going to try to repeat that. Cheers."

"One more. *Za ubliudkov.*"

Her brow furrowed. "What does that mean?"

"The first one was, to your health. The second one was, to the bastards."

She blinked.

Pike smiled and drained his glass. "Always the second drink for Russians." He stabbed his finger at her. "Never forget the conquerors."

"And toast to their health?"

"The wheel turns," he said philosophically, spinning one index finger. "There are a few ways to toast someone's health, eh?"

Walker downed the glass in a gulp. "All right. I'm drunk enough for confessions now."

"No, you aren't. And you're not Catholic enough."

"I'm more Catholic than the frickin Venetian Pope. Shut up."

He shut up and sat back, resting his vodka glass on his chest and gestured for her to keep talking.

"The bastards," Walker said. She could indeed feel inebriation coming on like a hard acceleration burn. Two and a half glasses of whiskey and two glasses of vodka. This was going to go poorly.

Might as well get the confession out while she could still talk.

"Here's what I hate." She scratched at the back of her head. "I want to go back," she said. "I want to not go get the Dawning. I want not to give him th'excuse."

"He would've killed us all anyway," Pike said.

"Doesn't matter. I want to take it back." She paused, and decided to admit it: "I'm scared, Bill. Don't want to die. Fugged everything up."

Pike shook his head. "Would've done it anyway," he said again. "Eventually. Kill all the livestock. Very expensive." He started laughing, until a quick knock on the door startled him.

The door opened. A girl stood there: *the* girl. Eyes overlarge and black. Sunburned nose. Skin tanned and pale brown hair. Pictures didn't do justice to those eyes.

Walker shivered as the girl held out a tiny piece of equipment—it looked almost like a data pad, except ... different.

"What...." Pike tried to speak normally and gave up.

She held up one finger and then closed her eyes. Her hand clenched over the equipment—Telestine make, Walker thought, her mind still sluggish with alcohol—and slowly, it began to light up. Colors flickered over the black surface and the girl's face screwed up in effort.

"What's she doing?" It took Walker a couple of tries to stand up. Pike's arm came around her side and they leaned to hold one another up.

The girl had opened her eyes. She pointed, almost pleadingly, at the equipment.

"I don't understand," Pike said.

It came to Walker in a flash and she pushed herself up, nearly tipping both of them over in the process.

"That's ... Telestine equipment, isn't it?"

The girl nodded, very quickly, her eyes pleading, suggesting there was even more to the story.

Walker dropped her glass, the vodka splashing all over the carpet. "Oh my god. You think that's Tel'rabim's."

The girl nodded, clearly pleased.

"So?" Pike looked affronted by his near fall.

"So she's learning to *use* it. She's learning how to connect to Tel'rabim's technology—not just the regular Telestine shit, but Tel'rabim's." Walker explained patiently. She looked around herself. "We need coffee. Lots of coffee. We have a war to plan."

CHAPTER FORTY-ONE

Venus, 49 kilometers above surface
Tang Estate, New Zurich

The piece of Telestine electronics lit up again, like Christmas, and went entirely inert again a moment later. The girl gave a pleased smile and looked around at all of them.

The smile faded slightly when she saw Nhean's face.

"It's ... promising." Nhean's voice betrayed an inner struggle as he watched the girl's demonstration. He sat back in his chair. "It has potential."

"The question is, is that data pad from Tel'rabim's group, or is it just regular Telestine make?" Walker said, eyes closed and rubbing her temple.

Nhean nodded. "Oh, it's definitely from Tel'rabim's faction. This particular piece was left behind accidentally by one of the food delivery crews Tel'rabim regularly arranges to be sent out. My tech people have tried connecting to it ... to no avail."

Pike winced. Nhean's movement had allowed a particularly bright shaft of sunlight to find its way directly into his eyes. Thanks to a veritable cocktail of drugs, he was feeling more clear-headed every minute, but the pills didn't so much stop inebriation as accelerate it.

Right along with the hangover. He took another gulp of water and concentrated very hard on not throwing up.

"The question, of course," Nhean murmured, "is how we use that skill."

"Isn't that obvious?" Walker also looked like she was hoping for a quick death, but she was managing to sit upright, hands clenched on the arms of her chair. "She does what she did at the lunar base again."

"She doesn't yet have that much skill," Nhean said flatly. He looked over to the girl. "Do you?"

She looked down, a faint flush on her cheeks, and shook her head.

"She has time between now and then to practice," Walker insisted. "And any edge she gives us will help, especially if we catch their fleet unawares."

"And do you know where the fleet is?" Nhean tilted his head to the side. "Do you know where we could get her access to a computer terminal? Do you have a strike team that can guard her on her way there? Her success at the lunar base was due almost entirely to the fact that Tel'rabim made her to be invisible to their military's technology. But surely she is not invisible to Tel'rabim's technology."

The girl looked away, and Pike felt a stab of sympathy. She had gone to the lunar base of her own free will, walked into danger to help her own kind, and they still talked about her as if she had little to do with the outcome of the last battle.

"Those are skills she can use." Walker was clearly not going to back down from this idea. "The skill set is there, it's just attuned to the Telestine military. If she—"

"What, rewires herself?" Nhean snapped. "She can turn this shard on and off, but that's *not* part of his fleet. We have no idea if there are fail safes to keep her from doing this to his actual ships, or if the machinery is something she can control entirely on her own. We have *no* idea if what she just did can be used offensively. I need information on that machinery, and more importantly, I need information on what Tel'rabim is planning. He's shut the Telestine communications military and civilian systems down entirely. There is no communication with the human stations and I have no links."

"The Secretary General will be wondering what's happened." Commander Delaney's voice was quiet. He gave a look at Walker and his lips tightened; he clearly did not approve of her condition. "We should tell him."

"What's the point?" Walker asked him. Her gaze, if pained, was at least clear-eyed. "There's nothing Sokoloff can do. We don't have the transports to get humanity off the colonies, and even if they escape the destruction there, they can't possibly outrun the Telestine fleet. Either one." She held up a hand to forestall Delaney's argument. "If by some miracle they manage to escape, how long can they survive in stuffed cargo tankers? And, more importantly, where the hell do you think we're going to run to?" she asked him.

Delaney fell silent.

"And in any case...." She took a gulp of water and her

mouth twisted bitterly. "Calling him will only win us another lecture on how we're endangering everyone. We don't want to give him a chance to send a message to the fleet, recalling them."

"You think they'd listen?" Pike frowned.

"It would create uncertainty. We can't risk it—and if anyone at Mercury hears and believes him, they could sabotage the shipyards.

"The admiral is right." Nhean's admission was grudging; he did not look pleased. "The last thing we should do is reveal where we are and what we're doing. Not to mention, it would create a needless panic."

Thus spoke someone, Pike suspected, who had never lost loved ones without having a chance to say a proper goodbye. He looked down at the glass of water in his hand and scowled.

Walker reached out to tap the glass. "Keep drinking," she murmured. "It'll help."

"Right." He took a sip and tried to ignore the feeling of hopelessness. The room had sunk into silence. There was nothing to be done, clearly.

He should have stayed drunk.

"I need someone to get me one of Tel'rabim's ships," Nhean announced.

Everyone looked over at him.

"We have someone who can, at least, interface with them." Nhean gestured at the girl. "She will stay here and we will assess her capabilities, and the ship *should* give us a window into their communications network. The pieces I already have, I am afraid—" he gave a regretful look at the shards of machinery on the desk "—are not enough."

"We'll go," Walker said wearily. "I'll take the *Intrepid* and —"

"No." Pike looked up at Nhean and nodded. "I'll go."

"With what ship?" Walker looked at him like he was crazy.

Pike managed a lopsided smile. "I know a guy. Who knows a guy."

The rest of the group looked unimpressed by this description.

"My ship. The *Aggy*." Pike shrugged. "Rychenkov. Good captain."

"Mr. Pike, your ship—"

"Is a cargo hauler with a well-established record." Pike cut Nhean off. "It's registered. It frequently passes close to the Telestine military. There won't be any questions. It's our best chance to get close enough to grab one of them."

"Unless they've been informed by their new commander in chief that it's open season on human ships," Nhean said tightly.

"*Any* ship faces that problem now. I didn't say it was foolproof, I said it was our best chance. And far more discreet than a military ship."

"Pike's right." Walker nodded. "Pike—do you know where Rychenkov's ship is?"

"It had a run to Mercury to deliver food and water. It might still be on its way, actually, or maybe on its way back to Ganymede." Pike tried to do the math in his head. "I can check."

"It's settled, then." Nhean did not look overly pleased with the plan. "I will forward you the most recent patrol schedules I have, some of which involve Tel'rabim's ships, and you will begin your search. Meanwhile, we will ascertain all we can about the Dawning."

"No." The words were automatic. Pike looked over to meet the girl's look of mute appeal. "She comes with us."

"Mr. Pike—"

"For the last time, it's *Pike*. And I have no intention of—" Pike bit back the words. *Leaving her here with you.* He did not dare look at Walker for fear of what he would see in her eyes. She could be as calculating, in her own way, as Nhean.

Pike drew an unsteady breath.

"I said we had the best chance to grab a ship, but as you said, it's not a good one. We have no idea how far away the signal reached from the lunar base. The patrols out there could still be standard Telestine military—in which case, she's going to be invaluable."

Nhean considered, his fingers tapping on the desk.

"Not to mention...." Pike was warming to the theme. "If she can interface with Tel'rabim's technology and set up an FTL information stream from the ship, you can start hacking into his systems almost immediately. You wouldn't have to wait for us to get back."

Nhean sighed and nodded—which was good, Pike reflected, as he had rather run out of arguments at this point.

"Fine. Get me the registry information for the ship and I'll see what I can do. You're sure you can get this cargo hauler to let you use the ship for this? This man, Rychenkov—will he cooperate? Cargo haulers are a rather ... independent bunch."

Pike tried not to let his face show just how much he was doubting himself on that one. Rychenkov was eminently practical, a man raised—so he said—through generations upon generations of dictators. He often opined that the best thing to do with dictators was just outlast them and not make a fuss. He was, at least, not going to be pleased by Pike's mission. On the other hand....

"It's the end of the world." Pike lifted a shoulder. "It's this or die in Tel'rabim's sweep. I can't imagine he'll put up too much of a fight about it."

Hopefully.

Nhean gave a curt nod. "Very well. Go prepare the team. Admiral, commanders—we have much to discuss while Pike and our guest are gone."

They were clearly dismissed. Pike jerked his head at the girl —an ill-advised motion for someone in the throes of a hangover—and ushered her out before anyone could change their mind.

"What *is* your name?" he asked her as the door closed behind them.

She gave a shrug.

That was one of the saddest things he had ever seen—she didn't even know her own name. He cleared his throat and tried to come up with something to say. "Well, come up with one. We can't just call you the Dawning."

She blinked at him and gave another helpless shrug.

"Dawn," he decided. "For now."

The look she gave him was not impressed.

"I never said I was *clever*."

She seemed to agree with this assessment.

"You're too kind."

A grin was his only answer. She led him into the bustle of what had become a makeshift common area and a shout caught their attention.

"Pike." Charlie Boyd pushed his way through the crowd. "Just overheard you're going on a mission. Some order just went out to get a ship ready?"

"It's ... yeah. Nothing important."

"Nothing important?" Charlie seemed incredulous. "We just took down most of their fleet. Come on, man." He leaned close. "What's our next move?"

"I...." Pike rubbed at his forehead. "We just need to go get a Telestine fighter. Capture one."

"Why?" Charlie frowned.

"Well...."

"Nah, nah, you don't have to tell me. But—can I come with you?" Charlie shook his head and looked left and right as if to make sure no one was listening. "I'm going crazy here, man. There's nothing to do, and ... you understand—it's cramped. No sky. No solid ground. You know what I mean."

He understood all too well. "Right. Right." Pike nodded. "Of course. Come on, let's get this show on the road."

CHAPTER FORTY-TWO

Halfway between Earth and Venus
Freighter Agamemnon

It took them three days to reach the *Aggy*, and less than four minutes for Rychenkov to turn them down flat.

"You're insane," he said, by way of explanation. "You are a crazy fool, and you will die like a crazy fool." He liked to play up his Russian accent when he was displeased, and it was now strong enough that Charlie was squinting, trying to make out the words.

As Rychenkov strode away toward the cockpit, muttering about crazy bastards who would doom themselves for lost causes, Charlie leaned over. "Is this guy for real?" He kept his voice to a murmur so as not to be overheard by the crew, who were staring at them with flat expressions.

The girl nodded to echo the question.

"Unfortunately, yes." Pike gave a bright smile around at

the crew as they trickled into the *Aggy*'s bay. "Hey, guys. James. Gabi. Mr. Howie Howe. Good to see you all again."

"*Hola, guapo*," said Gabriela. She brushed her purple-tinged hair aside from her cheek.

"Hey, man." Howie smiled warmly, creasing the tattoo of Earth covering his left temple. The others followed suit.

James tipped his hat. "Good to see you, cowboy."

Pike turned back to Charlie and Dawn. "Look, you two stay here." He held out a hand to keep the girl back. "I'll ... go talk to Rychenkov."

"Better call him *captain* when he's in this mood," Howie offered.

"Thanks." Pike tried not to think about the yelling that was about to happen.

"And if you think he's going to kill you, try to make it down here so we can all watch."

"Sure." Pike hightailed it out of the docking bay and up the narrow flight of stairs to the cockpit.

Rychenkov was in the copilot's chair, reassembling a rifle. He did not look up when Pike appeared in the doorway.

"Captain Rychenkov."

Rychenkov's hands slowed on the gun for a moment. He still did not look up.

With a sigh, Pike dropped into the pilot's chair.

"You come onto my ship and take the pilot's chair like that? Who do you think you are?" Rychenkov shot him a look with those trademark pale eyes.

"Just hear me out."

"No." Rychenkov jabbed his finger into the air for emphasis. "It's a crazy plan. I don't make crazy plans."

"You love crazy plans," Pike corrected him.

"Since when?"

"Since three years ago at least." Pike raised his eyebrows.

Three years ago, Rychenkov had been the mastermind behind a plan that took down one of the main drug cartels running between Mars and a remote lab in the asteroid belt. The plan had involved three decoy ships, a computer virus, and a painted goat, and if Pike hadn't seen it himself, he would think the whole thing was a bald-faced lie.

It was crazy, and it had worked.

Now, however, the captain of the *Aggy* only gave an elaborate shrug. "That is different." His voice was fairly dripping with the accent. "Those were humans. Humans have the same weapons. The fuggers are different. They can shoot us out of the sky: one, two, three, go home for dinner."

"And they do," Pike said, with a sudden burst of inspiration.

"You're shit at negotiating, you know that?"

Pike only grinned. He hadn't been told to leave yet, and no one had taken a knife out. He was doing pretty well, by his estimation. "It doesn't make you mad that they treat us like this?"

"I've told you about this." Rychenkov gave him a look. He finished cleaning one piece of the rifle and set it aside carefully before picking up the next. The rifle, like everything on the *Aggy*—except the propulsion system and the inertial dampeners—was old, low-tech, and scrupulously maintained by Rychenkov himself. It had taken him eight years to find a mechanic he trusted, and Howie still complained that Rychenkov checked his work every night before letting him go off-shift.

"So, tell me again." Spacers liked to talk. Pike had learned to let them.

Rychenkov scowled. "You too stupid to remember? You don't fight dictators, *durak*. You wait them out. They get their palaces and their women—" He stopped, struck by this. "You think they take our women?"

"They aren't interested in our women," Pike said wearily. "And it's not a palace, it's our *planet*."

"Don't interrupt, it's rude."

Pike narrowly refrained from rolling his eyes.

"They get everything they want," Rychenkov continued. He gestured with a metal brush. "And then they piss off one too many people and someone kills them in the night."

"Yeah, but then what?"

Rychenkov shrugged. "Then there is another dictator. And while he consolidates his grip, we stay under the radar and get our shit done."

Pike was opening his mouth to retort when he realized that this was, in fact, an eerily accurate read on their present situation. He blinked and scratched at his head.

"We don't want another dictator," he tried.

"It is the way of things," Rychenkov advised him. "You stand up, you get crushed like a bug. Best just to live your life, *da*? Enjoy the little things?"

Pike sank his head into his hands.

"Cheer up, *durak*. Someday you will die, and this will not trouble you anymore."

"You have a way with people, my friend." Pike picked his head up. "Is anyone listening to us?"

Rychenkov's hands paused on the rifle. He considered Pike for a moment before reaching out to press a button. The door slid closed.

"Not anymore." The accent was fading, and Rychenkov gave him a serious look. "What's your secret, then?"

"We're screwed," Pike told him simply. "Totally, one hundred percent, anally screwed."

"Who'd you piss off?" Rychenkov finished the cleaning and started reassembling the pieces. "You piss off the fuggers and then come here?"

"Well...." He had, but not quite the way Rychenkov meant. Pike held up his hands. "They're not coming for us."

"They'd better not be." Rychenkov peered down the barrel.

"They're coming for everyone."

Rychenkov stopped. "How?"

"You were right about another dictator. There was a coup. A Telestine coup."

"Oh?" Rychenkov looked interested. "Lots of dead Telestines. You see? It all comes around in the end."

"They still have Earth," Pike reminded him. "And the guy who took over thinks that humanity is just too much of a pain in the ass to keep around."

"So, what—he comes to kill all of us?" Rychenkov gave a snort of laughter. When he saw Pike's face, the smile died slowly. "No. There are too many of us. They did not before— why now?"

"Does it really matter? He's right. We never stopped planning to take Earth back. We're too dangerous to keep around."

Rychenkov stared at him for a long time, his eyes narrowed. "That's what this is," he said finally. "You *did* piss the fuggers off. That mission you were on, you showed your hand, now they think *all* humans are part of the Rebellion and they crush us all. This is *your* fault, you and your ridiculous Exile Fleet."

"No," Pike said desperately. "Things would have gotten to this point eventually, in any case. I swear. This guy has been planning it for ... forever. He made a weapon to take down their military's fleet, and he has his own fleet."

"You get off my ship." Rychenkov's voice was ugly. "Off my ship, Pike. You have an hour before I airlock you, you hear? You get us all crushed. It is always the same with revolutionaries, they think of no one else but their ideals."

The door slid open, and he turned with an oath.

The girl stared at him quietly. She had climbed the stairs without a sound, barefoot on the metal.

Rychenkov stared at her. "Who the hell is this?"

"This is...." Pike looked down at his hands. It was useless.

The touch on his shoulder was light. The girl looked down at him and nodded at Rychenkov.

"It's not going to make any difference," Pike warned her. She shrugged.

"Fine." He looked back at his one-time captain. "She was raised in the labs. Telestine labs. You see those scars? The guy who took over, he *designed* her to take down their fleet, to interface with their technology. She's going to learn how to disable his systems, too—that's why we need the fighter."

"So *she* came out of some lab? A Drone?" Rychenkov looked worried.

"She's not one of the—" Pike waved his hands. "Look. We gave him an excuse, but he didn't need one. He controls them now—their military, even their government, I think, and he wants us all dead. Running's gonna get you a couple of weeks, tops."

Rychenkov considered. His gaze went back to the girl. "He telling the truth?" he demanded.

She nodded.

"You don't talk, huh?"

A head shake.

"Any reason for that?"

She shrugged.

Rychenkov considered. "*Fine*," he said savagely. "But I am not happy about this."

"I'm not happy about it, either," Pike offered.

"Yeah, yeah." Rychenkov paused. "So where are we going?"

CHAPTER FORTY-THREE

Halfway between Earth and Venus
Freighter Agamemnon

Pike eased the *Aggy* along from the comfort of the co-pilot's chair, eyeing the Telestine formation warily. *Fly casual*, Rychenkov had told him. What the hell did that mean?

He'd spent his years after Earth on the right side of the law, filling out registration forms and making sure his ships followed the prescribed routes, but every time he saw a Telestine patrol appear outside his ship, he was sure they would find out his history—that he'd escaped from right under their noses. You never lost your instinctive fear at the sight of those ships. The black hulls were jarring on Earth, and even more terrifying in deep space. You could hardly see them: little shadows blocking out the stars as they moved, an absence of light.

Today, they were accompanied by three feathers. Not a

single one broke formation as the *Aggy* came out of hard burn on their tail and fell into line.

"We should go." Charlie's voice was tight. "This is too risky."

Rychenkov threw an annoyed look over his shoulder and Pike was hard pressed not to do the same. Charlie had been melting down since he found out the details of the plan a few hours ago. In the past five minutes alone, he had accused them all of being crazy, he had suggested that they should contact the admiral for an alternate plan, and he hadn't once stopped fiddling with the pen he carried with him. A good luck charm, he said.

Weak, Rychenkov called him to his face, and from the look in his eyes, he'd finally had enough of this.

"Get out of my cockpit." His accent was back, and strong.

Charlie opened his mouth to protest, saw the evident unity in the rest of the crew, and visibly deflated. He left with a clatter on the grating.

Only the girl hadn't looked at him. Pike turned his head to watch her. *Dawn*. She might laugh, but the name suited her: the silent, pale pause before morning's fire in the sky, eyes black as night.

Right now, she was furious. Those black eyes were fixed on the Telestine ships with a simmering anger that told Pike this was not a woman to cross. Wherever she had been raised, she would never forgive Tel'rabim for what he had made her.

It occurred to Pike now that she was the most human of all of them. She was human by instinct alone.

"All right. Last chance to call it off." Rychenkov looked around at all of them. He locked eyes with each of the crew first. James and Gabriela Carson. Howie. Finally Pike. That had been one of his stipulations: *they say no deal, then no deal.*

Pike couldn't tell if Rychenkov was surprised or not when the crew agreed.

"We're with you cowboy," said James, tapping his hat. Howie nodded his agreement.

"I'm with *guapo*," said Gabriela.

From her place in the copilot's seat, the girl drew the shard of Telestine technology out of her bag. It gleamed black in the dim light of the cockpit, and everyone leaned forward to watch. Pike heard Howie catch his breath.

"What is that?" Charlie's eyes grew wide. He held up his hands when Rychenkov swung around, startled to see he'd returned. "I won't ... freak out. But what's that?" His voice changed. "Is *that* the Dawning?"

Pike didn't answer. It was close enough, and he didn't want to disturb Charlie's near-reverence. He nodded to the girl.

The pads of her fingers spread onto the surface of the machinery and the light began, but she didn't even look. Her eyes were fixed on the ships in front of her as her fingers moved. She drew them independently of one another, reminding Pike of a video he'd once seen—a piano concert from a time when humanity had more space than it knew what to do with. She moved as if the shattered piece of a computer she cradled in her hands was an extension of her.

Maybe to her, it was.

The ship shuddered. In the video screen, Pike watched the cargo claw begin to extend and splay.

The last ship drifted out of formation slowly. There was a faint *tip-tilt*, and a few seconds later it had gone noticeably off course. The girl drew a deep breath and pressed her fingers down onto the computer, *hard*.

The black ships lifted and scattered into a defensive formation, and the feathers began to turn. They were on to them.

"*Now*," Pike said. His fingers were white-knuckled against the chair.

Rychenkov slammed his hand down on the EMP button. It was the only weapon the cargo ships had, passed secretly among them, entirely forbidden. Since humanity had learned to shield itself from EMP, they had done everything in their power to keep this one piece of defense hidden.

Light flickered across the hulls of the feathers and they went dead on their trajectory. Pike had a visceral moment of horror, thinking of the pilots trapped in ships gone dead. What did it feel like, if they interacted with the machinery as instinctively as the girl did?

They were his enemies, he reminded himself. Enemies. And the effect of the EMP wouldn't last more than a few minutes—the Telestine's electronics seemed to be … self-healing.

The *Aggy* put on speed and banked expertly. Rychenkov snatched a dead ship out of the vacuum and was already accelerating as the claw began to retract.

"I'll take care of the pilot." Pike's stomach heaved—he had never liked killing—but this felt like his task somehow.

He did not want to consider the idea that he'd been looking forward to another round since he killed the first Telestine a few weeks back. He tried to keep from remembering how it felt to feel the body go still beneath him.

So many years of anger to channel into violence.

So many lives to pay back.

"Pike. *Pike*." Charlie was hurrying after him.

"What?" Pike did not look back.

"It's her, isn't it?" Charlie grabbed his arm to swing him around. "She's the Dawning. Why didn't you tell me?"

Pike wanted to laugh. "It must have slipped my mind," he said shortly. *What with all the genocide.*

"She's...." Charlie shook his head. "And she's really helping us?"

"Look." Pike resisted the urge to shove the man out of the way. "I have a pilot to kill before he manages to get his gun out."

"Right. Right." Charlie stepped back. "I'll ... better you than me." He looked faintly queasy.

"Go sit," Pike advised. "And hold on. I'm pretty sure we'll be burning back to Venus as hard as we can."

"Of course." Charlie shook his head. "I'll, uh, go see if Rychenkov needs any help."

That might help Rychenkov's opinion of the man. Pike made a mental note to drop a quiet word to Rychenkov about Charlie's family. He knew there would be bluster—*world doesn't stop when people die*—but he also knew Rychenkov would go easier on the man. Rychenkov was that kind of captain.

The Telestine ship sat on the floor of the cargo bay, tilted awkwardly on one side. Pike readied himself, knife in hand, and when someone touched his arm, he jumped and swore.

The girl bit her lip and looked away, trying not to see his evident embarrassment. She plucked the knife out of his hand and put it back in the sheath, and crossed the floor to open the fighter's cockpit with a press on some hidden button.

There was no pilot.

"Are *all* of them remotely guided?" Pike asked. His heart was pounding with relief.

She shrugged and went to drag Nhean's computer terminal across the floor.

Pike had gone to help her when the ship gave a sideways lurch and acceleration drove him to his knees.

"*Everyone hold on down there.*" Rychenkov's voice blared over the loudspeakers. "*We've got company. Big company.*"

CHAPTER FORTY-FOUR

Halfway between Earth and Venus
Freighter Agamemnon

The *Aggy* had no weaponry beyond its tiny EMP generator. No guns, no cannons, no laser arrays. All it had was raw acceleration, and Rychenkov had made sure it had that in abundance. The only drawback to raw acceleration was that the inertial dampeners could barely keep up. Well, that and the nasty drug cocktail that prevented them all from vomiting and collapsing in the intense vertigo.

"*Telestine cruiser just popped up out of nowhere, seems like. Probably running dark, dead in space. Is now accelerating to match our course*," came Rychenkov's voice through the comm.

"How long?"

"*Fifteen minutes?*"

Pike shook his head, trying to force his way through the vertigo. "Ok. I'll get her linked into this fighter. Hopefully by then she'll have learned enough about them to … do … something."

"And Pike, that's not all. There's a Telestine formation that just left Earth and is heading to us. If that first ship doesn't catch us, those bastards will. Whatever she got up her sleeve, now's the time."

Pike managed a grim grunt. "Got it."

The acceleration made him feel like he was moving through molasses, and the inertial dampeners were beginning to cause the faintest bit of nausea. But at least he wasn't goo. He shuddered to think what would happen if the dampeners suddenly gave out, or even momentarily blipped. One blip, and they'd all be smears on the wall.

He crawled across the cargo bay floor with a fair amount of effort and locked his fingers around the handle of the second computer terminal. The girl looked at him woozily. They hauled it over; it seemed heavier than it should be, or maybe that was them being heavier than they should be … somehow everything was heavy sideways, with a strong pull toward the floor. When they pushed the computer terminal into place at last, they were both panting like they'd been running sprints.

"I have to—" Pike looked slowly up to the bridge. Gesturing seemed like a lot of effort right now. So did talking.

Her hand clamped around his arm. She shook her head. She looked at the computer terminal and then the Telestine fighter.

"*I* don't know how to put it together!" Not to mention, he didn't want to die from a shot he didn't even see coming.

Gravity shifted, as if the *Aggy* was swerving into a new course, and they both sprawled—him onto the floor and her over the edge of the fighter and into the cockpit. Her head popped up a moment later and she waved him over, more emphatically this time.

"Okay, but then I have to go."

Rychenkov's voice rang out from the speaker. "*Pike. Some guy named Nhean on the radio. Wants to know if there's a data stream yet.*"

"We're setting it up," Pike called toward the comm unit.

"*Well, hurry it up and get that chick back up here. We could use some help with this fugger ship. It's almost matched our course—ten minutes, tops.*"

She shook her head morosely, but Pike wasn't about to tell Rychenkov that there was nothing he could do.

"Once you've seen all of this data, maybe you *can* help the captain," he suggested. "Maybe you'll learn something, be able to take down those bastards out there, huh?"

She looked pleased by that thought. She was hauling a truly staggering array of wires into the cockpit, each with a pad at one end and a plug on the other.

Pike peered into the cockpit, intrigued, steadying himself as the *Aggy* swerved again. Rychenkov was no longer on the comms, but they could hear the man swearing in Russian even from here.

He could see why no one had bothered retrieving much Telestine weaponry. The entire cockpit was as smooth and gleaming as the wall terminal he had seen on the lunar base, and they knew from the shard of technology upstairs that it was just as featureless all the way through.

To them, anyway. He rested his chin on his hands while she peered very seriously at different areas of what looked—to him—to be a completely identical white alloy, and at last she began to place pads carefully on different sections. She handed him the other ends of the wires carefully, each plug destined for a port of the same color on the back of Nhean's terminal.

"What do all of these do, anyway?"

She considered, face screwed up for a moment, and then waved her hand. There was no way she was going to be able to explain this to him, apparently.

That was fair.

"And does the terminal need power?"

A nod. She sorted around in the cables and pulled out a heavy power cord.

Rychenkov was guiding the ships in several high-g turns, so Pike gave up on walking. He crawled across the floor to plug in the power cord, then returned to plug another few colored lines in.

There was a pause as the girl considered all of this. She nodded decisively and peered over the edge of the cockpit, gesturing at the power cord.

The whole thing blazed to life, and the beeps and whistles on Nhean's unit seemed to correspond with the light show in the Telestine fighter.

"*He says he's getting data,*" Rychenkov called.

"Good." Pike leaned down to the girl, who seemed to be watching the data stream with great concentration. "I'm going back to the cockpit, okay? You good here?"

She didn't even look up at him as she nodded. Her gaze was riveted on the computers, and he could only hope she was learning more about Tel'rabim's systems.

Good. Maybe they had a chance now. Pike braced himself

against the wall and made for the cockpit as quickly as he could. Rychenkov was still flying evasive maneuvers, trying to set new, random courses to throw off their pursuers.

Charlie met him in the hallway, white-faced. "We can't outrun them."

"We have to try for as long as we can—Walker might be able to send backup." If they were burning this hard for Venus, that backup might even arrive soon. Or the pursuing ship might run out of fuel, or they might break off the chase. A good pilot knew that every moment alive was another moment his opponent might make a mistake.

Charlie might as well have read Pike's mind. "Your Captain Rychenkov's a good pilot," he said, "but he's trying to take on feathers. We *can't* outrun them."

"Are you sure? They haven't caught us yet."

"I think...." Charlie grabbed for Pike. "Slow down."

"I have to get to the cockpit."

"Pike, wait!" The man's voice was weak. He tried to whisper as Pike took the last few stairs to the cockpit. "What if they're here for *her*?"

He'd tried to be quiet, but everyone swung around. Even Rychenkov's head turned.

Pike felt his heart squeeze. "You think they can sense her?"

"I don't know!" Charlie looked away, shrugging. He looked at Pike helplessly. "But they aren't shooting! Why aren't they shooting?"

"The man has a point," Rychenkov said slowly. "They aren't shooting. They've matched our course and are closing in. But they're not shooting, even though they're in range."

"Is there anything more you can do?"

"Not much." Rychenkov sighed. "Not enough," he said, more exactly. "They match my every move."

"There's one thing." Charlie spoke quietly.

"Oh?" Pike looked at him curiously.

"You're not going to like it," Charlie warned.

"Spit it out."

Charlie looked around himself, gauging support, and took a deep breath. "We could give her to them."

"*What?*"

Charlie was shaking, Pike realized. But his chin lifted. "We could *give* her to them," he repeated.

"We need her," Pike said wildly.

"*The data stream is nearly complete.*" Nhean's voice broke through the cockpit suddenly. "*Captain Rychenkov, there are Rebellion ships making for you, moving to match your course, but if you have any other modes of acceleration, now would be the time to use them —we're reading more inbound ships, larger than your pursuer.*"

The line cut. Everyone stared at the comm unit.

"We can give her to them," Charlie said. He stabbed a finger for emphasis. "She's the big weapon, isn't she? They want her back. And Nhean said he'll have all the data he needs soon."

"No." Pike could see the crew wavering. He swept his eyes around the cockpit.

"Listen to me, she's valuable to them." Charlie was shaking his head. "They want her back, they don't care about us."

"All the more reason to keep her aboard! As soon as she's gone, we're just a bunch of humans who killed some Telestine fighters, have a piece of illicit tech on our ship, and are using banned weaponry. We're toast, Charlie."

Charlie looked at him, cornered. "They'd … they'd be grateful we gave her back."

"The same people who want to exterminate all of humanity? Yeah, I'm sure they would be—but I don't think that means what you're hoping."

Charlie looked down at the floor. He was rocking back and forth.

"They want her," he repeated. "We can't stop them."

"We just have to hold them off," Pike said, as gently as he could. Then he remembered it wasn't Charlie he had to convince—Charlie, who'd grown up running, who might never believe that they would have a chance against the Telestines—but Rychenkov and the crew. "You saw what she did to some of the fighters," he said. He looked around at them. "With this data, with that fighter down there in the hold, she might be able to learn to do it to the rest. We can stop now and get shot and lose her, or we can keep flying and have a chance not to have those fuggers around anymore."

The crew looked at one another. The nods were wordless.

"Hold on—hold on—oh, shit." Rychenkov looked up from the scanner. They're extending an umbilical. They're going to board."

Ground assault. Perfect. Pike finally grinned—this was something he knew how to do. "Ok. Let them in the bay. Howie? Charlie? With me. We'll ambush them, toss a grenade onto their ship, then fly like a bat out of hell."

Rychenkov hesitated, then nodded. "Fine." The three turned to leave. "But Pike?"

He turned back to glance at his captain. "Yeah?"

"You blow up my ship, and you're on my shit list."

CHAPTER FORTY-FIVE

Venus, 49 kilometers above surface
Tang Estate, New Zurich

The data stream flickered and Nhean glanced curiously over at another screen. He hadn't been above putting a scanner on the *Aggy*, embedded in the computer terminal, and he was intrigued to see the technology Rychenkov had managed to construct. Their inertial dampeners had been calibrated in a way Nhean would never have tried, but they were clearly working, compensating for the acceleration enough that the inhabitants of the ship were not only not goo, but not vomiting or even reeling from the vertigo. When the ship arrived back at Venus, he'd have to come up with some reason to keep the ship at dock for a few days while his engineers went over it.

"What's going on?" Walker had seen him looking. She was pacing like a caged animal near the windows.

"There must have been another patrol nearby, and they're calling in everyone they can." Nhean shook his head. "It *should* be hard to get a lock on a ship at that speed. Honestly, I didn't think it was possible unless one was watching out the window, and even then, she'd have gained on them enough that that would be hard...."

"Get to the point."

Soldiers. He gave her a look. "My point is, I'd like to know how they're managing to stay on our ship's tail. The pilot's done a few maneuvers that should have shaken them, and they're sticking like glue."

Walker frowned. "Do you think it's the girl?"

Nhean raised his eyebrows. He should have thought of that immediately. But—

"No." He frowned. "They were looking for her like crazy after the lab crashed. If they could see her on their scanners, they'd just have run one pass over the Rockies and called it done when she wasn't there. She's just invisible to them, I think."

"Huh." Walker flopped back on a couch and shrugged.

"You're not curious."

"I am, but I've gotten used to being outmatched in technology." Surprisingly, she smiled at him. "And as usual, we just have to compensate ... with clever tactics."

It was a surprisingly sensible perspective from her.

He looked over to where the data were streaming in, still translating in his system, and he decided to take a gamble.

He still didn't know her end game. "When this is all over, what do you think you'll do?"

She raised her eyebrows. "Why?"

Nhean made sure his smile didn't so much as flicker, but his hackles went up. "You're in the Rebellion," he explained with a shrug, as if he didn't much care. "I figured you'd build up the life we all *should* have—but I don't sense you have something to get back to."

"Ah." She looked away, and then gave a shrug. "I hadn't thought about it."

Now she was lying. Nhean watched her. Should he press her on this? Now? He could have the doors locked without a word, it would be so easy—

"To be honest, I don't expect to be alive much longer." Walker met his eyes and there, at last, was the honesty. She lifted her shoulders again, helplessly. "All I've thought about is what I can do to give humanity a fighting chance against a hostile universe."

How to put those pieces together? Nhean looked away.

"What about you?" Her voice was almost wistful. "Would you stay here?"

"No." The answer was more vehement than he liked. He took a moment to compose himself before he looked back. "I'd go back to Earth."

Something—*something*—flashed in her eyes, and was gone the next moment. She hesitated.

"You wouldn't want to see the stars? Travel to distant planets?"

"No," he said firmly. "Earth is where we belong."

"I see."

She was a child of the stations, he remembered. She had grown up in variable gravity and been used to the sight of stars and black. Her dreams had not been for a planet she had never seen, but for the stars that might hold an escape.

Interesting. He had never considered this about Admiral Laura Walker.

The computer was flashing at him and he swiveled back to it. His smile was immediate.

"As long as that fighter in Rychenkov's hold stays ours, we have a window into their communications."

"That's good." Walker sat up. "And?"

"Working on that. This is much more information than I've ever received all at once." He sank his chin into one hand. "I'll have to look at how she placed the wires...."

"Are you going to let her practice on it?" Walker sounded interested now. "I mean, if it's just your communications array." Her voice changed. "Maybe we should have had them get two fighters."

"Too much of a risk. I never like to bring in things that might network." Nhean spoke distractedly. These messages suggested that the fleet was massing somewhere, but ... where? "Frankly, even letting her bring that shard was a risk."

"She's his machinery, too, isn't she a risk to network with it?"

"Unless she has guns embedded in her somewhere, not quite the same. Although I suppose she must send out some sort of signal...." He considered for a moment, then shook his head. First things first.

First things, like where the fleet was supposed to mass. He scrolled through the information as quickly as he could. The translation was partial and even then, sometimes he could make neither head nor tail of it. He'd never quite appreciated how much of language was metaphor until he began trying to translate the work of an entirely different species.

"Come on...." He tapped his fingers impatiently. "Come on, come...."

"You got something." Walker pushed herself up. "Should I —"

He held up a hand to stop her. His mind was racing. Hard burn to Mercury from here on her ships would take how long? He'd seen her Exile Fleet; it was a miracle they were still floating. Death traps, the lot of them.

He hadn't wanted to play his hand so soon, but it appeared he had no choice. He'd made his life on these compromises.

"I'm giving you a new fleet."

"A ... new fleet? Did I understand you right?" She sounded dumbfounded.

He met her eyes and tried not to wince at the thought of her maneuvers with his ships. She'd throw them all into the breach if necessary.

Then again, what were ships for?

He tried to still the racing of his mind. His eyes went to the screen again, to reread the information, to confirm....

There was no mistaking it.

"I'll have a shuttle take you immediately. You need to go at once. The Exile Fleet will come behind you." He pushed himself up, eyes still fixed, trying to glean any last details he could.

"A new—you have a *fleet*?" She couldn't get over that one point, it seemed.

"*Yes*. And you have some ships at Mercury, yes?" He was counting under his breath. It might be enough.

It would have to be enough.

"Yes, but only a few—we've only just begun spinning up the shipyards that will—" She broke off and snapped her head toward him. "How the hell did you know about our operation at *Mercury*?"

"It's what I do," he said with a brief smile before turning back to the data stream. "We'll have to make it work. I'll join you there as soon as I can. I need to go for Pike and the girl. Now." He was pushing his way past her out of the room.

"*Stop.*"

He stopped, much to his own surprise. He had never heard her issue a command.

She spoke slowly, carefully. "Whatever we're doing, it's worth nothing if we don't communicate a plan. What's *happening*?"

"They're starting the sweep at Mercury." Saying it aloud made it real. "Then out from there."

"From Earth, it will take them—"

"No." He cut her off. "They're already on their way. Tel'rabim's fleet left Earth *hours* ago. Five g burn. They'll be there in less than a day."

She went white.

"I have something that may work," he said quietly. "I've called it the Seed—it's a computer program that will infect their systems. I've been developing it since I was first able to get in contact with Tel'rabim."

A shadow crossed her face. "You didn't tell us?"

"I didn't have a way to deploy it before." He gave a rueful smile. "Now we have the Dawning. If I can get to her, we can put it on Tel'rabim's flagship."

Her eyes flashed. "And then ... it's all over."

He shrugged. "If it works. But yes, either way, it's all over. For either the Telestines, or humanity."

CHAPTER FORTY-SIX

Halfway between Earth and Venus
Freighter Agamemnon

Pike tossed an assault rifle over to Charlie from the ship's modest armory, and James handed him a spare magazine.

"You good?" James watched their guest struggle with the magazine before clicking it in place.

"Yeah, sorry."

James gave Pike a heavy look and tapped his cowboy hat before he reached into the armory safe and unlocked one of the compartments, pulling out two grenades. He handed one to Pike. "Sorry, Charlie. I think you've already got your hands full there."

Pike was worried that he'd be affronted, but Charlie took it in stride. The other man seemed too nervous to care about the slight. He would have supposed having nothing left to live for, that Charlie would be a little more … cavalier. Trigger-happy.

But instead he just kept alternating between checking his pockets and the rifle.

"*Status, Pike?*" Rychenkov said over the comm.

"Ready." He gave a quick nod to the other two men. They were only wearing their regular clothes—no time to pull on anything more protective. Not that they carried anything beyond simple vacuum suits, which wouldn't repel a bullet, so why bother?

But if one of those bullets pierced the hull in the cargo hold, they were screwed.

Details.

"*Their docking umbilical is latching on to the cargo hold hatch. You'll be wanting to get your girl out of there now.*"

"Roger that," said Pike, and he pointed down the corridor with two fingers. They passed the crew quarters, and the galley, descended the steel steps to the lower level, and they were there, in front of the cargo hold.

The doors were shut. Pike fingered the switch to open them.

They didn't budge.

"Ry?" said Pike, nervously. "Ry, what's up? The doors aren't opening."

Muttered Russian vulgarities drifted over the comm as Rychenkov fiddled with his controls in the cockpit. "*Piece of ... Pike, we've been locked out.*"

"How? Telestines?" He urgently punched the switch over and over again, hoping it was just a loose electrical contact.

"*Looks like it. They're broadcasting something. Jamming us. Wouldn't be surprised if they've tapped in somehow and locked us out of our own cargo hold. They must really want that girl.*"

Pike grit his teeth and forced himself to think. "Well they're not getting her." He looked all around for something to pry the door open. He toyed with the idea of shooting the locking mechanism. Something, anything, to get him through that door and get Dawn out of there.

The ship shook and he heard a clang reverberate through the metal walls. He knew what that meant.

"They've engaged their umbilical with our hatch. They'll be through any—"

Rychenkov didn't even need to finish. They could hear through the thick cargo bay doors that something was happening. A screech as the outer hatch opened. Footsteps.

And then all hell broke loose.

Gunfire erupted from several guns at once—at least, that's what it sounded like to Pike's ears. He heard the eerie, guttural sounds of Telestines shouting. Crashes, followed by solid thuds.

Pike banged on the door, and swiveled his rifle down to the locking mechanism. "Stand back," he said to the other two men. They took cover behind the corner of the turn in the hallway, and he unloaded five rounds into the lock.

The doors remained shut.

The storm of gunfire, along with the accompanying crashing and yelling, continued unabated, even as Pike cupped a hand over his mouth and shouted through the seam of the doors. "DAWN! DAWN!"

"Pike, what the hell is going on down there?" shouted Rychenkov over the comm.

One final crash, the sound of dozens of pieces of metal scattering over a metal deck, one final gunshot, then silence.

"I … I have no idea," said Pike.

The silence was almost worse than the earlier cacophony of gunfire and crashes. He started to fear the worst, and slowly raised his rifle, leveling it at the doors. James and Charlie followed suit.

"*Pike, I've regained control. Whatever was jamming us and interfering with our systems is … gone, apparently. Opening the doors now.*"

"Roger that," muttered Pike, peering down the length of the rifle's barrel, ready to drop anything that leaped out past the doors when they opened.

The locking mechanism disengaged, and, slowly, the doors pulled apart.

Pike's finger twitched on the trigger. A flutter of movement beyond the door….

The girl stood there. Dawn. A trace of blood, in stark contrast to her skin, streaked down her cheek from her forehead. He wasn't sure if it was hers, or….

In the cargo bay behind her, on the floor, lay the bodies of six … no, eight Telestines. Soldiers, by the looks of them. All either bleeding profusely, some with limbs at odd angles. And the bay was a wreck.

He lowered his rifle. "Dawn?"

Her face contorted, as if she were either in great pain, or unsure about something, but then she gave a solemn nod.

"You … you did all that?"

Another brief nod.

She collapsed.

CHAPTER FORTY-SEVEN

Venus, 49 kilometers above surface
Tang Estate, New Zurich

"All right." Walker shot a look at the clock in the corner and shook her head. "We have three fleets and ... about ten minutes to plan the most important battle any of us will ever be in."

Great.

"I don't see any problems." King's eyes were shadowed, but her smile was genuine. "You're the queen of crazy maneuvers. Go with your gut."

"And *you* make sure I don't leave my flanks open." Walker stared at Delaney and King in turn and waited until they both nodded. "Okay. We have Nhean's fleet, which is eight carriers with sixty-four fighters apiece, sixteen destroyers, and three smaller ships that do ... something, he wasn't entirely clear on that, we're just supposed to get them near the Telestine carriers and let them do their thing. Signal jamming or some such."

King gave a low whistle.

"Now, here's the first complication. He says whatever we do, we can't take down the flagship."

"*What?*" King's voice rose.

"That's what I said. He's going to attempt to use the Dawning and, he believes—hopefully correctly—that the flagship directs many of the other ships remotely. It sounds like an awful lot of their system works on networks." She held up her hands. "He's the expert, not me, and he says don't take down the flagship."

"You're taking that rather well," Delaney observed.

"I'm trying to focus on the part where it's an interesting puzzle, not on the part where things I don't understand could kill me." Walker squeezed her eyes shut for a moment and shook her head to clear it. "So who's in charge of the Exile Fleet, who's in charge of our Mercury fleet, and who's in charge of the Venus fleet?"

"I'll take the Exile Fleet." Delaney cracked his fingers and gave a tired grin. "Can't teach an old dog new tricks, right? I know these ships. I know what they can do. I'll do what I can with that."

"Good."

"I'll take the Mercury fleet." King was staring at the readouts.

Walker nodded. That made sense; King had been the most involved recently in testing their new fighters. She knew those pilots by name and she'd seen the maneuvers they could do.

"Anyway," King shrugged, "seems like commanding a new fancy fleet is a dream job for any admiral."

All of them chuckled. It was a weak joke—not really a joke at all—but they'd take any humor they could get right now.

"So what's the plan, boss?" Delaney dragged a chair over and sat. He looked weary, Walker thought, but he caught her looking and gave a smile.

She considered for a moment, and then began to tear the printouts into pieces, placing them into position on the solar system map on the console's screen.

"Here's the Telestine fleet. They'll be coming past us in about three hours, so it's a race to Mercury, but for now we're still closer. I'll split Nhean's fleet into three groups, with one of those fancy jamming ships in each. King, you'll go ahead with a skeleton crew on a few of Nhean's fast shuttles, get to Mercury first, retrieve the ships there, and get them up and running as fast as possible. I've already sent them an FTL transmission warning them of your arrival, but you'll only have about two hours. Delaney, burn as hard as you can around the planet clockwise and come at them in retrograde orbit. Hammer and anvil—we're going to smash them between the two of us ... more or less."

"I liked that plan until the 'more or less.'" Delaney leaned forward to look.

"We don't want to get caught in one another's crossfire, so here's what we're going to do. The Venus fleet and the Exile Fleet will both sink below the Telestine fleet. That way, we're both firing up in opposite directions, and the Telestines have to reorient their battle while staying in the crossfire, all while dealing with King and the Mercury fleet coming out of nowhere from the surface." She picked up the piece of paper representing the Telestine fleet and held it over the other two, to demonstrate. "Psychological, too. People protect the bellies of their ships more than they need to if there's a threat—and no one seems to fight in the lower hemisphere." It was one similarity between humans and Telestines that she was finally getting to make use of.

Delaney frowned. "They're going to go lower in orbit to compensate. Do we really want to draw them closer to the rolling cities?"

"It's a chance we'll have to take," said Walker. She hoped it was a risk worth taking—they'd spent an immense amount of resources building those shipyards.

"All right." King cradled her elbows. "What about me?"

"You're shooting straight up from the surface, right underneath them when their orbit passes over you, and after Delaney has made his first retrograde pass. By the time he's had a chance to swing the Exile Fleet back around, you'll be in the clear, holding station *above* the Telestine fleet, while I cover you." She moved more bits of paper into position.

King nodded decisively. "Those pilots have been training for this for weeks; the fighters got up and running a while back, and the carrier captains have been overseeing fighter formations and running simulations themselves."

"Good." Walker tried to match the woman's excitement. "But King, whatever happens, the shipyards *must* survive. Protect them at all costs. The future of humanity lies on Mercury."

"Admiral." Nhean's aide, Parees, hovered in the doorway. He bowed his head courteously. "It's time to go."

"Thank you." Walker looked at her commanders. Her two most trusted officers. "Any last questions?"

"None." King smiled.

"Good. Delaney?"

Delaney was staring at the map. His eyes were distant and sad.

Something was up with him. Walker turned to meet King's eyes. "Head out now with your people. See you at Mercury." She nodded to the aide. "Tell Mr. Tang I'll be there presently."

She waited until they were both gone before she looked over at Delaney.

"What is it?"

"I have a request." He pushed himself up, and she saw in a flash how much he had been hiding from her. It had been ten long years since they first joined forces in the Rebellion, and he hadn't been a young man even then. "But first...." He hesitated, and held out his arms.

She went to hug him without question, burying her face in his shoulder and blinking away unexpected emotion.

"I am so proud of you," he said, into her hair. "I always wanted children. Never got around to it; never found a woman I liked as much as my ships, I guess. But if I'd had a daughter, I like to think she'd have turned out like you."

Walker closed her eyes. She could feel a tear threaten to break free from an eyelid. "Thank you for everything." Her voice was a whisper.

"I am so proud of you," he said again. He took her by the shoulders and gave a chuckle. "Aw hell, don't cry. I've been a pain in the ass for the past few months and you know it."

"Uh-huh." Walker gave a watery chuckle and wiped at her eyes. She almost felt shame at having let down her emotional guard, but then she noticed his eyes were red too. "It's just...."

"That we aren't all going to make it out of this." His voice was suddenly grave.

She stilled.

"That's my request," he said quietly. "If you have to throw someone into the breech, someone to hold the door, or stand as a last defense while everyone else escapes to safety, Walker ... it should be me."

"No." Her denial was instant. "The leader sacrifices themselves first. That's the rule. The captain goes down with her ship."

"Damned stupid rule if so." His voice was sharp. "You've a mind for this, Admiral, a better one than I do, and better than King. You know today isn't the end unless we all go to the grave, and I'm not going to plan on that. I'm planning on *you* staying alive to take out the rest of the Telestines, right? My endgame is Earth, and you on it."

It was a good point, and one she knew. And still: "I can't just sacrifice you."

"Can't you?" She saw him force himself to gentleness. "Not all of these ships are going to make it out," he said again. "If someone's gotta die, it should be the old man. You're young. King's young. I'm an old fart. Use me. Make me your shield when it comes down to the end."

She closed her eyes. "That's why you took the Exile Fleet. The old ships."

"That, and it suits me." He was smiling, she could tell even without looking. "We're both a bit unpredictable, a bit broken. But we've both got a bit more in us than anyone's expecting. Walker—*Admiral*—say you'll do what you have to, when it comes to it. You'll know the moment when it comes. Don't hesitate. That's why I'm saying my goodbyes now."

Grief threatened to swamp her, and she heard her own voice distantly. "But you'll never get to see Earth again."

"Already seen it." He pulled her close for another hug and squeezed tight, almost crushing her. "You and King should get to see it too before you die, huh?" His voice dropped to a whisper, "And Walker ... it's beautiful. Like nothing you've ever seen." He craned to kiss her forehead. "Go. I don't want you to see an old man cry. I'll never forgive myself."

She nodded; she didn't trust herself to speak. But at the doorway, when she looked back, she could see that he knew everything she wanted to say. She nodded again, and left.

Parees showed her to the shuttle that would take her to the Venus fleet's flagship. And from there, Mercury. And battle.

CHAPTER FORTY-EIGHT

Halfway between Earth and Venus
Freighter Agamemnon

Dawn was ok. Rattled, shaken, and unable to tell them why
—Pike could only assume it was because she'd expended so
much energy fighting off the Telestines. Though how she'd
done it … didn't make any sense.

Who was this person? Was she a person?

They'd sedated her, along with everyone else on the ship,
in preparation for a hard fifteen g burn, since there was still
another formation of Telestine ships out from Earth on their
tails, and they had to beat them to Venus. The inertial
dampeners might keep them alive, but at that unthinkable
acceleration, they'd be spinning and retching and vomiting just
a minute into the burn.

The problem with hard burn, Pike considered
philosophically from his place on the cargo bay floor, was that

you didn't actually pass out. You lay there and had what could only be described as gravity nightmares, where your brain slowed to a sluggish crawl, and then you started to wonder if the human brain had really been designed for this sort of thing, and you came to the inescapable conclusion that it hadn't, and you started to picture it actually melting into goo—

He heard the too-quick footsteps of someone moving at a normal pace and then a searing pain as Rychenkov jabbed a cocktail of drugs into Pike's chest.

"*Up.*" Strong arms looped under his and hauled him upright.

"Wh'th'*hell.*" The protest was plaintive.

"Cockpit. Now." Rychenkov snaked Pike's arm over his shoulders, none too gently, and did most of the walking.

Pike was in full-on twitch mode by the time they arrived. The drugs seemed to have set his chest on fire, but his brain was still moving a bit too slowly for comfort while his legs and arms flopped around, having acquired a mind of their own.

He was glad Walker couldn't see him right now. He leaned over to look at the sensor screens and nearly banged his head directly into him. "There's a *ship.*"

"I know." Rychenkov hauled Pike's head upright. Pale eyes stared into his. "Drugs hitting yet?"

"Close." Pike's body gave a convulsive shudder. "Who's the ship? It's close."

"It's Nhean."

"He sent a ship?" The man's concern was oddly touching. Maybe that was the drugs.

"He's *on* the ship." Rychenkov made sure Pike wasn't going to fall out of his chair and then leaned back. "Says he needs to come on board, but he can't dock while we're at this acceleration."

"We'll get to Venus soon."

"We've still got feathers on our tail. We can't exactly stop in a residential area."

Pike struggled to pull his mind through the fog of the sedatives. "But … after we left that last ship adrift, they shouldn't have been able to track us. They're millions of kilometers away. How are they tracking us?"

Rychenkov eyed him with a heavy look. "That's the question, isn't it?"

Pike felt himself sober up in a hurry. He'd been on the *Aggy* long enough to see how Rychenkov operated. The man was quick to swear and throw things and get in fistfights. He got angry easily and then dropped his anger up readily enough, at least once someone's nose was bleeding.

Or so Pike had thought. It turned out, he realized now, that he had never actually seen Rychenkov when he was angry. When Rychenkov was angry, he went entirely, eerily still.

Pike rubbed his eyes. "You sound like a guy who knows something. What happened?"

"We should have known to look when this all started." Rychenkov looked away, movements tight. Pike could see him berating himself.

"What *happened*?" Pike repeated.

"There's a locator beacon on board." Rychenkov leaned back in his chair. "Someone on this ship … is sending a signal to the Telestines."

Pike went cold.

"Ours might have turned on when we—"

"It's Telestine-made," Rychenkov interrupted him. "Your fancy computer man Nhean figured that out right quick, once we knew what we were looking for. We've been trailing a big-ass sign behind us this whole damned time while we've been trying to shake 'em."

"We have to find out who it is." Pike pushed himself up.

"You got that right." Rychenkov sighed. "Look. He said I shouldn't wake you up for this. I promised I wouldn't, but ... you're my guy. Been a damned good first mate. Wasn't going to do you like that."

He froze. "What the hell does that mean?"

"It means ... we know who it's gotta be, right?" Rychenkov held up his palms, a gesture of peace. "Pike, I know you don't want to hear it. He says you've been traveling with her, you know her, right? But she was *made* by them. He sent over a scan of what she is." His fingers tapped at the screen.

Pike looked away, his heart pounding.

"Look at it. *Look* at it. And what she did in the cargo bay? I mean, our *former* cargo bay? She left quite a mess down there. And Pike," Rychenkov's voice was harsh, his anger barely contained. "No *human* could ever do something like that. Pike, you were the one who hauled me into this saying I had to accept the truth, right? Now it's your turn."

Pike forced himself to turn his head, and flinched.

"She's not human. She *can't* be human. She might look human, but whatever they did to her ... we just can't risk having her around. I mean, what if ... we're next?"

The scan must have been taken at dinner. Nhean was seated, hands forward and holding a fork and knife. He remembered the spread of food Nhean had put out, and felt anger churn through him. Light conversation, toasts ... and the other man scanning them the whole time.

He studied the scans. Pike knew his own frame in a moment, the tallest of the three. He could see the traces of his bones and a few screws and plates from the time his leg had gotten crushed in a cargo vise. He shuddered involuntarily at the memory.

The girl ... the girl was almost all metal. It lined her bones. It even extended partially into the ligaments and tendons and muscles. It lay along her bones in a tracery that was half grotesque, half beautiful.

Everything they built was beautiful. Pike's hands clenched. "She's not—" he managed.

"She's not what?" To his surprise, Rychenkov sat back, watching him.

"Does it matter? You're going to go kill her, right? Best way to turn off the beacon?"

"I want to know why you care. You care when you kill people, I know that. But why do you care about *her*, specifically?"

Pike dropped back into the copilot's chair. His legs were shaking. He let out his breath in a sigh and shook his head. It kept moving on its own: *no, no, no.* As if he could make it be just by saying the word.

"She wants to be more than she was made to be. She—we left Nhean's place because I didn't trust him with her, and she wanted to do the mission he'd talked about, anyway. I don't know what she saw on that lab, but I know I'd be bitter as hell if it was me. I'd never go back, I'd just run. She keeps going back. She wants to help us and she doesn't *know* any of us. She wasn't raised with humans, she just wants to help. She ... *is* human. At least, I thought maybe she'd have the chance to be one when this was all over." He met Rychenkov's eyes. "I wanted her to make it."

Rychenkov's shoulders slumped. He let out his breath slowly.

"You want me to leave you here? I'll do it quick." He'd taken out a handheld directional EM scanner, showing a spike of activity from the direction of the cargo bay.

"No. I'll come with you."

"You're gonna be seeing this in your head for years, buddy."

"I know." Pike lifted his shoulders. "But I have to see. I won't fight you."

"Right." Rychenkov stood. "Come on."

They both stared at the tracker as they walked. It blipped, faster and faster, as they came around the corner to where the crew lay sprawled and half-conscious.

She was in the corner, huddled alone and—Pike saw now —entirely defenseless. She'd chosen a tiny space, like any animal.

She wasn't a machine. After everything, she wasn't a machine.

He was moving toward her, as in a dream, when Rychenkov stopped abruptly.

"Huh." The man's voice was entirely baffled. "Well, I'll be damned."

Don't draw this out. Pike closed his eyes in pain. "What?" He didn't look around.

"You should see this." Rychenkov's face was a puzzle. He

held the tracker in his hand and looked up as Pike came to stand beside him.

The bar from the tracker pointed nearby, but not to the girl.

"This is why you don't shoot first, I guess." Rychenkov glanced over. "Fancy that, Pike. Wasn't your girl."

The bar pointed unmistakably at Charlie.

CHAPTER FORTY-NINE

Halfway between Earth and Venus
Freighter Agamemnon

The sound of the slap echoed through the cargo hold. Charlie jerked awake with a gasp. His cuffed hands caught on the chair and his face came up, white with shock.

Rychenkov examined his palm disappointedly, as if he could do better.

"Talk, you son of a bitch."

"What?" Charlie sank back against the chair. "I'm still ... I don't know—"

Pike held up the locator beacon. Charlie's pen. His "good luck charm." Now turned off, it was slim and elegant, a metal rod with a faint curve to it that suggested the stem of a plant, like the graceful line of an aspen tree. Pike's mouth twisted as he looked at it.

Charlie swallowed.

"Here's what I don't get." Pike crouched down next to him. "By the way, before we start, though ... you might be thinking I'm a straight-talking Earther, not all that good with lies, right?" He saw the flash of contempt in Charlie's eyes. "Yeah, you'd be right. Didn't see through you when I should've. Unfortunately for you, there's a few people here who are better at that shit than me."

"Who?" Charlie twisted and craned.

In the shadows behind him, two figures shifted silently. Howie and Gabriela. Pike saw the gleam of a knife.

"Not important. Just something to think about." Pike held up the locator beacon again. "So back to what I don't get—because I'm not all that good with the plots and the lies, you see—why'd you come with me? You didn't know what she was."

Charlie stared at him for a long moment.

The blow, when it came, sent the chair over sideways and Charlie gave a yell as the its side crushed down on his arm. He arched with pain. Blood was running from the corner of his mouth.

Rychenkov looked more pleased with that hit. He and Pike both tilted their heads to look at Charlie.

"It was the best bet." Charlie spat blood and glared up at Pike. "You smart enough to understand that? I wasn't going to get anything from that admiral if I stayed around. She keeps her mouth closed—so do all her officers. Wasn't going to get anything from the rich bastard, either, and his servant's a useless ass-wit."

"So you came with me, because...."

Charlie gave him a look that said he should know, but

flinched when Rychenkov raised his hand again.

"The more time we spent together, the more you'd trust me." His voice was desperate. "That was it, that was all. I thought when we got back, you'd find out what their plan was and where the Dawning was and then I could get you to tell me."

"That was what this was? You wanted to know—" Pike broke off. He could see it all in his head again: Charlie grabbing at him to demand if *she* was the Dawning; Charlie suggesting, over and over, that they should give her back; Charlie freaking out as the Telestine ship had approached. "He wants her back," Pike said slowly. "He's afraid someone in the Telestine military will figure it out, and he needs her back to take them down. That's it, isn't it?"

Charlie hunched his shoulders and twisted, trying to take the pressure off his arm. "Yeah," he finally said, his voice hoarse with pain.

"And you didn't know what she was. Must've been a shock. And then you realized you could turn her in. You turned on the beacon, waited for us to give in and stop running...." Pike looked around himself at the others. "And then what?" He looked back at Charlie.

"What d'you mean?" But Charlie knew. He had gone still.

Rychenkov hauled the chair up without a word. The knife appeared silently under Charlie's nose.

"You can cut a man a lot," Rychenkov said gravely, "before he dies."

Charlie glared ice at him. "Coward. Cock-sucking cow—"

"Wrong." Rychenkov twisted his hand.

Charlie screamed. Blood was running from under his eye.

"Next time I take the eye," Rychenkov said. "You don't need eyes to talk. You don't need anything but ears and a mouth. You remember that."

Pike's hands clenched. "Charlie." He tried to keep his voice level. "Talk."

"You're not this cold." Charlie's voice was desperate. "You wouldn't—"

"Yeah, maybe I wouldn't. I don't like this. So maybe you talk, and I persuade him not to kill you."

Charlie looked between them.

"Maybe if you talk," Pike said quietly, "he'll like your reason. We know you did it. You admitted you did it. We just want to know why, huh?"

Charlie's eye squinted in pain. "Fine." He hung his head. "But you should know."

"Revenge," Pike said promptly. "The lab crashed. We killed your daughter and your wife. That's it, right?"

Charlie began to laugh. His head dropped back. The blood left a jagged trace across one cheek before it dripped onto his shirt, then onto the floor.

"It was them. It was always them. But you didn't kill 'em." He turned his head, his face warped with hatred. "You would have. You would have left them to die when the labs went down. Just good luck they weren't there."

"So they really weren't there?" Pike shook his head. None of it made sense.

"Let *me* guess." Nhean spoke at last from the shadows behind Charlie's chair. Only the faint tremble in his movements betrayed the drugs coursing though his veins; otherwise, he was as elegant as always. "You received word from an anonymous source that your daughter and your wife might still be alive. It didn't specify *them*, of course—just that certain missing persons might be found in the labs. You didn't know who got you that information. It didn't come through on the normal Rebellion channels, it was just a whisper passed between the communities. Everyone had lost someone, of course."

Charlie had gone still. He didn't look behind him.

"You had a plan." Nhean leaned close to whisper in Charlie's ear. "You talked about it before you joined the Rebellion. You were going to use them. You hated the Telestines for what they'd done, so no one was going to expect it. You'd infiltrate the cell, kill a few Telestines, and then someday you'd get a shot. You'd be able to find your families again."

Charlie was shaking. His face was pale.

"You thought it was all there. That they were on the lab. And then...." Nhean stood. His face was a mask. "Then, when you went into the labs, there was nothing but a comm unit. The Telestine on the other end gave you a choice—he could find your family for you, but you would go back to the Rebellion as his agent. You would betray them when and where he chose."

"Yes. That was—yes." The words were quick.

Too quick. Pike frowned, confused.

But Nhean knew. "The others didn't want to do it, did they?"

Charlie's face went still. His shoulders were hunched.

"There were two others who went with you. Oh, yes, I know about that." Nhean's head tilted. "I saw it all. I wondered why it was that I saw two of them die and the other not. Of course, I was rather more occupied with Pike at the time. And I admit, it all rather fell out of my head after that. An oversight. I should have known when you showed up."

"He said he'd give them up," Charlie whispered. "You don't understand. He was doing experiments on them but he said he'd give them back to me."

"He was never doing experiments on them." Nhean's voice was cold as deep winter. "They were dead minutes after they were taken, you poor fool."

"No!" Charlie twisted in his chair. "Then why—"

"For this!" Nhean yelled the words at last. "For *this*. To make you betray us! He didn't know who, he didn't know when. He just knew that if he took enough, eventually one of the ones left behind would join the Rebellion—and there, they'd be ready to be turned into his agent. He *knew*. He's been planning this for *years*."

Charlie had slumped in the chair. His chest was shaking.

"Years." Nhean's voice finally calmed from the frightful and uncharacteristic rage. "Years, you poor, poor fool. He's been planning to use you for years." Nhean finally turned away.

No one spoke. Even Rychenkov had fallen away in the face of Nhean's rage—and Charlie's grief. The man was sobbing, the most broken sound Pike had ever heard. It echoed in the cargo bay as the others looked around, uncomfortable, but still angry.

The sound of the gun cocking startled all of them. Even Charlie jerked up, out of instinct alone.

"You ... were ... *not*," the girl said, shaking with rage, "the only person ... who lost someone."

The gun went off with a hollow *crack-boom* that raced around the cargo bay. The chair tipped with the force of the shot, and blood streamed away from Charlie's head onto the scratched and dented floor.

CHAPTER FIFTY

Mercury, outside New Seattle City
Mining Rover Fifty-Seven

Jeremiah Kim looked up to the sky and saw death approach, swiftly and silently.

Jeremiah was a practical sort of man. Work hard, keep your head down. Survive. You got whatever work you could, and you did it well, and hopefully your employer kept up their end of the bargain and paid you.

Did he want to be a miner? No. He'd heard mining was hot, sweaty work even on Earth, before the fuggers, but those mines had never come close to what it was like on Mercury.

Mercury, where the mines were automated, they said.

Automated. Yeah, right.

They had some vehicles, sure, little rigs you could climb into that kept you cool as you oversaw the array of bots climbing down into the depths and coming back up with cages of ore to dump onto the belts.

Problem was, those bots broke down pretty regularly. Something about it being four hundred and thirty degrees celsius on the surface in direct sunlight, and only hotter as you got down toward the core. That's why the rolling cities tended to stay just on the terminator between eternal night and day, where the weather was a balmy seventy degrees celsius. But sometimes you get left behind, the sun rises higher, and the parched landscape bakes to a dull, glowing red. That's when you hightail it back to the terminator. Keep the sun less than ten degrees above the horizon, and you'll live—that's what they'd told him.

They never told him what to do when a Telestine fleet appeared in the sky.

He'd seen Telestine ships show up before, sure, but always singly or in pairs. Never twenty or thirty at a time.

Jeremiah leaned back in the seat of his rig and stared up at the activity swarming above. *Ain't nothing for it,* he thought. *Nothing for me to do.* Let the city admins figure it out—he'd ask them what was up when he returned—assuming there was a city still there when he returned.

Chasm Five had an ore vein that ran deeper than any of the others, and every twenty four months when their long rolling day started over, he had to descend farther into the depths of Five. This was his third time here. The rig always seemed to climb slowly at the end of the shift, too, like it was tired; sometimes it wavered and paused, and he felt an uncharacteristic surge of fear that it would break down and he'd be stuck down here. Nineteen minutes, that's how long he'd have before the suit gave out.

Something serious must be going down, because all of the comm lines were lighting up. He propped his feet on the desk and closed his eyes, waiting for his mining bots to return. *Ain't nothing for it*, he repeated to himself. They'd call him if they needed anything, and he was far too old to fall for the excitement of everything going to hell.

You could only live in this world for so long before *that* novelty wore off. Hell, you'd think the mines would break anyone of the idea of excitement.

Ten minutes later, he drove the rig out of Chasm Five and when the scene fully unfolded to his view, he saw what everyone was on the comms about.

He'd known about the new Exile Fleet, known about the shipyards. Worst kept secret on Mercury. Then again, there weren't many people *on* Mercury, and most of them were like Jeremiah—they didn't care about anything unless it was about to hurt them. He'd never decided how he felt about the Rebellion, in truth. He knew he didn't buy the passionate declarations their pilots made in the pubs about freedom and dignity and honor.

But he also didn't care too much for the Secretary General's speeches about laying low. He wasn't the sort to slink around like he was apologizing for being born.

Yet, he had to admit, it was sure something to see that fleet lifting off. You forgot how big a spaceship could be. Hell, some of these even looked like stations, almost as big as the rolling city themselves. He held his hand up to shield his eyes from the glare as they climbed into the atmosphere, fighters swirling around them in elegant formations. There was something poetic about it. Something that almost made him want to join up so he could be part of this sort of thing.

It was probably too late for that, though. What with the Telestine ships blocking out half the sky.

Jeremiah wasn't a man who whistled a lot, or swore a lot, or—really—said much at all, ever. He didn't even like to talk to himself in his head. Right now, however, he had a pretty strong internal monologue, and it was composed almost entirely of awestruck swearing.

And then the first Telestine ship fired, and his mind discovered one instinct that never left the human race: survival. His rig was winding slowly around the tracks that led to the garage complex, and he would be helpless as he slid under the bulk of the battle that was clearly about to start. He watched a human frigate take a penetrating shot to its side and spin out of formation above and ahead of him. It careened and tumbled back toward the surface, righting herself only just before hitting the ground in a blaze of engines that liquefied the tracks ahead.

Goddammit. Jeremiah checked the seals on his suit, threw the door open, and tumbled out onto the baking ground. He pushed himself up and ran, cursing his old body, cursing every instinct that had brought him here, cursing himself for taking this shift. He cursed the reaction that was making his palms slick with sweat. He cursed the people who'd chosen Mercury as a place to build the fleet, and the Telestines who'd finally found them, and he ran as the massive ships above him blocked out the stars and swung into formation, shards of glass and metal and debris raining down as the battle was joined in earnest.

Only when he had pushed himself into the shadow of the

garage did he look up properly, and his breath caught in his throat. Missiles were streaking silently through the black. The wreck of a fighter—human or Telestine, he couldn't tell anymore—streaked toward one of the rolling cities on the horizon and hit the edge in a burst of silver and gold.

Another Telestine cruiser was orbiting just overhead, less than a a few dozen kilometers high. And it rained down mass-driver slugs heading toward him. Toward the city he'd come to call home. New Seattle, a massive rolling behemoth that specialized in steel smelting. Dozens of slugs found their mark: explosions ripped through the upper reaches of the city and stray slugs pounded the regolith all around him.

And just in time, two new Exile Fleet cruisers moved to intercept the Telestine ship, and the orbital battle was on, New Seattle now ignored and left to burn.

But it still rolled, slowly, inexorably, toward the terminator on the horizon.

And then he realized with a start that he was still alive. The Telestines hadn't wiped them off the map yet. Someone, somehow, was finally standing their ground.

It was the sort of thing that could give an old man hope.

CHAPTER FIFTY-ONE

Mercury
Bridge, Venus Fleet Ship Resurgence

"Ten minutes to Mercury orbit, ma'am. Deceleration burn almost complete."

"Thank you." Walker nodded over at Larsen. She raised her voice, out of habit. "We'll be——" She broke off with a laugh as she looked around herself at the vacant bridge. Walker cleared her throat and started again, volume lowered. "Our first priority is covering her team until they get the Mercury fleet up into orbit."

She spoke directly to Larsen. Aside from the two of them, the bridge was empty. Splitting her Exile Fleet personnel between not just one but two new fleets had stretched them thin. There were enough desks and chairs for a full crew, and Nhean had offered what people he had, but she had declined.

There was an engineer, somewhere below in the bowels of

the ship, and there were two women in the gunnery chambers. Nhean had explained that reloading was still one of the things that occasionally fouled up in maneuvers, as the g forces and inertial dampening slid the ammunition slightly out of place.

Before, on the *Intrepid*, she was continually running into people. Each crew quarters was crammed to capacity and the mess required almost round-the-clock shifts to keep everyone fed. But now she felt alone, on a ghost ship.

She hoped that feeling wasn't a premonition.

Larsen mumbled under his breath, fiddling with his chair. "Piece of shit ... this chair actually reclines. *Reclines*, Laura. And swivels. That bastard Nhean spared no expense with this fleet. Makes you wonder what else he's been holding out on."

She gave a smile at Larsen—she could always count on him to notice the little details. "I'm glad you're here, Scott."

"With you to the—" Larsen broke off and cleared his throat. "Glad to be here, ma'am."

"Oh, say it." She was actually smiling. "We may go down with the ship. It's the end of the world, Larsen. Any last words?"

He gave a brief look at his screens, and then actually considered the question.

"I miss Johnson Station," he said finally. "I miss being young—"

"You're twenty-seven!"

He shrugged. "Miss being a kid, that's all. Carefree, and all that, not having to worry about fleets and rebellions and shit. When we were kids...." He tipped his chair back and smiled lopsidedly. "You'll think this is crazy, but do you remember how we used to talk about going out to the stars? We'd talk about what planets there might be, or just finding an asteroid, making our own colony?"

Walker stood frozen, watching him. Her breath shortened.

"I never stopped dreaming about that," he admitted.

Her answer was quieter than she intended. "Neither did I."

He looked at her, and she remembered the child he'd been, white-blond hair and a curved nose from when he'd broken it playing "Hide and Retake Earth." He was practically her little brother and annoying as hell. He'd grown into a man sometime when she wasn't watching. He shrugged. "You? Were you thinking you'd settle down or something? You know, I always kind of thought you and Pike—"

Walker found her voice hastily. "That's enough of that."

"Right." Larsen looked away. He was holding back something that might have been a smile. "Cheer up, Laura. I'd say we've got at least double the odds we usually have of making it out of stuff like this. This ship's *nice*."

"That it is," Walker murmured, rubbing the soft leather armrest with relish. She brought up the holographic display and hesitated only a moment before dipping her fingers into it. She dragged the images until the shadows of the eight carriers lay broadside to the approaching Telestine fleet.

Her heart leaped as the ships glided smoothly into motion toward their assigned places. This had always been how she wanted to fight: directing ships like a composer. It was torture to shout commands and wait for the rest of the captains to bring their ships into alignment. She had dreamed of the formations she could wield and the maneuvers she could accomplish if only she could be the one responding to the whole battle by instinct alone.

And now, in what might well be her final battle, she would at last have that chance.

"Decel burn complete. Entering high Mercury orbit."

She nodded acknowledgement. "Tell me what you see, Larsen." Nothing had appeared on the screens yet.

"You have what I'm guessing is an incoming scout force: two destroyers and what's reading as a small contingent of fighters. We barely beat them here. And a larger Telestine force incoming behind them. Twelve ships."

"That's all?" She frowned over at him.

"I've been thinking about that." Larsen swiveled in his chair. "I'm pretty sure there'd be more if they had the Dawning. I don't think he built a whole fleet. I'm sure his new fleet is big and all—Tel'rabim doesn't seem like a bloke who does half-measures—but I think he was counting on being able to use her to control the usual military ships remotely."

Walker glanced over in surprise. "Hadn't thought of that."

"Yeah. Just a guess, but—" His voice changed. "Heads up, you should be seeing them on your screen in three, two … one."

They flickered into existence on the holograph, moving low and fast to cut around them and down onto Mercury itself.

"Oh, no, you don't," Walker muttered. She reached out to drag two of the carriers into a dive and zoomed in to start maneuvering the fighters.

Nhean had been reluctant to let her use his fleet, that much was obvious, and she could see why. If this was her ship, her program, she would never give it up. A ship, once moved, would scout its surroundings and choose its targets based on a calculation of the velocity, structural read, and assumed firepower of enemy forces, all automatically, only requiring direct intervention by a live crew member if something went wrong. Even the pilot-less fighter groups would change formation as they were picked off, and the targeting systems automatically guided ships out of one another's line of fire. It was a thing of beauty.

The two carriers plunged on her instructions.

Larsen whistled. "They move quick."

"Us or the Telestines?"

"Both. I tell you, I'm glad we have Nhean on our side. He's like ... what do you call someone who's the same, but different?"

"You've always had a way with words, Scott."

"A foil. Didn't you pay attention in English class?

"No. Focus."

He tapped at the screen and one of the Telestine fighters blipped out of existence. He gave a self-satisfied smile. "I *am* focusing."

"Show-off," Walker muttered. She opened her mouth to ask what he'd meant by foils, and then lost the question as the fighters engaged in earnest.

They danced. There was no other word for it. They moved together as if held by some invisible force, as if each formation was one being. They slipped between the Telestine fighters and curved around in tight arcs that manned ships would never be able to hold.

No limits. It was ship against ship now, and Walker allowed herself a small smile. Had Tel'rabim ever thought humans would make something like this—or had he thought they would roll over and die quietly as he sent his ships through the solar system?

It was time for payback. She dragged the other carriers forward to form a wall and gestured for all of them to advance.

She was pleased to see the Telestine destroyers adjust course within seconds. They were banking to avoid the wall of death moving toward them. Unfortunately for them, Telestine ships had their guns on the front, not the sides, and they had just presented a very appealing target.

"All batteries fire." Walker could not hold back her smile now.

"All batteries firing, ma'am." Larsen jerked his head at the window. "Why don't you go look?"

She turned her head away from the window and shuddered. "Because it is unnatural to have windows on the bridge, that's why."

But it was impossible to resist now that he'd said it. She indicated to the two outermost ships to begin flanking the Telestines, cutting off their retreat, and then she went to the window to watch the battle unfold.

Mercury shone below them. She could barely make out the glitter of the newly-built shipyards attached to a handful of the rolling cities far below, and she gave a quick glance at the clock. Would King have launched yet?

The cannons captured her attention. Rail guns fired a steady stream of slugs that streaked away into the night, detectable to the naked eye but marked by the computer. And the ion cannons—tech Nhean had stolen from the Telestines, no doubt—fired glowing orbs that traveled just slow enough for the eye to follow. Nhean's artillery systems, it turned out, were just as excellent as his ships.

"Ma'am—look." Larsen's voice was hushed.

Walker caught her breath. She had seen ships blink out of existence on the displays, and she had seen the destruction of her own fighters, but she had never watched such large-scale destruction with her own eyes. A Telestine destroyer blew apart. One was caught, and then the other. The first tumbled away and the furthest carrier turned its weapons accordingly. By the time Walker looked back, the second was gone as well in a little cloud of debris that began to fall toward Mercury.

"Just fighter cleanup now, ma'am."

She let out her breath slowly. "And then the main fleet."

"And then the main fleet," Larsen agreed.

"You know...." Walker looked over at him. "I'm beginning to think we actually have a chance."

He looked grim. "I can't help but wonder though, if that wasn't just a probe. A test. Tel'rabim's way of seeing what our shiny new fleet is capable of before he engages it directly with his main force."

She shrugged, and motioned the ships forward with a quick gesture of her hand. "I suppose we're about to find out."

CHAPTER FIFTY-TWO

Halfway between Earth and Venus
Freighter Agamemnon

"So how do we get out of this mess?" Pike leaned back against one of the cargo crates and looked over at Rychenkov. "You got any bright ideas?"

Rychenkov didn't reply for so long that Pike constructed the answer in his head. It was the answer he'd been waiting to hear, in truth, since they came on the *Aggy* two days ago: that this wasn't Rychenkov's problem. That they'd gotten exactly what they deserved for poking the bear. Pike had *heard* Rychenkov say that before. Granted, that had been while scraping Howie off the floor of a backwater Kuiper Belt bar, but the principle was the same. You didn't pick fights you couldn't win.

Rychenkov was tossing the locator beacon up in the air and catching it without looking. He was always moving. Never liked being still. His eyes were distant now. And then he tossed the beacon to Pike, who barely caught it.

"There's your answer."

"What is?"

"They're homing in on to the beacon, right?"

"They were. We ... I mean ... *she*, took care of that first scout ship. The other pursuing ships won't catch up to us for at least twenty minutes...."

"The fleet's assembling at Mercury," Nhean reminded them both. "As soon as our fleet shows up there, they'll know that's where we're taking her—they'll know our trajectory."

The girl said nothing. She hadn't spoken since she'd killed Charlie, and she had curled into a little ball on top of one of the cargo crates with one foot dangling. Pike looked up at her now and she managed a small smile.

Her eyes kept going back to the dark spot on the floor, though. *What the hell are you, Dawn*, he thought.

The body was wrapped in a tarp at the edge of the room, but they hadn't been able to get all the blood up.

Pike turned the locator beacon over in his hands while Rychenkov considered. "I thought you said she only worked on the feathers. The silver Telestine ships. At Earth."

"She does."

"So ... you *might* take her there."

"I told you." Nhean's voice was impatient. "I need her to help me deploy the virus at Mercury—that's where Tel'rabim's fleet is headed. She needs to be—"

"Yeah, but you *might* take her to Earth. I mean, if I were a Telestine, and I saw you taking her to Earth, I *might* think that you were planning on infiltrating their system *that* way...."

Rychenkov looked at Nhean.

"Ah," Nhean said softly.

There was a significant pause, and Pike looked between the two of them. "Someone tell me what's going on."

The girl's finger rose, pointing at Rychenkov.

"Yep, she's got the right of it." Rychenkov sounded annoyed. "Hell."

"*What?*"

Rychenkov stood wearily. He jerked his head at the crew, pointing at Howie, Gabriela, and James. "You all go with him."

Gabriela swore. "Hijo de puta…."

"Now listen here, cowboy—" James began, but Rychenkov cut him off with a flick of his hand across his own neck.

Pike swallowed hard. He could not possibly be hearing what he thought he was hearing. "Pyotr Nikolai Rychenkov, what the hell are you doing?"

"You know what I'm doing." Rychenkov's smile was sad. "You need to get to Mercury to do … whatever it is she does." His hands waved at the girl, and he bobbed his head. "No disrespect ma'am, mind you. It's a hell of a thing."

She managed a smile. Pike got the sense that she rather liked Rychenkov.

That only made him feel worse.

Howie was scratching at the tattoo of Earth on his temple, as he always did when he was weighing his words. "There's got to be another way…." But he had no alternative to offer.

Pike shook his head. "Ry, I can't let you do this."

"Of course you can." Rychenkov smiled, and under the habitual bitterness, there was real humor. "I'm expendable, aren't I? I can lead them on a grand chase, and then, while their sensors are confused, you can flit away with them none the wiser." He waved his fingers, as if performing a magic trick.

"Set the ship to go on autopilot."

"Autopilot's easy to detect and you know it. They'll see right through that. You need someone flying some corkscrews and shit if they're going to believe that she's with me."

"What if they don't believe?"

"At least there's a chance—better than no chance at all. Look, if they aren't following me, it's not like I'll pop on over to Earth and land. I'll come after you and chase them down and take 'em out if they try to shoot you down. Right?"

"The *Aggy*'s got no weapons—s"

"So I'll ram them. Geez."

"Right." Pike swallowed hard.

Rychenkov rubbed the back of his neck. "Didn't think I'd be going out like a revolutionary, but everyone's gotta go sometime. And hey—maybe I'll make it."

He wouldn't, and they both knew it.

"Maybe you will." Pike clasped the man's hand for the last time.

"If I don't, I'll take some fuggers with me, eh? Revolutionary's promise." The man made a mock salute. He plucked the beacon out of Pike's hand and switched it on, then looked around at all of them. "Get going. Go save the world."

"Come on." Howie ushered the rest of the crew toward the door.

Nhean held up a hand to help the girl down from the cargo crate. Pike watched them disappear, and watched Rychenkov make his way toward the cockpit. The man was murmuring to himself in a mix of Russian and English as he tossed and caught the locator beacon over and over again.

He knew Pike was still there. He turned in the doorway and gave a rueful smile. "Look at me, huh?" he said. He chest shook with a silent laugh. "Dying for something. Son of a bitch, right?"

And then he was gone.

CHAPTER FIFTY-THREE

Mercury, New Jakarta City
Fighter Bay, New Jakarta Shipyard

Tocks gave a low whistle as she ran her hand over the wing of one of the new fighter jets. She crouched to stare at the underbelly and rapped her fingers against the metal. She raised her eyebrows at McAllister. "You ever seen something like this? These are *slick*."

He shrugged. If he were being honest, his missed his junky fighter left behind on the *Intrepid*. She might be a bucket of bolts, liable to die on him at any moment, but the truth was that he'd gotten used to the feel of her. He knew how to cut one engine to spin on a dime—well, as close to that as you could come when you were going that fast—he knew her quirks and how she warmed up. These new Mercury fighters were slick—Tocks was right—but they didn't have much soul.

"What's the matter?" She stood up, frowning.

"It's nothing. We should get going. The sooner we're in the air, the better." The carriers were still warming up around them, each tethered by tenuous umbilicals to the shipyards at the top of the rolling city of New Jakarta, but everyone knew that as soon as they lifted off, it was going to be go time.

"Theo…." She bit her lip, and glanced over her shoulder at Princess, who was examining his own fighter across the cramped bay of New Jakarta's shipyard. "Look, you don't have to talk to me about this. I know you're not really a talker."

"You ever meet a fighter pilot who was?"

She laughed at that. "We're all talkers, just not about things that matter."

He cracked a genuine smile at that and leaned against the bird, crossing his arms. She was right.

"That reminds me, I'll tell you this joke I heard—later, though, after all this." She waved her hand at the sky. "Gotta have something to look forward to, or our lives are going to be entirely without meaning once the Telestines are all little smears." She cocked her head, considering. "What color do they bleed?"

"Tocks…."

"Right. Right." She sobered, sighed. "Look, you were closest to Fisheye."

"Don't—I can't—"

"I'm just *saying*, let's all fly like that crazy bastard today, okay?"

He blinked. He was *not* going to embarrass himself, here, on this strange flight deck. In his mind, to distract himself from Fisheye's memory, he did some quick calculations of the burn required to get into Mercury orbit with less than one-third g pulling them down.

"I can't think of a better way to honor him," she added.

"Huh?"

"Fisheye." She waved her hand in front of his face. "You in there? You need to be on point today. I said fly like Fisheye, not drink like him." She changed her voice to the dead man's accent. "Hey. *Che boludo!*"

McAllister gave a laugh. "Right. So you think we should all be crazy as shit, huh?"

"No one could do crazy like he could," she said, almost philosophically. "But we can try. And if we pull it off, man— the Telestines aren't gonna know what hit 'em."

He froze. There, across the bay, was a familiar shape. "Uh … right." He clapped Tocks on the shoulder. "I'll be right back."

She cast a look over her shoulder, seeing his target, and grinned. "Don't be too long."

He wasn't even listening anymore. He strode to the edge of the bay, shiny new flight suit boots thudding heavily on the metal, and he saw her look him up and down appreciatively.

"I wasn't sold on the uniform, but if you like it…." His grin died, and his voice trailed off. This wasn't the time for jokes. "How'd you know I was down here?"

"Where else would you be? New Jakarta doesn't have any pubs. Dry city, you know." King sounded like she was trying not to laugh. "And knowing you, if you're not at the bar, you're at work."

He nodded. There was the habitual distance between them, the protocol they followed rigidly, and all of a sudden, he realized how meaningless it was. He pulled her into his arms and felt hers come around him, holding tight.

"Promise me something." She had buried her face in the front of his uniform.

"Sure. Anything."

She picked her head up to look into his eyes. "Come back."

He tried to smile, and couldn't.

"I mean it," she said fiercely.

"You know I can't promise that."

She wrapped her fingers in his uniform and pulled him down for a kiss. "Don't give up," she said quietly, her mouth close to his. "You're the best pilot I've ever seen. I mean that. You've got more smarts than all of them. Don't go on some crusade for Fisheye."

"I do that, he'll give me an earful in hell for the rest of eternity." McAllister smiled and cupped her face in one hand. "I'm not going to go on some crusade, and I'm not going to give up. But you know I'm gonna go take a few of those fuggers out."

"Yeah." She smiled up at him. "I know."

"You come back too."

She smiled. "I'll try."

A klaxon went off, too-loud and right above them, and they both jumped.

"I think that's for me," he said, wryly.

"You think?" She was laughing. "I knew it must mean something." She kissed him again, fiercely. "Up to the bridge for me. Good hunting, Mr. McAllister."

He gave a salute and watched her disappear into the ship,

and then he turned and jogged over to their fighters.

"All right." He leaned in to the tiny contingent, glancing up at Tocks, Princess, and the other pilots he'd brought with him from the *Intrepid.* "Let's get these beauties in the loading tubes before all hell breaks loose."

CHAPTER FIFTY-FOUR

Near Mercury
Nhean Tang Shuttle

"No."

"Pike—"

"Absolutely *not*." Pike's fingers clenched. "No. I refuse."

"It isn't yours to refuse." Nhean's voice was as sharp as he had ever heard it. "We need to deploy this virus or we will have no chance at all of stopping Tel'rabim's fleet. Every ship we have is dedicated to holding him off long enough to get us onto the flagship. That plan is already in motion—the *entire* Rebellion is there and committed—all three fleets. Exile, Mercury, and ... mine. If you refuse to do this, they die."

"Deploy it remotely!"

"We *can't* deploy it remotely. She needs to be in direct physical contact, and deliver it in person." There were white lines around Nhean's mouth.

They had been over this three times during the course of the journey, each at increasing volume. The tiny confines of Nhean's shuttle were as gorgeously appointed as his estates on Venus, and the plush carpeting and filigreed accents were only making Pike's mood blacker.

"Try harder," he said now. His fingers twisted on the arm of the couch, and he hoped in some petty part of his mind that his nails would scratch the leather—where the hell did he get real *leather*?

"If we could, this would be different. If we could do that, we would have been able to spare the entire Rebellion fleet. We can't."

"But...." Pike tilted his head back. "I don't like it."

"You have my word that she will not be harmed by this." Nhean's voice was soft.

Pike looked over at the girl. She nodded at him gravely.

"You're running a virus made to kill Tel'rabim's machinery ... through someone built with parts of his machinery in her." Pike repeated the words, as he had three times before. Why did neither of them seem to understand how dangerous this was? "Why are you not worried about this?"

"Because...." Nhean stopped to pick his words carefully. "Because this is what I do," he said finally.

"So you're telling me there's no risk at all?"

"Not at all. We will likely face some opposition within the flagship, yes. You will be coming under fire. Are you not worried about that?"

Pike caught the deflection. "So there is danger."

"I'm saying there's danger to all of us from the aliens on

that ship. I'm saying this mission is dangerous." Nhean had the look of a man only barely controlling his temper. "And I am saying that there is no other way to accomplish this, and we have to work with what we have. Doing this in the middle of a battle isn't ideal, I will grant you, but I would sell *myself* into hell for this chance." He gave a sharp laugh. "I guess I am."

That didn't make Pike feel any better at all.

"Pike." Nhean's voice was uncompromising. "You care deeply for Walker, do you not?"

Pike felt his cheeks grow warm. "What the hell does that have to do with anything?"

"I notice you haven't protested *her* involvement in this plan," Nhean said simply. "Walker is just as vulnerable to the risks as the girl is, arguably more so."

"That's *different*."

"How?" Nhean gestured at the girl. "It's now obvious that she could have easily killed you after you rescued her. She could have taken a shuttle and left from Venus and never gone to the lunar base."

Pike swallowed hard.

"She's here because she wants to be," Nhean said. He looked over at the girl. "Is that correct?"

She nodded.

Nhean looked back at Pike.

"It's a risk," Pike said again, miserably.

The girl reached out to him. Her fingers were warm on his arm. The same fingers that had squeezed the trigger to kill Charlie. The same hands she'd used to take out a squad of Telestine soldiers—he wished they'd caught that one on camera. She smiled.

"*You* think you'll be okay?" Pike asked her.

She shrugged, but nodded easily. Her meaning was clear: *no, but what other choice is there?*

"Fine." Pike covered his face with his other hand, a futile attempt at shielding someone, anyone, from the reality of their situation. He lowered the hand and raised his head, nodding at Nhean. "Fine. What's the rest of the plan?"

Nhean shook his head, apparently pleased to be finished with that. A holograph appeared over the exquisite coffee table: a ship at once sleek and imposing. It was almost a teardrop, designed to fly with the heavy orb at the top and the directional jets down the point. In space, there was no need for ships to be aerodynamic.

A green dot flashed near the top.

"This is—*if* their structures hold true—one of the weak points in the system." Nhean pointed at it. "A hull breach will be easier there than anywhere else. Theoretically."

"If it's not?"

"Then we hope Walker is a miracle worker. But don't worry. My intel on this is *solid.*" Nhean lifted a single eyebrow and waited for an argument.

Pike only nodded. There were no good options, as Walker had predicted. *Make the best choice, and keep moving,* echoed Walker's voice in his mind.

"Once we get in, the control chamber will be very close. We were able to acquire some scans of the fleet as they went past Venus. All of them have a bridge with a window, near the top of the ship."

Pike raised an eyebrow. "A window? Really? That's risky in a military ship."

Nhean jerked his head toward the windows on their own ship and gave a shrug. "Their technology is better than ours."

"Still." Something occurred to him. "Couldn't we just breach the bridge?"

"Ah." Nhean looked almost pleased to be able to share this knowledge. "We have reason to believe the bridge will be unoccupied—that Tel'rabim is controlling the battle remotely. On Earth, through an FTL link. Also, I believe her contact with the interface needs to be directly with her skin for it to work, yes?"

The girl nodded.

"I will be able to locate the bridge once we're inside the ship, and you will need to hold the door while she and I deploy the virus. That virus should spread quite quickly, and will disable—though not destroy—the accompanying fleet. If we're very lucky, the effect will spread to the rest of the Telestine fleet at Earth and then through the rest of the solar system."

"Could we put a self-destruct in?" Pike pictured jammed cannons, air venting.

"We could if we had time, but that's one thing we don't have. Now, I've instructed Walker not to attack the flagship at all costs, but we should work as quickly as we can. These right here are cannons, and they will be devastating to any human ships they encounter."

"How do you know all of this?"

"I had some windows into the Telestine production, and was able to ascertain small details from the ship we acquired. Their technology is, in many ways, an extension of the Telestines, themselves. I'm still only beginning to understand it."

"So their ships can be remotely guided?"

"I think that's part of it. Many of the ships *are* crewed, so I can only assume that's a superior setup." Nhean gave a rueful smile. "That, or—like us—they're unwilling to sign over all of their control to a machine, even one they built themselves. Perhaps they have some of the same reservations regarding AI that we do. Either way, there *are* Telestines on board those ships, but Tel'rabim *is* guiding the battle from Earth—that much I know."

Pike stared silently at the ship before him. He would have to leave the girl with Nhean. The fact that he would be mere yards away with a gun did little to help. He knew how easily a situation could change—a stray missile, a crashing ship. There was no safety, and the thought that he would also die with her in either of those scenarios was no comfort.

He knew what it was to wake in the night, years later, with the cold knowledge that someone you loved had seen their death coming for them, and that at the end, they'd been alone and frightened, and that you'd been powerless to help them.

You'd been powerless to help them because someone else had lied to you. And you believed them.

He wasn't sure he could survive that again.

"Pike?" Nhean's voice was soft. "Any questions?"

"No." Pike cleared his throat and rubbed at his eyes. "Any uppers you have would be good, though. I think the first course Rychenkov gave me is running out."

"Parees will have some in the cockpit."

"Thank you. I'll...." Pike looked at both of them.

The girl smiled reassuringly.

"I'll go get some of that." Pike cleared his throat and left.

Outside the room, however, he leaned against the wall and let his eyes drift closed.

And after all the years, he could still smell the smoke wafting on the air from their fields. He could hear the screams on the wind.

He forced himself to breathe. *One, two, three*—deep breaths. Then he pushed himself up from the wall and made for the cockpit as Parees's voice came over the comms:

"Final approach. We will arrive in twenty-three minutes."

CHAPTER FIFTY-FIVE

Near Mercury
Nhean Tang Shuttle

"Are you sure you want to see this?" Nhean looked over at Pike calmly.

"Yes." Pike forced himself to stand the same way Nhean did, hands linked behind his back, eyes fixed on the battle unfolding below.

The fleets had joined together, and it was chaos. Pike, for all that he could hold his own in any bar room brawl, could make neither head nor tail of the formations hurtling themselves at one another.

It was difficult, he realized, to have the first idea of the *scale* of a fleet battle until you saw one. The fleets were within range of one another's guns, and yet so distant from one another that from Nhean's shuttle, high above, one could hardly make out the tiny specks of the fighters, except when they caught the sunlight and the reflection from Mercury's surface or when the flashes of firing and impact sparked briefly against the vacuum of space.

The scale of the battle twisted again once he saw the capital ship hanging in the center of the battle. It was unlike anything Pike had ever dreamed. It was as large as a space station and larger, an upside down teardrop with elegant spurs he knew were weapons of some sort. Still, Pike was Earthborn, and he knew that large ships, like large animals, lumbered slowly.

This was space. Nothing was normal here: the giant inverted-tear-drop ship glided into formation with the rest of the fleet without a trace of delay. It was Tel'rabim's flagship, though he was not courageous enough to be here himself.

Pike's mouth twisted.

"From here," Nhean murmured, "one can almost understand the way the Telestines see the world."

"How is that?" He was glad for the distraction from his anger.

"Chaos." Nhean's eyes tracked a ship tumbling end over end and his jaw tightened as it shattered against the hull of one of the Telestine carriers. "They see the world as chaos, and sentient life as that which brings of order—and it is that order they used to find us and appropriate our world, and that they use to hunt us still."

Pike looked away. He did not want to think the way the Telestines thought.

And yet—that was how he hunted, seeking out the signs of nibbled leaves and the patterns in the paths between the trees, the tiny, ordered spaces of nests and burrows.

Behind his back, his hands clenched.

"*Sir, I've made contact with the* Intrepid. *Commander Delaney has ordered the rearguard to hold fire until we reach the flagship.*"

"Commander Delaney?" Pike looked sharply at Nhean. "The *Intrepid* is Walker's ship—I mean, the admiral."

"The admiral is commanding my fleet." Nhean's voice was impressively dry.

"*Your* fleet?"

"My fleet." Nhean nodded to ships nearly as sleek as the Telestine carriers, and yet utterly different—unmistakably human. Behind them hung yet another fleet, built not for beauty but for crude effectiveness. "I'm given to understand that Commander King now has control of the new Mercury Fleet."

"Do you know their battle plan?" Pike's eyes locked on Nhean's ships. Six clustered in the center as two swung wide to flank the battle.

"I know only that they will not destroy the flagship." Nhean's gave an elegant shrug. "I am not a military commander. I did not ask for their tactics."

"They'll be good," Pike promised him. "When we were kids—" His voice failed him unexpectedly and he finished quickly, "she was good even then."

The girl had appeared at his side at some point, a silent witness. He saw her hands clench as the flagship loomed larger in the windows. The closer they got, the more jarringly massive it was.

"Where did they *hide* it?" Pike whispered. "How could we not have seen—"

"How do you know no one did?" There were white lines

around Nhean's nose. "Why would anyone comment on it if they did? The Telestines were never prohibited from building weaponry or a fleet. Even if a few lone ships passed through the wrong region of the asteroid belt during a strange alignment, who would the humans out there tell? Who would they *think* to tell? Of course, that's assuming they weren't shot on sight."

"If Tel'rabim had been shooting down human ships.... " But his outrage trailed away into weariness. Who would have stopped Tel'rabim? Who would have even thought to ask if it were him? Ships were lost all the time out in the black. Humanity was new to space, and space was famously unforgiving of both mistakes and bad luck. No one would even think to ask questions if some of the lost cargo haulers and transport ships had stumbled across things they were not meant to see.

The flagship was so close now that he could see the patterned markings on its black hull. A wing of fighters soared past them, human made: protection for the shuttle and its irreplaceable cargo. There were no cockpits that Pike could see, and he had a memory of Walker spinning in the very center of Johnson Station, head dropped back, hair floating, her fingers dancing as she composed battles only she could see.

He swallowed against the lump rising in his throat and his fingers closed around the barrel of his rifle.

Today, they would end this. There would be no more Walkers, dreaming of a re-conquered Earth. There would be no more William Pikes, ushered onto shuttles by fathers who had numbly accepted the loss of their families.

The sound of the hull clamp was jarring, and all of them

stumbled.

"It's time." Pike's voice surprised him. He said to Nhean, "I'll go set the charges."

Nhean only nodded.

At the door, Pike turned back for a moment. Nhean was contemplative in his fury. Like Walker, apparently, he had learned to feed on it. The girl, he thought, was new to all of this. Her hands were clenched, her spine ramrod straight. Pike stared at her for a moment, silhouetted against the elegant hull of Tel'rabim's flagship, before he turned to make his way to the cargo bay.

Today, they would end this.

CHAPTER FIFTY-SIX

Mercury
Bridge, Venus Fleet Ship Resurgence

"They've reached the flagship, ma'am." Larsen swiveled in his chair. "Should I open a line to all ships?"

"Please." Walker waited for his nod before pitching her voice to carry to the comm unit on the desk. "All ships, this is the admiral. Remember our target. Remember your orders, which ships to hit and which *not* to hit. Yet." She spoke carefully, not wanting her meaning to be picked up by the Telestines.

She paused. Her eyes fixed on the Telestine fleet, glowing faintly on the holographic display. Their carriers and destroyers whipped back and forth in formations designed to destroy the human ships that were now coming at them from both sides. *Even predators have an underbelly to slice. They may have forgotten, but we have remembered.*

"The battle that is coming will be long." Her voice sounded distant. "We have been made exiles in our own land. We have been hunted almost to extinction. We have been given a slow death sentence. Today we launch the first strike to end our captivity. Today, we begin to make humanity anew. It is a new dawn."

"We are facing an enemy who has pretended to be our friend, who has pretended to speak for us. He has used our trust and our friendship to learn our weaknesses, and he hopes to kill us all in the dark blackness of our makeshift homes."

"Today, we show him that he does not know the first thing about betrayal. We show him that humans are more cunning and more terrifying than he could have imagined. Today, we show him that we are not prey, but predators, and that our retaliation will begin the end of him and his kind. The Telestines came to take our home with superior technology, and with superior force. Over those years, they have made only one mistake: we lived."

"Today, they pay for that mistake with everything they have. Take their future from them."

She heard the cheer go up on two dozen bridges as she cut the line. Larsen was staring at her, a boy again, listening to her speeches on the station. For a moment she thought he might contradict her.

"They should never have let us live," he said finally.

She nodded, and pressed the button to reopen the channel.

"Commander Delaney, are you ready?"

"Aye-aye, ma'am." She could hear the grim certainty in his voice.

"Very good. Commander King, keep your forces ready to swing. All units begin formation. Walker out."

The hair on the back of her neck stood up as she watched it unfold. Nhean's ships—no, *her* ships, her gorgeous new ships, slid down in an elegant curve under the bulk of the Telestine fleet, and Delaney's ancient Exile Fleet, ugly and lumbering, nonetheless danced through the swarm of carriers and fighters to do the same.

Walker wondered if it pained the Telestines to lose ships to something so ugly, so inelegant, as the first Exile Fleet.

The Telestines had thought that if they removed the memory of war from humanity, they would be safe. They had never realized that humanity carried war in its very DNA. They had not understood one vital fact: a weapon was not simply a machine made for the purpose of killing. Anything could be a weapon—and for humanity, anything *was*.

Tel'rabim's fleet scattered and reformed into a new formation. It was like the flight of birds, the way Pike had once described it to her. The ships split their focus, trying to drop onto the plane of battle Walker and Delaney had created, and finding themselves in the line of fire of their own ships.

"All fighter wings, engage." Walker felt the satisfaction in her voice. "Stay out of the line of fire and...." She paused. Her eyes narrowed as she stared at the screen. Was the flagship turning?

"Ma'am, the flagship is—"

"I see it." Walker cut off Larsen. His voice was high and panicked, and she gave him a look. "Stay with me." Her fingers danced over the keys. "It's facing our group, yes?"

"'Facing' is a—"

"Yes or no, Larsen? Tell me where the cannons are!"

"They can move—all the way around. They're aiming."

Walker swore. "Delaney, split your team. Get out of the direct line of fire of that flagship, we're trying to—"

"They're firing!"

But it was too late. The shot slammed into the *Resurgence*, a bolt of energy around a metal core that buckled the hull and ripped it open. Stars burst against her vision as Walker was thrown against the back wall. Could she hear screaming? Was it her own?

"Gunnery is venting!" Larsen shouted. Soon, he was crawling to Walker's side. "Admiral?!"

"I'm okay. I'm okay." Walker pushed herself up on his shoulder and hauled him to his feet. The world was tilting. "We have—we have to get out of the way. We can't take another hit."

The floor buckled beneath her feet and she froze.

"*Bridge sealed*," announced an AI voice.

Both of them turned, slowly, to the technical readouts.

What had been a ship was now a husk. The engineering decks were shredded, the cannons were gone. She could only assume the skeleton crew was all dead, or dying.

"*Walker!*" Delaney's voice came clear on the radios. "*Walker, get out of there!*" His voice was distant. "*All batteries fire, draw their attention! They cannot be allowed to take out the admiral's ship, do you hear me? Protect the* Resurgence *at all costs!*"

Her fingers clenched around the desk. She took a moment to marshal her thoughts. One must always take a moment to think before acting out of fear. When the room went dark, she looked up at the single window. She expected to see a Telestine ship hovering over them like a bird of prey, but it was the shadow of Mercury itself.

She straightened her shoulders.

Let instinct be your guide. Her fingers began to move through the holograph. Her ship groaned in complaint as near-crippled engines and thrusters tried to maneuver, and the other ships of Nhean's fleet moved forward to cover her.

She was the only one who could direct all of them. She had to survive at least long enough to cover for Pike's team.

"Life support systems experiencing Grade II failure," the AI informed them.

"Is that better or worse than Grade I?" Larsen asked acidly. The AI did not respond.

Walker began to laugh. She laughed as they fell back, as the other ships engaged, and then she stilled herself and opened a channel again. She could feel the cold from the darkness now. Life support was failing, and they were sliding ever further into Mercury's shadow. "Here's the real question: should I try to get us out of the shadow so we can boil to death instead of freeze?"

"Let me get back to you on that one."

Neither of them were smiling, but at least they were trying for humor, and it was enough to keep them going. They didn't even have to keep going very long, either: just long enough for Pike's team. Long enough for the Dawning to do her work. That was all.

"All ships, this is the admiral. Don't worry, the damage looks worse than it is. Focus on your mission. Forget about the *Resurgence.*"

Larsen's head whipped around and she gave a sharp shake

of her head. Delaney and King could *not* be distracted by fear now. Now was the time for cold, rational decisions, and Walker intended to enable that.

"Everyone mark the position of that cannon. Should it aim, make evasion your primary tactic—none of the Exile Fleet ships can survive a direct hit from that thing." Her eyes caught a hint of movement on the screen. "King, what are you doing?"

"Shielding you, ma'am." King's voice was composed. "Your ships have superior firepower to mine. They must survive as long as possible."

"King—"

"Ma'am, you know—"

"I *know* that we need to protect the shipyards." Walker's voice was sharp. Fear squeezed around her heart, and she knew she could not let King hear that.

Don't be seduced by fear. Was it best for King to take the hits?

No. It was best for King's fighters, human and able to spot the tiny shifts in the arrangement of the Telestine fleet, to be the first line of defense against any ships dropping toward the planet.

"I need you to keep formation," Walker said crisply. She was shivering now; the blood on the back of her head was cooling quickly. She touched her hair and her fingers came away wet. Could she smell smoke? "You'll need to keep the ships from breaking my formation and going to the shipyards. King, every chance we have of rebuilding is on Mercury. We cannot let those facilities be destroyed. We'll handle the flagship."

There was a pause.

"Yes, ma'am."

Larsen swiveled in his chair to point to a private comm line that was flashing.

"King?"

He nodded.

Walker picked the phone up. "Listen to me."

"Walker...." King sounded afraid. "I can *see* your ship. Your life-support is out."

"It's not as bad as it looks," Walker said quietly. Her teeth were nearly chattering now, and she pressed her hand over the receiver to mute the noise of the AI's pre-recorded dire warnings. "We're all right. Just *do your job*."

A pause.

"Yes, ma'am." King cut the line.

CHAPTER FIFTY-SEVEN

Mercury, High Orbit
Telestine Flagship

The charges went off with a blast that sent them staggering back from the walls.

Pike was the first to move. Nhean watched from behind one of the iron columns as the Earther went to check his handiwork. The man examined the debris carefully before nodding in satisfaction.

"We're through the hull and the seal is holding. We need to move *now*, before they can vent the area—or get a team up here. Everyone take cover."

They had already dragged the ship's furniture into the docking bay and Pike's crewmates took up position, rifles lying along the tops of the furniture. Klaxons wailed as the doors began to open. Howie peered down the length of his rifle's barrel. Gabriela swung hers back and forth over the hole in the

Telestine flagship's hatch. James looked like he was praying, silently mouthing the words as he fingered his trigger.

Despite himself, Nhean felt a flicker of interest. He had never paid attention to the petty matters of smuggling and piracy, secure in the knowledge of his own weaponry and supply routes. In any case, piracy was a matter of supply and demand, numbers on paper, a hazard to be accounted for; he had not bothered to think of it in terms of bullets and human lives, breathless fear and the hunt.

But there was a practiced air to the *Aggy*'s crew, and it was impossible not to be drawn into the moment. The betrayal of the Rebellion soldier, the makeshift rifles—humanity was, indeed, devouring itself.

It always had been, he supposed. Only now they faced an enemy even more deadly than humanity.

He knew he was only trying to keep from thinking of what would happen when the Telestines finally responded to the boarding attempt. Nhean was no soldier. He could manipulate fleets and distant supply routes with detachment, but it was surprisingly uncomfortable to watch other humans take up arms while he huddled in the shadow of a doorway.

The girl had moved to shield him with her body. Her fingers tightened around the grip of a pistol and she nodded reassuringly at him. *You're safe. I will protect you.*

"No," Nhean murmured. His voice hardly registered against the clank of the doors. He hesitated, and then he drew out the computer chip and pressed it against her palm. "You will figure out how to deploy it," he assured her. He took her shoulders to move her into the shadows, his body out. It was a meaningless gesture; one human body would stop almost nothing in the way of Telestine weaponry.

It was still important. It was a choice. For once, he couldn't shield them with data or information, so his frail body would have to do. He pressed close as the sound of footsteps caught their ears.

The first shots were human. He knew that sound, at least. Five bursts—he couldn't help but count them—before a new sound shot past him and embedded itself in the door behind them. Nhean jumped and swore, and the girl gasped suddenly.

"Don't be frightened," Nhean murmured. There was no point. It would help nothing.

They held one another and shook as the bullets flew outside, their hands clasped.

A yell of pain came from deeper in the cargo hold.

"We have to move!" Pike's voice was ragged. "That was one group, and there will be more on the way. If we don't get out now, we'll be trapped here."

The girl was the one to move, dragging Nhean out.

"Which way out of the doors?" Pike asked.

The girl pointed left.

He nodded. "James, Gabi, you swing right and set up a rearguard. Howie, you and I will go first."

All four hefted their weapons and began to move. They were practiced; Nhean caught a flicker of gestures rippling through the air as James and Gabriela disappeared from view.

"Clear!" A call from their direction.

"Clear!" Pike's voice. "Come on!"

The girl dragged Nhean forward and into the alien corridors.

There were no words for the discomfort. He had not been

made for this ship. It was his enemy's home, in spirit if not in body. Tel'rabim had pretended friendship, and all the while he had been planning humanity's annihilation.

It was a thought one felt clinically, because it was too large for emotion. Nhean stumbled and was pulled to his knees while Pike advanced. The corridors curved around the top of the flagship, leading inward....

His mouth was dry. His heart was pounding now. He could not do this, he was not the soldier.

"Move—*move*." Pike hauled at him. "Go, go, go. Howie!"

"They're coming behind, cowboy!" James's call was half roar. "Go, we'll hold them off!"

A burst of gunfire, and a woman's yell. "*Go, guapo, go!*"

"Come on!" Pike shoved Nhean forward. "Howie, anything up there?"

The only answer was a burst of gunfire. They pounded around the curve, following in Pike's wake, and found Howie crouched behind a corner at a cross corridor. Gunfire was peppering the back wall and he leaned out to shoot before reloading.

"I'll cover you as much as I can. Go. Get across." He tossed a look over his shoulder, pointing to the cross-corridor.

Nhean froze, but Pike's grip was like a vise. "Ready?"

From behind them, gunfire and another scream. Gabriela, he thought. Ahead of them, Pike burst across the opening, shielding the girl running beside him. She threw herself to safety behind the far corner and Pike skidded behind cover a split second after. He was grinning, a feral grin.

"Took out two! Three coming behind them!" Howie yelled.

"I'll cover you! Grab him!" Pike pointed to Nhean. Howie reached back, grabbed him, and propelled him into motion across the opening as Pike put down cover fire.

He didn't remember it later. It passed without thought—he acted on instinct alone. He ran and he heard the bullets go past; the air burned with them, a hot, dry wind. He ran for safety and he hit the curving wall without feeling it. His whole body was trembling.

The girl was standing with her hand over her mouth.

Nhean looked, and froze. Howie's body lay twisted on the floor behind them. Three wounds, or four, or—

A bullet hole square in the center of the tattoo of Earth on his temple. Blood oozed out like an ocean.

"*Move.*" Pike grabbed the two of them and shoved. "James! Gabi!" His shout echoed behind him. "Need you here!"

"Can't—" James's distant voice was cut off in a barrage of bullets.

"Come on."

"He's dead," Nhean whispered.

"Better him than you," Pike said brutally, but his face was white. "Tell me we're close."

The girl grabbed his hand and they ran, the pair of them. Nhean could almost see the rough ground of the Rockies under their feet. She was still wearing the clothes they had found her in, the clothes Tel'rabim had given her. Her hair rippled behind her like a lion's mane.

Nhean followed. He didn't need to be a soldier to know that the only thing behind them was death—and it was catching up fast.

They rounded a corner to find a lone Telestine guard. He

was still raising a pistol when Pike slammed into him shoulder-first. They tumbled over on the ground and Pike yelled something indistinct. The girl sprang over their bodies with an almost inhuman grace, making for a broad door behind them.

Pike was smashing the butt of his rifle into the Telestine's face, trying to hold him back as the guard fought to get to the girl. Blood spurted from the alien's eyes and Nhean felt the uncomfortable rush of pure, visceral enjoyment.

They were here to kill his kind. And so they deserved everything they got.

The doors slid open silently at the girl's touch, even as Pike slammed his rifle down one last time. The Telestine's body lay silent and broken and Pike stood, air entering his lungs in a wheeze.

"I'll hold them off." He pried the Telestine's fingers off the alien pistol. "Get in there. I'll...."

He tried to smile at the girl and she tried to smile back. She beckoned Nhean into the control room, and her eyes never left Pike as the doors slid shut.

It was when she turned, tears in her eyes, that Nhean realized she knew. She knew the cost. He hadn't told her, since he wasn't even sure himself, but she knew anyway.

Guilt stabbed, deep in his chest.

"If there was any other way—" he began.

She cut him off with a single shake of her head, and held out the computer chip.

"I hope I'm wrong," Nhean said awkwardly. He felt like a child, helpless. "I hope it doesn't ... I hope you'll be fine."

She only shook her head.

"You knew all along," he said quietly.

A silent nod, and her fingers opened a port from the featureless wall of machinery. She pointed.

He swallowed. "If—"

A head shake. She jabbed her finger.

No more words.

He began.

CHAPTER FIFTY-EIGHT

Mercury, High Orbit
Telestine Flagship

Pike turned as the door closed. He couldn't meet her eyes. Howie was dead. Either James or Gabriela was down—he could only hear one human weapon from the corridor.

He was going to die, too. And the old scar on the side of his head ached at the thought of leaving Dawn back there in that room. Out of his direct care. He'd just have to trust Nhean. Trust him to protect her at all costs.

Pike dragged the Telestine's body behind makeshift cover —a metal chair, better than nothing but significantly worse than anything else he'd tried to take cover behind in his life— and readied his weapon. He must only shoot when he was sure it was a Telestine target. He could not afford to take down his one remaining ally if they somehow made it to him.

"*Pike.*" A familiar voice in his earpiece.

"Laura." He breathed her name. His fingers trembled on the gun. He could hear the tramp of feet. Shock troops were approaching. His line fuzzed, and snatches of other voices came to him. A man was roaring orders, a woman was giving some crisply. "Walker, how is it—"

"*Are you in?*" Her voice was desperate. He could hear her teeth chattering.

"Walker—"

"*I have to know.*" Her voice was hoarse—he could hear the desperation there, and pain. For the first time since he'd known her, there was weakness there.

He swayed at the silence and readied his finger on the trigger. "We're here. I'm holding the door for them." He was miles from her through empty space and yet he could feel her wave of relief, almost crippling.

She gave what sounded very much like a sob. "*Thank god for that.*"

"You're hurt." It wasn't a question; he knew without asking. He'd never heard her like this before.

She hesitated before answering. "*My ship took a hit, early on. Pike—*"

And then the first Telestines came around the corner and Pike could spare no thought for anything but them. Black uniforms, face guards—an echo of grotesque features.

They'd been trained to kill. They were here to exterminate an entire species and they didn't have any goddamned right. A hollow roar burst from his chest and his gun slammed back against his shoulder as he squeezed the trigger.

"Eat shit!" God, he'd wanted to say that for ages. "Eat ... shit ... you ... god ... forsaken ... sons ... of ... bitches! ...

Fuck ... you!" Each word was punctuated by a burst of fire from his rifle. He ducked behind the chair as shots ricocheted overhead. Almost out of ammo.

Shit.

He could hear something that sounded half like a laugh, half like a sob. Had that come from him, or Walker? He didn't know. He could hear her voice only faintly now. She was calling something to someone else on the bridge. Her voice was weak. He could hear the other voices fading in and out in response.

Walker shouted. "*No!*"

No time to ask what that meant. Pike reloaded and came back up—face to face with a Telestine shock trooper. Black eyes peered out from behind the mask, eerily similar to the girl's. The words it spoke were smooth, utterly alien, and yet Pike had no doubt what they meant:

You die now.

At the age of seven, Pike had been checking on rabbit traps when he turned to see a bear behind him. It wasn't one of the black bears that scampered near the camp looking for berries. It was a brown bear, and it was starving; he could see that in its eyes. It sized him up, and it knew him for prey.

His father had been there before Pike knew what was happening. The man had gone at the bear in dead silence, rifle at the ready, and the bear reared up, a giant in shaggy fur with its paws out while Pike screamed and screamed.

No hesitation, his father said later. *The only way something knows you're prey is if you tell it so by running.*

The pistol was in his hand and at the Telestine soldier's head before the soldier knew what was happening. It went off with a roar and the body flopped away.

The other soldiers fell back with a hiss and Pike brought the gun up to shoot again, again, again. His arm was on fire; recoil jerked his arm back in its socket and his fingers and palm were bruised with it.

But the pain was fading. He looked his enemies in the eyes and he smiled, and he knew he was laughing. In his earpiece he could hear the screams of his compatriots out in their ships— their metal coffins. There was the distant boom and shudder of cannons going off, the answering calls of the humans as they watched the rounds streak away into space.

And here, he reminded himself, he wasn't trapped in a ship with the Telestines. They were trapped with him. He could hear them loading their guns, huddling behind the curved wall, and he took cover once again.

"You are going to regret the day," he growled softly, fiercely, "that you let us live. Eat … shit." He leaned out from he curve in the wall and sprayed the attackers—no, the prey— with fire.

They couldn't speak English, but he knew they understood him.

He dragged the rifle close to him and leveled the pistol at the open corridor. He did not look back at the door behind him, but he felt the urgency shaking through him.

Come on, come on, come on. Dawn, do your thing. Get it done.

"*All ships hold formation!*" Walker's voice was in his ear. "*The team is on the flagship, all exile ships hold formation!*"

Just a little longer. He only had to survive a little longer.

He wished he had said goodbye.

CHAPTER FIFTY-NINE

Mercury, High Orbit
Bridge, Venus Fleet Ship Resurgence

"*Eat shit!*" The voice echoed in her earpiece. She listened to Pike's vulgar battle cry with glee, in spite of her violent shaking from the deadly cold.

Walker tried to laugh around the tears in her throat. She was rocking back and forth in a desperate attempt at movement. The chills were shaking her whole body now, and her breath was clouding in front of her face. She had to stay conscious. She had to stay awake. The Telestine fleet had spread outward into a claw, trying to outflank her, and her fingers trembled as she tried to drag her ships to compensate. She had to stay in the shadow of one at all times, but which one? Her mind was beginning to feel sluggish.

An explosion of yelling, and her eyes focused on a strange swirl of activity in the Telestine fleet.

"Ma'am, they're breaking off the attack on Delaney's ships." Larsen was shaking his head. "They're ... retreating?"

"No." Walker shook her head. She gave a hoarse laugh. "They can't be, we aren't winning." Her fingers clenched and released and she squinted through the cloud of her own breath. "Where are they going, though?"

"Delaney reports that they're making for the flagship, ma'am. Maybe to dock, or—"

Her heart seized.

"To take it down. They know what we're doing." She grabbed the comm unit and it nearly tumbled from her frozen fingers. "All ships, form up. We need to get between their carriers and the flagship, they're trying to take it down."

"They know," Larsen whispered. His face was horrified. "They know what's happening and—"

"And it's *working*, or they wouldn't be trying to take the flagship down." Savage satisfaction kindled in her stomach. "They know if the signal gets transmitted, they're dead in the water." The comm unit dropped and she forced herself to move. Her fingers dragged her own fleet up and around in an arc. "We need to get *there*. Tell Delaney to mirror us."

Larsen obeyed, but his face was white with fear. "We don't have time—we aren't going to be able to cut them off. We don't have *time*."

"Focus, Larsen!" *We only have a few more minutes alive in this world, and that's how you're going to go out?* She forced herself not to spit the words at him. Like hell she was going to die knowing her plan had been a failure. She snatched up the comm unit herself. "Delaney, do you read? Get between them and the ship."

"Ma'am—" King's voice cut in.

"King, you stay! Keep them away from the shipyards! Keep that Telestine back, don't let them get around you! Delaney—"

"Yes, ma'am." He had been the storm and fury for this fight, roaring orders to his ships, and now, at the last, he was composed. "We're moving into position, ma'am. Nothing will get through us."

She saw the *Intrepid* begin to climb toward the Telestine carriers that were now closing in on the Telestine flagship—the key to the whole operation was now itself the target of its own fleet.

"Good hunting, Commander Delaney."

"And you, Walker."

Walker set down the comm unit and surveyed the battle. At last, now, she was calm. Their death was coming quickly, and she cleared her mind to ready herself for it. Nhean's carriers were climbing at full burn up toward the rounded bulk of the flagship. All batteries were firing.

Nothing to do but wait. She clasped her hands together and went to the window. The ship was falling down in her view, or they were rising toward it; her world tipped and tilted and she splayed one hand on the window to keep herself upright. Frost collected at the corners of the glass.

To go out fighting was a good death. She had always believed that.

But they weren't going to make it in time. She could see that from here. She watched Nhean's ships ahead of her pick up speed and, with the clarity of approaching death, she knew that even they were not going to succeed. The Telestine carriers would beat them there.

Delaney, his ships coming into view at the corner of her vision, would not even be close. The Exile Fleet had gone too high ... and the Telestines had sunk lower. They would batter the vulnerable control room at the top of the flagship, and they would destroy whatever chance humanity had had to disable them.

There were tears on her cheeks.

"*Full burn, full burn!*" She could hear Delaney's words only distantly. "*That carrier is picking up speed; get between it and the flagship!*"

Harris called something back, indistinct. Walker could only hear the impression of the helmswoman's voice through the comm.

They weren't going to make it.

The ventral cannons on the spine of the flagship turned toward her ship like giant, unseeing eyes, and Walker stared back at them.

So this was how it ended.

This was how it ended.

The Telestine carrier nearest the flagship closed to weapon's range and opened fire at the top of the ship. At the Dawning. At humanity's only best and only chance.

It happened so quickly that she hardly saw it. The scream caught her unawares: Delaney crying out a single, hoarse word, and a human ship came out of nowhere. A gleaming new Mercury ship.

No.

It slammed into the Telestine carrier. Glass and metal exploded beneath her gaze. Both ships were carried sideways with the force of the collision: the Telestine carrier crumpled against the onslaught of the human ship even as it came apart at the seams. Both erupted in a series of muted explosions, which the vacuum quickly snuffed out.

"No!" Delaney's yell. He was sobbing, she could hear it.

It didn't make sense, the pieces weren't connecting in her head. Someone had made it, to intercept the carrier, but who? None of the ships in the Venus fleet's offensive group or the Exile Fleet had enough time to get into the right vector. No one should have been able to make it.

A piece of debris tore from the side of the ship and tumbled past her, black letters marred by twisted metal and scorch marks. But she could still read it, and the word was like a punch in the gut: *Indomitable.*

The new Mercury fleet. King. Arianna King.

She had forgotten them, ordered them to stay back, to protect the shipyards. But the shipyards were safe, she saw, and now, under King's orders, they were intercepting the real threat. Another ship soared past, and another, each going unflinching to make the interceptions only they could. How many human lives?

Delaney's cries were hoarse in her ear. *If someone has to go into the breach,* he'd said, *let it be me.*

There was only ever the best choice, and King had made it without blinking. She'd made her choice, and saved them all. Walker felt the tears take her.

The ventral cannons on the Telestine flagship were beginning to heat again, priming for fire, and she opened her eyes to stare them down. She would watch her death. She would not run from it.

CHAPTER SIXTY

Mercury, High Orbit
Telestine Flagship

The screams were in his head and they wouldn't stop. The pistol went off and Pike shrieked his fury at the soldiers that kept coming. He caught the latest assailant in the shoulder. The thing dropped its weapon with a cry of pain and staggered as Pike took aim, pulled the trigger....

Nothing. *Shit.* The thing was still coming toward him, and who knew when the next one would arrive? He ducked. His hands searched a dead soldier's uniform desperately. There had to be more ammunition. There had to be more.

The other soldier was fumbling for the gun with its other hand, and there was no time. Pike launched himself across the hallway; his knuckles cracked against the Telestine's head and there was the sickening sound of a jaw splintering out of place. The thing screeched in pain. He ignored the searing pain from his own hand—he'd surely broken a bone or three.

"What ... the ... fuck ... do ... you ... know ... of ... pain?" He pounded its face again and again and again, his fist bloodier with each blow. The Telestine blocked his blows, fighting back with its good arm, its speed and strength knocking Pike's own attack aside. Pike didn't care. He changed course abruptly. A kick. A brutal knee to the thing's broken face. Another kick.

The glint of a pistol caught his eye—the bloodied soldier's sidearm fallen to the ground. Pike stumbled down to retrieve it, and sent a bullet through its brain before lurching across the hallway to avoid another volley of shots from the arriving soldiers.

The ongoing clamor in his earpiece wouldn't stop: the man yelling, Walker calling orders desperately before her voice fell away. There was a ship coming for them in the control room and there was not a goddamned thing Pike could do about.

It made him furious. As another soldier came around the corner, he grabbed the fallen soldier from the floor and threw the body with all his might. They were either lighter than he thought, or the adrenaline made him a super-human.

It wasn't just humans who hated having their own dead near them. The Telestine flinched, and the pistol round tore through the body a moment later. Pike staggered forward. He'd caught a round at some point. His shoulder was bleeding. He couldn't feel his legs at all, though maybe that was adrenaline too. He stumbled his way over the pile of bodies. He'd killed them all.

"Pike, listen. The Telestine carriers are closing in on the flagship. They've figured it out. They're going to take it, and you, down," said

Walker in his earpiece.

He stared at the bodies. He couldn't bring himself to care one way or another about that. He couldn't bring himself to care at all. Death was seconds away. How close were those Telestine carriers?

Pike rushed around the corner with his teeth bloody and two of their own guns in his hands, and the Telestines there shrank back.

They'd been setting a bomb. That's why there'd only been one or two of them at a time. These one looked more like techs, judging by their uniforms. He stared at the partially-set device, swaying on his feet. None of them had their guns out. They stared at him in mute horror.

"Your buddies are coming to take the ship down," Pike said. He slumped against the wall. There was a laugh somewhere in his chest but he was too exhausted to give it life. His knees buckled. He looked up to meet black eyes. "Did you know that? They're going to destroy this ship, and you're all going to die. They're just throwing you away. Throwing away your worthless, shitty lives, like the little shits you are. Good riddance."

The lights flared, and went dark, and he heard the sound of footsteps. They were running. The lights were going crazy and he couldn't make sense of what he was seeing. He tried to stand—he wasn't dead, and he wasn't crushed into goo—and resorted to crawling.

The lights flickered on. Lights. Power. It had to be them— had to be Dawn. Was there cheering in his earpiece?

"Dawn?" His voice was hoarse. Bodies slid out of the way beneath him as he brutally shoved them aside. "Dawn!"

The door opened for him with a hiss.

Nhean did not look around. His eyes were fixed on a giant screen before him—and on the Telestine who stood framed there.

"—traitors," the Telestine was saying. His words were crisp and exact; he had learned English, this one. "Faithless," the alien said.

Nhean laughed. The sound was wild. "Faithless? We never signed that treaty, Tel'rabim."

"You did."

"Our leaders did—and even that was nothing. You put their hands to paper and a gun to their heads. What choice did they have?"

"They signed it!" The Telestine's voice was losing its crispness. "And I saw the lies in them even then! I told the others you couldn't be trusted—and I was *right*. *Artalbath hecardah lasan*—faithless, honorless, nothing in you but lies and violence. Animals!"

"*Essocar lorasai tragerve junari.*" Nhean straightened his shoulders. "Oh, yes, Telestine. I know your tongue. Call us what you will. You came and you consigned us to death. A slow death. A death without death—and a life without life. You left it to us to roll over and die. Does it surprise you that we did not? Does it surprise you that there is life in us yet? Life enough to seek yours as payment for your crimes?"

The cheering in his earpiece was deafening. Pike tore it out and stumbled forward. His arm wasn't coming up. He wanted to raise the gun, show the Telestine his death.

"Not in the least. I was the one who knew to watch you." The Telestine's lips stretched in an eerie grin. "I was the one who saw your potential—oh, yes, you have potential. What did you think the labs were for, *human*? What did you think the slaves were for? There's intelligence there. There's cleverness and some strength. But you aren't stupid enough to be brute labor, and you aren't clever enough to align yourself with a superior species. You're unpredictable, you have a desperate need to win, and to win alone. You think you should determine the rules of the game when you have no right. You can't be broken reliably."

"The word," Nhean said simply, "is pride."

"Pride." The Telestine pronounced it like a curse. "And you revere this thing?"

"It's one of our sins." Nhean laughed bitterly. "A deadly sin, we call it. And one of our greatest virtues. A paradox, really."

"It will be your undoing. The one thing you all do is die."

"It will be *your* undoing. You should have killed us all when you had the chance. Now you'll never get it back. Where are you, Tel'rabim?"

The Telestine stared at him silently.

"We will find you," Pike said. His voice sounded rusty. He jerked his head back to the corridor. "There's a pile of dead Telestines out there to show you how it's going to go for you."

Tel'rabim's face twisted with rage.

"You failed." Pike started to laugh, and stepped forward, into the view of the video feed's camera. "All of you. You said you wanted to exterminate us all. I bet you didn't even think you'd fail. You built this flagship to hover in the skies and terrify us, so our last thoughts would be of our own death bearing down. You spent all that time studying us, and you never realized we'd fight back?"

"He says we're clever enough, but he never thought we'd be clever enough to win." Nhean looked over at Pike with a small, satisfied smile.

"You haven't won," Tel'rabim spat. "You've only hardened the Great Race's resolve to terminate you. You've only seen a quarter of our fleets. Believe me, human, death is coming. You should have kept the faith, Nhean. Neither of you would be here today but for us. You'd have died in the void, and yet you won't keep faith. Even *she* didn't keep faith."

"You made her a weapon." Nhean lifted one shoulder. He reached over to take the gun from Pike's hand. "A weapon with a mind. And as you say ... humans cannot reliably be broken. We may not have her any longer, but we are coming for you, Tel'rabim. We will meet you at every battleground and we will best you. We will come for your cities and we will prove you right. You should have killed us when you had the chance." His arm came up and the gun went off with a crack; the screen shattered into hundreds of pieces.

And Pike caught sight of the girl, lying motionless behind the interface.

"Dawn." He was at her side in an instant, shaking her shoulder. "Wake up, you have to wake up."

"Pike—"

"*Get* away from me." He snarled the words. "Dawn, please." Her chest was moving, but only faintly. Her eyes were wide and staring; she saw nothing. "Dawn...." He rounded on Nhean.

The man was staring at him, pity in his eyes. "She knew, Pike. She was prepared."

"You swore." He gathered the body in his arms. The heart still beat, but there was nothing there. "You *swore.*"

Nhean bowed his head, focusing instead on the flickering readouts of the Telestine interface.

"*Pike? Nhean?*" Walker's voice cut through.

Pike flinched, his arms clenched around the girl's body. He hadn't noticed when they came in, but a bruised and battered James stood nearby, hat-less, supporting Gabriela who was bleeding from several points on her leg.

Nhean waited, and when Pike did not answer, the man walked through the rubble to pick up his commlink.

"It's done, Walker." he said quietly. "We'll meet you on the *Intrepid.* It's done."

CHAPTER SIXTY-ONE

Mercury, High Orbit
Shuttle Bay, EFS Intrepid

Walker was shivering now as the sweat dried on her skin. The shuttle the *Intrepid* sent for them had seemed like heaven —her idea of a summer's day on Earth, but an hour later the chills had hit her again, and she couldn't stop remembering the cold leaching the strength from her, and the memory made her shiver all over again.

The mad crush of bodies pushing their way through the *Intrepid*'s shuttle bay—the survivors of the various broken ships of their three fleets—helped to warm her, at least, and representatives from each of the surviving intact ships were coming for a hastily-called meeting on what to do next. A council of war, essentially.

They still had dozens of dormant Telestine ships floating all around them, and a decision to make.

She wiped her eyes and pushed her way through the crowd on tiptoe, which was useless—she was too short for that to work in her favor, and no one seemed to be noticing *Admiral Walker* trying to push her way through them. Still, she might see....

Not what she'd expected. She was looking for Pike, for Nhean, but her eyes rested on an inconsolably weeping form on the floor leaning against the wall. McAllister's face was wrenched tight, eyes red, and shaking. Tocks and Princess sitting with him on either side, as if in vigil.

They'd won. But for some, the pain would be too much to bear for a long, long time.

There—the distinctive sight of Pike, taller than the rest. Walker let out her breath in something that might easily have been a sob and forged across the stream of people, brushing off attempted handshakes and congratulations. She didn't want those now. She would let the people here have their celebration, though there was worse to come and they had already lost things they could not afford to lose. People needed celebration after victory, she knew that.

But she wanted to see Pike. She wanted to know where he had gone, what had happened aboard that ship. Until thirty seconds ago, she'd been afraid that he was dead, and that Nhean simply wouldn't tell her.

The crowd parted in a swirl of people and she saw the three of them: Nhean in his too-nice suit, still somehow looking passably dignified, in spite of the spatters of blood covering the fabric. And Pike was there, bloodied and battered.

And the girl.

Walker did not ask whether she was alive. She watched,

saw the faint rise in the girl's chest, and then turned to yell for a medic. She was pleased to see her people scramble out of the way as a medic unit raced toward them—they were still a military of a sort. That was good—they would need that discipline in the days to come. She watched as the girl was laid carefully on a stretcher, and Nhean pried Pike's fingers free for the medics to take their patient away.

At the look in Pike's eyes, Nhean stepped back. There was pure venom there, a cold fury that was nothing like the Pike Walker knew. In her experience, Pike ran hot. He yelled when he was angry. He solved problems with fistfights and shouting. Now he was her kind of angry: icy cold. Holding a grudge. Nursing a frozen hatred.

She said nothing for a moment, watching him.

He looked at her and something in him seemed to snap. He lifted his shoulders helplessly. His head was shaking back and forth. He wanted action, wanted to *do* something, but there was nothing to be done.

She opened her arms and pulled him close. It didn't matter how ridiculous it was, her all of five feet tall and him towering over her. It mattered that they were solid and human and both alive and she was glad to see him here.

"He promised," Pike said quietly. "He said she wouldn't be hurt. I should have known." He paused, and added darkly, "just like before. Just like Thomas."

He always called his father by his name, never by *dad* or *father*. Walker said nothing. There was nothing to say.

"He said she knew." There was a simmering anger there now in his whisper.

She stepped back as she considered this. "If she had

known, what do you think she would have done?"

There was a long pause.

"She would have done it anyway," he finally admitted.

Walker nodded silently.

"There was a traitor in the Rebellion," Pike said, as if he'd only now remembered that piece of information. "Someone from the surface. Charlie, you remember him. Tel'rabim sent him to get the Dawning back."

"How?" It mattered.

"He told Charlie he'd give his family back. Nhean said...." Pike's face darkened at the thought of the other man. "He said it was how the Rebellion got word of families on the labs. Tel'rabim was just stealing people, hoping to drive the ones left behind into the Rebellion, and then use them later. With their families as ... bait. Leverage."

Walker closed her eyes; she didn't want Pike to see the admiration in them. It was damn clever, that was the thing. She didn't want to admire anything about Tel'rabim.

But it was the sort of thing she would have done to the Telestines, if she could.

She looked down at the floor while she composed herself.

"I should go to the med bay," Pike said. His eyes seemed to take in Walker's bloody uniform, the sweat still dying on her skin. He saw the shadow of tears in her eyes. "What happened?"

"A battle happened," she said dryly. It was all there was to say. She shook her head and turned to look as a rippled hush went through the crowd. "Go. I'll catch up with you later."

She pushed her way back to the wall. Only her rank got her through, and it was slow going. Everyone was huddled around a comm unit.

It was when she saw Delaney's face that she knew.

The message was on a loop, repeating over and over again in the stillness. She would have recognized that voice anywhere; her hands clenched.

"—a full surrender," the Secretary General said. "We must beg forgiveness for our breach of the Treaty. I encourage anyone with any information whatsoever about the Rebellion, its fleet, and its members to come to me or to the Telestine government. I have negotiated a full surrender. We must beg forgiveness—"

The comm unit switched off. Nhean's finger was on the button, shaking.

"Get me on the comms," Walker said. Her lips were numb. "I need to tell the fleet—"

"It's too late." Delaney's voice was quiet. "Three of the ships have already jumped out to surrender to the Secretary General. Venus and Mars have issued their own surrenders. The stations at Jupiter are in negotiations. Everyone is scared shitless that the Telestines are coming for blood. And all the planets and stations are sitting ducks, so why wouldn't they be?"

"I have to go back." Nhean's voice was tight. "I'll get Venus on our side."

"I don't think you will." There was no cruelty in Delaney's voice, only weary certainty. "There's a price on your head now. You, specifically. You, me, the admiral. All of our officers. Bill Pike. The girl."

And the three ships that had jumped … knew every secret there was to know: the dark places in the Telestine array, the flight patterns, the technology.

Even as the whispers started around her, Walker's mind fastened on one thing. They didn't all know about the girl. They didn't all know *how* the Telestine flagship had been taken down, or about the divisions in Telestine society. They didn't know....

There would be time for a full catalog later. Time to make a different set of plans. Now, she needed to stabilize, to reassure. She needed to stop the panic in its tracks. She raised her voice as well as she could, and was pleased to hear the whispers stop.

"Today, we stood our ground against an enemy determined to begin the genocide of our entire species."

Silence greeted her words.

"You—every one of you, your crewmates both here and on your ships—stepped into the breach to say, *no more. We are not prey. We will no longer turn and run.* We took back something today: our pride, our honor, our humanity. With or without Earth, as long as we fight for our freedom, we will be human."

There were tears in her own eyes, though they did not fall. "Many of our number made the ultimate sacrifice today. There will be a time and place to grieve for them, but it is not today. It is not now. There is no time for us to rest yet. *Now* is the time for us to honor them by continuing their fight." She swept her gaze over the crowd and, met the eyes of those whose faces were pale with fear. "Make no mistake, fight we will. And fight hard."

Her voice seemed to swell in the space. "I have no intention of abiding by a treaty we signed with a gun to our head and our children in chains. Now is not the time for us to surrender to fear, to tell ourselves that the yoke that hangs heavy around our neck and drags us to a slow death is better than an open fight. Now, in the face of our victory, is the time to stand tall, and firm, and resolute. Unflinching." She swept her gaze over the crowd. "We will win this. We will win freedom for humanity, and today, we have already won the first victory of the great war of liberation."

The clapping began quietly, hesitantly, and then it gathered momentum. Stamping began, whistles and cheers and shouts of the fighter squadron slogans, and the Rebellion's anthem, voices carrying the chorus high.

Let them have their celebration. One by one, Walker sought out the ship captains and caught their eyes. She nodded her head toward the passageway that led to the CIC and led them away from the celebration.

Now was the time to prepare.

Epilogue

It was some hours later that she sat back at last, rubbing at her eyes. Her head ached fiercely. The celebration in the main hangar bay had not abated, as she expected. It had spread to the mess. Shuttles had arrived from the other ships, bearing the fruit of a dozen illicit distilleries, and the songs and cheering only seemed to grow louder as the party went on. There was another incoming Telestine fleet, and she had recommended full destruction of the Telestine ships that were sitting ducks, against Nhean's vehement opposition. But there was not time to study.

Even when the first orders went out and the fleet started into an acceleration burn, the party did not stop; thankfully, the helmsmen still seemed to be sober enough to set coordinates.

"We've done all we can," Delaney said firmly. He nodded his head at the stack of papers on the desk: rendezvous points, schedules, and patrols of their own. "We have a few hours until we change course." He nodded at the other captains. "We'll handle getting the crews back to their ships."

"During this burn?"

"We'll pause the burn momentarily. Well, and it'll take a while to wind the celebration down, anyway. I'll go be the grumpy old man and crash the party. You all get some sleep."

"*Ma'am?*" The comm unit buzzed and crackled.

The med bay. Walker exchanged a quick glance with Delaney and pressed the button. "What is it?"

"Something you need to see," said the doctor.

"I'll be right there." She didn't like that tone. She nodded at one of the captains. "Change of plans. Noringe, you get to be the grumpy old man. Get people back to work. Delaney, come with me."

As she strode through the empty hallways her heart began to race in her chest. She didn't like this, didn't like it at all. When they got to the med bay at last to see Pike pacing and Nhean jiggling a foot anxiously, her misgivings deepened.

"What's going on?"

"It's … bad." Nhean met her eyes. "The girl—"

"Let the doctor tell it," Pike said flatly. His tone said that he wasn't ready to give up his grudge yet.

Nhean fell silent, gaze down. He didn't seem to think this was a fight worth having, and Walker didn't have time for it anyway. She sought out the doctor's eyes and raised her eyebrows.

Doc LaScalla brushed her black braid over her shoulder. "She wasn't responding to standard treatment," the woman said quietly. "So I ran an analysis on her DNA—there are sequences that can signal different treatment options."

"And?" Walker frowned.

LaScalla sighed and tapped a button. A display came up on the wall, lines of code blinking an angry red in between the strands of different shades of green. "These," she said, pointing to the dark green, "are very standard. Match plenty of things in the database. These lighter green ones … well, we'll get to that in a minute. But *these* don't match anything in our system at all. The ones marked red."

Walker shook her head. "So…?"

"So, we've got the genomes of millions of humans in here. The odds of even one sequence being this far out of normal, much less nine? Vanishingly small. And I looked at them myself, just to make sure."

"Cut to the chase, LaScalla."

"They're not *human* genes." LaScalla delivered the news with a wry smile. She looked a the girl, still lying prone on the bed. "She? Is not all human."

Walker had to force herself to speak. "That can't be right. Looks pretty damn human to me."

"Trust me, I checked my work. A *lot*."

Walker stepped closer, shaking. She looked so human, that was the thing. She looked so human, and she wasn't. Was that even possible? "What do they do? Those sequences."

"We don't know." LaScalla was honest, at least. "That's where the other part comes in. The ones I've marked light green here." She pointed at the flashing sequences.

Walker's fingers tightened on the railing. "It's worse, isn't it? That other part."

"Yeah. It is." LaScalla looked down. "They match … one very specific group."

"Spit it out, LaScalla."

"The drones." It was Nhean. He stood at last.

"The ones we got out of the chain gangs on Earth?"

"The same. No one noticed at the time. That seemed like the least of our worries when we got them off-planet. We couldn't get them to do much of anything, really, so how they responded to chemo and the rest was ... not something we paid attention to. We essentially just forgot about them."

"Does it matter?"

"You tell me." His eyes met hers. "Where did they all go? Once we got them off-planet?"

Walker shrugged. "All over the solar system, I guess." She looked over at Delaney, who lifted his shoulders as well.

"I think some of them went to Venus," he continued. "We tried to give them government jobs. They were ... vulnerable. People were using them the way the Telestines did. They went all over, though, really. Mars. The Jupiter Snowballs. The stations. Asteroid belt." Nhean looked white, and grim. "They're everywhere."

He glanced at Pike, and for just a moment, there was a shadow of understanding between them. Walker traced the look.

"What *is* it?"

"Perhaps we shouldn't say *she* matches *their* DNA," Nhean suggested. "Perhaps we should say that *they* match *hers*—very, very closely." His eyes held hers. He saw the dawning horror there, and nodded. "Yes. We've checked. Every one of them has the non-human sequences as well. The *same* non-human sequences."

The world had dropped out from under her. Walker felt

her fingers clench around the metal railing on the girl's bed.

Everywhere. They were everywhere by now: hundreds, possibly thousands, of human-Telestine hybrids on the stations —cleaning the government offices, fixing the life support systems, doing maintenance on the cargo haulers. There wasn't a hope in hell of tracking them all down. And they knew now what those hybrids were capable of.

A horrified silence stilled the med bay.

The girl's eyes snapped open.

Thank you for reading Mercury's Bane.

Sign up to find out when Jupiter's Sword,
book 2 of the Earth Dawning Series, is released:
smarturl.it/nickwebblist

Contact information:

www.nickwebbwrites.com

facebook.com/authornickwebb

authornickwebb@gmail.com

Made in the USA
Middletown, DE
02 November 2020